Shadows Cast by Stars

Shadows Cast by Stars

CATHERINE KNUTSSON

Atheneum Books for Young Readers

NEW YORK LONDON TORONTO SYDNEY NEW DELHI

ATHENEUM BOOKS FOR YOUNG READERS
An imprint of Simon & Schuster Children's Publishing Division
1230 Avenue of the Americas, New York, New York 10020

ATHENEUM BOOKS FOR YOUNG READERS is a registered trademark of Simon & Schuster, Inc.

For information about special discounts for bulk purchases, please contact Simon & Schuster Special Sales at 1-866-506-1949 or business@simonandschuster.com.

The Simon & Schuster Speakers Bureau can bring authors to your live event. For more information or to book an event, contact the Simon & Schuster Speakers Bureau at 1-866-248-3049 or visit our website at www.simonspeakers.com.

Book design by Hilary Zarycky
The text for this book is set in Fairfield.
Manufactured in the United States of America
First Edition
10 9 8 7 6 5 4 3 2 1
Library of Congress Cataloging-in-Publication Data
Knutsson, Catherine.
Shadows cast by stars / Catherine Knutsson.
p. cm.
Summary: To escape a government that needs antigens in aboriginal blood to stop a plague, sixteen-year-old Cassandra and her family flee to the Island, where she not only gets help in communicating with the spirit world, she learns she has been chosen to be their voice and instrument.
ISBN 978-1-4424-0191-4 (hardcover)
ISBN 978-1-4424-0193-8 (eBook)
[1. Science fiction. 2. Indians of North America—Fiction. 3. Spirits—Fiction. 4. Family life—Fiction. 5. Brothers and sisters—Fiction. 6. Twins—Fiction.] I. Title.
PZ7.K7873Sh 2012
[Fic]—dc23   2011038419

For Mikel

ACKNOWLEDGMENTS

Writing a book is a collaborative task. I am so grateful for the many eyes and hands who have touched this story as it made its way from idea to book.

To Caitlyn Dlouhy and her team at Atheneum: my gratitude for helping me polish this story until it shone.

To the River Writers: Shari, Kristin, Diana, and Sheena, for all the laughs and support and advice along the way.

To my international cast of writer friends: Deb, Jo, Rabia, Ryan, Cat, and Jen, for reading the various drafts and offering such sage and generous advice. And especially, my undying thanks to Elena, for pushing me and encouraging me to break the rules I had created for myself. I am a better writer and better person for knowing you.

To the women of SIFM: such shining examples of strength! My gratitude for your unwavering encouragement, support, and friendship.

To my sister, Carmen, for always being there, no matter what.

To Diana Fox: my heartfelt thanks for all that you have done. You have been a true champion and friend through all this. I couldn't have done it without you.

And, last but never least, to Mikel Knutsson, for picking me up when I fell down (repeatedly!) and for never losing faith in me, even when I had lost it myself.

CHAPTER ONE

We live the Old Way. Our house, constructed of wood timber and roofed with asphalt shingles, straddles the boundary where the wasteland and the northernmost edge of the Western Population Corridor meet. This land was once my great-grandfather's farm. Once was. Hasn't been for a long time.

Every morning, my brother and I rise before dawn, make the trek to the mag-station, and ride into the Corridor to attend school, where we plug into the etherstream via the chip in our forearm. By law, our chip-traces can't display any information about race, religion, or sexual orientation, but our classmates have always known that Paul and I are Others, of aboriginal descent, marked by the precious Plague antibodies in our blood.

Every afternoon, we make the return trip, riding the mag-train to the end of its line before walking back home along the old dirt road. Behind us, smog from the Corridor reaches north, stretching its ugly yellow fingers as far as it can as it tries to snatch up the last of the habitable land. Not long ago, a reserve was here, lodged in the Corridor's throat, but all that remains now is our home. We are the only ones who have stayed, clinging to what little is ours, defiantly living as we always have, without computers and etherstreams and data-nets in our home, without food gels, without central heat. This is our choice. This is what it means to live the Old Way.

Today the walk seems longer than usual, because Paul isn't talking to me. He got into a fight earlier in the day, but it's not his split lip or his gashed knuckles that have me so worried. Paul's on disciplinary action for fighting and truancy as it is, which is tough on both of us. *Why can't you be more like your sister?* the teachers always say to him. *Why can't you help your brother?* they say to me. We're twins, Paul and me, but we're not alike—not anymore, at least. Paul's always had a short fuse, but lately it's gotten shorter.

Now he walks beside me, slump-shouldered as his battered raven flies next to him. The raven is Paul's shade, his spirit animal, and it always shows up after something bad happens to him. Today it was some kid who was looking for a scapegoat to blame for his brother dying of Plague. The rest who joined in? Well, no one in the Corridor needs an excuse to stick it to an Other.

Paul notices me watching him. "What's wrong?" he asks as his shade casts him in the wavering light where spirit and flesh merge. The raven looks as beaten and bruised as Paul.

"Your raven. He's back."

Paul glances over his shoulder, but there's nothing there for him to see. Only I can see the shades, even though I don't seem to have one of my own. Paul's gifts run a different path. "Well," he says with a sigh, "at least it's here and not at school."

He's right. When shades come to me, they sometimes take me under into the twilight world of spirit. More than once, I've been trapped there, unable to find my way back to my body. I fear that one day I'll drown in the heavy darkness of the other side. But not today. Today I watch Paul's raven and worry, for there's one thing I know: When a shade comes to visit, something is about to change.

We round the last corner of the road, and the moment our house comes into view, Paul's raven takes flight, leaving my brother lighter, unfettered. Paul may not like it here, but this place is good for him. Under the watchful eyes of the old windows, my brother is whole. He races inside to change out of his school clothes, the old floorboards creaking under his movements. It's not long before he pounds back downstairs and flies through the kitchen, grabbing the last biscuit from breakfast before disappearing outside.

I always leave the last one for him.

I wait until I hear the sound of Paul's ax striking wood before I go inside and close the door, leaning against it to seal the Corridor, school, the Band, the entire world outside. We have made it through another day. Our family is still together, if not whole.

For one complete minute, I allow myself to pretend we're safe. The minute ends, as it always does, and reality sets in. Time for chores, but first I need to hide the contraband in my schoolbag: twine, twigs, old pencils, paper clips, elastic bands, tossed-away shirts, a red ribbon, a bundle of rusted keys. The family magpie, my father calls me. He doesn't like that I take castaway items hiding in the school basement or in the lost-and-found, forgotten, homeless. No one may want them, but it's still stealing, he says.

I do it anyhow. One day I might need an elastic, or a scrap of leather, or a length of wire. That's what I tell myself, but most of these things, ancient and obsolete, will end up in a weaving, or a basket, or a dream catcher for Paul. This is how I pass my time when the night falls and we're left in the dark, because I don't need to see to work with my hands. I need only to feel.

The twine and paper clips and the other cast-off junk spill onto the table the moment I unbuckle my school bag. Sunlight glints off the keys, and for a moment they seem to wriggle like bright blue herring, a fresh catch, ready to be devoured.

I blink and they are keys again.

The Old Way is a way of work. We have no electricity, no running water, no garbage collection. Our luxuries are born of our own hands. The Old Way keeps us honest, my father says. It keeps us connected to the earth.

That doesn't stop me from thinking about a day, a week, a lifetime in the Corridor. Even with the rolling blackouts, they have heat in the dead of our brutal winter. Their bones don't ache when the rains come, nor do they have to haul in wood when squalls descend from the north, blanketing the world with snow—not to mention it's a lot easier to hide from the searchers among the millions in the Corridor. Here, we're exposed, and there's not much stopping them from coming to gobble us up.

In the Corridor I would find a job, and with the money I earned, I would buy my father a new armchair so he had somewhere comfortable to sit after a hard day of work. I would buy myself a new wool coat and a pair of boots to keep my feet warm in the winter.

And for my brother?

For Paul, I would buy peace of mind and freedom from the dead, except that's not for sale in the Corridor. That's not for sale anywhere.

But we don't live in the Corridor. We live here, on this farm, with its aging roof, its slumping porch, its sorry, sorry garden that I go outside to tend. Paul and my father have no talent for coaxing food from the depleted soil, so the task is left to me. I weed, I till, I plant, I nurture, and if I am lucky, the earth rewards me with a meager bounty in the fall: some squash. Apples, if the spring was warm enough for bees. Turnips, cabbage—there's always enough of those. But not like the old days, when this land was among the richest on earth. The rivers ran so thick with fish a man could walk from one shore to the other without ever getting his feet wet, they say. Bears gorged themselves on berries until they were food-drunk. Sweet rain fell like manna from heaven.

Now our squash vines are stained with white mildew. Tomatoes won't grow. Potatoes do, sometimes, if blight doesn't get them first. But still, we stay. This is our land. This is home.

Our father refuses to supplement our diet with nourishment gels. Only whole food, real food for us, he says. The UA-distributed stuff will rot our guts, rot our souls.

I agree with him on that, at least.

Our father returns home after dark. The table is set, dinner made, the fire stoked even though it's the beginning of June. The chill stays later and later each year as the earth dies her slow death.

Paul gobbles down his dinner while our father washes the ash and dirt from the plastics refinery off his body. This is a clever ploy on Paul's part, because if he's not here, my father can't ask him about the swollen eye that Paul still won't talk about.

I spoon stew onto my father's plate and then my own, sitting down at the table, ignoring Paul's empty spot. The stew was Paul's idea. I wanted to make soup, which isn't as filling but stretches the food remaining from last year's harvest further. We argued about this earlier, and in the end, Paul won out. As my father sops up the thick, heavy stew with a piece of biscuit, I can't help feeling that Paul was right and I was wrong. My need to be thrifty, to dole out our lives in careful measures, would have prevented my father from enjoying tonight's dinner, and goodness knows my father can use every little bit of enjoyment he gets.

"I have good news," my father says as he chews. "I might be up for a raise."

"That's great, Dad," I whisper. I refuse to look at him. He is an unabashed romantic, my father, always holding on to hope, whistling that song about the bright side of life despite the fact that sunlight is a murderer and poison rain her accomplice.

A hand reaches out to take mine, and I resist the temptation to flinch. It's covered with sores and burns. It couldn't possibly belong to my father. "Maybe there'll be enough money to take a vacation," he says. "Just you and Paul and me. Somewhere nice. What do you think?"

"Maybe." That's the best response I summon up, because it's only a matter of time until my father's position at the plastics refinery is rendered obsolete. They don't know he's an Other. I'm not sure how he's concealed it, but he has. Sooner or later someone will catch on, and my father will be entered into the UA inventory too. Either that or a machine will replace him.

It could be worse, I suppose. It could always be worse.

Later, long after my father has fallen asleep, I creep through the dark, searching for Paul. Our house was built back in the days when fertility rates were still high. It has four bedrooms. Mine is at the back, overlooking the garden. My father sleeps on the old, threadbare sofa downstairs, and Paul? Well, Paul has always been a wanderer. I never know where I'll find him.

His voice drifts out from what was once my parents' bedroom. "I'm in here. Put out the candle and come look at the stars."

I take a seat beside him on the windowsill and stare at the sky, stained gray by the Corridor lights. "There isn't much to see. Too much smoke."

"No, look. There's Orion's Belt." He points. "Mintaka, Alnilam, Alnitak."

"Sure, I see them." But I don't—not really.

But then the clouds shift and a few stars appear, along with the half-full moon. Her thin light illuminates Paul's face. Our faces share the same sharp planes, Paul and me. Both of us have hair the color of dark honey. Our teeth are white and straight, a reminder of what our father has sacrificed for us. Our father's teeth are brown around the edges now, and sometimes I see him spitting blood.

"Dad's talking about a raise again," I say.

"About time."

"You know he won't get it."

Paul turns. His eyes are dark and I see a raven's wing drift through them. "You would have to say something like that."

"Someone's got to be the voice of reason in this family."

"Naysayer, you mean."

"Truthsayer." I toy with the hem of my nightgown and shiver, suddenly cold. "But no one ever listens." I don't want to leave my brother here alone, but unlike him, I'm no good without sleep. So I rise and creep to the door, but when I turn to say good night, Paul's already forgotten about me. His eyes are fixed on the night sky. His head is tipped to one side, as if he's listening to something only he can hear, and I wonder—not for the first time—if the stars talk to Paul. He's never mentioned it. I've never asked, but what I do know is that when my brother's like this, deep in communion with something I'll never hear or see, I worry for him—even more than when I see his raven, because when Paul enters that world, he does so alone.

And one day I fear he might not come back.

CHAPTER TWO

$\mathcal{M}$orning is my least favorite time of day. Even in June, the air outside my bed is cold and damp. I rush to dress, rush to wash, rush downstairs to make breakfast for Paul and me.

This morning my brother is nowhere to be seen.

"Paul! We're going to be late!" I call up the stairs as I scramble about, stuffing leathery apples into lunch bags—paper, not plastic. My father doesn't allow plastic in the house.

Eventually Paul wanders down the stairs. His hair is a mess and his eyes remind me of thunderclouds. He's still in his pajamas. "We're not going," he says.

Paul never wants to go to school. He's always made excuses, ever since he was a little boy—the school smells, it's too hot, he has a stomachache, he doesn't learn anything anyhow. Over and over again, and I'm the one who ends up having to tell my father. "Do we have to do this again? Really? Do we?"

"So don't, then." He slumps in his chair and stabs his spoon into his porridge.

It's a flippant answer, one that would normally set off an argument between us, but today it doesn't. Today it twists my stomach into a knot. There's a reason Paul doesn't want to go, a reason that extends beyond his black eye or the bullying from the other kids or just plain not liking school. "Tell me why," I say. "What is it?"

"Your hair is falling out of your braid."

"Don't change the subject." I touch the back of my head anyhow and sure enough, a strand of hair drifts free.

"Told you."

"You're still changing the subject." I rip the hair band from my braid and start to retwist it, but Paul takes it from my hands.

His long fingers weave themselves into my hair, dividing it into three new strands. "I had a vision," he says.

I bite my lip. He's done this deliberately, trapping me like this so I can't whirl around and glare at him. We both get visions, Paul and I, but Paul's are different than mine. Mine are like dreams, surreal, strange. Sometimes, when they come while I'm awake, they show me the stories of people's lives, whether I want to watch or not. But Paul's? They're like prophecies, terrible and violent and brutal. They leave him broken in their aftermath. "When? Of what?"

"Does it matter?"

"You know it does."

"There. Not quite as good as what the Corridor girls do with theirs, but not bad." He takes the hair band from me and he snaps it around the end of my braid. "Just let it go, Cass."

I should, but I can't. Paul has always shared his visions with me—up until recently. One more item on the growing list of things he won't talk to me about anymore. "Come on," I say. "Tell me. You always feel better when you do."

"Do I?" He snorts. "Do I really? Since when do you know how I feel about anything?"

"Paul," I say, because what else is there to say? It's not about figuring out what his vision means. It's about dividing its weight in half so we shoulder the burden together.

"Cass," he says, "would you quit trying to be my mother? I had one. She's gone. I don't need another."

"That's not fair, Paul. You know that's not fair."

And like that, he snaps. "Damn it all, Cass!" His fist

pounds down on the kitchen table, sending a glass fly-ing. It shatters across the floor. Sunlight catches on the fragments skating toward me, casting prisms around the room. My vision blurs, and it takes everything I have to make sure I stay here, attached to the earth. Spirit is coming for me. Spirit wants to take me under.

Slowly the world settles back into place as I bend to pick up the shards of glass. My hands are shaking—from anger? From fear? I'm not sure. Both, maybe.

Paul must sense this. He crouches beside me and slips the glass carefully from my hand. "Let me do this," he says. "Go outside. Do what you need to do."

I feel myself nod and will my legs to move. My head is light, fuzzy, like it always is when spirit comes to call, as if a veil has descended in my mind, detaching me from my body. I hate this feeling, like I'm no longer part of myself. Paul hates it too, because sometimes when this happens, it's not just spirit that takes me. When I was younger, I'd have seizures—another reason why we still live here, close to medical help—and though I haven't had one in years, every time this happens, I brace for them, for the loss of myself, for the force that takes hold of my body and shakes me free of it.

For some reason, setting my hands on the earth, dig-ging my fingers deep into her soil, as if I might grow roots myself, staves off the seizures. Keeping spirit away, though, isn't so easy. If it wants me, nothing I do will stop it from taking me under into a world of blackness and shadows and monsters.

This is my problem, my curse, the counterpoint to Paul's visions. My mother said it was a gift, but I think she was wrong.

Later, after the glass is swept up, after I've come inside to wash the dirt from my hands, Paul makes tea. This is his way of making amends.

Our tea isn't really tea at all, but an infusion of minced dandelion root—not what anyone would drink by choice, but real tea hasn't been imported into the UA since continental quarantines were implemented after the first outbreak of Plague. Since my father refuses to deal with the Band-controlled black market, we're left with our sorry substitute. Puts hair on your chest, my father always says, to which we reply: *Gee, Dad. Great. Just what we've always wanted.*

"It needs to steep," Paul says. He refuses to look at me. "I'm going to the tree."

I want to tell him it's okay, that I know he didn't mean to break the glass or upset me. Instead I just go upstairs and get a basket of found things, add it to the tea tray, and head outside for the telling of Paul's vision.

Vision doesn't really describe what happens to Paul. Sometimes the lost whisper to him in his dreams, telling him their sorrows, their grief, as if he's their confessor. Occasionally they ask him to release them. These encounters leave Paul worn and grim, but it's the other visions, the ones that foretell the future, that trouble us both. We decode them together, trying to make some sense of the bizarre symbols, the totems, the omens. Most times we don't decipher what they mean until afterward, when it's too late, but we still try, hoping that one day we'll unlock the code. This is what torments Paul, that he has the power to stop things, terrible things, if he could only decipher what he sees. I understand how he feels. What good is a gift when you don't know how to use it?

We settle under the apple tree, the one where we spread our mother's ashes, school long forgotten. Paul builds a fire as I take the basket in my hands and ask the items inside what they want to be. The keys whisper to me, and so does a length of twine. As I wait for Paul to speak, I begin to twist the twine into knots, stringing the keys between them. I will give it to Paul once I'm finished, and knowing him, he will feed it to the fire. But that's okay. I know these things I create with my hands aren't for me to keep. It's the giving that's important.

Today I don't have to wait long for Paul to speak. He rushes into the words as if he can't stand to keep them inside himself any longer. "I was a raven, and I was flying," he says.

I close my eyes. Key and knot, key and knot. A key to open the door of Paul's vision, and a knot to close it firmly behind him.

"I was above our house," Paul says, "circling over and over again, waiting for you to come home, but I knew you wouldn't. No one would, except me because I was already here, and every time I tried to fly away to find you, to find anyone, I couldn't. It was like there was an invisible rope tying me in place. And then someone shot me and I fell."

"Oh." The keys drop from my fingers, falling on the earth with a metallic clatter. I know Paul is waiting for me to say something, but I can't find words. They're trapped in my heart. This is not a good vision. I don't know what it means, but I feel the warning in it. Something bad is on the way. I grapple for the keys, as if they really do open another place, a place where we might be safe, but they keep slipping out of my grasp.

"Here," I say when I finally get ahold of them. "Put them on, Paul. You need to wear these."

But before he can take them from me, our father's

truck rattles down the driveway, going fast—far too fast.

Paul gets up first, and when he breaks into a run, I follow. Our father leaves for work before dawn, long before we wake for school. He gets off after dark. He would never come home from work so early unless something terrible had happened. The worst kind of terrible.

We draw to a halt just as the door groans open. My father slides out. If he's surprised to see us at home, he doesn't show it. Instead, he's pale. "You two get in the house. Now!"

Paul arches an eyebrow at me, but we do what our father asks, springing away like frightened deer. Once inside, we hover behind the front door, peering out the window. As the dust cloud dissipates, we see my father's not alone. A woman gets out of the truck, hauling an ancient leather bag with her. She's about my father's age, judging from the gray at her temples; squat, but not fat, and grim.

"Who is she?" Paul whispers.

"I don't know." I feel as if I should, though.

"Do you see anything?" Paul asks.

I let my eyes drift out of focus and scan the sky, but it's free from anything hinting of spirit involvement. "Nothing. Nothing spiritual, anyhow." Our father draws an old rifle, still as lethal as any modern weapon, from behind the seat of his truck and glances our way. "Searchers?" I say.

"Maybe." Paul turns away from the window. "I haven't seen him like this in ages."

"Me neither." My heart flutters at the thought of the last outbreak, when we were almost taken in a search. The searchers caught up to us at the mag-station on the edge of the reserve, only a mile from our home, at the same time the Band men found us. For three long hours the Band hid us in the bowels of the mag-station, safe beneath the layers of earth blocking the searchers from tracing the signals from our chips. When they finally escorted us home, we found our father sitting on the porch, cradling his rifle. He pressed us to his chest, and then pushed us inside so we wouldn't see him cry. He wears the same look now—ashen faced, jaw clenched tight, a worried pallor framing him. The sight of his frailty hits me in the gut.

His footsteps are heavy on the porch. He heaves the door open as if it weighs as much as the world itself and looks at both of us slowly, as if time is winding down. "Pack your things. Only what's absolutely essential— clothes, food, tools."

Paul makes for the tool shed. I dart upstairs and begin pulling things from drawers, my mind spinning as I try to decide what we need. Clothes. Needles. Thread. Soap. Underwear. Socks. Shoes. What else, what else? I run from room to room and back again, frantic, panicking at the idea that today, this very afternoon, we are leaving. What if we never come back?

When I finally come downstairs, I set the boxes next to a sack of potatoes and a duffel of tools. Will this be enough? What have I forgotten? What would my mother have taken, if she was here? The china? The curtains? The photograph of my grandparents? I don't know, I just don't know.

"Cass."

I turn to find my father standing there, looking like he's on the verge of tears.

"That'll do, starshine," he says. "Come into the kitchen."

I follow him, and then wish I hadn't. An array of surgical instruments is spread over the kitchen table. The woman from the truck stands at our sink, washing her hands. She doesn't look up.

"Cassandra," my father says, "this is Madda."

I should acknowledge her, but I can't. All I see are needles and scalpels, a neat row of silver. My throat's so thick with fear that I can't even ask what's happening.

"Cass?" my father repeats. "You okay?"

Slowly, I raise my gaze to meet his. "What is going on?"

"Tell her," the woman says. "The short version. We need to get this over with if we want to make the tide."

"Plague," my father says. "A new strain. Airborne, they think, because it's jumped the quarantine grids."

I close my eyes. In my mind, I see Paul's raven circling our house. Is this what his vision was trying to tell us? My father is still speaking about the searches, how there aren't enough full bloods in the Corridor, how the UA is now rounding up half-bloods, how we're not safe. I hear him say these things, but what he's really saying is we're leaving. We're leaving our home, the only home we've ever known, the one we've worked so hard to keep.

"You know what happens to the ones the searchers take," he says.

I do. Every Other does. We die.

"Where are we going?" Paul asks. He's standing just outside the kitchen, as scared as me, but at the same time practically shaking from excitement. He knows the answer to his question already. There is only one place *to* go.

"The Island," my father says. To treaty lands. To the Band.

"We're removing your chips," Madda says as the kettle starts to whistle. "No chip, no way to track you. Besides, best you have nothing of the Corridor left on you. They don't look kindly on that sort of thing on the Island."

"I'll go first," I say, but Paul pushes past me, rolling up his sleeve, exposing the chip in his forearm that allows us to connect to the UA etherstream. He takes a seat at the table and offers up his arm like a sacrifice to the gods.

Neither of us makes a sound as Madda slices our skin and digs out the chip, but we're both pale and shaking afterward. My father and Madda load the truck while we sit on the porch, wrapped in blankets, sipping at Madda's flask of whiskey. I hate alcohol, but when the only thing to cut the pain is willow bark tea, even I will allow myself a sip—but just one. Paul cradles his bandaged arm close to him. I hold mine out to the wind, letting it cool the heat rising from the wound. Later we'll both have scars. This is how they'll know where we came from when we get to the Island, that we weren't born there, that we weren't raised native. The Band might open its arms wide to us now, but they'll never, ever let us forget that we came from the Corridor first.

CHAPTER THREE

*P*aul and I ride in the back of the truck with our belongings. Our route takes us along roads that haven't been used in years. Trees reach out toward us, snatching at my hair, at Paul's arms, as my father drives over the potholes faster than he should, forcing us to cling to each other as much as to the truck. We are running, and every time I look up, I expect to see the sleek silver searchcraft bearing down on us.

Only a few Others taken by searchers have ever survived the rescue missions staged by the Band, and the tales they tell are harrowing—wards where row upon row of Others are hooked to harvesting machines to be drained of their blood. For some reason, the powers that be can't manufacture a vaccine. We're it. Our blood is injected into Plague victims, who cross their fingers and hope to survive. Sometimes they do; sometimes they don't, but it works often enough that they keep using us, even though they can't keep us alive.

But consider, the UA government says, the greater good. What is the loss of one when that person can help so many?

When my father finally stops the truck at the end of the road where a trail cuts into the brush, I allow myself to breathe. Maybe he was wrong. Maybe we can still go back. Maybe this has all been a mistake.

But the aching wound on my arm reminds me there is no going back. Removal of a chip without UA consent is punishable by law. Like it or not, we are now fugitives.

We work quickly, unloading our boxes and lugging them down to a sheltered cove where a weather-beaten herring skiff rests in the shallows. Madda hops into it, taking our belongings from us until there's none left. She then begins the careful task of moving the stuff around, adjusting the boxes until she's happy with the balance, leaving us with nothing to do but fret. I sit on a nearby rock, watching her work, wishing I had something to do with my hands. I've always known that belongings are expendable, that stories and memories are the true treasures we carry with us, but seeing what little we have loaded onto the boat leaves me feeling very poor. Paul stands beside me, his rifle resting in the crook of his arm, staring out across the expanse of ocean. I can sense he feels the same way.

It's some time before my father returns. He took the truck deep into the forest to be reclaimed by the land, but not before draining the fuel tanks. Fuel is too precious to sacrifice, even to the earth.

No one speaks.

Silence is our talisman.

It takes time for the tide to rise, but once the skiff is floating we climb aboard. The sun descends behind the thunderheads hugging the western horizon. Behind us, to the east, mountains rear up, demanding that we return home. *There is no coming back once you cross to the west,* they say. *We will remember that you abandoned us, and we will exact revenge if you return.* Their peaks are blackened maws stretching skyward to snap at the stars. As fearsome as they are, I can't help staring at them. This may be the last time I look at those mountains, those peaks I've looked up at every day of my life. I wish I could say good-bye, but even if I did, I don't think the mountains would listen.

My father and Paul use oars to pole the skiff out into

deeper water. It's hard work. My father's breath comes fast and heavy as he fights against the tide.

Once we're far enough out for Madda to risk starting the motor, Paul takes a seat beside me on the cold metal hull, and reaches out to take my hand. He knows I don't like the ocean. The first time spirit took me was while I was swimming not far from here. If it weren't for Paul hauling me to the surface and dragging me back to the beach, I would still be there. Even though that day was years ago, when we were only six, I can't shake the feeling that if I touch the water, I'll be drawn back down into the shadows of the old cities below. They aren't friendly, those places: Vancouver, Victoria, Seattle, Los Angeles. Their deaths were sudden and painful, shaken loose from the land by terrible earthquakes. Below, in the inky fathoms, they're reaching toward me, raking the water with their gridiron hands.

One look at Paul tells me he remembers too. The buildings aren't all that lurk below. The lost live amid the barnacles and sea wrack, and they, too, seek a new home. That day, when he swam into the dark water to save me, was the first time he encountered the lost. That was the price of my life, that Paul be haunted by those who have died and yet not passed over, and that price is something I will try to repay for as long as I live.

Our father turns from his watch at the stern. "Is it bad, Cass?"

"Yeah," I murmur.

"It'll be better when we're out a bit farther," he says.

I smile and nod, because that will make him feel better. My father has enough to worry about already.

Once it's dark, Madda flicks on a single red light on the port side of the boat. "There's still some traffic out here," she whispers, "so I've got to put it on, but if you need to say something, keep your voice down. The ocean does strange things to sound, especially on a night like this."

I know what she means. The water is glassy smooth, and as the boat slices through it, the ripples turn red around us. My mind swims as spirit pulls at me, demanding I give in. *Look,* it whispers. *Remember. You've seen this before.* And I have, this red flame surrounding a boat plying a dark ocean. But when? I've never been to the Island before, but that's not it, exactly. There's something deeper to this feeling.

Paul sets his hand on my arm and gives me a questioning look. I shake my head. No, I'm not going under. I'm still here, but that doesn't mean I'll watch the bloodred wake anymore. I train my gaze on the darkness to the west, where the Island looms. My father lived there once, long ago. He doesn't talk about it much. My mother used to, though. She said it's beautiful there, peaceful, a haven from the Corridor and its smoke and noise. But there's trouble on the Island too. Back then, the Band ran wild, until Arthur Eagleson got them organized, but that was after my parents returned to my grandfather's farm, and now Arthur Eagleson is gone as well. He disappeared two years ago, and it didn't take long for some of the Band to revert to their old ways, ways that prize violence over temperance, ways that mirror the UA tactics more than they'd care to admit.

And the Band has already stolen so much from our family—our two uncles, for one, and our safety, for another. Two years ago, the Band signed the treaty land surrounding our house back to the UA, and left for the Island. Since then, they just showed up whenever they wanted, marching into our house, taking it over like they owned the place, and while I retreated upstairs and locked myself in my bedroom, my brother and father sat with them, drank with them, listened to their stories about how, one day, the Band would overthrow the UA and take back the land that was once ours to begin with.

It's not the boasting, or the drinking, or even the guns they brought into our house, though I hate all of them, too. It's that the Band men filled my brother's head with dreams, dreams of being a warrior of the Old Way, when what they really want is to use my brother as cannon fodder. They don't tell him about the boys who die when they raid the facilities where they hook us Others up to machines and drain us of our blood. They don't tell him about those who return home broken, those who take to drinking rather than face a day sober. But I know. My mother told me.

What would she say if she were here right now? Does she know how much it hurts to leave her behind, sleeping beneath the apple tree at the house? Sometimes when I close my eyes I think I hear her talking to me, but I'm too scared to believe that might be true. I wonder if she speaks to Paul. If she does, he's never said. Would he keep something like that from me? I wish I knew. Sitting here in the boat, holding hands, it's like we're children again. When we were little, we were inseparable. I kept my hair short so I'd look just like Paul, because back then, I wanted to be him, the funny one, the happy one. I didn't want to have seizures. I didn't want to cross into the spirit world and see the things I saw, things I don't truly remember.

But now, my seizures have all but left me behind and sometimes I find myself wanting to walk those spirit paths, if only they didn't scare me so badly. But I don't tell Paul that. Paul thinks I'm brave. I let him. One of us has to be strong, and Paul doesn't believe it's him.

As I think this, I look up and find Madda watching me. She's frowning. If I closed my eyes and allowed my spirit sight to come, I think I'd find her looking for my shade too, and that frown tells me she's just as puzzled as I am about why it's missing.

Sometime later, just as I'm about to doze off, Madda kills the engines. We float, helpless under the watchful eye of the waning moon, as something pricks at my temples. We are crossing the boundary.

In the old times, sailors used to tell tales of sirens. My mother told me about them, the women who sang songs to lure men to their deaths. Perhaps the boundary is part of that, a siren of sorts; for if I was on my own, I'm not sure I'd be able to leave. Spirit is thick here, calling to me, blinding my eyes, whispering words that my mother once used: *My gentle girl. My starshine child. Stay with me. Don't go. Don't leave me alone. Don't leave me behind.*

When Madda starts the engines again, I almost weep. I don't want to go. I want to stay here and listen to my mother's voice, even though part of me knows it's not really her. I'm only hearing what I want to hear. *It's the boundary*, I think. It's lonely. I would be too, if I were out here all by myself, waiting, watching people pass by, never to stay.

My father takes the helm as Madda sits beside me, watching me with night-dark eyes. Paul snores, his head leaning against my shoulder.

"You felt it, did you?" Madda whispers.

I nod.

"Ah. I should have known." She looks back toward the boundary. A glimmer of phosphorescence marks our wake. "Non-Others can float right up to it and never know it exists, you know, unless they try to pass through. Then the boundary pushes them away, although to them it feels like the current, or the wind. Well, that's the way it used to be. Not quite like that anymore—there are gaps now that didn't used to be there. But our blood has always allowed us to pass through, and that permits us to bring non-Others across if we want to. But to feel it, to hear it, that's something a little different."

"How?" I whisper.

She looks as if she won't answer but then changes her mind. "The boundary is made of spirit, and if you feel it, that means you've got a strong connection to the spirit world. Sometimes, the spirits of the ones we love, the ones who have passed on, can come through here. But you didn't need me to tell you that, did you?"

She makes her way back to the wheel before I can answer, because I don't need to. I see the pinch of her mouth, the way she's holding her breath, the shadow of loss in her eyes.

She's heard the siren's call too.

Dawn rises like a gray dove. The air is cold and I haven't slept at all.

The Island looms before us. As the sun rises, its mountains ripple with golden light, with crimson, like a christening, a great homecoming. I wish it was both, but I know it's neither.

There are five treaty territories, established more than two hundred years ago, before the world fell apart. All of them are protected by the Band. The Pueblos far to the south still grow food by dry-till methods. The eastern Mohawk Nation is the oldest, and the most militant. They always have been, those Mohawk warriors. They were the ones who created the Band to begin with, and it was their idea to negotiate the treaty territories before it was too late.

The third is the Shu, in the heart of what once was British Columbia. Far to the north is the fourth, the

Bix'iula. Some wonder if it still exists. No one has heard from the Bix'iula in years.

And then, there's the Island.

My father moved to the Island when he was a child, after my grandmother left my grandfather. When my father went back to the farm in the Corridor, his brothers, my uncles, decided to stay on the Island. One day they disappeared. Just like that—gone, without any explanation from the Band. Once in a while, I think I can feel their totems following me, but when I look back, nothing's there.

I sometimes wonder if the Island took them, for it is an angry land. Once, ages ago, a great tsunami swept its lower half into the sea. The Island has never forgiven the ocean for this, and eventually she'll seek retribution.

Paul wakes as Madda guides the boat into an estuary. He's always wanted to come here. "Told you it would be beautiful," he says, as a heron, startled by the engines, takes to wing. "Told you."

A wharf looms out of the morning mist. Boats flank it, rocking at our approach. The jangling of their rigging breaks the eerie silence.

Madda pilots the skiff into a berth as my father jumps onto the wharf, catching the mooring line as Paul throws it to him, and tows the skiff into place. "Start unloading," he says to me once the skiff is moored. "I'll be right back." He jogs up the ramp and vanishes into the mist.

I climb over the gunwales to take a box from Madda. "I knew you a long time ago, when you were a little girl," she says as she hands it to me.

Paul catches my eye as I bite my tongue. Meeting me as a child hardly constitutes knowing me, but I swallow those words. It's been a long night, and we're all a little owly.

Once everything's unloaded, my father reappears and helps move it all up the ramp. There's a truck waiting there. A white man is at the steering wheel, and beside him, a girl about my age, with long blond hair woven into braids. Neither of them gets out. They just watch us load our belongings into the back, making it clear that they think they're better than us, and when I notice the scar on the girl's arm, it's all I can do not to give in to my anger. That scar tells me she lived in the Corridor once, so she knows what it's like to lose your belongings, your home, your everything, and she doesn't even have the decency to say hello?

When we finally have the truck loaded, we climb into the back with our boxes. Madda tells us she'll see us in town, and heads back down to her boat. The man turns the key. The engine chugs a few times, and then coughs.

He turns the key again, with the same results. Chug, chug, cough, nothing.

"Want me to take a look?" my father says.

"Nope. It does this sometimes," the man replies, but it's not long before they've got the hood up and they're both bent over the engine.

I wander back toward the wharf, picking up an old piece of salt-crusted rope that someone's tossed away as I go. The rope's stiff, but with a little work, I unravel it into strands and start to knot it into a chain.

On the beach a short ways down, something catches my eye as I work—a blur of black against the thick, dark firs. I squint. It's a raven. He's tugging something from under a rock. He cackles and hops, dancing his awkward, funny jig, until he finally pulls his prize out. Then he rises in the air, a black arrow, and drops something small, something white, to its death. An oyster, I think.

"Paul," I say. He's talking to the girl, and looks annoyed that I've interrupted him, but strolls over anyhow, the girl sliding out of the truck to trail after him. "What?" he says.

"Look at that raven," I say.

"Raven?" Paul tips his head to the side. "What raven?"

I look again. It's not there. "It must have flown away," I say quickly, though Paul narrows his eyes. He knows I'm lying, but to admit I'm seeing shades in front of this girl that neither of us knows is a bad idea. Strangers don't always take kindly to someone who sees things that aren't there, and there's something about this girl, now that she's close to me, that strikes me wrong.

But the girl didn't hear my slip. Her attention is focused on the chain of knots in my hand. "What's that?" she says.

"Oh." I hold it up. "A necklace, maybe? I think it might be long enough." I smile and hold it out to her. "If you like it you can have it when I'm done."

She pulls a green stone on a leather thread out from under her shirt and dangles it for me to see. It's beautiful, and she knows it. "I've already got one. I don't need another," she says. She tucks the stone back in place and strolls off to the truck.

My brother follows her, casting me a glance that says, *Oh well.*

My hand forms a fist around the knotwork, and when I'm sure no one is looking, I throw it as far as I can. It floats on the water for a brief moment before it starts to sink. Madda, who's still down on the docks, notices and fishes it out. She tucks it into her pocket and then turns back to her work.

I ball my hands into fists. Why should I care if the girl didn't want the necklace? But it wasn't the refusal. It was the way she refused it that's left me feeling hollow inside. She's back in the truck now, the door open. Paul leans against it, smiling. I should be happy that he's making a friend, but I'm not, though I'm not sure why. Maybe it's that she didn't help us. Maybe it's the look in my brother's eyes, the one that says he's smitten. Maybe it's the look in her eyes, the one that says she knows.

The engine finally roars to life. "All right, everyone back in," my father says as he slams the hood down.

I cast one more look at the estuary. The ebbing tide has created ripples of green water that look like a humpbacked monster, and a seal floats away on the current.

But no raven. Maybe there never was.

I turn away and refuse to think about what that might mean.

CHAPTER FOUR

*O*ur path takes us through the forest. Ancient firs reach toward the sky as if they want to claim the sun for themselves. This forest is a dark, still place. The only sound is the truck, rumbling and grinding its way along the road. The trees aren't happy that we are disturbing their slumber, so I close my eyes and wish for them to rest, to sleep. *We mean no harm,* I say. *We only want to pass through.*

Whether the forest understands my silent request, I don't know. I have no idea whether it does any good at all, but an offering, even one as meager as a thought, is something at least.

And then the forest gives way and the town appears.

The town had a name once, but names have little meaning anymore in this world where humanity is crammed into population corridors, where numbers designate quarantine grids, where people are divided into Others and non-Others. A main street runs east to west, disappearing into more old forest. Buildings flank the street. Some of them are derelict, with broken windows and sloughing paint. One, in better repair than the rest, has STORE painted in blue across its pediment. A dark-haired girl sits on its steps, weaving a basket. A little ways away, sunlight glints off the bell in an old church's belfry. Scorch marks race up the church's side, and boards over the windows prevent anyone from looking in or the church from looking out.

Standing at the top of the street, closest to the forest, is the longhouse. A green-and-red thunderbird rests on the apex of its roof, and flanking each corner is a watchman, gazing down on us with stern eyes. Their arms are not raised in welcome. No one may enter.

I may not enter.

Across the street, a path leads out to a park. Women stand out there, clustered around a fire, where racks of oolichan cure above the coals. The whole place reeks of smoke and fish, and my mouth fills with saliva. We haven't eaten since yesterday evening, and even though I don't really like oolichan, right now, I'm not choosy.

The man stops the truck at the store. He gets out,

nods at my father, and stomps up the steps, disappearing inside.

My father watches him, then jumps out. "I've got something to take care of," he says. "Wait here." A man in a cowboy hat meets him halfway up the steps. They shake hands before heading inside. The girl on the steps doesn't even look up. She just keeps weaving her basket.

Paul and I exchange curious looks. We've heard of this place all our lives. It was a mining town long ago, filled with Chinese immigrants who came to dig coal from the earth's bones, but Others lived here long before that, steeping the land in their legends, their stories. Our father told us those stories, of a raven pulling a man from a seashell, of mountains that swallow people whole, of the lake, just beyond the trees, that has no bottom. Rumor has it you can still catch steelhead on the rivers around here. Rumor has it salmon still run and elk call in the fall.

But rumors aren't real. All they do is make a person hope for something that can't be, and what's the sense in that?

Paul jumps off the tailgate and approaches the passenger side, where the blond-haired girl still sits, legs dangling out. I join him. If we're going to be here for any length of time, we might as well make a friend or two, and I'm willing to try again. "I'm Cass," I say, offering her my hand.

"Avalon." She stares at my hand as if it's covered in Plague marks for a moment, then jerks her chin toward the girl on the steps. "That's Helen over there. You should go talk to her."

I'm sorely tempted to tell this Avalon that she doesn't get to order me around, but the girl on the steps has looked up. She has a beautiful moonface, open and sweet, but a blush is crawling up her neck. She heard what Avalon said, and she's afraid I don't want to talk to her.

But I do. Unlike Avalon, who makes me wary, this Helen reads like an open book. I feel like I can see right down into her soul. She shuffles to one side to make room for me to sit down, then takes up her basket again, working a new strip of dyed cedar into the pattern. "I knew you were coming," she says. "Madda's my auntie. I live with her." She looks at Paul and purses her lips. "I see Avalon's got her hooks into your brother already."

Paul is grinning from ear to ear as Avalon laughs at something he said. "Corridor girls never really noticed Paul," I say. My gut tightens into a knot.

"Corridor girls." Helen snorts. "If the rest are like her, he should consider himself lucky. I'm sorry you had to leave your home behind, though," she adds quickly. "Was it hard? Leaving?"

I don't reply, because a lump has formed in my throat, hard and raw and threatening.

Helen nods. "Sorry. Dumb question. I've never been there, you know, though I've heard a lot about it." She inspects her basket and picks up another strand of cedar.

I sit down beside her. "That's going to be a good basket. Your weaving is tighter than mine."

Helen looks up. "Oh, you weave?"

"Yes. My mother taught me."

"Here." She holds the basket out to me. I take it, along with a thread of blackened cedar, and work it in and out of the spokes. Helen smiles. "Madda's going to like that you're good with your hands."

I'm about to ask why that would be, when someone at the far end of the street whistles. A dozen or so men emerge from the forest. They're all wearing packs on their backs, and most have belts of ammunition hanging from their hips. Most also carry rifles. Band men.

Helen takes the basket back from me. "They were out at the boundary, at the south end of the Island," she says as she stands. "I've got to go. If Madda comes here looking for me, tell her I've gone to back to the cottage, okay?"

"Okay," I say, but Helen doesn't hear my reply. She's already jumped off the porch, rushing away in the opposite direction. The Band men don't even notice her. A man with a vicious scar cutting across his face leads the men up to the store. He thumps his way up the steps and goes inside. The others follow, fierce and grim and dirty, though now that they're closer, I see a couple aren't much older than I am.

One by one they go into the store, except for the last in the line, a boy about my age. He has thick auburn hair, and hovering just behind his shoulder is a kingfisher cast in shadow. He looks at Avalon in the truck before shifting his gaze to Paul, and then to me. His eyes are the color of ash. He looks like he's about to say something to me, but before he can, the door creaks open and a stout boy leans out. "Henry wants you in here. Now."

The auburn-haired boy casts a half-smile in my direction, as if he'd rather stay, before ducking inside.

"Gotta go," Avalon says, pushing her door open suddenly, forcing Paul to jump out of the way. She runs up the stairs and into the store without another word.

Paul scratches his head. "What was that all about?"

"Don't know." But I want to, despite myself. It's not just Avalon's reaction or that our father's inside the store with all the Band men—it's that boy, the one with the kingfisher shade. I've seen him before. I don't know where, but I feel like I know him.

Paul shakes his head as I creep up the steps to press my ear against the door, in hopes of hearing something—anything. "You could just go inside, you know." He yawns. "What are they going to do? Kick you out?"

I'm trying to find a smart reply when the door opens. I jump back as my father steps out. He gives me a funny look. "What are you doing there, Cass? Eavesdropping? You know what they say about curiosity, right?" He takes me by the shoulder and steers me back toward the truck. "In you get. You too, Paulie. We've got a house to go see."

"Don't we need our driver?" I ask as I shuffle along the hot vinyl seat.

"Nope." My father grins as Paul climbs in beside me and slams the door shut. "The truck's ours. And just wait until we get to the house! I know you didn't want to leave, Cass, but trust me—things are going to be good here. You'll see."

I want to believe him. I want to believe him with all my heart. But good things don't happen to people like us, and so my heart just hurts instead.

CHAPTER FIVE

Something changes as we head out of town. My father drives with one hand on the wheel, steering with careless ease. His other hand dangles out the window, tapping the door of the truck as he whistles "Alouette."

Paul can't help himself and starts to sing.

"Alouette, gentille Alouette,
Alouette, je te plumerai!"

Our French is more *patois* than pure, but it marks us as what we are: Métis. Once the children of the *coureurs de bois* and their Indian wives of convenience, we are now just what the name means: mixed. Half-breeds. Not red enough to be red, and not white enough to be white.

We don't have a native tongue. Our myths are a curious twist of European tales and plains folklore, and never do we dance until we become one with the spirit world. We jig instead, hopping and skipping to fiddle and spoons.

The truck rumbles past house after dilapidated house. "We're looking for a big rock with a petroglyph carved into it," my father says.

Paul spots it first. "There!" he says as we whiz by the granite boulder jutting out from the forest.

A cloud of dust surrounds us as my father slams on the brakes, throws the truck into reverse, and parks by a driveway running downhill into the trees. "You two wait here for a minute," he says between coughs. "I'm going to check things out." He hops out and marches off.

I slide out to stare at the rock. The petroglyph is a raven, carved deep into the granite, with outspread wings and an open beak reaching toward a circle that I think must be the moon. With my eyes closed, I set my hand on the raven and trace its ridges with my fingertips. Memory threatens to wash over me. Ravens, always ravens. They follow me everywhere, laughing at the girl who has no shade, no spirit animal, taunting me, whispering that if I follow, they can show me where my soul is hidden.

Paul's raven is the lone exception. He has never spoken

to me, but to Paul? Yes, I think my brother has heard the trickster's lies.

Paul pulls my hand away from the granite. "Not now. Not with Dad around."

He's right, but it would be so easy just to slip away, surrounded by the thick, dark forest of fir. I open my eyes. Beyond the trees, the lake is a sheet of quicksilver, so bright it blinds me. Surely I would be safe here. Surely I could cross and find my way back.

But a breeze ruffles the hair at the base of my neck, reminding me that I'm only a moment away from spirit taking hold of me and using me as it chooses, so I hold tight to my brother's hand until the raven releases its grasp on me.

It's not long before my father returns and we pile into the truck again. Neither Paul nor I mention the raven.

The truck lumbers down the steep driveway, and when the house comes into view, I wince. It's in shambles. Glass is missing from several of the upstairs windows and the roof is blanketed with a thick coat of fir needles. Who knows what lurks underneath? Paul eyes it, knowing that my father will have him up there tomorrow to see what needs to be repaired.

Paul jumps out once the truck groans to a halt, and pushes open the door to the woodshed. A raccoon darts past him, skittering away into the bush. Paul laughs, but then the acrid scent left behind by the raccoon wafts out. *This is my home*, it says. *Trespassers will not be tolerated.*

Paul's laughter fades. My family doesn't take omens lightly.

My father draws a deep breath, then nudges me. "Go see what we're dealing with inside, Cass," he says. "Paul and I will start unloading."

A path runs around one side of the house, leading to a door that's stuck fast, its hinges rusted shut long ago. I find another path, but it leads down the steeply sloping hill toward the lake, where a boathouse sits in the shadows, its dock extending out like a crabbed finger.

Next I try the sundeck that runs across the front of the house, hoping to find a window ajar, but instead I end up standing at the railing, staring down at the water. Sometimes the beauty of the earth is so profound, it steals my breath away. In the Corridor, there's not much of the natural world left amid the concrete and the asphalt and the steel, but here? Here I almost feel like I belong, high above the firs and the bracken and the salal.

"What's the matter?" my father asks as he sets a box down next to the door.

"The door's rusted shut." Which is true, but the real problem is that I can't seem to take my eyes off the silvered lake. Reluctantly, I turn away.

"Only one way to fix that." He shoves his shoulder into the door, cursing when the door doesn't move. After a bit of discussion, Paul attacks the door with an ax. Doors are replaceable, but broken shoulders aren't easily mended, no matter how much my mother taught me about healing.

I go back to the truck while Paul hacks away. A spark of light passes through my field of vision as I pick my way up the path, forcing me to shake my head. *Please, let it just be a speck of dust,* I think, but no, it's there, just in the corner of my eye. "Stop it," I murmur. "Just stop it. I'm not going, and that's that."

The spark sits there a moment longer, and then vanishes. I slide a box from the truck and return to the house, blinking, hoping that the spark is truly gone. Paul is pulling pieces of the door from its hinges, but stops what he's doing to peer at me. "You okay?" he says.

"Yeah." I force myself to look at him. "Just not feeling quite right."

"I know." He looks around. "It's almost like this place isn't fully here. I feel it too."

We both shiver, and then laugh just as our father approaches. "What are you two up to?" he says, grinning. "Must be nice, standing around while I do all the work around here. Come on, back at it."

I'm still laughing as I make my way back to the truck,

but for some reason I glance over my shoulder. Paul's still standing there, motionless, staring at the shadows in the trees. My laughter dies.

By the time I return, the last of the door has been cleared away. My father's inside, already sizing up a broken window. "Put that down over there," he says, nodding at the box in my arms, "and then take a look upstairs. There's a bedroom up there with a good view of the lake."

"How do you know that?" I ask.

My father rubs his forehead with the back of his hand. "I've been here before, back when I was about your age." He motions to the stairs. "Go on. You'd better go claim that bedroom before your brother does."

Paul would never claim a room for himself, but still, I go upstairs, knowing that my father hasn't told me the whole truth of this place.

Pinecones and skeletal leaves cover the floor, but my father was right. In this room, I am high above the lake, closer to the sky than the earth. My old bedroom only had a view of the apple tree, but this? This is a view that sings to my soul, and instantly I feel guilty, as if I have betrayed our old house and our life there. That apple tree is where my mother rests. Am I ready to exchange her for the view of this lake so quickly?

No, I decide as I throw open the window and let the

wind rush in. Not just yet, though I can't help wondering what my mother would think of all this. She worked so hard to make sure we had a home at the Corridor. She didn't want me here. She wanted me in a place where I would have a future that didn't involve marrying a warrior and bearing him babies, a future that didn't condemn me to working my fingers to the bone and aging far before my time. That's what she told me, at least, but then, she didn't live to see what happened with the searches. Would she still have made the same choice if she knew what we know now?

On the far shore, several cottages nestle into the trees. Just beyond them, a plume of smoke rises from the forest, a smudge of gray against the expanse of green. The house creaks around me, its bones shifting in the afternoon sun, as on the lake, a single canoe breaks the watery mirror in two. It's heading this way.

"We've got company," I call out the window to where Paul has taken over the job of unloading boxes from the truck.

My father rounds the corner of the house and peers up at me. "Company?"

"There's someone in a canoe down there."

"Hmm." He scratches his head and frowns. "Well, you might as well go down and see what they want."

I don't like the look of that frown, but I try not to think about it as I make my way out of the house and down the hill, out onto the dock, where I stop short. The canoe is tied to it, bobbing in the gentle rhythm of the waves as the boy from the store, the one with the auburn hair, lifts a cage holding three fretful chickens. His kingfisher shade flutters at his shoulder, and now that I'm closer to it I can see that some of the feathers are new, as if they're just growing in over recently healed wounds.

"Oh, hi," he says when he notices me standing there. He sets the cage down, wipes his hands on his shorts, then holds one out to me. "Heard you were moving in and came to see if I could help."

I open my mouth, shut it, and open it again like a landed salmon. His kingfisher has begun to change shape, sending a wave of unsteadiness swooping over me. I close my eyes to fight it off.

"Are you okay?"

"Yes." I open my eyes to face the images hovering over the boy's shoulder, one morphing into the next: the kingfisher, swirls of mist, a green stone, a strange dark shadow. I have never met anyone with more than a single totem before.

"Well," he says, nodding at the chickens. "Madda sent these. Where do you want me to put them?"

"I don't know," I say, while I grasp for anything that will bind me to reality.

"Okay," he says. He's trying hard not to laugh at me, I think. "How about the boathouse? I'll move them there, for a price."

"A price?"

"Your name. Tell me your name."

Finally, something I can answer. "Cassandra. Cassandra Mercredi."

Relief colors my voice, and he laughs again—but not in a cruel way. More as if he understands. "Mercredi . . ." He rolls the word on his tongue. "Mercredi, like Wednesday? You're French?"

"No. Anishinaabe. Métis."

"Ah. Half-breed. Me too. My dad's full-blood, but my mom's white." He shrugs. "Well, welcome to the Island. I'm Bran. Of the Band, I guess. Lead the way, Cassandra Mercredi." He hoists the cage up and nods toward the boathouse.

I set off, Bran following behind me. Bran. It's an unusual name, even by native standards, but I've heard it often enough when the Band men stop to give my father news of the Island. Is this the missing leader's son? Only one way to find out. "Bran, as in Eagleson?"

"Yep," he says. "That's me." The disappointment in his

voice isn't hard to miss. But why? Because I know who he is? And who his father is? Probably. It's hard having a ghost follow you wherever you go. I know. My family has ghosts of its own.

The boathouse isn't the best place to set the chickens loose, but they flutter up into the rafters, happy to be free of the cage. Bran doesn't speak as we step back outside and make our way up to the house. I can feel him watching me as I climb. What is he thinking? Why doesn't he say something? Why do I want him to say something?

Paul greets us as we round the corner of the house. Quick introductions are made with my father, then I duck inside to unpack our belongings because I know what happens next: Band talk.

Their voices drift through an open window as I carry a box of clothing upstairs. I pause, and look down to see Paul, my father, and Bran sitting on the tailgate, sharing a canteen of water.

"And so they're building more outposts to the south?" my father asks.

Bran holds a hunting knife by its blade, only to flip it into the air, grabbing it by the hilt just before it can embed itself into his thigh. "Yep. They've had some strange reports coming out of the Mohawk and Pueblo reserves, so they figure it's time to strengthen the south, though that's part of my father's plan anyhow. Make ourselves strong, so we're not dependent on the boundary, just in case. The reports have just moved up the pace, is all."

I step back. I don't like the look in Paul's eyes, the desperation to prove himself to Bran, to show that he's a warrior too, that he's strong, that he can fight. Suddenly it strikes me that all of this has been too easy. We've only just arrived, and already we have a house and a truck and chickens. But at what price? My father? My brother? Is that what the Band will charge us for this new existence far away from the Corridor and the danger of searchers?

I don't know, but I don't want to be here anymore. I wish there was someplace else *to* go, a place where I wouldn't have to worry about my brother turning hard and bitter.

Except there is no other place. It's here, or nowhere.

But that doesn't mean I'll sit here and listen to them.

I'm halfway down the hill when Bran catches up with me. "Hey," he says, giving me a curious look. "What are you running away from?"

I stop in my tracks. "Why do you think I'm running from anything?"

"Whoa." He holds his hands up. "It was just a joke. But seriously, are you running?"

I look out over the lake. Am I? "I don't know," I say. "Maybe."

"Hmm. Well, don't go too far. I haven't had a chance to get to know you yet." He peers at me. "My mother would like to meet you too. She asked if you would visit her tomorrow." He bites his lip. "Would you?"

I manage to nod. I don't want to like him. He's part of the Band. But I can't help it. I do like him, and I want him to like me, too. Me, who has never cared what anyone thought about her, who has never given a guy the time of day, and here I am, nodding. I can't seem to stop myself.

"Good." He smiles. "I'll come get you after lunch, okay?"

I shouldn't go tomorrow. We've only just arrived. There are still so many things to do. I have to help my father. I can't go with Bran.

But I don't say a word. He assumes my silence is assent, and by the time I find my voice, the only thing that remains of Bran are the ripples of his canoe.

CHAPTER SIX

We work by candlelight. I mop the floor while Paul brings buckets of water up from the lake. My father prowls the house, opening cupboards, taking stock. He's in the crawlspace right now, crowing about something he's discovered.

"Whatcha got down there, old man?" Paul says, hanging his head into the darkness.

My father pops out of the hatch, grinning from ear to ear, and motions for Paul to get out of the way. "Close your eyes," he says. "Both of you. Go on, do it!"

Paul groans as we do as my father asks. He grunts as he pulls himself up through the hatch, and then I hear the snap of a latch and the scrape of something against wood.

"Come on, Dad," Paul says. "We've got work to do."

"Just a moment longer," my father responds. His voice is positively crackling with excitement. I laugh. I haven't heard him like this in ages, and soon I know why. The notes of a jig fill the room. My father has found a fiddle.

He pauses to retune, and laughs. "Not bad for an old scrap of wood, huh? All those years under this house, and it still sounds good!" He draws the bow across the strings again, then peers at Paul and me, beaming. "Well? You two think I'm going to play for nothing? Go on—dance!"

And so we drop the mop and the bucket and the wash-cloth to dance while our father plays. His fingers aren't certain at first, the fiddle squealing as his bow slips across the strings, but we don't mind. When he plays the final chord, Paul and I are panting and sweaty and the happi-est we've been since our mother's passing.

"I can't believe this is still here," my father murmurs as he sets the fiddle back in its case. "I just can't believe it."

"What's that, Dad?" Paul says, reaching into the case before my father can snap it shut. He pulls out an old photograph.

"Oh. That." My father won't look at it. "It's of me and your mother and your uncles, back when we were all here on the Island."

I peer over Paul's shoulder. Staring back at us is a young

man who looks a lot like me. My father, probably not much older than I am now. Two men stand next to him—his older brothers, whom I only remember as tall and serious. My mother is pretty and fair and laughing. She reminds me of Paul. There's one more person in the photo I don't recognize, another man, younger than my father, with enough similarities that he must be related to us too.

"Who's that?" I say, pointing at the one I don't know.

"Oh. Just some kid," my father says, taking the photograph from Paul's hand and setting it back in the violin case. "I can't even remember his name."

As my father snaps the case shut, Paul and I share a look. My father is a terrible liar. He knows who that young man is, and I know Paul is thinking the same thing I am: Why won't he tell us?

But soon the mysterious young man in the photograph is forgotten as we take up mop and broom and bucket again. We have so much work to do. Cleaning the house is just the start. Our only source of water is the lake. There's no outhouse. We have no beds, or any furniture for that matter, and no wood for the fireplace. There's no garden to grow our own food, and nothing to feed the chickens with. What little joy we had while we danced to the tune of my father's violin has vanished, replaced by the truth of our predicament. In the Corridor, we had enough wood for two winters stored up at all times. Our garden had been planted. The apple tree had already bloomed and would, with luck, produce some fruit, for I'd fertilized it by hand myself.

Here? We are not just starting over. We are starting from scratch.

I set the mop down again and stare at my hands, where blisters are already rising. Is this what this place holds for me? Am I all that I'll ever be?

"Dad," I ask as he passes by, "is there a school here?"

"Oh." He pauses. "Don't know. Probably nothing formal, but we'll figure something out for you and Paul, okay?"

"Okay," I say, even though I have a sinking feeling in my gut. No school means no university, and no university means . . . that my only future is here, working my bones into the earth, all to live the Old Way. And what then? Will I be married off to some Band man? Am I destined to tend the homestead? Keep the hearth warm? Wait and see if my warrior returns from war? The treaty lands are full of women like that, most broken at the hands of their Band husbands. Those men have seen things in battle, the Elders say by way of an excuse. Bad things. Terrible things.

This is why my mother never wanted to live here. She never wanted this future for me, and I don't want it either.

Later, when I've taken out my frustrations on the floor, my father comes and slips the mop from my hand. "That's enough for tonight, Cass. Why don't you go get washed up?"

"Okay," I say, turning to head outside, but pausing and turning back. "I almost forgot—I know I've got work to do, but Bran invited me to his house tomorrow. Is it okay if I go?"

Paul bounds down the stairs. "He invited me, too," he says as he stops to pick up the bucket of dirty water at my feet, and then continues on outside.

"Oh," I say before I can stop myself. It's good that he asked Paul too, so why do I feel so disappointed?

My father doesn't notice. "Sure! Might as well start making friends because we're going to be here for a while." He reaches out to ruffle my hair. "Go on. Get cleaned up. I'll dig a sleeping bag out for you, okay?"

"Thanks, Dad." I lean in to kiss his cheek, and then head out into the night.

Outside, the waning moon spreads silver wings over the forest. When I was little, my mother told me the story of the princess of the stars, who sat on the edge of the heavens, listening to the cry of a wolf. When the princess reached out to catch the wolf's song, she fell to earth and was captured by a demon, who took her to the bottom of a great lake. I never learned if she escaped. Is she out there, that princess, trapped beneath the still, black water? This lake looks like the sort of place a demon might lurk.

Stop dreaming up nonsense, I tell myself as I pick my way down the hill.

On the opposite shore, a fire burns bright and bloody. The sound of throbbing drums races across the lake. Band business, no doubt. Whose fate are they deciding tonight?

I crouch and plunge my arms into the water. The wound site where Madda removed the chip aches, and as I stare at the black spidery stitches, the impulse to cut them from my skin overwhelms me. It's too soon, I know, so I leave them alone, but they're such a strong reminder of what was once there. How could I have let anyone plant a chip under my skin?

Gravel crunches on the hill. I don't have to look to know it's Paul. He squats down beside me and holds his arm out next to mine. His stitches are already gone. Even in the flickering light of his candle, I can see the edges of the incision have separated, exposing pink flesh beneath the dry, crusted blood.

"You shouldn't have taken them out," I say. "That's going to be an ugly scar."

Paul pulls his sleeve down to cover the wound. "I know," he says almost triumphantly, then wanders away.

• • •

Something wakes me. I sit up, straining to listen to the silence around me, but there's nothing to hear. Still, something is amiss.

I rise and dress, and slip downstairs. It's early. Night hangs heavily over the forest. Down by the boathouse, a fire burns. A solitary figure stands beside it.

Paul.

I pull on my shoes and go outside to join him.

He crouches by the fire, feeding slivers of cedar bark to the flames. He doesn't look at me.

"You're up early," I say.

He shrugs. "Couldn't sleep."

He must have had another vision, but with the memory of last time still fresh in my mind, I just poke the fire with a twig instead, stirring up sparks. "Hungry?"

"Nope." He stands, unfurling his long, thin arms, stretching toward the sky. He's barefoot.

"Where are your shoes?" I ask.

"In the house. Got to toughen myself up if I want to run with the Band."

"By going barefoot?"

"They'll never hear me coming." He drifts away, and he's right. As he leaves, he doesn't make a sound.

I sit by the fire, watching the sun rise, wondering if

Paul will return. He compares himself to me, Paul does. He beats himself up that he can't weather his visions like I can, even though, by comparison, mine aren't nearly as bad. His, though—his are terrible, but if I could, I would trade in a heartbeat.

I just wish we understood why. Why have we been given these gifts that we don't know how to use? I think of the shades that I see, following people around, and wonder, why do I see them? There must be a reason, but what that reason is, I don't know. And Paul—why does he dream of the future? Is it so he can change it? If that's the case, the future would be wise to send Paul visions that make sense, because every time, it's not until afterward, when it's too late, that we understand.

Not long after the sun has risen above the trees and turned the lake to gold, my father comes down to join me at the fire, bringing along a bowl and some flour and a little oil for bannock. We wrap dough around willow branches and stick it over the coals, and though it's nothing more than a flour paste, something about cooking it over open flame turns it into the best-tasting treat I can imagine.

"Should I call Paul?" I ask as I pull the bannock from the fire.

My father stares up toward the house, which still sits

in darkness. "Leave him be," he says. "He'll come back when he's hungry enough."

But he doesn't—not after we've cleaned up, not after my father goes back to hammering the old house back together, not after I turn the chickens out to scratch and begin to mark off the corners of a garden plot. I can hear him, though, the thump of the pickax in the soil as Paul digs the pit for the outhouse, swearing up a storm as he does battle with the rocks and the roots.

Finally, around noon, he reappears, covered in red, iron-rich soil. I'm back in the kitchen, mopping the floors again.

"Guess you should have worn your shoes after all." His feet are filthy, and I raise an eyebrow at them.

He wiggles his toes. "A little dirt never hurt anyone."

"That won't be the case if you step on my clean floors."

"Yours?" He inches a toe toward the threshold.

I brandish my mop like a sword. "I wouldn't do that if I were you."

He shrugs. "You win. Going to get cleaned up before Bran gets here? You're a mess too."

I hand him a bucket of filthy water. "Since when do you care about my appearance?"

"Since Bran Eagleson came to call. You know who his father is."

"Who he *is*?" I straighten up and shake my head. "He's

been gone two years. Two years, Paul. Do you really think he's still alive after all that time?"

Paul's smile falters. "I wouldn't say that too loudly if I were you." He brushes his hair away from his eyes, and the smile returns. "Come on. The house is clean enough. Do you want me to heat up some water for you?"

"Thanks, but no." Sweat rolls down my forehead, stinging my eyes. "I'll bathe in the lake."

"Then you'd better hurry. No matter who his father is, Bran Eagleson doesn't get to see *that* much of my sister."

"Hah. Funny." I toss a rag at him.

Paul ducks outside. The rag hits the wall instead, and harmlessly drops to the floor.

The lake is wreathed by heathered mountains. A glacier, which supplies this land with water, is the sole exception. It stretches between peaks, a brilliant expanse of white amid all the green. How it survived when the other glaciers of the continent died their rapid death is a mystery, but then, the Island is steeped in mystery. One of the mountains up there is called Forbidden Plateau. My mother told me its story. They say long ago a group of women and children took refuge there during a war, but when their men came back to get them, they were gone, never to be found again. I stare at the mountains, trying to find the forbidden one, but they all look forbidden to me.

Heat radiates from the dock as I slip off my shoes and stroll to the end, where I sit and test the water with a toe. It's icy cold, but I plunge my feet in anyhow, smiling as minnows come to investigate my toes. Then, in a bright flash, the minnows vanish.

Below, a shadow glides through the water.

I jerk my feet up. The shadow is huge, easily twice as long as I am. It drifts under the dock, unhurried, emerging on the other side and circling back again before slipping out toward the center of the lake.

Too big for a trout. Too big for an otter. Too big for anything logical.

Water does strange things, I think. *It plays tricks on the eye.*

But I'm not convinced. I run back to the boathouse, picking up my shoes as I pass them, and end up crouching on the shore to wash, staring out at the lake.

Myth doesn't live in lakes or descend from stars, I tell myself, and even though logic says the shadow isn't a monster, logic has never been my strong suit.

CHAPTER SEVEN

Paul and I wait in the shade of the boathouse, staring out at the lake, waiting for Bran. Paul is whittling a piece of wood. I'm trying to figure out a way to make a necklace out of a piece of weathered glass I found on the lakeshore and the ribbon I brought from the Corridor, though that's only to give me something to do while I debate whether to tell Paul about the shadow in the lake. It's one thing to see something irrational, but to actually articulate it? Just the thought makes me feel stupid.

Bran's canoe sidles up to the end of the dock just as the sun reaches its apex. Paul pulls on his shoes and runs down to meet him.

"Oh sure, put your shoes on now," I grumble as I fasten the ribbon around my neck and make my way down the dock, taking my time, feigning complete disinterest in Bran Eagleson, even though it's hard work not to look at him. Guys aren't something I know much about. At school, they avoided me as much as I avoided them. So this, the way my stomach suddenly flip-flops, is unexpected, and maybe would be even a bit unwelcome, if it weren't for the way he watches me.

Paul grins at me when I draw close, as if he's privy to some great secret.

"What?" I say.

Paul just shrugs and steps into the canoe, though that cheeky grin doesn't leave his face.

"Do you want the stern?" Bran asks, flashing me a bright smile.

"No. I can paddle, but not well," I admit, watching as my brother settles himself into the bow of the canoe with uncanny ease.

"Then I'll steer. You sit in the center. Paul and I will bear you across the lake. Like royalty, hey, Paul?"

Paul snorts. "Don't give her any ideas."

Bran offers me his hand.

I falter. The last thing I want is to take his hand.

The only thing I want is to take his hand.

"Well?" Bran raises an eyebrow.

My cheeks burst into a furious blush as our fingers

touch. I turn my face away to shield myself from Bran's cinder-gray gaze as I take my seat. The canoe teeters as he steps in and I hold my breath, remembering the shadow that passed under the dock.

"Don't worry," Bran says. "I've been doing this all my life."

I want to believe him and that certainty in his voice, but the shadow in the water is still fresh in my mind. "So, is the fishing good in this lake?" I ask, steadying my voice so the question sounds like nothing more than idle conversation.

"Yep. Sometimes we even get sturgeon."

With that one word, my gut releases the knot it's been holding. Sturgeon. A lovely, logical explanation. The bottle-green depths no longer seem quite so menacing.

Paul and Bran dip their paddles and the canoe glides away from the dock. They spring from the same branch, Bran and my brother, matching each stroke with the same strength, the same cadence.

I close my eyes. I can no longer see the lake, or the water, or what might lurk below. Instead I am flying alongside a raven and a kingfisher, who leave a space between them for my own absent shade.

Bran's house sits on the southern edge of the lake. While it might have been grand at one time, the shutters now hang at odd angles and the windows appear filmy, as if they watch us with the milky eyes of the aged.

A woman in a billowing fuchsia dress strolls along the strand. She is rail-thin, and her hair, as long and white as a sun-bleached bone, streams behind her.

"That's my mother," Bran says.

She's nothing like what I expected. She looks as if she has been left behind by time.

The canoe runs up the beach and Bran holds it steady so I can hop out.

His mother doesn't even notice me. She only has eyes for her son. "My darling," she whispers, reaching out to touch him and then withdrawing her hand as if she was about to make a mistake. "I've missed you so!"

He stows the paddles, ignoring his mother altogether.

Paul gives me a questioning look. We stand side by side, waiting awkwardly. Finally Bran wades up onto the shore, wipes his hands on his shorts, and sighs. "Mother, this is Paul and Cassandra Mercredi. They've taken the place with the boathouse on the northern side of the lake."

Her eyes fall on me. They're blue, but not like any blue I've ever seen—almost crystalline, pale, translucent. Unearthly. "Cassandra, Cassandra," she says, rolling my name about in her mouth, the words catching on the odd lilt of her voice. "The entangler of men?" She looks me up and down and gives me a withering smile. "No, I suppose not. Well, come up to the house, then." She doesn't move, peering at Paul for a long moment before clapping her hands. "Call me Grace, darlings! Come along!"

Bran trails behind me, and though I'm not sure, I think I feel his fingers brush my arm.

Grace watches me from the corner of her eye. "You don't say much, do you? Well, Bran has that effect on girls sometimes." She stops, twirls around, and plants a kiss on Bran's cheek before he can escape. "Darling, why don't you and Paul go find something to do? Take him to your workshop, maybe. I'm sure he'd like that." She eyes me. "I want Cassandra all to myself for a little while."

Paul mouths *Sorry* to me as they take off.

"Don't be late for tea!" Grace calls after them. "Boys. They'll always come back for food." Her laugh is a brittle sound that sets my nerves on edge. "Now, my dear, tell me about yourself." A queer smile crosses her face. "I imagine you're from the Corridor, yes?"

I duck my head rather than answer, letting her guide me toward the house. She wants something.

"You do have a voice, don't you? Are you a mute?"

"No."

"Ah. Good. I was afraid you were damaged. Well? Tell me about your family."

"What would you like to know?"

"Well, you're native. I can tell that just by looking at you—those cheekbones, you see." She stops and cups my chin with a hand, turning my head one way, then the other, inspecting me. "Let me guess. Cree?"

I am stunned by this. How dare she inspect me like I'm a fatted calf? When I find my voice, I take care to sound polite. This is Bran's mother, after all. "No. We're Métis."

"Hmm." She sniffs, releasing her grasp. "Your father's side, or your mother's?"

"My father."

"And your mother?"

"She died five years ago."

"Ah, my dear." Grace clasps her hands to her breast, but the gesture is hollow. "I *am* sorry. Was it Plague, then?"

My eyes glide to the placid waters of the lake. That is one question I will not answer.

She takes my silence as an affirmation. "You should have moved to the Island a long time ago. The Band would have made sure your mother was safe. Ah, well!" She draws me into an embrace, only to push me back, holding me at arm's length. "That can't be undone now. So, do you like to read? Please tell me you like to read, because if you do, I have just the thing for you. A job, you know. Everyone needs a job, don't they?"

I want to snap at her, or flee, or something—anything— but I can't. I just stare at my feet and mutter "I guess" before sullenly following her inside.

My father says a home is a reflection of a family. Our home on the mainland was always spartan clean, and nothing ever went to waste. What was broken, we mended. What was dirty, we scrubbed. *Waste not, want not*, my father also says, though it's pretty hard to waste not when there's nothing to waste in the first place.

He'd be horrified by Bran's house. Grace leads me through a maze of unwashed dishes, decaying food, tables and chairs that block doorways, boxes of bric-a-brac, and everywhere, dirt. I search for Bran's presence in this mess, but I can't find it. It's like he doesn't live here.

Grace chatters at me like a squirrel, saying things that I don't really hear. I peer through the cracks of doors, hoping to spy Bran's room. Darkness stares back at me.

"Don't mind the mess," she says, waving her hands as if the disaster will magically disappear. "There's plenty of time to clean when I'm dead."

I wonder if she's dead already. I haven't seen a hint of her shade. Sometimes that happens with those who aren't native, but I expected something considering what follows her son around.

She pushes her way through heavy cock-eyed doors. "The library!" she announces, only to whirl around, her eyes comically wide. "You aren't a prophetess, are you?" She laughs before I can say anything. "What? You don't know your own mythology? That's something we'll have to rectify immediately. I know something about these things, you see. Come along, darling. I'll be your teacher."

I step into the room. Rows of books line three of the walls. Sunlight peers through the dusty curtains, staining the room sepia, casting the masks on the fourth wall in an unearthly light. They are old, these masks, carved a long time ago. I recognize some of them: Crooked Beak, with his deadly snapping jaws. Eagle, the one who soars the highest. Thunderbird. Bear. Sisiutl, the double-headed serpent. These are the masks of Bran's people, of the tribes from this coast. Spirit is thick on them, carved right into the wood, steeped into the paint.

"So," Grace says as she creeps up behind me, "you like them? They're from the old times, back when people remembered how to dance, how to carve. They say if you put one on, you become the creature the mask resembles. Would you like to try? Who would you like to be, Cassandra, my young prophetess?"

"I'd like to be myself," I murmur as I force my eyes closed. The masks are reaching out, whispering that it's safe here, that they will protect me, but I know better.

That's when Grace crosses the room and shuts the doors behind us. "Well then," she says, smiling a smile so sweet that I know better than to trust it, "you don't know who you are. I think we should fix that. Open the blinds. We need light!"

I do as she asks, pulling the drapes back so that sunlight spills into the room, breaking the spell of the masks. I'd like to open the windows, too, and release the old spirits trapped here, but I don't dare. This is Grace's home, and I can tell she expects me to do as I'm told, nothing more.

She browses the bookshelves, her fingers tracing the spines, until at last she says, "Aha, this is the right one!" and gestures for me to sit down on the floor. I don't want to. The carpet's filthy, but my father has taught us to respect our elders, so I do as I'm told.

"Let's see here," she says as she paws through the pages. "Oh yes, here we are. Cassandra. Your namesake. Daughter of King Priam. Twin sister to Helenus. She told her father that Troy would burn if they opened the gates to the wooden horse, but he wouldn't listen to her. Apollo gave you the gift of prophecy by licking your ears, you see, and then took it away when you refused to sleep with him. Not nice, that Apollo." She holds the book out toward me so I can see an illustration of a man of great beauty. On his shoulder sits a raven.

"Why is that there?" I say, pointing at the raven as my heart thuds. I don't like how Grace assumes that the legendary Cassandra shares more than my name.

"The raven? Oh, that's a guise Apollo was known to take, but not this version of Apollo. This is the Hellenized version, the clean, pretty one. The old version, the primal one, was a wild man, king of the hunt, king of the land, before the Greeks got ahold of him and made him a god in their own image. That's what people do, you see. If a god doesn't fit with what they want, they rewrite the myths until they're more to their liking. But the raven, that's a symbol older than time. Did you know that almost all the cultures of the world feature the raven in their mythology?" She smiles down at the bird. "This is what I used to be, once upon a time, long before I came here, a scholar of myth." Her voice takes on a melancholy note, and just as I think she's about to say something more, something important about me, she snaps the book shut and tosses it aside. "Enough of that. There are other stories you should hear."

The next book she pulls from the shelf is thick and old, though gilt still trims its pages. She opens it to a ribbon marker and then hands it to me. "Read," she says. "Aloud."

The first story is about a man with a shrunken arm, which includes a poem that she makes me skip over. It's followed by a tale about a long-dead king, and then a story of a man who tries to bring his wife back to life, but doesn't trust her to follow him, and so he fails.

She interrupts me to wave at the rest of the books. "Bran's father brings me these," she says. "He's such a generous man, always thinking of me and Bran, always making sure we have everything we need. Did you know, when he first brought me here, back when I wasn't much older than you, he brought me flowers every day? And made sure I had real tea? And when Bran was born, the look on his face! He knew his son would grow up to be as strong as him, a real leader, someone who had the fortitude to walk in his footsteps."

I glance at her, wondering why she speaks of Arthur Eagleson in the present tense, but her gaze is elsewhere, as if she's listening to something that I cannot hear. But then she blinks, like she thought I was someone else. "Continue," she says.

So I do. When my tongue stumbles over a Latin

passage, Grace corrects me, eyes closed, hand dancing in the air as if conducting a symphony. "Repeat after me: *Hic jacet Arthurus* . . ."

She knows the book by heart, and yet I'm still required to read?

This is a test. I'm acutely aware of that, and if I pass, Grace will permit me to spend time with her son. Fail, and I will be deemed unfit.

Am I worthy stock? Are my cheekbones arched high enough? Is my hair the right color? My breasts supple enough to feed the hungry sons I will bear, sons destined to become warriors for the Band?

Her answer to those questions? I may never know. But I care. I shouldn't, but I do.

Just when I think I can't bear it any longer, Bran and Paul burst through the door like tempests, breaking the oppressive atmosphere. Paul leans against a bookcase while Bran flops down next to me and tugs at my shoe-lace. He smells of varnish and sawdust. "Why are you making Cassandra read to you, Mother?"

"Because, my son, reading aloud is a cultured pastime. We may live in the wilds, but we are not savages."

"Speak for yourself," he says, giving me a wicked grin. "I like being savage. When's tea? We're starving."

Grace glares at him. "When I make it." She sighs

dramatically, then takes the book from my hands, places it on a shelf, and drifts away.

Bran nods at Paul, who turns and tiptoes after Grace. "She's outside, smoking," he says when he returns.

"Never smokes in the house. She's afraid she'll damage my lungs or something. She didn't give you too much of a hard time, did she, Cass?"

"A bit," I say as I find my way to my feet. "But I managed."

"You shouldn't have to manage," he says. "Sorry about that." He steps past Paul into the hall, then quietly opens a door leading into a darkened corridor. "This way," he whispers. "Time to get out of Dodge."

CHAPTER EIGHT

We walk into town. Cicadas rise up before us like gilt-winged heralds, singing of our approach. I carry a book under my arm. Bran ran back to get it for me. He and Paul want to play football, and he was worried I'd be bored.

We pass a garden so beautiful I can't help but stop and stare. Sunflowers in full bloom reach to the sky. Apples dangle from their trees, green and glossy and waiting to ripen. Cabbage. Tomatoes. Squash. Pole beans dotted with scarlet blossoms, and everywhere, the sound of bees. I haven't heard a bee sing since I was a little girl. I've always had to fertilize our plants by hand, going from flower to flower with a tiny paint brush.

The garden is full of women working, bent backed,

their heads bobbing up and down between the rows. I look for Helen, the girl from the store, among them, but she's not there. A few of the women look up as we pass, and the resentful glares on their faces leave me wanting to tell them I will work, I will work hard. I know that the Old Way takes care of those who toil, but I suspect, even if I spoke the words, they would not hear me.

Bran doesn't say anything when I start walking again, but he does smile.

When we reach the town, I settle in the shadow of an ancient chestnut tree while Paul and Bran jog across the park, hollering at the boys who sit in the shade on the other side.

Bran immediately takes charge. He divides the players up—Bran and Paul on one team, with the stout, dark-haired boy I first saw at the store captaining the other. The opposing team strips off their shirts and uses them to make goal lines while Bran and Paul talk strategy. I sigh wistfully and open the book. At least I'm spared from seeing Bran without his shirt. His mother's words still sting my ears. *An entangler of men? No, I suppose not.*

Something drops on the ground near me and I look up to see the stout boy throwing shirts not far from where I'm sitting. His shade, a muskrat, peeks its head out from behind his shoulder. The boy has a coarse face and his body is heavy with muscle. *Strong like bull, smart like rock*, my father would say. The boy glances at me, then jogs away.

I don't like him. He makes me feel the need to curl up into myself like a snail. A sudden headache pulses at my temple, reminding me that I was uprooted and transplanted only a day ago. I'm sensitive and edgy, none of which has anything to do with the muskrat boy. Judging him when I'm in this condition isn't really fair, but something is pricking my mind in warning, and I can't ignore that, either.

The game gets under way. Bran tackles a tall, long-haired boy, flinging him to the ground with careless ease, and apologizes as he gives him a hand up a second later.

I turn another page, and a gray feather, almost the same color as Bran's eyes, slips into my hand. I twirl it between my fingers. A bookmark, or a gift?

The latter, I hope. I wish.

I yawn, and let my eyes close.

I dream.

I dream of a woman, crabbed with age. She cuts my hair. "Sit still," she says. "Squirm and I'll end up cutting you."

I place my hands on the red vinyl seat and do my best not to move, but as my hair drifts around my shoulders in newly shorn wisps, I can't help myself. It tickles my neck, my ears, my arms. The old woman issues another warning and swats my ear. I try, I try. "I can't help it," I say. "It's beyond my control."

She takes her shears and snips my earlobe. Blood courses down my neck.

"Now you've done it," she says.

Shouting wakes me. I bolt upright and touch my ear. A sugar ant falls into my hand and without thinking I squish it under my thumb as I seek out the source of the commotion.

Paul stands behind the far goal line, crowing, while Bran performs a celebratory war dance. Some of the boys join in, whooping and hopping as the other team huddles together in conference.

The muskrat boy's head pops out of the scrum. "Penalty on the play. No touchdown!"

"Says you, lead-foot." Paul tosses the football to Bran.

The muskrat boy's face screws into a scowl. "Whatever you say, apple."

Paul freezes. I can see he's fighting himself, that he wants to walk away, but he can't. Apple. Red on the outside, white on the inside. One of the worst insults an Other can throw. The muskrat boy thinks he's gotten the best of Paul and turns away, and that's when Paul attacks him, taking him by surprise so they both fall to the ground. Bran jumps in, and by the time I've made it to my feet, all the boys are fighting, a swarm of fists and elbows.

A man walking by shouts at them to stop. When he's ignored, he dashes off and returns with two more men in tow.

I run over and stare, helpless.

"There'll be no reasoning with them," the tallest of the three men says to me. A scar runs down his face like a great, angry river. "Better cover your ears." He puts his fingers to his lips and lets loose a piercing whistle. His two companions cross their arms and wait.

The fight slows, and then stops. Bran emerges from the pile first, dragging a bloody-lipped but grinning Paul after him. The others stand and line up, beaten, bruised, and shamefaced. The worst off is a towheaded boy who cradles his limp right arm in his hand. I can tell it's dislocated. Paul gives me a look that's full of warning, demanding that I stay where I am. I hesitate, take a half-step forward, and then stop.

I have tended wounds since I was old enough to stand. My mother was a nurse, and she passed what she knew along to me—or, as much as she could. I can suture a wound as neatly as any physician. I could pop that arm back in place without a thought.

The men take to lecturing the boys, but what they say, I don't hear. If I do what instinct begs of me, word will spread. Even though I'm only sixteen, the Band will want to know why I'm not working for them, stitching up war wounds. But fate makes the decision for me. The boy's face turns ashen and he drops to the ground like a felled tree.

I am at his side in an instant, and I know, without looking, that the shadow hovering over me is Bran. "He's all right," I say, checking the boy's breathing. "Bend his knees." Bran does as I instruct. "His arm's dislocated. I can put it back." I glance over my shoulder at the scarred man, waiting for his permission.

He nods. "Do what you can. His name is Adam."

Adam's unconsciousness is a blessing. I pick up his lifeless arm, suck in a deep breath, brace myself, and give the limb a mighty tug and twist.

His eyelids flutter open. He looks from Bran to me, turns his head, and vomits.

Bran holds him up, waiting for him to finish, and then slips his belt off and hands it to me.

"You've done this before," I say as I fashion the belt into a makeshift sling.

Bran shrugs.

The scar-faced man points to two of the boys. "Carter, Jesse, take Adam to Madda."

"Thank you," Adam says to me as they help him up. He's blinking back tears. I squeeze my eyes shut, forcing back my own. Healing hurts. There's no two ways about it.

When I open my eyes again, I look for Paul. He stands at the edge of the group, kicking at a tuft of grass. Blood still oozes from his lip and his left eye is already swelling shut again. Tomorrow it will be purple. Before I can take a step toward him, he glares and shakes his head.

I stay where I am.

"You the Mercredi girl?" the scar-faced man asks. I nod. "Good work." He turns his gaze to the boys. "No more football. Get."

The boys scatter, save for Bran and the muskrat boy. The men stroll off, their leather boots leaving a trail of dust to chase after them.

Bran whistles under his breath. "Not often the Elders say something nice to anyone. I was sure we'd get hauled down to the slurry and put to work."

"Best place for half-breeds," the muskrat boy says.

"I think you'd better leave," Bran says.

"Or what, Eagleson?"

Bran's smile is cold and feral. The other boy tries to return it, but he blinks first, and stalks away.

The remaining boys head to the lake to soak their war wounds, Paul included. When I move to follow, Bran catches my arm. "I'd like to show you something," he says.

"But Paul . . ."

"He'll be fine," Bran insists, brushing his hair away from his eyes. "Paul needs some time with them. Without me. He did well against Cedar. They'll honor that." His eyes meet mine. "Where's your book?"

It still lies in the shade, tossed aside. I run to retrieve it. Bran watches. A small, guarded smile crosses his lips, a smile that gives me the feeling that the gray feather was a gift after all.

"We'll go this way, then." He steps off the road. "It's nicer in the forest."

We follow the narrow, twisting path through stands of fir and cottonwood. Bran sets a fast pace, and though I don't want to admit it, I'm struggling to keep up. "Sorry," he says as he stops to help me over a log that blocks our path. "I keep forgetting you're not from here, that this is new to you." He purses his lips. "It just seems like I've always known you, you know?"

I nod. I do know.

"Close your eyes," he says. "Tell me what you hear."

I do as he asks. The stiff leaves of a poplar rustle in the wind. A jay cackles in the cottonwoods, and if I concentrate hard enough I can make out a subtle hum just below the level of hearing, as if the earth is singing a song of its own. It's . . . beautiful. "It's like a hymn," I say.

"See? You belong here." His bangs drop in front of his eyes; I wish I could see them. "Come on. It's not much farther."

The trees fall behind as we climb a granite ridge worn smooth eons ago by the slow slip and slide of a glacier. The lake opens out below the ridge like a blue fan. On a whim, I wander to the edge. The wind rushes past, begging me to take flight.

CHAPTER NINE

*E*ddies of heat shimmer around us. We walk side by side, making small talk and carefully avoiding mention of the fight. I'm not sure why, but I can sense Bran doesn't want to talk about it. But I do. I'm practically itching to know who the muskrat boy is. No friend of Bran's, that's for certain, and no friend of my brother's, either. All the more reason to learn about him—*know thine enemy*, my father says. Well, I plan to.

"Warm today," Bran says, breaking my thoughts. "You're not used to it." He points to a bead of sweat winding its way down my forehead.

"Not yet. The rain keeps the Corridor pretty cool most of the time."

Bran's hand steadies me. "Don't want you to fall. Your brother would kill me."

"He probably will anyhow, once he notices we're gone."

"Nope. He knows to meet us at my house later."

I try to prevent my eyebrow from arching, but it pops up anyhow.

Bran doesn't notice. He pushes his hair out of his face before taking a seat and patting the spot beside him. "Sit. We can talk up here."

"Only up here?" I ask, plucking some grass before settling down beside him, and begin to work. Two stalks, bent in half, for spokes, and a blade to weave with. I'll make a sun wheel, a Brigid cross.

"Well, no, but up here, there's no one to interrupt us." He casts me a sidelong look. "Being an Eagleson comes with baggage. Everyone talks, no one listens."

So, that's it. I'm his confessor. I should have known. I'm not the type of girl someone like Bran would ever be interested in. I'm too tall. Too thin. Too intense. Still, I hope. My mother was beautiful. Paul resembles her far more than I do, but I can't help hoping that a sliver of her beauty was passed on to me.

Bran shifts, moving close enough that the grass bent by his frame tickles my forearm. Bees, fat and laden with pollen, drift around us. A hummingbird hovers overhead before soaring off in a blur of metallic wings. I watch it as my hands weave.

Bran laughs. "Thought we were flowers, I bet."

"Maybe you. Definitely not me."

"If you're not a flower, then what are you?"

I shrug. "I don't know." The conversation is running too close to me. Time to redirect. "I don't suppose you'll tell me what that fight was all about?"

"For someone like Cedar, there doesn't need to be a reason." His voice is flat with anger. "He's always looking to pick a fight." He yawns and stretches out onto his back, hands cradling his head. "Like he has something to prove."

"Such as?"

"That he's better than me because he's full-blooded Indian. I'm only a half-breed, and some people around here think that makes me less than them. There's talk, you know, about what happens if my father doesn't come back, who'll lead the Band then."

"And someone wants to give you the job?"

"Yeah." He picks up a spider that's crawling on his leg and carefully sets it on a leaf. "Some days, I think I might do okay. Most days, I think I'm too young, that I've got too much to learn. But, the Elders, you know, I'm not sure about them, either. They always looked to my father, who looked to the people. Now they look to no one except themselves. See that spot down there? Where the river runs out of the lake?"

I nod. The water turns murky there, as if the river is leaching life from the lake.

"That's where my dad met the bear."

"What bear?"

"A grizzly. The only one ever found on the Island. They can swim here, you know, all the way from the mainland. Pretty long way. Tough animals. That's how the Elders knew my father was going to be chief, they say. Grizzly sought my father out, and fought him to see if he was strong enough. I guess he was. He used to let me play with the claws when I was little. He was going to give them to me before . . ." His voice trails off.

I hold my breath. Before what?

Bran gazes out toward the lake. "I'm still waiting to find my bear."

But Bran's shade isn't a bear. It's a kingfisher, and a stone, and other things too, things I've only seen glimpses of. Should I tell him? Would he want to know what I've seen?

No, I decide. What good would that do? Look at Paul. How much help have I been to him? So far, no help at all.

More than once, I've wished I understood why I see what I do, and in this moment, I wish it more than ever.

"Do you want to be chief?" I ask, because I don't know what else to say.

"I don't know." He shrugs. "Maybe. I guess it depends if the Elders want me. Besides, Henry Crawford's chief until my father comes back."

If he comes back. The unspoken words hang between us until Bran says, "But, maybe one day. When I feel I'm half the man my father was. Is." He looks down at the sun wheel in my hands. "What's that?"

"This?" I hold it up and inspect it. "I call it a sun wheel. My mother taught me to make them. She called it a Brigid cross. It's supposed to protect you from evil."

Bran laughs. "Does it work?"

"I think so. Maybe. Here." I reach out and take his hand, setting the sun-wheel in his palm and curling his fingers around it. "It's for you."

He stares at it for a long moment before looking back at me. "Thank you," he says, like he really means it.

I start to say that it's nothing, that it's made only from grass, but I stop myself and just smile instead.

Bran sweeps his hair back and stands, offering me his hand. "Well, we should probably be getting back, I guess."

"I guess." Though I could stay here forever, on this hilltop, with the grass swaying in the wind, the hummingbirds, the flowers.

But I still take Bran's hand. Our palms meet, and this time, even after he's pulled me up from the ground, we don't let go.

Paul sits beside the beached canoe, smiling as we approach. "I thought you two had run off together," he says as he touches his swollen lip.

"Thought about it. Figured you'd hunt us down before long." Bran gives Paul a friendly punch to the shoulder. Paul stands up and punches him back. They both laugh.

This is how things are meant to be, and I would stop time right now if I could. My brother is happy. I am happy.

But time doesn't stop.

And everything changes.

CHAPTER TEN

Sometimes, I think the earth can hear my thoughts. There are days when I wish for a storm, or for a clear sky to see the moon, and the wish arrives.

Today I wish for wind—a brisk wind, fierce, even—to bear us across the lake, to raise whitecaps so high that Bran is trapped at our house, and it comes, rushing over the hills, bending the firs, showering the lake with needles as Bran and Paul paddle the canoe toward home.

My father greets us and holds the canoe steady while we scramble onto the dock.

"Help me lift it out, Paul," Bran says. "Last thing I want is for these waves to swamp it."

Doesn't sound like such a bad idea to me, but I don't say so.

"The wind will die later," my father says as clouds slip across the sky.

Not if I can help it.

My father brought down a brace of grouse while we were away. Bran and Paul pluck them while I light the fire.

"Tell us a story," Paul says as we settle in. The grouse sizzle and pop each time Bran turns them.

My father doesn't look up. "Maybe later, Paulie," he says, though we know from the tone of his voice that "later" really means "no."

I love my father's stories, but he seldom tells them anymore. Some things are best left to die, he says. Stories haunt the living and when my father turns his gaze back to the flames, I can see he's no longer with us. Words hold power—everyone knows this—but perhaps those who tell stories know it better than the rest, for through their voice, the dead live again, resurrected like that story of the woman Eurydice, except there's no Orpheus to lead the way back to the world of the living.

Just as well—he didn't do a particularly good job of it.

"You tell one then, Cass," Paul says. "You tell a story."

I'm not sure why, but the look in Paul's eyes tells me he needs this story from me, to hold him to the earth, to tie him to something solid. Stories do that, my father says.

They make the impossible real. That's why my father's choice to not tell stories anymore hurts both Paul and me. Some days we need to believe in the impossible.

But when I try to find the words, none will come. I try, but all I can think of is that my father looks so sad tonight, staring into the fire, remembering. I know the story he would tell, if he could speak, the one of how he met my mother and knew, in an instant, she was the one he would marry. He's told it to us often enough, but tonight, for some reason, he can't, and neither can I.

Later, against my wishes, the wind dies and Bran leaves. My father leaves as well, but Paul and I stay by the fire. Paul stares at the coals pulsing gray and gold. The fire has stolen him, drawing him down into the world of vision.

Above us, stars crowd the heavens. When we were little, Paul wanted to be a star. I don't know where he got that idea, but stars were the one thing he never tired of learning of at school. He learned all the myths, of Andromeda, of Calliope, and, especially, of Orion. The stars of Orion's belt have always been his favorite. My father says his father told him those three stars were once three ravens, crossing the heavens. *To go where?* I wonder. *To do what?*

A branch breaks in the forest behind me, as if in

answer to my questions. I whirl around, but there's nothing there.

My movement rouses Paul. "What's the matter?" he asks, rubbing his eyes.

"I heard something behind us." A shiver slithers up my arm. "Probably just a deer."

"Probably," he says, yawning, but I see the worried wrinkle of his brow as he turns his gaze back to the fire.

What does he see in the embers? I wish I knew, but I must wait until he's ready to tell me. And I hate waiting.

He knows this and lies down, leaving room for me. When we were little, our family would spend nights under the stars, lying with our heads together to create a star of our own. The top of my head touches Paul's, and my arms stretch out at my sides, filling the space our parents would have claimed. Satellites swoop through the heavens, as bright as fireflies.

"Do you think they're watching us?" Paul asks.

"I don't know," I say. "I hope not." But I get up and head for the house anyhow.

I bolt awake.

Moonlight spills into my room, painting the floor a milky white. The grumble and roar of my father's snoring rises from downstairs.

Paul isn't in the house. I can feel it. Something is wrong. Altered.

I slip from my sleeping bag and tiptoe downstairs. Sure enough, Paul's sleeping bag is empty again.

Outside, the lake stretches out like a silver gauntlet, beckoning me.

I step over the threshold, out into a night full of frog song. But then, the frogs stop singing. The night goes silent. I stand completely still. Paul is out there somewhere. I want to search for him, but fear grips me and all I can do is stare into the depths of the forest.

A rock bounces out of the shadows, nearly hitting my leg.

"Paul?"

"Go back inside." His voice drifts up from somewhere down the hill. There's no way he could have thrown that rock.

"Paul, what's wrong?"

"Cass, go back inside."

"But . . ."

"GO NOW!"

I flee, tripping over the threshold and falling into the house.

My father wakes up and stumbles from his room to stare at me. "What's going on?" he rasps.

I don't answer. I don't have an answer. Sparks of spirit

float around my head, trying to warn me of something I don't understand. My father draws me into his arms, but I can't see him. The sparks press in on me, droning like a swarming hive, so thick I might drown.

And then I feel it, way down in the bottom of my gut: only a tickle at first, but then it grows, crescendoing to a rumble, forcing me to my feet as I drag my father after me.

The world is about to change.

The floor shudders and suddenly my father understands. "Up to the road!" he shouts.

Stones bite into my bare feet. I slip, fall, skin my knee, my hands, as I try to stand. My father hauls me up. The sparks coat my eyes, my ears. I feel like I'll retch, but I can't. Not yet.

We fall on the old, broken asphalt.

My father wheezes, "Paulie?"

In reply, the world begins to sway.

When the earthquake finally stops, I scramble down the hill to search the lakeshore while my father scours the woods that flank the house. No Paul. The look on my father's face when I meet him halfway up the hill mirrors my own. We are panic-stricken.

"Back up to the road," my father says. "He's probably waiting for us up there."

But the road is no longer a road. Asphalt lies in heaves and gullies, and trees are strewn about like spent matchsticks. An earthquake is always a reminder that we humans are as expendable as anything else, and if a fir that has weathered five hundred years of existence can be toppled, so can we.

A whistle from behind makes me whirl around, and there Paul is, stepping out from the forest, covered in scrapes. He holds his left forearm with his right hand and the dark seep of blood stains his shirt. A piece of wood is embedded in his skin.

We run to him.

"Leave it," he says when I move to examine his arm.

I give him my sternest look. "Only if you want it to fester. You'll lose your arm." I can't tell him how relieved I am, how worried I was.

"Fine," Paul snaps. "Get it out, then."

We head back down the driveway and stop at the truck. Paul paces, waiting as my father fishes our precious supply of whiskey out from behind the seat, as I stare at the house, looking to see how it fared. In the predawn darkness, it looks okay, but what damage will daylight reveal? None if we're lucky, though I know that's too much to hope for.

"Here, Cass," my father says, handing me his jackknife. "Use this."

Paul watches as I dig the wood from his flesh, and doesn't wince—not once, not even when I pour whiskey over the wound and stitch it with deer-gut thread.

"Another scar," I murmur as I tie off the knot.

He grins. "Good."

Our house, by some miracle, is unscathed. Below, the boathouse has come loose from its moorings and the dock is partially submerged, but it's nothing that can't be fixed.

Only then, after we've surveyed the damage, do I let myself think of Bran, of Madda, of the people in the town. If the wind listens, if the sky hears my words, surely they will see them all safe.

Paul touches my arm. "Relax," he says. "It'll be okay."

But I see the raven in my brother's eyes, and I know more is yet to come.

CHAPTER ELEVEN

*D*aylight breaks after we've begun the long walk into town. Fallen trees litter the road. Our father makes us stop at each one, inspecting it carefully while Paul and I pace. We've been through earthquakes before, and we all know what the aftermath brings. Our house might be safe and we might be unharmed, but what about everyone else? What about Bran? Helen? Madda?

Paul carries an ax, and my father a machete and a shovel. I bring a basket holding bandages, a bottle of whiskey, needles, and thread. No one speaks, allowing me to run through the things my mother taught me: how to start a heart. How to stanch a wound. How to tie a tourniquet. How to stitch a person back together. Some of these things I've never done, but my mother made sure I knew how to, just in case.

The smell of smoke reaches us long before we arrive in the town. Something's burning. When we finally emerge from the forest, we see it's the church. The roof has already collapsed and smoke billows from its shell. People have formed a fire line and swing buckets of lake water from hand to hand, dousing the house next to the church, but I fear it, too, will go up in flames before long. Someone will then have lost a home, and all their belongings along with it. My heart squeezes tight at the thought. I know what that feels like.

Down the way, in the park, a tent has been set up. It seems to be a hub of activity, so my father steers us there, but once we step under the canvas awning, we realize the tent is a hospital. My father pats me on the shoulder before he and Paul step back outside. He knows I'll be able to help here.

A huge woman barking orders spots me and waves me over. "What's wrong with you?" she says.

"Nothing." I hold the basket I carry out to her so she can see inside.

She cocks an eyebrow at me. "You know about healing?" She plants her hands on her wide hips and assesses me with muddy eyes. "What do you know?"

"I can stitch wounds and set bones."

"Good enough. I got work for you." She nods at a man in the corner with a bad burn on his hand. "See to him. Oh, and my name's Adelaide Corry. Holler if you need anything."

I sit down before the man and wince. The burn's not terrible, but still, it must hurt. There's not much I can do but clean it as carefully as I can and wrap it in a clean bandage.

"What about butter?" he asks. "That's supposed to be good for burns."

I shake my head as I tie off the bandage's knots. "No. The skin's got to breathe to heal. Butter will just give you an infection. There." I sit back to admire my handiwork, and then offer the man a swig of whiskey. "Keep it clean, and wash it tomorrow. And no butter!"

He nods as he heads out of the tent, but I'm pretty sure from the look he gives me that the first thing he'll do when he gets home is find a pat of butter and smear it all over his hand.

Next is a little girl with a cut on her arm, followed by a woman with a bad bump on the head. I do the best I can, stitching and bandaging and hoping that I'm helping. My hands have work to do, and it's good work, needed work. Important work. I feel like myself for the first time since we arrived here.

As the day wears on, the number of people needing help diminishes. The temperature under the canvas climbs, so when we can, Ms. Adelaide and I sit outside, watching what's going on in the town while we wait for our next patients to arrive. I look for Bran, but he's not among the people passing by.

Ms. Adelaide tells me who they are. "Sidney Morrow," she says, nodding at a man carrying a length of hose. "Lives out toward the gravel pit. Missus has three girls, another on the way. Pretty lucky that she can pop babies out. Not many women can do that anymore. Madda's probably out there right now, seeing to her. Their house is a ways away. Don't know why anyone would want to live so far from town, but I guess people need to live somewhere. Oh, and there's Peter Vickers. He does woodwork. Made me the most beautiful table . . ."

I'm busy cleaning a gash on a little girl's leg when Bran finally appears. Soot is smudged across his cheeks and he looks exhausted, but he's safe.

"Ms. Adelaide?" he says. "May I borrow Cassandra for a moment?"

She sits down and takes over. "Go on, girl. Chief's son wants to see you."

"Thanks, Ms. Adelaide." I set down the rag and smile. "I won't be long."

She snorts and waves me away.

The air outside reeks of smoke. I start to ask Bran whether he's okay, whether his mother is safe, but he just takes my hand and pulls me into a run.

"Where are we going?" I say.

He only tightens his grip.

Together we race across the park and into the under-brush, crashing through willows and fireweed until we reach the shore of the lake. He drops my hand and starts pacing while I try to catch my breath.

"What's going on?" I ask.

He doesn't answer. Gravel crunches under his sneakers. His gray eyes never leave mine.

I take a seat and wait.

The earth is still. Waves do not lap upon the shore. Birds do not call in the trees, nor does wind stir the forest. The earthquake has disturbed the order of things and it will be some time before the earth's clock resets. Bran's agitation mars the stillness.

Minutes slip away. Finally, I can stand it no more. "I should probably get back." I push myself up and dust off my pants.

"No." Bran catches my hand and turns it over to examine my palm. "Stay a little longer?"

"Let go," I whisper. "Please. Let go."

"Why?" He traces my lifeline.

In answer, I lean in and kiss him. I have never kissed a boy before, but I am possessed by immediacy. Now or never.

He smells of ash and tastes of blackberries.

I pull away and dash back to the tent, startled by what I just did and too scared to wait for Bran's reaction.

Ms. Adelaide looks up from the little boy she's tending when I step back inside, and gives me a puzzled look. I duck my face and begin rolling bandages. I'm blushing. I know I am, and Ms. Adelaide's chuckle tells me she knows too.

The little boy leaves, and Ms. Adelaide motions for me to join her back in the doorway. She doesn't say a word, though I feel her looking at me before turning her attention across the way. I look too, wondering what it is she's focused on. The church is still smoldering, but it looks like the house next to it will survive after all. Down by the store, a couple of women have built a fire, a proper one for cooking, and have prepared a haunch of venison to roast over it.

"Working hands have empty stomachs," Ms. Adelaide says. "No better way to knit a broken world back together than to share a meal."

I nod as my gaze comes to rest on the men gathered at the general store. They're waiting for something. My brother is standing among them. Already Paul is fitting in here better than I ever could have imagined. Bran stands next to him, pushing his hair away from his face. I wish I were there too, but I'm not. I'm here in this tent, left to watch from a distance. My hand finds its way to my mouth and I touch my lips, remembering. I kissed Bran. I'd like to kiss him again. I'm sure of that, but what I'm not sure of is if he'd like to kiss me, too.

Ms. Adelaide nudges me. "So, Bran, huh? Well, be careful of his mother. Crazy as a loon, that woman. Oh. I almost forgot. Madda stopped by on her way back from the Morrow house. Seems all that shaking shook Mrs. Morrow's baby loose. A little girl, healthy as can be. Who would have thought, on a day like today?" She smiles and shakes her head. "Madda said she'd like to talk to you."

"Do you know about what?" I ask.

Ms. Adelaide shrugs. "Maybe about healing? I told her you did good here. Why don't you go find out for yourself? She's up at her cottage—know where it is?"

"No." I'm only half listening as more men gravitate toward the general store. My father is there now too, standing on the far side of the group, hands on his hips, legs wide. His *concentrating pose*, as he would call it. Everyone's attention is on the tall, scar-faced man I met the other day.

Ms. Adelaide nods at him. "That's Henry Crawford.

Bran's daddy's best man. The new chief, since Bran's daddy left. They'll be going soon."

"Going?"

"Yup. To the boundary, or even to the Corridor. If the quake was bad, people will be heading this way, looking for refuge. But don't you mind that. Madda wants to see you. That's all you have to concern yourself with now. Down the street, turn left at the old post office, and keep on going until you can smell roses. That'll be her cottage. Go on. I'll see you around, okay?"

"Okay." I like Ms. Adelaide. I hope she's right, that I will see her around, though my mind is already drifting back to Bran. He smiles at me as I pass. I smile back, but my smile fades when I see Avalon standing at the back of the group. Though she doesn't look the least bit friendly, I wave. She doesn't wave back.

Madda's gray cottage is hidden behind a mass of blackberries. A stone path crested by a pergola once led to the door, but so many blackberry canes have fallen from their pinnings on the pergola that the path is impassable. A wooden chest with a heavy leather strap sits next to the gate along with a basket of blood-soaked linens, but there's no sign of Madda.

"Hello?" I call.

Madda's head pops out of the brambles. "Over here," she says. "I can't even get to my door! Help me, would you? Goddamned things." She snarls as she heaves a newly shorn bramble out of the mess. "They were gnarled before, but with all that shaking, they're hell-bent on taking over the cottage. There's another set of shears over there somewhere, if you can find them. Helen!" Madda calls. "Can you get the back door open yet?"

"Not yet," Helen calls from behind the house.

"Bloody hell," Madda mutters as she ducks back into the blackberries to continue her fight.

I don't find the shears, but I do find a hatchet, and start to hack away.

"So," Madda says as she rips another length of cane out of the mess. "You have a way with healing, and you have a way with spirit." She peers at me. "True?"

I nod. "But my mother said I shouldn't talk about it."

"Wise, that bit of advice. But I dreamed of you, a long time ago, before I even met your parents. You have a mole just under your right shoulder blade."

I blink at her. She's right.

"And you're much prettier when your eyes aren't bugging out of your head. Go on. Tell me about what you see."

"My mother said I see into the spirit world."

"I don't want to know what she said. I want to know what *you* say. Is it true?"

"I don't know." Because that *is* the truth. My mother said I played with imaginary friends when I was small. The shades came later, when I shed my first moonblood. I've puzzled out what they are on my own, but I certainly don't have any control over what I see, or when spirit decides to intrude into my life. And if the shades are supposed to presage something, I don't know what. Sometimes I'm pretty sure I don't want to know.

Madda nods and steps back, pulling another long, rambling vine from the mass of brambles. "I can help you, teach you the spirit paths. I'm a witching woman—a medicine woman—and I need an apprentice, someone to take my place when I'm gone. I haven't had one for years—too many years."

I cast my eyes to the ground. This is one of those times I don't want to see a shade.

"Oh, I don't mean that kind of gone!" She pats my arm. "Sometimes I have to leave—spirit quests, gathering medicine, that sort of thing. Sometimes I just need to be alone." She smiles. "What do you think?"

"But," I say, pitching my voice lower, "what about Helen? Isn't she your apprentice?"

Madda's gaze hardens. "No. Helen is a good girl and

she's good with the ways of spirit too, but becoming a medicine woman isn't the path for her. It's not an easy job, you see, and I don't just mean it's hard work. I mean, you have to walk the truth, no matter what people think, no matter what they want you to do, and that's a lonely life. Sometimes a medicine woman has to make hard decisions . . . unpopular decisions. People think they know what's good for them, but not always. It's like the best medicines—they taste awful, and no one wants to take them, but that's what you've got to do in order to get better. So? What do you think?"

"I need to speak to my father first."

"He already knows. I asked him about it when I saw him in town earlier, but I don't care what he thinks either. What do you think? The sooner you start speaking your mind, the sooner you'll figure out how to use your gift."

I blink at her. What *do* I think? Is this what I want? Is this what I'm meant for? Back in the Corridor, I never thought about what would happen after I finished school. There was always too much else to worry about, like trying to survive, or Paul's visions, or keeping him out of trouble, but here? Maybe Paul will find his own way. That's what I wish for. That's what I've always wished, for Paul to feel complete unto himself—not half of a whole.

Not the flawed twin, which is what Paul calls himself. Maybe, just maybe, Madda might teach me what I need to know to help him achieve that. "I'd like to be your apprentice," I say, surprising myself with the certainty in my voice, so I say it again. This time I can't help smiling.

"A smile? Now, would you look at that?" Madda chuckles and takes a deep breath. "All right. Just a little more to do, and we'll be inside. I'll brew us a pot of tea, and then you can head back to town to see what your dad and brother are up to. I'll come with you. Folks will get a better impression of you and your family once we're seen together. There's talk, eh?" Her shears bite into another length of blackberry.

"What sort of talk?"

"Well, a new family comes to town. They're given a house, a truck. The girl's seen with the chief's son, the boy is his new best friend. Breeds jealousy, that sort of thing. I imagine you've been warned about Grace?"

I nod slowly.

"Well, take care with her. Her spirit is tainted. I tried healing her once, years ago, but she just won't have it. Good thing Bran's more like his father than her. Now, get back to work. These canes aren't going to go anywhere by themselves."

It's not long before we have the last of the blackberries cleared away. I follow Madda into the cottage. A rustle of wings follows me, but I don't look back. I don't want to see the ravens lined up on the fence, watching to see what happens next.

After tea, Madda and I head into town, leaving Helen behind. I sense she'd like to come too, but something's stopping her. What that is, I can't say, but it troubles me.

The town is all but deserted when we arrive.

"Hmm," Madda mumbles. "Must have reached a decision quickly. Better get home, then. Come see me tomorrow morning."

I run along the broken asphalt as fast as the heat allows. I can't wait to tell Paul what's happened. An apprentice! The more I think about it, the more excited I get. I run with my arms extended, two featherless wings, bearing me away from the Corridor, away from my old life, and as I swoop down the driveway, I know I've come home.

My excitement vanishes the moment I step inside the house.

Paul and my father sit on the floor. Ammunition runs along the floorboards like a deadly brass river. Paul is cleaning his rifle. My father is fitting his back together.

"No guns in the house," I growl.

Neither of them will meet my eyes.

"You promised me to never bring those in the house!"

My father peers down the bore of his rifle and then sets it aside. "Paul's joined the Band. He and Bran are going to patrol the boundary." He says it as if that justifies the breaking of his promise.

"By themselves?" I ask in my most sarcastic voice.

Paul still refuses to look at me. My father glances up and scowls. "Watch your lip."

"Right." I turn on my heel and march outside, only to run right into Bran, who's materialized at the door. He holds an armful of books. Two slip from the top, falling between us.

"Did you put him up to this?" I demand as he bends to pick up the books.

He straightens and hands them to me. "These are for you, from my mother; and no, I didn't put him up to this. I told him to stay."

Suddenly I'm overwhelmed with fatigue, as if the world is pressing down on me. Bran somehow senses this. He takes the books from my hands, sets them on the counter, and then leads me back outside. "He'll be fine. We shouldn't be gone long—a week, at most, and all we'll be doing is looking for refugees. Searchers hardly ever show up after this sort of thing." He draws a deep breath. "I'll see him safe."

I want to believe him. "You promise?"

Bran laughs. "Of course I promise. This isn't the first time I've done this, you know."

"I'll hold you to that. Everyone in this family seems to think nothing of breaking promises." I say the words loud enough for my father to hear.

"He'll be fine."

"I'll be fine," Paul echoes.

"And who'll make sure *you're* safe?" I demand, poking Bran smack-dab in the center of his chest.

"Finally!" Bran flings his head back and whoops so I can't help but smile. "The girl is worried about me!" He grins as he rubs the spot where I poked him, and heads inside.

And that's that.

But that doesn't mean I'll remain inside with those guns. I meant what I said. My father promised me. Paul promised me. I've never asked anything of them except this one thing.

And now that promise is broken.

Later, at dusk, Paul joins me down on the dock. "I'm sorry" is the first thing out of his mouth. "I have to do this," he says.

A hatch of gnats hovers over the lake. "Why, Paul?" I ask. "Tell me why you have to go."

He doesn't answer at first. I can tell he feels he doesn't owe me an explanation, and yet he'll offer it anyhow. "Do you remember," he says finally, in the pained tone of memory, "when Mom was still here, when she would make me wash my face and I'd cry and cry?"

I nod. I do. It wasn't that Paul was a dirty child. It was that he painted his face with mud, in stripes and circles, a mask of dirt. It was his way to hide, he used to claim, but hide from what?

He never said.

"It's like that," he says. "I know you hate guns, Cass, and I do too, but you don't know what it's like to be lost all the time, to never know what's inside of yourself."

I do, Paul. I know that feeling all too well.

"If I go," Paul says, "maybe I'll learn something. Maybe I'll figure out a way to leave all the lost ones behind. Maybe I'll figure out how to read my visions. Maybe I'll come back someone else. You know, different."

"I don't want a different brother," I whisper, but Paul has already stood up and turned away. I watch him leave, my younger brother by four thin minutes, tall and brooding and haunted, and wonder just who it is he wishes he could be.

CHAPTER TWELVE

I'm awake and out the door before the sun has even crept over the trees. I can't wait to get to Madda's, but more than that, I want to be away from the house, from the weight of Paul's absence.

I try to think of what Madda's going to teach me as I walk into town, but no matter how hard I try, my thoughts keep turning to Bran. *What was I thinking? What was he thinking? I kissed him. What does he think of me now?*

Robins accompany me part of the way, swooping ahead in search of worms, and a jaybird takes over where they leave off, hopping from tree to tree, cackling at me.

"What do you want?" I say to it. "I've got nothing for you."

The jay tips its head to one side, listening, and then flies off.

Another hatch of gnats rises over the road where it dips close to the lake, so I break off a branch of cedar, using it as a broom to clear a path. I like cedar, its strong, resiny scent, so I keep the branch, swinging it back and forth until I reach Madda's.

"You're here early," she calls from a patch of dill as I step through the gate. "What you got there?"

"Oh." I toss the cedar branch aside. "Nothing."

"That didn't look like nothing to me. Go get it and bring it back inside. You've just chosen your very first lesson."

That doesn't sound good, I think as I go back outside and retrieve the cedar branch, shaking it free of dust. Madda points at the kitchen table where Helen sits, spinning a length of wool. I set the cedar bough in front of Helen, who gives me a worried look before rising and heading outside, taking her spinning with her.

"So, cedar. A very useful tree." Madda motions for me to sit. "What can you tell me about it?"

"It smells nice," I say, picking my words carefully. Madda's setting me up for something. "It grows near water. People use it for houses and canoes."

"Yes, this is all true. Cedar is a good tree, a helpful tree." She narrows her eyes. "So, did you ask to take that branch from it? And, did you say thank you once you did?"

"Ask?"

"Yeah." She picks up the cedar branch and shakes it at me. "Before you picked it, this branch was alive. Now, it's not. If you're going to kill something, the least you can do is ask first, and then give thanks afterward. The trees, they have long memories, and they talk to each other, you know. They'll remember you, and next time you take something without permission, they might not be as willing to just let you go. So your first lesson is to go back to this tree and apologize."

"Apologize to the tree?" I echo.

"Yep. Trees have spirits too, and going around breaking bits of them off without giving them a bit of common courtesy is rude. You've got some dark roads to walk, Cassandra, and you need all the friends you can get. So make amends. A little gratitude goes a long way, and the trees, they remember." She picks up the cedar branch and runs her hands over it. "Just think of what this branch might have become if you hadn't taken it—a nest for a bird, for example. Its cones might have fed a squirrel. Maybe, one day, if the tree was tall enough, this branch might have held someone's body after they passed over. That's a mighty powerful thing, don't you think?"

I make myself nod. Madda sets a hand on my shoulder as if to say it's okay, but her touch just leaves me feeling worse. She gives me a kind smile. "If you want to be my apprentice, you've got to know that you are responsible for all your actions now, and spirit holds you to higher standards than it does other people. That's the price you pay for what you're going to learn. Best decide now whether you're willing to do that or if you'd like to go back to being like everyone else. So?" She sets the branch back down on the table. "What's your decision?"

"I want to be your apprentice." I can barely speak the words, I feel so stupid.

"Good." She taps the branch. "When you go home this afternoon, stop and bury the branch when you find the tree you took it from. And, tomorrow, I want to hear about every single living thing you encounter once you leave here. Not just the obvious ones, like birds and bees, but other things too. Here's a piece of paper. Take notes."

I stuff the paper and a pencil into my pocket. This wasn't how my first day was supposed to go. Tomorrow I'll have to do better.

For the rest of the morning, I'm assigned the task of weeding Madda's garden. Helen sits not far off, working on her spinning, watching me work. I'm not sure whether we're allowed to talk or not, so I don't. I'm already in trouble. I don't want to find myself more.

As the day approaches noon, Madda comes outside, bringing a large basket along with her. She sets it next to me and squats down. "So, weeding. Why do we weed?" She holds up a length of ivy that I've just ripped from the rosemary. "Why is it okay to rip this plant out of the ground, but not to take the branch of the cedar tree without asking?"

I sit back, but keep my hands rooted in the dirt. "I don't know."

"Well, I know you don't know. But you've got a brain, don't you?" She shakes her head. "A perfectly good one, I'm assuming. What good is that if you don't use it? Think, girl."

My cheeks go hot. Behind Madda, Helen gives me a sympathetic look. "Because," I say as I grapple for words, "of what the ivy does? It takes over and chokes out the other plants?"

"That's part of it." Madda inspects the vine. "This is a tough plant. On one hand, we've got to honor that. It's a survivor. But that doesn't mean it gets to go wherever it wants. You're right—ivy kills other plants if it's allowed to take over. Like me and my blackberries—they taste good, but they aren't native to this land. They were introduced here by white men, and they need to be managed carefully, or soon all that's left are blackberries. Spirit work is a little like that too. You got to take care of yourself—tend your own weeds, in a matter of speaking. It's easy to go too deep, to go too far, when you're trying to help a person, and all that does is weaken you. A healer has to be strong, and not just in the ways of spirit. Strong in the body, strong in the mind. So that's why I've got you out here, working in the garden. Dirt," she says, picking up a handful and rubbing it between our fingers, "isn't just dirt. It's us. Healthy soil makes healthy plants. Unhealthy soil? Only the weeds will grow in that." She straightens up, groaning, and points at the basket. "That's yours for now on. Take it wherever you go. Gather what you find, whatever you think might be useful, even if you don't know why. Things come to us for a reason—never look a gift horse in the mouth." She starts to turn away but changes her mind. "You're free to go. Come back tomorrow morning, and don't forget your list. Oh, and I think there's something Helen wants to ask you." She winks at Helen, and heads inside the cottage.

Helen smiles at me. "Tomorrow afternoon, some of the women are getting together to make baskets. Do you want to come?"

"Sure," I say, returning Helen's smile. "I'll see you tomorrow, then?"

Helen nods, but in a way that makes me think she was expecting me to say no. "Good," she says, almost to herself. "Tomorrow."

"How did it go?" my father asks when I walk in the door.

I drop the basket, now full of rocks and flowers—all of

which I've said thanks for—and the list of birds and berries and rocks, on the counter. "Don't ask."

My father eyes the basket, but doesn't say another word.

Later, as we sit by the fire under the stars, I want him to ask. I want to talk, but I'm so afraid. *Maybe I can't do this. Maybe I'm not the person Madda thinks I am.*

Maybe I can't help Paul.

And if I can't, what then?

I don't know, but just the thought of that possibility turns my stomach to stone.

The next morning I return with the paper Madda gave me. Both sides are covered with notes. She takes it, inspects it, and hands it back. "Not bad," she says with an appreciative nod. "Wind, stones, good. What, then, does something need to be considered alive?"

"I guess it depends on a person's perspective," I say, adding quickly, "but if you ask me, it just needs to exist. Everything has a piece of spirit in it."

"Good. Very good." Madda fills her kettle and sets it over the cook stove. "So, why is that, then? Why does a rock have a piece of spirit?"

I take my time answering. It's a good question. Why *does* a rock have a piece of spirit? "Because," I say slowly, "spirit is part of existence?"

"Sort of." Madda sits down with a huff and examines her hands. "You ever hear people speaking of auras?"

I nod.

"Well, it's sort of like that. Everyone has a signature, an aura. Scientists, they call it an 'energy field.' What I was taught—and I haven't heard a better explanation yet—is that each of us has a little piece of the old times, when supernaturals were with us, when the animals walked and talked like people. Somewhere along the line, the supernaturals got a little tired of all our bickering and squabbling, so they created the division between our world and what we now call the spirit world, and headed off for a little peace and quiet, but they didn't cut us off completely." She stops to clear her throat. "A few, like you, like me, can still travel to the spirit world. Most people, though, just have that little piece of spirit in them. Not everyone, mind you. Some people have given their spirit away, to greed or crime, to addiction, or to just something as simple as forgetting that us and the earth are one. And that's when you see a person get really sick. If your spirit's healthy, if you walk in harmony with the world, then you're healthy too. That's one of our jobs as healers, to bring that piece of spirit back." She taps the table. "But as far as we're concerned, this table here has as much spirit as you and me. Anyone who says otherwise just hasn't looked well enough."

"When I see shades then," I say slowly, "is that what I'm seeing? That bit of spirit?"

"Shades?" Madda frowns.

"Totems."

"You can see totems?"

I nod.

"Without going into the spirit world?"

I nod again. I don't tell her that I can't see hers. It's there, hovering just above her shoulder, but it's out of focus, like a shadow trapped behind mist. Madda gets up and lifts the kettle from the cook top, setting it to one side before taking the teapot down from a shelf. She knows I'm trying to make out her shade, but she doesn't say a word. Neither of us does.

"So," she says when she turns back to me.

I hold my breath. Is she going to ask me what her totem is? What will I do then? Will she doubt my ability when I tell her I don't know?

Madda smiles. It's as if she can read my thoughts. "So," she says again, "do you want honey in your tea?"

"No, thanks," I say.

She laughs and turns back to the teapot, but not before I see a shadow pass through her eyes, a shadow that seems to have eyes of its own.

CHAPTER THIRTEEN

$\mathcal{H}$elen's been working at the orchards all morning. She returns just as Madda and I set out a quick lunch of greens and salmon jerky. Madda gobbles her food, and then pushes herself away from the table. She looks tired, and somehow distant, like her mind is far away and troubled. "Off you go," she says once Helen and I have finished eating. "I'm going to go for a walk in the woods. Cassandra, take the morning off tomorrow. Come by after lunch. I'll have work for you then." She attempts a smile, but her lips barely move.

Helen casts her a worried look as she picks up a basket of cedar bark and bulrushes sitting by the door. "You sure, Madda? I can stay, if you want."

Madda just waves us away before wandering out the back door.

Helen sighs as we head out.

I glance back, but Madda's nowhere in sight. "Is she like that often?"

Helen purses her lips, as if trying to decide whether to tell me. "Sometimes," she ends up saying, "though it's been more often lately. I wish I knew what was troubling her. She used to tell me when I was younger, but not anymore."

I nod. I understand how that feels.

The sun is hot and heavy on the town's dirt-packed streets. No one's about. Helen and I turn from the lane and make our way to the chestnut tree in the park, where a group of women have gathered. Most are closer to Madda's age than ours, but a few are younger. I look for Avalon among them, but she isn't there. All the heads are dark, coppery brown or black or sleek like sable. At the far side of the group is Ms. Adelaide. She flashes me a grin.

"Who's this?" a woman asks Helen when we get close enough.

"This is Cassandra," Helen says, turning to smile at me.

"Hi." I wave.

The woman peers at me as if I've grown an extra limb. "What's she doing here?"

"I invited her." Helen sits down beside Ms. Adelaide and takes out a strip of cedar bark. I sit down too, because already I can tell that this isn't going well. Helen hands me a bundle of rushes, and I quickly arrange them into spokes for a basket, hoping these women see I'm capable, that I could be one of them, if only given a chance. It's easy to think you can stand alone when you're by yourself, but now, sitting here, feeling their gazes on me, gazes that single me out as a stranger, someone not to be trusted, I realize that maybe that's not simple after all.

The older women go back to their work, while the younger ones divide the cedar into narrow strips and pound them until they're pliable. They watch me as Helen passes me the strips and I weave them between the spokes, pulling them snug, pressing them down for a tight weft. It feels good to work with the bark, to know I'm creating something from the tree I wronged yesterday.

"Jada," Helen says when the last strip she brought is gone. "Would you hand me that dyed cedar? The stuff that's black? I'm going to teach Cassandra the running raven pattern."

Jada, the woman who asked who I was, glares at me. "She doesn't get to learn that. Not yet. Look at that basket. It's uneven. It'll probably fall apart the first time someone puts something into it." She gets up and takes the basket from my hand to inspect it. "My five-year-old son can make a basket better than this." She throws the basket on the ground, and then, keeping a wicked grin trained on me, steps on it, snapping the spokes in half. "That's what we think of people who come to our town and take over. Remember that." She turns on her heel and leaves.

One by one, the other women get up and follow her. I glance at Helen, who has averted her gaze, and then at Ms. Adelaide, who's intent on her own basket. Did they not hear what she said?

"Just pretend you didn't hear," Helen mumbles under her breath. "Don't say anything."

I couldn't, even if I wanted to. I'm too stunned by what just happened.

"Give them some time," Ms. Adelaide says. "In the past, new people have come to town and done more damage than good. They haven't forgotten. Just be yourself. They'll come around. You'll see."

Will I? They've settled on the other side of the park, right in the blinding hot sun. I want to get up and go over there—to do what, I'm not sure, but Helen stops me.

"Please," she says. "Just let it go for now."

It's the pleading note in her voice, a note that I don't think is there just for me but for her, too, that keeps me where I am. For a moment Helen's shade appears behind her, a hummingbird with matted, broken feathers feebly trying to hover in place. I blink and it's gone.

What would do that to a person's shade? Madda's explanation of totems is still fresh in my mind. Is that what I'm seeing, a shade that has been damaged at the hands of others?

Helen, what have they done to you?

The next morning I decide to return Grace's books. Between Madda's lessons and the work that still needs to be done at the house, I don't have time to read them. Besides, the one attempt I made told me what I suspected: These aren't my stories. The only book I've kept is the one Bran gave me, the one that had the gray feather tucked inside of it, though today that feather is woven into one of my braids.

The walk into town seems longer than usual, the books growing heavier with each step, and when I set foot on the main street, they tumble out of my hands. "That's just great," I mutter as I crouch and pick them up. The last thing I want is to return them dirty and ruined. That will really impress Bran's mother.

A group of women walks by as I'm trying to brush the worst of the dust from the covers. I look for Avalon, but she is not among them. Helen is, though, and so is Jada. They carry hoes, shovels, baskets. One pushes a wheelbarrow. They stop to watch me. Not one cracks a smile or offers to help, except Helen. She looks at me, then back at the other girls, hesitating.

"Helen," Jada says. "Come on."

Helen gives me an apologetic look as I gather up the books. When I set off again, my cheeks burn with shame. I don't blame her. I can tell she's trying to regain her place here, and I can understand that. It's the other woman, this Jada. I allow myself to glance back, once. A few shades flutter around them—a doe, an otter—but what I really see is anger and jealousy, nothing hinting at the possibility of friendship. Except for Helen. She glances back too, and looks about as lonely as I feel.

I try to pretend it doesn't matter, and quicken my step.

A few hot minutes later, I turn onto the lane leading to Bran's house. I wonder what his mother will say when she learns I haven't read her books, but then, she didn't ask me if I wanted to read them in the first place, did she? At least I have the excuse that my studies are taking up all my time, though even if they weren't, Madda's books are far more interesting than Grace's. I haven't read them all yet, but I have glanced through every one: a collection of stories about Madda's tribe, another on the history of this land, and, the oldest and my favorite, a slim book on Chinese meditation. There are secrets in that little book, Madda said, wonderful secrets, nothing like the dusty, dry tomes I hold in my arms. Grace's books died a long, slow death ages ago.

I find her sitting on the beach, smoking. She turns her head just a fraction of an inch as I approach. "Well?" she says as she crosses her arms.

"I've brought your books back."

Blue smoke curls around her head. I scan the air for her shade, but it's missing. She coughs, and then takes a long, slow drag. "What did you learn?"

"Um," I stutter, trying to find something to say, all the while sensing that no matter what answer I give her, it's going to be the wrong thing.

"Um?" She shifts so suddenly her feet leave arcs in the sand. "That's all you have to say? Um?" She raises an eyebrow and looks ready to laugh in my face.

I clear my throat. "Actually, I've been so busy with my studies that I haven't had time for these." I set them down next to her. "I thought you might need them back."

This time she does laugh. "So, you do have a bit of a backbone after all. That's good." She grips the cigarette between her lips and pushes herself up off the beach. "Come inside. I'm thirsty."

I trail after her. She stops to grind the butt of her cigarette into the dirt and then meanders into the kitchen, clawing her hair away from her eyes. The house's condition hasn't improved since my first visit. In fact, it's even worse. A rotten smell like the odor of unwashed bodies hangs in the air, forcing me to breathe through my mouth so I won't gag.

Grace uncorks a bottle of murky wine, pours it into two dirty glasses, and hands me one. "Bottoms up," she says.

I slide the glass onto the counter. "I don't drink."

"Oh, really?" She frowns. "I never trust a person who doesn't drink." The frown loosens into a catlike smile. "Are you sure you want me to distrust you?" The tone of her voice conveys she's serious. She leans against the counter, watching, waiting to see what I'll do, leaning so close that I catch a whiff of her breath. She's drunk. "Go on," she says. "It won't kill you."

"I know." My finger traces the stem of the glass. The wine might not kill me, but botulism certainly could. I grapple for an excuse. "It just gives me really bad headaches."

Grace snorts. "Well, if you drink the whole bottle by yourself, it might. Do you have a problem with alcohol?" She leans on the word *problem*, and I blush.

"No, I don't." My voice trembles. "I mean that only a little bit gives me a headache."

She drains her glass and pours another. "Ah, yes. I've heard that line before."

"No, really . . ." I don't bother finishing the sentence. "I should get going."

"But you've only just arrived." She laughs. "Come along, my pet. Stay with me a little while. It's so lonely here when Bran's away."

I don't want to go with her, but I do, because of Bran. This is his mother. I may not like her, but I can treat her with respect, if only for her son's sake.

She leads me into the library and motions to the sofa. "So, now, I notice that the story of Arthur isn't in the pile you returned. Might I assume it's to your liking?"

I nod, though the reason I kept it is because Bran gave it to me, nothing more.

"And what did you think of his legend?" She flops down beside me and lights another cigarette.

"It's good," I say as I try to figure out a polite way to waft the smoke away from my face. "An interesting story."

"Story?" She leans toward me. "It's much more than a story—truth is hidden beneath those words. That is my history you speak of. What stories do you have? Is your family's history written down in books?" She exhales and bats at the cigarette smoke. "And why not? Because it isn't worthy. History has taken no notice of your ancestors' passing."

You're wrong. My blood runs back to Louis Riel. My blood almost changed the fate of a nation, I think, but before I can say a word, someone near the door clears her throat.

Grace jumps, and then snarls, "What do you want?"

Madda's standing there, frowning. "I think that's enough," she says.

Grace takes a quick, desperate drag of her cigarette. "Do you mind? We're in the middle of a lesson here."

"Last time I checked, Cassandra was my apprentice, not yours." Madda locks eyes with Grace. "The only lessons she attends are with me."

I press myself into the sofa, hoping that it'll swallow me whole.

"This one knows nothing," Grace says, dismissively flicking her ashes onto the floor.

"She knows more than you think, but how do you expect her to answer your questions when you're doing all the talking?" Madda gives me a quick half-smile before returning her attention to Grace.

Grace's eyes shift to me. They widen a little, as if seeing me for the first time. We sit like that for what seems like several minutes—Grace looking at me, Madda looking at Grace, and me wishing I was anywhere but stuck on the sofa in this library.

Finally Madda clears her throat again. "Grace, I've got a matter I need to discuss with you. Band business. Cassandra, would you wait for me outside?"

I force myself to take slow, even steps as I cross the room and slip into the hall, but when the library door doesn't close all the way, I creep back to listen.

"How do you know she's not the one?" Madda asks.

"She's a half-breed. She said it herself." Grace coughs. "Bran can do better. He *will* do better."

"She might be a half-breed, but she's also touched by spirit. I would have thought that would be enough for you."

"I'm looking for pure blood. That's what Bran needs to step into his inheritance—a woman whose lineage I can be sure of. Spirit has nothing to do with it. I am rebuilding what should never have been lost. I'd think you'd understand, considering you trade in myth and legend. The old myths are being reborn. You know that as well as I do."

That's when the door slams shut. When I press my ear to it, all I can make out is the murmur of their voices. I sigh, and go outside to wonder what it is that Bran is supposed to inherit, and why I'm not good enough to be part of the equation.

CHAPTER FOURTEEN

"Well, that was a bloody waste of an afternoon," Madda says as she comes storming out of the house. "Why I have to be the go-between for the Elders with that woman is beyond me. Come on, Cassandra. Keep up."

I trot after her as she pounds her feet into the earth and fumes, leaving me to wish I could ask her what was going on without revealing I had been listening in. She glances back at me. "How much did you hear?"

"Enough." More than enough.

She stops, glances at me, looks as if she's about to set off again, but then shakes her head and takes a seat on a fallen log. She pats the spot beside her. "Look, you have to know Grace has had a bad go of things. When she first came here, she had a really hard time fitting in. Arthur wasn't supposed to marry some white woman, especially not one like Grace, and it wasn't long before she started talking about all this legend stuff. Arthur came and asked me to do some healing work with her. I can't tell you what came of that, but I can say there's a reason why Grace is as she is. She isn't harmless, that's for sure, but she doesn't always mean to be unkind, either."

"But what does that have to do with Bran? What's he supposed to inherit?" I ask.

"Ah." Madda closes her eyes and turns her face to the sun. At first I think she won't answer me. I try to wait patiently, but my vision has begun to blur, just a little at the corners, like a starry night pushing its way through my eyes. I attempt to blink it away, and when that fails, my hands start to twitch. The need to set them in soil is overwhelming, so I take the only thing available—a section of my hair—and braid it. When that braid's done, I begin another. What will I do when I run out? I don't know. I only hope Madda begins to speak before then.

"I suppose," Madda says at last, "that you'll find out sooner or later. Grace believes Bran is the reincarnation of some dead king from her homeland. She thinks he's destined to become a greater leader than his father, that he'll save our people or something like that."

I know the legend she's talking about. I know because

it's in the book Bran gave me, marked by that gray feather. The once and future king, the one who is supposed to come again during the world's greatest need. "Does Bran," I say slowly, releasing the braid in my hand, "believe he's this king?"

Madda purses her lips. "Not that he's ever said. It's not the sort of thing anyone would want to talk about, you know. Bad luck, for one thing, and for another, no quicker way to get branded as crazy than to start spouting that you're some dead king come to life again. It's not that people around here don't believe a person can live more than once, but everyone's got to make their own way in the world—no free passes. If Bran wants to lead the Band, he's got to prove himself. The trouble is, his mother doesn't believe that, and she's made problems for Bran more than once."

"Problems?" I look up at Madda. "Like what?"

"Like demanding the Elders make him chief in his father's stead. That's why I went to see her today. Henry Crawford's the chief here now. I don't care for him much, though he's the best of the bunch. However, he's not about to let some kid push him out of the way. Bran is a good soul—kind, smart, fair. Special, really. He tries to do the right thing, no matter what. He'll make a good chief one day, but he has a lot to learn before that time, like the fact that compromise isn't necessarily a bad thing. And besides, no one," Madda says, nudging me, "should grow up too quickly. You included." She yawns. "Speaking of which, don't you go changing to fit with Grace's crazy ideas. She's been waiting a long time for some girl to arrive, the one she thinks will awaken the old stories within Bran."

"So that's why she hates me? Because I can't do what she wants?"

Madda smiles a very sad smile. "She doesn't hate you, Cassandra. If she hates anyone, it's herself. She thought she was the one who could do all this awakening, and I don't think she's ever forgiven herself that she couldn't. But that doesn't mean you should just go along with whatever she wants. Why did you stay in there? Why didn't you leave?"

"I don't know. I thought it would be rude, I guess."

"Rude? What Grace did was rude, Cass. You getting up and leaving is you taking care of yourself, and if you're going to be my apprentice, if you're going to be a healer, you have to learn that taking someone else's crap because you're afraid of hurting their feelings isn't just wrong— it's dangerous."

She pushes herself up and we set off, walking in silence until we reach the cottage. Then, Madda instructs me to sit at the table and stare into a bowl of water while she works outside. Helen still hasn't returned, and I find myself thinking about her. What is wrong with her shade? What could have done that to her? I wish I could ask Madda, but I'm supposed to be focusing. I try, over and over again. It's hard to concentrate with the sound of Madda's shears snipping as she does battle with her garden, a battle I'm pretty sure she'll never win. The blackberries are determined, and every day they edge closer to the cottage. I wonder what's so wrong with just letting them take over. As long as a person can avoid the thorns, what's the harm if they climb up the walls and over the roof? An image of Madda doing just that pops into my mind, and I laugh.

"I hear that," Madda hollers. "Get back to work! Nothing that you're doing right now should be funny!"

"Sorry," I say as I force my gaze back to the water that just sits there in the plain, chipped bowl, looking like water and nothing else at all. I try to keep my eyes on it, but they keep wandering away as Grace's words echo through my mind. *Half-breed, half-breed, half-breed.*

I slump in the chair and wonder what Bran thinks about all of this. I could ask him, but would he answer? Would I, if I were the one carrying around such a burden? If he asked me about totems and shades and the spirit world, would I tell him how I can see people's souls? How sometimes I'm here and then, I'm not?

I don't even have to think about the answer. Yes, I would. I would tell Bran anything he wanted to know.

Madda marches into the house, bringing the scent of sun-warmed earth with her. "Well?" she demands. "See anything?"

I glare at the water. "Nothing."

Madda grunts, picks the bowl up, and dumps the water out the window. "Good."

"Good?"

"Yeah," she says. "Good. You weren't supposed to see anything. It's just an exercise in concentration. You've got a busy mind, girl. Gotta learn to get it under control, just like a cowboy taming a wild horse."

I groan in frustration.

"Oh, none of that," Madda says. She pulls two mugs from a cupboard and sets them on the table before filling them with sun-tea. "Gotta earn your stripes, you know? Besides, you haven't exactly had success on your own, have you?"

"No."

"Oh, stop being so sullen, for god's sake."

I draw a deep breath. "Sorry."

"And stop saying sorry." She sits down and scratches her head. "You're just going to have to trust me. This isn't an easy process, especially with someone like you who's been fiddlefarting along on your own. Oh, don't worry." She holds up a hand. "I know you've done the best you could, and that's why going back to basics is hard for you. Hard on me, too, you know. It's been a long time since I've had an apprentice. The last one . . ." She pushes her chair away from the table and I can tell what she's about to say next is really important. "Well, the less said about that, the better. What counts is now." Madda stares out at the garden where the wind ripples the purple heads of the lavender.

Minutes pass, and still Madda stares outside. She looks lost, and that's when I begin to worry. I clear my throat, and then reach out and touch her hand. "Madda? Are you okay?"

"Yeah," she says, giving my hand a quick squeeze. "Just thinking. The last one, well, I didn't do such a good job. We'll just have to do it right this time." Her words come out full of breath, like she's not talking to me anymore. She blinks, and then rubs her eyes, and she's back in the room. "So, patience. Patience for me, patience for you. Nothing good happens quickly. When it seems things are taking too long, remind yourself of that."

"Right." I yawn. It's been a long day. My eyes feel dry and itchy. "So, what's next?"

"Next is to start walking the spirit paths, but I need

you to promise me something." She clenches her hands into fists and then releases them, spreading her fingers wide on the tabletop. "I need you to promise not to go into the spirit world until we've worked through a few things. You can probably tell spirit runs a little different here on the Island, hey?"

"That's a bit of an understatement."

Madda chuckles. "Yes. Yes, it is. That's the boundary at work."

"But, Madda," I say as I push my mug away from me, "sometimes I have no choice." I think about when I touched the petroglyph on the rock by my house, about how it almost drew me under, and about the sparks that overwhelm me whenever spirit comes to call. "Sometimes spirit comes for me."

"That's what I'm talking about." She reaches behind her, takes a book down from the shelf, and pushes it across the table to me. "I don't mean to scare you, but there are powerful creatures in the spirit world, and not all of them are nice. Right now, you don't have any control there, and if you cross, they'll be able to use you as they want." A frown pinches her brow. "We might not have a lot here in this world, but one of the most precious things we do have is the right to choose how we live, and part of that is choosing the paths we walk on. If you choose to walk on over to spirit, that's one thing, but how often have you done that?"

A lump forms in my throat. "Not often."

"That's what I thought." She pats the book before me. "I want you to read this. I had planned on giving it to you when you were a little further along in your studies, but some things can't wait."

I pick up the book. It's old and worn and the cover is missing. The title page reads: *Medicine Country: A Guide to Healing.* "But I know how to heal," I say.

"No." Madda shakes her head. "You know how to fix. There's a difference. It talks about it in there, but what I really need you to read is the chapter on grounding, on attaching yourself to the earth so that nothing can break you free. The book has some exercises, too. Try them on your own, and when you come back, you can tell me about them." She rubs her eyes and I realize that she's tired too. "Time for you to go. I need to spend a little time with my own spirit guides tonight. Lots to think about. Lots to consider." She tries to smile. "You're going to make a very good healer. Just take your time. Time is one thing we have an abundance of right now."

"Okay." I tuck the book under my arm and move to get up, but change my mind. "Madda," I say slowly, "something happened with Helen."

"Oh, the basket-making incident? Yeah, I heard about

that. She wants to apologize, but she's afraid, you know?"

I nod. "Did something happen to Helen?"

Madda draws a deep breath. "Yes. Something did."

"Something bad?"

Madda nods again. "Something very bad. Look, Cassandra, I can't tell you. Right now, Helen and you are friends, and if I tell you, that'll change—not that you'll think any different of her, but you will pity her, and Helen, well, she doesn't want that. She just wants a friend. She needs a friend. One day, she'll tell you; I'm pretty sure of that. But for right now? Let it be. You've got enough to think about, and Helen, she does too. Trust me, all right?"

"Okay." This time I do get up. "Though, would you mind telling Helen I'm not mad? That there's nothing to apologize for?"

Madda smiles. "Sure. I will."

"Thanks. I'll see you tomorrow?"

"Yeah," she says. "That'll be good."

When I reach the end of the path that leads away from the cottage, I look back. Madda's still sitting at the table, her head cradled by her arms. I hope it's just fatigue, but I suspect something's troubling Madda, and I have a funny feeling that something is me.

CHAPTER FIFTEEN

dream.

I dream of Paul sitting on a rock. His raven has wrapped its wings around his shoulders so I'm not sure where the raven stops and my brother begins. One eye is swollen, and from time to time Paul touches it, gingerly, and smiles.

Bran joins him. They talk, but what they say, I can't make out. Then Bran produces a knife, his hunting blade. He makes an incision in his forearm, right in the spot where a chip scar would be if he had one, and as blood wells up and drips onto the rock, he hands the blade to Paul, who embeds the point right into his chip scar. They press their forearms together, melding their blood, the water of their body.

Then Paul's raven looks at me, and with a blur of wings, forces me away.

• • •

I have always dreamed like this. The next day, when I arrive at Madda's, it's the first thing I tell her.

"That's your soul walking," she says. "Powerful stuff, that is."

"So, what I saw, was it real?" I rub the chip scar on my arm. It began to hurt this morning and hasn't stopped since.

"Real?" Madda sets down the bowl she's been drying and turns to me. "Define 'real' for me."

Define "real." I roll the words over in my head, and realize I can't. "I don't know how," I say. "I mean, I had my dream, so it was real to me. Did it actually happen, what I saw? That I don't know, but that doesn't make the dream unreal, I guess."

"True that," Madda says. "Dreams are real, but some dreams are more real than others, if you know what I mean. Did you feel like you were actually there?"

I nod.

"Well, then, maybe you were. Who's to say? Best wait until your brother gets home and ask him about it. Then you'll know for sure. Dream-walking is a strong gift, though, and you need to make sure you can come back to your body. That's what that raven did—sent you back into yourself—but you can't rely on him every time. And a raven, even if he's in the dream world, will want something in return for his help."

"So what do I do?" The hair on my arms has risen. What would happen if I didn't return to myself? I've never considered that dreaming, something that is as natural to me as breathing, something I have no control over, might not be safe.

Madda takes a seat. "You just make up your mind that you're coming back. Decide before you go to sleep, and make sure you give yourself a reason to come back. Dreams can be tempting, you know. Sometimes they're so sweet we don't want to come back to our bodies." A shadow passes behind Madda's eyes, and I get the sense she's experienced this temptation more than once. "From now on, I want you to write your dreams down. And, go get yourself some lemon balm. It's good for making sure all of you is inside your body again. Take some home with you. Put it under your pillow. See what happens."

So I go outside, full of questions that I don't know how to ask. If I have lemon balm under my pillow, will it mean I won't dream at all? What if I want to go dream-walking? What then? Just make up my mind and I'll wake up? Can it really be that simple?

And what of Paul? All this time, I've been thinking about Bran and his mother and my studies and Madda, and yet, I've forgotten why I want all of this in the first place.

My thoughts are broken by the sound of footsteps, and I look up to see Henry Crawford at the gate. He nods at me, and then at Madda. "We're back. Elders meet tonight."

"I'll be there," Madda says as he strides off. Madda looks at me. "Well? Get on home."

Paul is down at the lake, washing up. He turns when he hears me. A grin is etched on his face and with the two very black eyes he sports, he's a jack-o'-lantern come to life. A rather sunburned jack-o'-lantern. That's what three days on open water will do.

"What happened?" I say as he splashes water over his shoulders. Bubbles of soap rush down either side of his backbone.

"Nothing that hasn't happened before." He shakes his hair, deliberately spraying me. I laugh and splash him back, and it's not long before I'm drenched too.

My father stomps down the hill, hammer resting on his shoulder, and grins at us. "Being away didn't do much for your appearance," he says to Paul.

My brother laughs. "I'm so tired—didn't get more than an hour or two of sleep a night the whole time I was gone." He wades to shore and gathers up his soap and towel.

It should be enough for me that he's safe, that he has only a couple of shiners rather than a bullet hole in the leg or a puncture wound to the gut. It should be, but it's not. I force a smile on my face and give him a hug, and then glance down at his forearm. There's a scab there, right over his chip scar. So it was real, my dream. That's never happened before; not that I can remember. My stomach drops. What does that mean?

"You okay?" Paul says, tipping his head to one side to give me a curious look. "Bran's fine, you know."

"Good," I say, pasting a smile on my face as my father takes the towel from Paul's hand and shoos him up the slope, demanding that Paul share his war stories.

We sit in silence as my father builds a fire, and only when the flames are leaping high does Paul start to speak.

"There were boats everywhere, bobbing along the boundary," he says. "The Band took me into the Corridor, made me be their guide. Searched for Others, mostly." He shrugs. "Didn't find many. The northern part of the Corridor was hit pretty hard, but from what we heard, it was even worse to the south. They say the waves were as bad as the earthquake itself, but what did they expect? Buildings as tall as the sky? They're going to fall down sometime."

I check the kettle that's steaming over the coals. "What happened to the refugees?"

"We brought a few back."

Paul's use of *we* doesn't escape me, but I let it slide for now.

"And the ones they turned away?" my father asks.

I look at Paul expectantly. I was about to ask the exact same thing.

"They're on their own," he says. "We don't need people who can't take care of themselves here."

"Paul, that isn't fair," I say. "What if it was us?" This doesn't sound like Paul.

"If it was us? Since when did anyone ever help us?" he says as he stabs a log in the fire. "You speak of fair— when did anyone in the Corridor ask *us* about what's fair? The UA turned their backs on us Others a long time ago. Why should the Band look after the ones the Corridor's spat out?"

"I don't know," I admit, but I can't help wondering, how many are injured? How many without food, without homes? Here we sit behind our boundary, safe and fed, while others suffer, all because they have the wrong blood in their veins? "It just doesn't seem right to me."

"Cass, you can't possibly take care of everyone." My father reaches over to touch my hair. "I know you'd like to, but take care of those close to you first, hey?" He settles back to watch the waves on the lake. "When are you going to Madda's next?"

"Tomorrow."

Paul glances at me from the corner of his eye. "You know what they say about her, right?"

"I imagine you're going to tell me."

"She can curse you with a glance."

"And that's supposed to scare me?"

Paul frowns. "It should. Bran's afraid of her."

I laugh. "Bran isn't afraid of anything."

"That's what you think." Paul pitches his stick into the bushes and stalks away.

"What did I say?" I ask my father.

He shakes his head. "Leave him be. I imagine he saw a few things that he didn't expect while he was away. All that bravado is just covering up hurt. Give him a bit of time. He'll come 'round."

He's right, but I can't help wanting to chase after Paul. I could help him, if I were only a little further along in my studies, and that brings Paul's words about Madda to mind. "Do you think it's a bad idea for me to learn from Madda, Dad?"

"Not at all. Madda is respected by the Band. Feared, too, but that goes with her position. She'll teach you well—better than some of the other people around here. I heard what happened with Bran's mother. I won't tell you what to do, but I don't think you should see her anymore. She seems harmless enough to me, but she has high aspirations for Bran. If you don't fit in with them . . . well, I just don't want to see you get hurt." He bends to pull his fishing rod from its case at his side. "The midges are hatching. Dusk is the best time to try." He bites the line between his teeth and threads a fly on, peering at me all the while. "Bran's a good sort, Cass. Just be wary, that's all. With a mother like that . . . well, it's bound to rub off somehow," he says, before he wades out into the water and casts his line. The rod swishes from six to twelve, fast to slow, and the line spins out, sparkling in the last light of the day. Once, twice, and then he releases it, gathers it in, and starts again.

I go to sit on the lopsided dock, where before me the dance between line and fisher blur in my vision.

Just be wary, that's all. The words play on my mind, over and over. This is the third time someone's warned me about Bran's mother. The third time's a charm, but a charm for what?

I'm rolling the thought around in my head when the dock jerks beneath me, jolting me alert. *Another earthquake* is my first thought, but nothing else seems wrong.

The trees don't sway; the water just continues its gentle lapping as the dock lurches again.

Something is moving it. Not the waves, not the wind, but something large.

I am standing on the shore before I know it. I had no idea I could move so fast.

"What's wrong?" my father asks, reeling his line in.

"Something bumped against the dock . . . s-something big," I manage to stutter. Every hair on my body is standing on end.

"Stay here." He jogs off, but I'm right behind him, our footsteps echoing on the wood planks. When we reach the end, my father crouches, staring into the depths, cocking his head to one side as if listening for something. "Probably just shifting from your weight," he says as he straightens up. "Paul and I will fix it up tomorrow, okay?" He tugs my braid and wanders off.

But something deep within me whispers that it wasn't just my weight. It was something else, something from the depths.

Something that is hunting me.

CHAPTER SIXTEEN

Calendula is a tonic for the liver, gall bladder, and uterus. Heather is a diuretic and can ease the pains of rheumatism. Mallow is an expectorant.

I turn the pages of Madda's book of healing—her herbal, she calls it—slowly, reading, trying desperately to commit all the knowledge to memory. Poultices, tinctures, alexipharmicals, coagulants, abortifacients. The book holds the secrets of life and death, and will I ever know which is which? One plant heals, the next kills, and that's all before I walk into the world of spirit and encounter what lurks there.

Give me a broken arm, I'll mend it. Give me a wound, I'll suture it. Those are concrete things, things I can hold and touch. This stuff of mystery is no province of mine.

Madda hovers nearby, adding sage bits of advice that I scribble in the margins of the herbal. "It's already there," she says when I write *poisonous in large doses* under the heading of digitalis. "I wrote those exact words myself." Sure enough, her thin, spidery script crawls around a hastily sketched foxglove. "I didn't learn it all in one day. You aren't expected to either."

I nod, wondering when I can leave herbs and lore behind and begin to wander the paths of spirit. Didn't she say that was what we were doing next? I suspect if I ask about it, she'll answer with an enigmatic comment about seeking the way of water or some other Zen thing, so I don't mention it and wait.

I feel like I'm waiting for everything.

Madda sits across the table from me and watches as I read. I raise an eyebrow at her. She laughs. "Well? You gonna stare at that book all day, or are we going to talk about spirit?"

I open my mouth. All that comes out is a hiss of air. I try again, but my throat is tight. I don't think I've ever realized how frustrated I am. Why couldn't my abilities have come with an instruction manual?

Madda reaches out and takes my hand. "Take your time. You've been holding a lot inside you, and these past few weeks haven't been easy. Nothing says you have to give words to all of it right now."

"Thanks," I say. She offers me a handkerchief and I blow my nose. "Things *have* been different since I came here."

"This is an old land," Madda says with a nod.

"The other day, when the earthquake came? I could feel it. Before, I mean."

Madda sits back and strokes her chin. "You could? Hmm . . ." She hums to herself for a moment and then nods. "Let's not worry about that right now. I'll have a chat with my spirit guide about it tonight. What did yours say?"

"Who?"

"Your spirit guide."

Something outside the window behind Madda catches my eye. It's a raven, roosting on the fence. He watches me watching him, and I'm pretty sure I see him smile.

"I don't have a spirit guide," I say, knowing the raven can hear my words.

Madda frowns. "Have you asked it to come forth?"

"Yes!"

She laughs. "Okay, let's try a little something here." She pushes herself away from the table, turns, and spots the raven. "Hey, you! Get out of here!" The raven bobs his head and cackles at her, but doesn't move. She runs to the window, clapping her hands. "Go on! Get! We don't want your tricks here!" The raven croaks at her again but this time, flies away, his wings whooshing through the air. "Gotta watch those ravens," Madda says. "They seem to like you a little too much." She takes a bowl from the windowsill and sets it on the center of the table, then stuffs it with sage. "It's gonna get smoky in here. You don't have asthma or anything, do you?"

"Nope."

"Good." She lights the sage and then blows the flames out. Smoke curls up from the smoldering leaves. Madda wafts it toward me. "Breathe it in, and close your eyes."

I try not to cough as I inhale. My eyelids seal away the world, but I still try to look through them. Somewhere out there is my spirit creature, my shade. Madda said a shade is a bit of the divine, that spark that gives a person her soul. If I have no totem, what does that mean? That I'm soulless?

"Stop looking," Madda snaps. I can hear her take a seat and shuffle around until she's comfortable. "Looking's my job right now. Yours is to breathe."

Gradually my breathing steadies as my mind drifts. I see a pool of water so black it's blue. A lake. It stretches out as far as time. A single drop of water falls into it, sending ripples racing across the darkness. I follow the ripples, I become the ripples, I am the water, I am sinking down, down . . .

Madda touches my hand. "Open your eyes," she whispers.

I do, though it takes several seconds before I recognize the room I'm sitting in, and several more before I feel like I fully inhabit my body.

Madda fixes me with a serious stare. "You learned to do this by yourself?" she says.

I nod.

"Hmm." Her hand returns to her chin. "Herbs might have to wait for a bit. Take this." She turns to grab a pouch on a string from the counter. "I was going to wait to give this to you, but you need it now." She pushes the pouch into my hand. "This is your medicine bag. There's something inside, but don't look at it—not just yet. You'll know when the time is right. You can add your own stuff as you go along, things that have deep meaning to you. Remember what I said about dreaming, about having something to lock on to, to get back? This is part of it, like home base in a way. It should do the trick." She pauses to give me a hard look. "Don't ever take it off."

I slip the string around my neck, wondering why I can't take it off or look to see what's inside. How, exactly, is a pouch going to protect me? "Did you see anything?" I ask.

She shakes her head. "I was told that I shouldn't

interfere. Well, they used terms a little stronger than that, but you get the idea. This is between you and your totem. You have to figure it out. That doesn't mean we can't work on the other stuff. The roads to the spirit world are many. We can walk the other ones together while you figure out what your totem is. But I think that's good enough for today, don't you? Off you go." She fans the remnants of the sage smoke away and then nods to the door.

I try not to think about the pouch hanging around my neck on the way home, but with every step I take, it bounces against my breastbone, begging me to open it and see what's inside. I make it halfway home before I give in. After all, Madda said I'd know when the time was right, and though something in my mind whispers that I should wait, I don't. I can't. The pouch and its contents are driving me crazy.

Inside is a carving, a tiny woman's face chiseled out of cedar. Her eyes are pebbles and her lips are painted red. I tuck the carving back inside the pouch as a feeling of dread pours over me. Madda's right. I should have waited. I should have heeded her words. As I set off again, a whisper takes up in my mind, one that doesn't come from within me. If I didn't know better, I'd say it came from the tiny carved woman in the pouch. What she says, I can't make out, but she's there, tickling my mind, laughing at me because I don't know what she's saying. How can something like this protect me? Maybe Madda was wrong. Or, maybe, I'm the wrong one. I should have left well enough alone, and I didn't.

I try to ignore the whispers as best I can, but by the time I reach the top of our driveway, I can't stand it anymore. I slip the pouch off and tuck it into my pocket. The whispering stops as suddenly as it started, and relief floods through my body.

Will I tell Madda what I've done? No. I've managed this long on my own.

But when I fall asleep that night, the whispers flood my dreams. The first thing I do when I get up is walk down to the water and throw the pouch into the lake.

And though I know I should, I won't tell Madda that, either.

CHAPTER SEVENTEEN

*M*adda and Helen surprise me by arriving at my house just after breakfast. They both wear baskets strung across their backs. "We need willow. There's a good grove near here," Madda says. "I used the last of my supply removing chips from the new Corridor people."

"How many new people?" I ask as I grab my basket.

"A half dozen." She yawns. "Kept me up most of the night. You'll see them at the gathering tonight."

We don't speak as we follow the road along the lake's edge. Madda glances at me from time to time, but doesn't ask what I'm thinking about, though I can tell she'd like to know. What would she say if I told her I threw away the medicine pouch she gave me? I can scarcely believe it myself. How could I have done that?

Because it was talking to you, I tell myself. *It was driving you crazy.*

So shouldn't I have asked Madda about it first?

Maybe, but it's too late now, and I'd almost believe that, if it wasn't for the sick feeling in my stomach.

The willow grove is on the shore of the lake. We squat in the mud and ask permission to take the willow before we begin our work. The mosquitoes arrive soon after, and even though Madda sprays us down with a mist that smells of camphor and lemon balm, they're hell-bent on eating us alive.

Helen drifts close to me, and I can tell she wants to apologize so badly it's killing her, but she can't seem to find the words. So I find them for her. "It's okay," I say when Madda conveniently wanders out of earshot. "I understand."

Helen's on the verge of tears. "No, you don't," she says in a thick, choked voice. "You haven't been anything but nice to me, and they . . ."

"Haven't?" I arch an eyebrow. "That's not hard to believe, considering how they treated me." A tear slips down Helen's cheek, so I bend to cut another branch of willow, giving her time to wipe the tear away. "I'm used to being alone, Helen. I've never many friends—just Paul, really, and if they don't like me, so what? But you—you've known those people for a long time. If it's easier for you to pretend you don't like me when they're around, I understand. Really, I do. Doesn't mean we don't know the truth." But it still stings just the same.

Helen sniffs and shakes her head. "No," she says. "I'll do it right next time. I will. I promise."

That's when Madda rounds the corner and wades her way back through the shallows toward us. "That's enough for today," she says, batting the bugs around her face. "Time to get back to the cottage."

"Okay," I say, though I take a moment to give thanks before we leave. Helen copies me. Madda nods in approval. If she only knew.

Once we're back at the cottage, Helen and I are assigned the task of stripping the leaves off the willow branches. There's a gathering tonight, and Madda wants the bark to make a tea for the hangovers she'll have to treat tomorrow.

She works at her mortar and pestle, crushing feverfew. "Make sure you don't drink any of that firewater the Band brings tonight—horrible stuff. Impure. It'll give you a terrible headache. When you're finished with that, bind the white sage over there into wands. Oh, and take this." She slides a sheathed knife across the table to me. "It'll come in handy. You never know when you might need to gut a fish or strip some bark. I never go anywhere without mine. Neither will you, from now on."

I slip it onto my belt, feeling oddly pleased. The knife makes me feel like I'm an initiate of a secret order. Maybe I am.

Someone raps on the door. I rise to answer it, hoping that maybe it's Bran. I haven't seen him since he got back. Madda waves me away. "Just keep doing what you're doing."

"Fine," I grumble. I'm tired of doing what I'm doing, but when I see who's at the door, I find I'm very glad to be stripping willow. It's Avalon. Helen slips out the back door at the sight of her.

"Hi, Madda," Avalon says. "My dad said you'd have his medicine for him. He's almost out."

"Oh lord." Madda shakes her head. "It completely slipped my mind. Come in, come in. I'll make it up right away." She bustles about, pulling jars from cupboards as Avalon and I eye each other.

"Hi," she says.

"Hi," I say back.

"What are you doing?" Her gaze flickers to Madda, who's pounding something into a pulp, as I set one willow switch aside and take up another.

"Getting these ready for Madda. They're for . . ."

"Headaches. I know. I used to help Madda before you came."

"Oh." I don't know what to say. She's working hard to be nice, I can tell, and I wonder if she knows Madda's taken me as her apprentice.

"Do you," she says carefully, "miss it?"

"It?"

"The Corridor." She rubs the chip scar on her forearm. "Being connected. Having friends. You know. Having hot water." She laughs.

I don't have the heart to tell her that the only hot water at my house was boiled on the cookstove, that my father didn't allow etherstream devices in the house, and friends? Can't say I ever had those, either. She's talking about a different world than the one I knew.

"Okay, here you go." Madda hands Avalon a jar of salve. "It's best if he can let it steep for a couple of days. Tell him to come see me if it doesn't do the trick."

"Thank you," Avalon says, though she doesn't move to go. "Will you be at the gathering tonight?" she asks me.

"Yes," I say. "Will you?"

"Yes." She smiles at the jar in her hand. "Make sure you come say hi, okay?"

And with that, she leaves. I watch her make her way

past the roses and out into the lane. Madda watches her go too. "A troubled girl, that one," she says.

"Is she?" As if I didn't agree.

"Yep." Madda closes the door. "I had thought about making her my apprentice before you came, but she isn't the right sort. Too much ambition. Too hungry for power. A girl like her, she'd lord her gifts over everyone else, use them for punishment and reward. Didn't take it well when I told her you'd be taking her place. Can't blame her, I guess. These ones from the Corridor, they just have trouble fitting in here. You—you grew up living the Old Way, knowing what it's like to do without. Her—she never had a day when she worried about where her dinner would come from, and she hasn't quite forgiven her father for bringing her here." Madda moves to the window. "Avalon hasn't fit in with the other girls, but she seems to be making an effort with you. Try with her, would you? She could use a friend—someone who has a bit of moral fiber."

"Okay," I say, though I doubt friendship is what Avalon has in mind. Still, Madda has asked, and so I'll do my best.

"Now," Madda says, "you head off home too. This gathering tonight is important for you and your family. You want to be at your best. A little bird told me that someone's looking forward to seeing you there too."

"Someone?" I force myself not to smile as I get up and wipe willow juice from my hands. "Someone who?"

Madda doesn't answer. She just grins as she steers me toward the door.

The house is empty when I arrive home. My father has left a pile of rocks by the door, arranged to indicate he'll be back soon. I move them, restacking them to say I'm home safely, and then run down the hill. The lake beckons.

But I draw to a halt at the boathouse and stare at the dock, the memory of it lurching beneath me suddenly fresh in my mind. A merganser and her chicks float by, watching me with their queer red eyes. I step out from the boathouse's shadows, and they scurry away, leaving ripples in the otherwise seamless water. Little by little, I inch my way out toward the end of the dock, pausing with each step, listening, waiting for the dock to move, but it doesn't. Nothing happens at all, so by the time I sit down and dangle my feet in the water, I'm laughing at myself. My father was right. It shifted under my weight, nothing more. Docks don't just move without reason.

The sun is hot, and the water, so cool against my bare legs. I pull off my shirt, and then, with a quick glance back at the house just to make sure no one's come home,

I pull off the rest of my clothes and slip into the lake.

It's icy cold, but soon my flesh numbs. I float on my back, naked, until I feel the forest watching me, and then I dive. The merganser flashes past me in a blur of red, chasing a school of fish. I take comfort in that and linger underwater as long as I can while my lungs tighten. Green waterweeds wave back and forth. The sun trickles down as if it's made of water, and the lake, of glass.

I wait there until my lungs feel like they're about to burst, and then I set my feet on the lakebed, bend my knees, and push off, jettisoning myself to the surface. The merganser chicks scatter as I break through the water. I laugh, and then notice the shadow hanging over me.

The muskrat boy stands on the dock. "I didn't know there were mermaids in the lake," he says.

I push myself underwater and swim to the end of the dock, my cheeks burning against the chill of the water as my mind races. *How am I going to get out with him standing there, and just what did he see?* When I surface, I press my chest against a piling so only my head's visible.

"No need to be shy," he says as he strolls toward me. "I didn't see much. These yours?" He points at the heap of clothing at his feet.

"What are you doing here?" I demand.

"Came to see your brother." He leans toward me,

smiling at my discomfort. "Not coming out?" When I don't answer, he shrugs. "Suit yourself." He grabs the hem of his shirt, as if he's about to take it off.

"What the hell do you think you're doing?"

"Well, if you aren't coming out, I have to come in, don't I?"

"Like hell you do." I spot Paul walking across the sundeck up at the house. "Paul!" I scream. "Paul!"

It takes only a second for him to assess the situation. He bounds down the hill, snatching an ax from the woodpile along the way. By the time he reaches the dock, he's going for blood. "Cedar, get away from my sister!"

The muskrat boy drops the hem of his shirt and holds up his hands. "What's the matter, Mercredi? I'm just having a bit of fun!"

Paul pulls his lips into a snarl. Cedar takes another step back, inching toward a rowboat tied to the other side of the dock. "Listen, man, I was just messing with her. No harm intended."

"Get out of here." Paul heaves the ax from hand to hand.

"I'm going. I just came by to tell you that the Band's meeting tonight at sundown. At the park. Be there." He returns Paul's snarl with one of his own, steps into the rowboat, and rows away.

Paul waits for him to leave and then turns on me. "What the hell are you thinking? Swimming naked where everyone can see you?"

"Don't yell at me! He's your creepy friend. Besides, I didn't know anyone was home."

"Dad and I just got back, and he's no friend of mine." Paul swings the ax up onto his shoulder. "If you want to swim, wear a swimsuit next time." He starts down the dock, but draws up, favoring his right foot.

I wince. His sole is bleeding. He must have cut it running down here. I wait until he's gone and then haul myself out of the water, dressing as quickly as I can so I can follow Paul and see to his foot, but by the time I've scurried up to the house, he's left.

"Leave him be," my father says when I ask where Paul's gone. "He's struggling to find his place."

"His place is here with us," I mutter as I storm around the house, searching for something to wear tonight that's not threadbare or a crumpled mess.

"Yes, but he also has to figure out how to live with everyone else. We don't exist in a vacuum." My father nods at the dress in my hand. "Wear that. It reminds me of your mother."

"This?" I frown at it. "It's too creased."

"Here. Give it to me. I'll see what I can do about it."

"Are you going tonight?"

My father smiles one of his rare smiles. "Yes. Should make an appearance, being one of the new families in town, shouldn't we?" He drapes my dress over his shoulder and meanders off, humming to himself.

CHAPTER EIGHTEEN

*T*don't know how my father did it, but an hour later, I'm wearing a wrinkle-free dress, the only dress I own. My mother wore this dress once, and gave it to me before she passed. It was too big then, but it isn't now, and I wonder what she would think, me standing here, old enough to wear a dress she wore when she was my age. When I come down the stairs, my father's there in the kitchen, looking up at me with tears in his eyes. He brushes them away, and clears his throat. "Tickle from the dust," he mumbles. "You know."

I smile. I do know.

Just then the kitchen door creaks open. I turn, expecting Paul, but it's Bran—Bran like I've never seen him before, with a collared shirt and clean shorts. He's even slicked his hair back out of his eyes.

I don't know what to do. The last time I saw him, I blamed him for Paul getting involved with the Band. The time before that, I kissed him.

"I was hoping," he says. He pauses to swallow, and I realize this is new to him. But then again, this is new to me, too. "I was hoping I could take Cassandra to the gathering," he finally says, forcing the words out so quickly that my father can scarcely stop himself from laughing.

I look at my father. He looks at me, arching an eyebrow as if to say, *Is this what you want? Are you sure?*

Yes, Dad. I'm sure.

"Well, I guess that's okay. Go on. Have her home sometime tonight."

I kiss my father's cheek and follow Bran outside.

We walk down the hill in silence, both too shy to speak. He holds the canoe for me, and once we're both seated, paddles us out into the lake. Bran's humming, just under his breath, a sound that should calm me, but it doesn't. My hands have found the sides of the canoe and grip it so tightly that I can't feel my fingers anymore, but not because of Bran. It's the shadow I saw in the water. I'm looking for it now, and I can't shake the feeling that it's looking for me, too.

Bran taps my shoulder. "Are you nervous?"

For a moment I wonder how he could know, until

I realize he's talking about the gathering. "A little," I admit.

"Don't worry. I'll make sure you have a good time."

From somewhere on the other side of the lake, a raven cackles. If Bran hears it, he gives no sign. "You don't mind, do you?" he asks.

"Mind?"

"About me coming to get you?"

"No," I say. He can't see my smile. I don't mind at all.

Bran continues to talk while he paddles. My brother is a good wood worker, he says. That's what they've been up to while I've been with Madda. He tells me about the totem pole they've been working on, the images he's carved, the paints he's using. I close my eyes and the pole appears in my mind, an enormous grizzly holding a salmon in its mouth, a raven, a kingfisher. I wonder if Bran is aware that he's talking about his own totem, and Paul's, too.

"Would you like to see it?" he asks. I look back at him and nod. He grins as a blush stains his cheeks. Something in my chest tightens at the sight of it. "Good. Maybe Paul's surprise will be ready by then."

"Surprise?"

"Oh. I shouldn't have mentioned it."

Maybe not, but that's okay. I like surprises.

We arrive at the beach all too soon. Bran stows the canoe under the lazy boughs of a willow before taking my hand and leading me toward the park.

Dozens of people mill about. Someone is playing a drum, but everyone else is talking, waiting. Tents have been erected near the road, and the aroma of food wafts toward us. "Hungry?" he asks. I nod. "Good." Bran holds the flap to the nearest tent open for me. "Inside. Ms. Adelaide will feed us."

"How can you be so sure?" I say, poking him.

"Just go." He pokes me back. "You impressed her when you helped out after the earthquake. She likes you."

Ms. Adelaide mans a cook fire out the other side of the tent. Stacks of venison ribs are arranged over a metal grate, sizzling as fat drips onto the coals. "Meat's not ready yet, kids," she says with a broad smile, twisting her massive body to push past a table.

"Doesn't matter." Bran settles himself on a crate.

"Hiding out then, are you?" Ms. Adelaide gives us a cockeyed stare and laughs.

Bran shrugs. "Nope. Got any of your doughnuts kicking around, looking for a home?"

"I knew you were after something, Bran Eagleson." She shakes a finger at him, and then draws a large box out from under the table. "Here. One each. Just don't tell anyone where you got them from. This is a special batch for the Elders—for after."

Bran hands me his doughnut so he can fumble for something in his pocket. "Stay here," he says to me as he retrieves the doughnut from my hand. "I'll be back in a minute."

"Where are you going?"

"Need to give something to someone. I'll be right back. It's okay if she stays with you, isn't it, Ms. Adelaide?"

"Sure, if she doesn't mind doing some work—and eat that doughnut before anyone sees!" she hollers, waving a basting brush at Bran's back. She hands me the brush and a bowl of sauce. "Go on, that meat won't cook itself." She sits down on a crate with a groan, and mops her brow. "So, you going around with him?"

I slather the sauce on the meat, thinking of her question, then take a seat beside her. She smells of heat and blood and perspiration. "I don't know." Because I don't. But if not, what is this, then? Just Bran being nice?

She waves her hand in front of her as if the answer's obvious. "You aren't sure, huh? Well, if you ask me, you are. He wants to, at least. What about you?" She peers at me. "What do you want?"

What do I want. I look outside. Paul is making his way through the grounds, walking with Avalon. "What I want," I say slowly, "is for my brother to be happy."

"Ah." Ms. Adelaide follows my gaze. "And you think he'll be happy with her?"

"No. I don't." But he looks happy, and that's got to count for something.

"So, now I know what you want for your brother. How about you?" She laughs. "Look at me, pestering you with questions. But if I could go back to your age, there is one thing I'd do." She fixes her gaze on me with such intensity that I can't look away. Her shade is a bear, a great mother bear, reaching over her shoulder to touch me. "It would be to listen to my gut and follow it, no matter what. You're a thinker, I can tell, and thinking is good, but if you don't listen to your gut, well, you don't got much." She pokes me in the stomach. "You ask your gut what it thinks about Bran, and you follow its advice, and don't let anyone, not Avalon or Bran's fool mother tell you otherwise." She pushes herself up, taking the bowl of sauce with her to slop more on the ribs.

Listen to my gut. I want to. It's what told me to kiss Bran the day of the earthquake, but the trouble is, what if it's wrong?

"Talk to him," Ms. Adelaide says, though she doesn't

look at me. "Going 'round and 'round in your head will get you nowhere at all. Talk to him, and then you'll know what's what."

"Talk to who?" Bran steps into the tent. He's grinning from ear to ear.

"Speak of the devil," Ms. Adelaide says. "You look like you just swallowed a canary."

"Nope. I just found out my mother's gone home with one of her headaches, so tonight, I'm free!" He pulls me to my feet and spins me around in a circle. "Free!"

"Go on then, free boy. You're going to get into trouble if you stay around my kitchen. Out!" Ms. Adelaide shoos Bran from the tent, but grabs my elbow before I can leave. "Now, girl, listen to me," she whispers. "They'll be bringing out whiskey later—stay with Bran and don't let him drink any. He's just kicked it, and for him to go back to the bottle? Tragic." She shakes her head. "Shame we have it here at all. Probably best if you just get Bran to take you home after Madda does her thing. The men, well, things can get out of hand, and you're new—different." She cups my chin with her wide, firm hand and gives me a searching look. "Promise?"

"I promise," I say, shocked at everything she's just implied. Is that why Bran's shade is so strange? Because of whiskey? If so, what does that mean for Helen's own newly healed shade? Did she have the same problem, or is it something else entirely?

"Good." She squeezes my chin. "I knew you had a good head on your shoulders. Make sure you have a little fun tonight."

Bran waits for me a few paces away, twirling a blade of grass between his fingers. "What did Ms. Adelaide want?"

"She said that things can get out of hand sometimes, and if they do, you're to take me home."

He nods. "That's true. And I will. But for now let's go and get a seat. The drumming will start soon, and then the dancing."

"Do you dance?"

"No." He purses his lips. "Not until my father returns."

"Why is that?"

"Don't know." He picks a pinecone up off the ground and throws it as far as he can. It bounces into the trees. "Just doesn't seem right without him. He's the one who taught me."

The longhouse is already full of people when we step inside, but space is made for us near the fire. This is my first time inside the longhouse. Heat rises from the coals in invisible ribbons, making the sisiutl, the double-headed mythical serpent, painted on the far wall look alive. Already the transformation from here to the time of myth has begun, and when I look around, I see that other people feel the shift too.

The drummers have all ceased playing, save for one lone man. He's ancient, and as the shadows of the fire ripple across his face, I can see his shade, a raccoon, hovering so close I can't tell where it ends and the man begins. He beats a slow rhythm on his drum—*ba-bump, ba-bump*—like a heartbeat. I feel it deep in my chest, deep in my bones. Those sitting around me feel it too. I can tell from the way their breathing shifts, the way they close their eyes and listen.

Above, through the smoke hole, the moon peers down at us: Cree, Dene, Anishinaabe, Métis, white, half-breeds, some with the names of their native tongues, some with the names given to them by the white man, some with names that I've never heard of before. We're a strange stew, but we all wait together to see what the moon has to say. The Elders have been cloistered away in a sweat lodge all evening. The crowd's on edge.

Never takes this long, someone nearby whispers.

I take it that's not a good sign.

Bran leans into me. The solidity of his shoulder, the heat of his skin, settles into me, helping me stay attached to the ground. I set my hands there, not caring that they'll come away dirty. In my mind, great roots creep down from my body. Tonight is not a night for spirit to overwhelm me. Tonight, I wish I had kept Madda's pouch. I have a feeling I could use its strength, whispers or not.

The cadence of the drum changes and the crowd parts. The Elders, wrapped in cloaks of woven cedar bark, stagger up to the fire. Firelight glints off the shells sewn to the capes, shells that have become eyes of the creatures painted there. The Elder's faces are covered with red ocher and soot, giving them a nightmarish, menacing look. Madda comes last. Her eyes are vacant, and I can tell just by looking at her that only her body is in this world. She looks exactly like Paul when he goes to his place of visions. I scan the crowd, looking for him, for my father. I can't find them, but I know they're here, hidden in the shadows.

A woman walks before the Elders, waving a branch of burning sage in the air as another woman hands out smudge sticks to the crowd.

"What do I do with this?" I ask Bran as he hands one to me.

"Wait and see."

"We've been waiting all night," I murmur.

He smiles. "Time moves differently in the spirit world. You should know that better than me." He shifts his weight and wraps an arm around my shoulder. I close my eyes as he whispers, "We'll light them in a bit, after Madda speaks to the Old Ones, asking them for guidance."

"Guidance for what?"

"For the coming winter, for the path of our people, for healing the world around us—who knows, really. The Old Ones choose what they want to reveal. Madda will deliver their messages, and then the celebration will begin. Dancing, drumming, you know. Then, when you're ready, I'll take you home, safe and sound."

The air around me stirs with a wind that doesn't come from a natural source. This is the spirit wind, the breath of the world, come to the longhouse to speak its secrets to Madda. I feel it drift past me, then stop and double back. *No,* I think, *I'm not the one you want. She's over there, under that cape, waiting for you. Please, not me. I'm not ready.*

In my mind, I see the wind nod and continue on, looking for the one who has given up her body for its purpose.

The drum changes cadence again and a man starts to sing. Others add their voices, and as Bran joins them I can feel the rumble of his bass coming through his chest, right into my back, echoing out through the longhouse, to the moon, the stars, the sky.

The Elders circle around the fire, supporting Madda as she takes shuffling steps. Her head droops to one side, her mouth slack. The singing grows louder and louder. Her eyes roll back, and every muscle in my body tenses. I know what's happening. I know, because it's happened to me. She's about to have a seizure.

"Won't be long now," Bran whispers in my ear.

But then Madda lifts her face to the moon and shrieks. The men let go and she falls to the ground, crawling on her hands and knees, grasping at things only she can see. Then, she whirls around and points at me. All I can see are the whites of her eyes as she bleats, *Hoo, hoo.*

Bran nudges me. "She's calling you."

Everyone's looking at me as I push myself back, but with Bran right behind me, there's nowhere to go. This creature isn't Madda. She's someone else, someone who terrifies me.

"You must go," Bran says, more insistent this time as Madda shakes her finger in my direction.

I creep forward. She lunges at me, wrapping me in her arms and cackling. I don't know what to do. Her grasp is firm and tight, and I can't breathe. She rocks me back and forth, faster and faster, until the world blurs before my eyes. The singing becomes chanting as the earth tilts and whirls. I squeeze my eyes shut because I feel like I'm falling, falling . . .

Madda howls. She releases me now and I drop to the ground, panting, as she bays at the moon.

And then, without warning, she collapses in a heap.

That's when I notice the silence. Everyone stares at us as I crawl forward and check Madda's breathing. It's shallow, but regular. "What do I do?" I ask the Elder nearest me. He's staring at Madda, his eyes wide with fright. "Please—what do I do?"

Madda groans and sits up. "Start the dancing," she croaks. "Go on, start. Start!" she barks at the nearest person and the drumming begins again. "Henry, help me up."

Henry Crawford rushes over and lifts Madda to her feet. "You did good, kid," she says to me as I follow them outside, half-running to keep up with Henry's long strides. He stops when he reaches the back of the long-house and gestures for me to open a door that leads into a meeting room. There, he sets Madda down on a table.

"You did real good," she says to me as she struggles to sit up. Henry presses a cup of water into my hands, and I hold it to her mouth. She drinks, coughs, then blinks at me.

"Was that calling down the moon?" I ask.

"No," Madda says. Her voice is tight with concern. "I'm sorry." She looks at Henry. "I'm sorry. That shouldn't have happened."

I agree, though I wish I knew what it *was* that happened. "But you didn't do that on purpose," I say.

Madda shakes her head. "No, I didn't, and let that be a warning to you not to go messing with things that aren't yours to mess with. Now, go on back. I'm fine," she says, giving me a push. "The dancing's started, and I need to talk to Henry. Alone. I'll see you tomorrow, Cassandra."

Madda gives me another push. I don't want to go. I want to stay. I want to make sure Madda is all right, that she's truly back in her body and attached to the earth. I want to ask her what happened to make her scream like that. What could the Old Ones have told her that would have brought that madness to her eyes? And, is that what will happen to me if I go walking in spirit unprepared? I'll go mad and not even know it?

I make my way back toward the longhouse. The dancing has spilled outside and with it, whiskey. I can smell its scent on the air. Bran's nowhere in sight. I look inside the longhouse for him, but right away I'm overwhelmed with the sparks of spirit. There is no barrier between our world and theirs tonight, and one glance at the dancers, whirling so fast that I can't tell where dancer stops and spirit begins, tells me what I already know: I am not ready for this yet.

You have no choice, the thunderbird guarding the door seems to say. *This is what has been given to you. You cannot give it back. Ready or not, here it comes.*

I turn and rush outside, bumping right into Paul. "Hey," he says, taking my arm and steering me into the park. "You okay?"

"No." I look over my shoulder at the longhouse. "Were you there? Did you see?"

"Yeah," Paul says. "Not the best way to introduce you to everyone, was it?"

"No." I cross my arms. Suddenly I'm very cold. "Do you know where Bran is?"

"No," he says a little too quickly, and when I follow his gaze, I see two shadows just a little ways off. Firelight flickers across them. It's Avalon and Bran. She passes him a bottle and leans in, kissing his neck.

"Cass," Paul calls as I pull away from him. "Cass, come back!"

But I don't. I find my feet and run into the night.

CHAPTER NINETEEN

*H*alfway home, my dress soaked with sweat and my legs burning, I stop running. What am I running from? I'm not even sure. The sight of Bran and Avalon? Yes, that's part of it, but it's Madda, too, how she singled me out. She might not have said a word to me, but in those howls I heard despair, and confusion, and sadness for me and for her. What did the Old Ones show her? What could have been so terrible?

I stand there, panting, thoughts of Madda giving way to Bran again. How could I be so stupid? I try to tell myself he doesn't matter, he's just some dumb guy, but that's a lie. He does matter now. I promised myself that I wouldn't let this happen, that I wouldn't care, that I wouldn't become like the women who live here, the ones who pine after

Band men and get nothing in return. So I won't. No matter what I feel in my heart, I won't go back to that.

Bran's not like that, a small part of my mind whispers.

But the image of him and Avalon passing the bottle, sharing a kiss? It mutes that whisper. I know what I saw, and no matter how strong I wish I was, it still hurts.

Above me, the night sky is awash with stars. When I was little, my mother told me that when people died, they became stars. I'd like to believe that my mother's up there somewhere, watching me at this very moment.

Mom, if you can hear me, make this right. Make everything all right. Make me strong enough to do what needs to be done. Make me brave enough to weather whatever is heading my way.

I'm still staring at the stars when I hear someone coming up the road. For a moment I think about stepping into the forest and hiding, but I don't. There's only darkness there, so I break into a run again.

It could be Paul. It could be your father. It could be . . .

But I don't let that whisper take root. All hope needs is a spark, and I'm too smart to allow that.

I don't stop until I reach our house, my heart pounding, my skin cold with fear. Whoever is chasing me hasn't let up, and isn't far behind.

I round the corner and am halfway down the hill when Bran calls my name. I don't stop. I'm past the house, the boathouse, out to the end of the dock as fear transforms itself into fury. How dare he chase me, after what I saw in the park? How dare he!

His footsteps echo behind me. "Cass! It isn't what you think," he calls from several steps away, as if he's afraid to approach.

"Isn't it?" My words come out as a hiss. "I saw you with her. What was all this about, coming to get me, holding my hand? What was that all about? I'm not like her. I'm not like *that*." I spit the last word at him.

"I know. I know you aren't," he says, his voice halting, unsure. This is not the Bran I know. He holds his hands out toward me, pleading. "Please, Cass. You have to listen. She has ideas, Avalon. She won't listen. She kissed me. I didn't kiss her, and I'm sorry you had to see that. There was something between us, once, but it hasn't been that way for a long time. That's where I went when I left you with Ms. Adelaide. She had something of mine I needed back, and I had something of hers. I thought she'd understand, but . . ." His voice trails off.

I want to believe him. I want to believe him so badly it hurts.

"Ask Paul," he says. His eyes are full of desperation. "Please. He'll tell you."

I turn toward Bran. A green stone hangs at his throat.

The one Avalon wore the day I met her. With two quick steps, I stand right before him, catching the stone in my hand. "Then what is this?"

"That?" He meets my gaze. Moonlight reflects in his eyes. "That is mine. Avalon took it months ago, and I've been trying to get it back ever since. That's what you saw—me, trying to get it back."

"And the whiskey?"

"I didn't drink any." He whispers the words, and I can tell they're true, but I can also tell that he can taste the memory of whiskey on his lips. If a bottle appeared in my hand and I offered it to him now, he'd drink. "I'm trying, Cass," he says. "I don't want to be like my mom, but it's hard. It's so hard sometimes."

We stand like that for several minutes, me gazing into his eyes, searching for—something. I don't know what, exactly, and finally I sigh and pull him close, resting my forehead against his.

"Did you find what you were looking for?" he says.

"I think so," I say.

"Good." He traces my arm with a single finger. "I want you to have . . ."

The sentence remains incomplete as the dock suddenly lurches. Bran makes a desperate grab for me but misses, and we both tumble into the water.

I try to swim back, but my hand slides off something smooth and slick that blocks my way. It writhes in the water, churning it to white as I kick with all my strength, trying to get away.

"Here!" Bran screams. He's back up on the dock. "Give me your hand!"

I swim toward him, stretching my hand out to his, but as our fingers touch, I'm hit square in the stomach and borne to the bottom of the lake, pinned there by a glittering mass of black.

I kick and try to scream, but water fills my mouth. My hands rake across leathery skin as clouds of sparks fly at me, misting my vision so I can't see anything as I lash out, fighting with all the strength I have. The creature bites me right in the stomach and I scream, and scream again, even as water gushes into my mouth, down into my lungs, consuming me whole. The lake is my coffin, and I am about to die.

No, I think. *No, this isn't how it's supposed to be! I will not be trapped here in the dark with that creature. I want to live, so I can hunt it down and do to it what it's done to me!*

And with that, I start to kick—kick with all my might. *I will not die here. I will not die. This is my life. The lake and her creature will not steal it from me.*

My hand finds the knife Madda gave me and

unsheathes it, blindly lashing out at whatever is pinning me down. I strike and strike and scream and forget that I can't breathe underwater. I don't care. I will kill this thing that seeks to kill me.

And then, it's gone. I float. Up, down, I don't know. I don't care.

CHAPTER TWENTY

$\mathcal{H}$ands lift me from the water. I drift above my body, looking down at it, at Bran, at my father running down the dock, at Madda chasing after him.

I think I might be dead.

Bran presses his mouth to mine and blows air into my lungs. I know this, but I don't feel it. He tries again, and then Madda takes over, pushing Bran out of the way. My father holds him back while he moans, "Oh Jesus, oh Jesus, Cass. Oh Jesus . . ."

A strong voice whispers in my ear, "You aren't going anywhere yet. Get back in this body right now!"

All at once, I'm pulled in two directions simultaneously, and then with an audible *snap* I am back inside my body, staring up at Madda as she blows breath tasting of whiskey and wood smoke into my lungs.

My body jerks and as she draws back, lake water gushes out of my mouth, all over me, all over her, all over the dock. I retch and retch as if my lungs have drunk the entire lake dry and now they've decided to give it back.

Arms grasp me, strong arms, and I look up to see my father. He rocks me back and forth. "Oh sweet Jesus," he whispers. "I thought I had lost you, too. Not you, too."

My throat aches, but my rib cage aches more. "You're hurting me."

Madda pulls my father back. "Lou, let her go. I need to check her over. Bran, step back. You're in my way. Go get my medicine kit. It's up at the house. Go!"

Bran thunders down the dock and disappears into the shadows.

Madda eases me down. Pain sears my skin as she peels back my wet shirt. She sucks in a breath. "Cassandra, I need you to stay very still. You're bleeding quite badly. Lou, get something for a stretcher."

I reach out for my father's hand, but all I touch is nothingness.

• • •

They carried me up the hill on an old door. But I don't remember this. I don't remember anything except the blackness that stood over me like a stalwart soldier and refused to let consciousness draw close.

Madda sits beside my bed. Her eyes are closed. Her face is pale. I'm not sure whether she's asleep or not, so I don't move. If she is sleeping, I don't want to wake her.

Every inch of my body hurts. Sparks float before my eyes, threatening to draw me back under when I move my head. I try wiggling my toes. I shift my body a little to the left, a little to the right, just enough to know I can move but not enough to upset the sparks that buzz about me like flies.

Madda's eyes flutter open. "You're awake," she says. Her voice is hoarse and her eyes are bloodshot. "Let me get your father." She rises slowly and leaves the room.

I hear them talking, but I can't make out the words—just the low rumble of my father's voice and Madda's gravelly response. Then, footsteps echo down the hall. Madda enters first, followed by my father. He looks as bad as Madda. "Hey, starshine," he says. "You gave us quite a scare."

I force a smile onto my face, though it hurts so much. "I'm sorry," I whisper. "I didn't mean to."

"Don't be sorry," he says as he bends to kiss my forehead. "I love you, Cassandra."

I try to find words, but they won't come, so I nod.

"Okay, that's enough for now," Madda says, gently pushing my father back. "Now that she's awake, we need to have a talk."

Madda herds him out the door. I hear him walk away and wish he'd come back.

Madda kneels at my side and draws the blanket down. Then she lifts me up a little, just enough to wedge a pillow under my back. "I need you to see what happened," she says.

But I don't want to. I squeeze my eyes shut.

Her hand is cool to the touch. It falls on my stomach where the cool vanishes, replaced by blistering heat. It hurts so much. I moan. I can't help it.

"Sorry," she says. "This is going to smart, but you need to see."

I force my eyes open and look down at a bandage bigger than my hand. Madda peels it back to expose a perfect circle of brown dots, each bearing a single stitch.

"What is it?" I whisper.

"A gift," she says. "Open your hand." She spills thirteen translucent pearls into my palm. "One for each one of those dots," she says. "Had a devil of a time getting them out, and used up most of your father's whiskey in the process. Good thing you weren't conscious. It hurt me to do it."

"What did that to me?" The words scrape against my throat and I want to go back to sleep, but I can't. I need to know.

"Sisiutl." The word is sibilant, as if Madda has taken on the voice of the double-headed sea monster.

"But . . ." I touch one of the dots. It hurts, but not as much as my head.

"Yeah, *but* is right. They're the meanest of the mean in the spirit world. Looks like you're one of the lucky ones, though. It marked you—that means it will never harm you again, sort of like choosing you as its own."

"Great," I say. "I've always wanted to be a two-headed serpent."

Madda chuckles. "That's not quite what I meant and you know it. My people believe sisiutl chooses the most powerful warriors to fight alongside it."

"Warriors?"

"Sure. Sometimes, people call us healers 'spiritual warriors.' Sounds about right, don't you think?"

I shake my head. "That wouldn't be me."

"Well, I don't know about that. You fended it off, after all. You fought back."

"Thanks to you. It was your knife that did it."

Madda purses her lips. "I knew you were going to need that knife. I just didn't think it would be for this." She gently pats the bandage into place and draws the blanket back up. "Now, you need some rest. Sisiutl gave you more than that love bite—you're covered in bumps and bruises and I'm pretty sure you've got a concussion. You're to stay in bed until I say you can get up. Got it?"

I smile. "Yes, ma'am."

Madda snorts and moves to leave.

"Wait," I say, though sleep is already pulling at my eyes. "Bran—?"

"Is outside. He hasn't gone home since it happened. Thinks this was his fault. Always does." She shakes her head. "But don't you worry about that right now. Just go to sleep, all right?"

"All right," I manage to say, before I drift off.

Sometime later, I wake. Light stabs at my eyes. I raise a hand to cover my face. My body feels as if every square inch of it is swollen and raw.

"Cass?" A hand touches my cheek.

Bran.

"The light hurts," I say.

"Oh." I hear him rummage about and then the light goes away. "Is that better?"

"Yes." I open my eyes slowly, testing them for pain, only to see that Bran's shirtless. I raise an eyebrow at him.

"Oh." He glances down at his chest. "I used my shirt to cover the window."

"Ah." I try to laugh, but it becomes a cough.

Bran's face drains of all its color as he watches me. Then, as my coughing subsides, he bends to help me sit up. "I'm sorry," he says. "I'm not very good at this."

"You're doing just fine," I say. "You're here, aren't you?"

"I haven't left," he says. "God, Cass, I'm so sorry. This is all my fault."

His head drops so I can't see his eyes and I know he's fighting back tears.

Madda's words drift back to me. *Thinks this was his fault. Always does.* I want to say something to change that, but all I can manage is to take his hand and hold it tight.

CHAPTER TWENTY-ONE

There is no pain quite like the pain of healing. I walk up and down the sundeck, Paul at my side, holding my hand while I gasp for breath. Madda decided one of my ribs must be broken. She's plastered my rib cage with boneset and honey and now I have to wait for it to heal. It hurts so badly, but it feels good to be up and moving.

Bran is asleep on my bed right now. He still hasn't gone home.

"Are you tired?" Paul asks as I reach out and take the railing. He's been distant since the night of the attack. I think he feels a little guilty that he wasn't around to help. In fact, he didn't return until late the next day, from what my father says, and left as soon as he saw me.

"Hey." Bran stands by the kitchen door, running a

hand through his hair. "Why didn't you wake me?"

"Thought you could use a break," Paul says. "Divvy up the duties of taking care of this pain in the arse."

"Hah," I say, nudging him.

"That's the best you can do?"

"Yeah." It is. Even that hurt. "Let me try walking on my own, okay?"

Paul smiles and releases his hold. I shuffle toward Bran as if I'm ninety. If this is what it feels like to get old, I want no part of it. Bran takes my hand and tucks it into his. "You should be back in bed."

"Madda said I should get up and move around."

"In small doses." He looks at Paul. "Tell her."

Paul waves us away. "You're on your own, man. She never listens to me."

I stick out my tongue at him as Bran and I step inside. Paul's laughter drifts after us.

"You're looking a lot better today," Bran says as we pause for me to catch my breath.

"I'm feeling better." It's not much of a lie, really. He draws a chair up for me and I sit, gazing out at the lake. A skiff divides the silver water in two. A canoe bobs in its wake. On the far shore, smoke drifts lazily above the evergreens. The mountains watch. Everything is deceptively peaceful, for somewhere out there is the sisiutl, and the longer I stare at the lake, the more I'm convinced it's waiting for my return. Despite what Madda said—that I'm safe from it now—I don't believe it one bit.

Bran stands behind me, stroking my hair.

"Have you seen what the sisiutl did to me?" I say, though what I really want to ask is, *Are you here because you feel responsible, or because you really want to be here?*

He shakes his head. "I don't want to look. Not now."

"But you'll have to someday."

He takes a deep breath. "Yes. Someday."

I reach up and take his hand, giving it a squeeze. He squeezes back.

A week later, Bran leaves to do battle with his mother (as he put it). My father has been busy building the outhouse, and who knows where Paul is. When I ask my father, he just shrugs and frowns.

Madda has been back to our house almost every day under the pretense of checking on me, but really I think she's here to see my father.

It's been five years since my mother died. Five years of my father wandering through days without blinking, without thinking of anyone but me and Paul. At first, after Mom, he stopped living too, as if his life was a house and he no longer came home. Each day he returned to us a little more, but for five years I haven't seen his shade. It's a robin—the first true shade I ever saw—and as I stand at the window, watching Madda and my father survey the garden they've planted, a lump forms in my throat. My father's robin sits on his shoulder, warbling its heart out.

Madda glances up at me and heads toward the house. "Well?" she says when she arrives, huffing from the climb up the hill. "Have you learned all you can from that herbal I lent to you?"

"I've memorized it."

She sniffs. "Memorizing isn't the same as learning. Come to the cottage tomorrow. We'll see how much you really know." She pulls something from her pocket. "Before I forget—this is for you."

I take the little cloth pouch from her outstretched hand.

She nods at it. "Open it. See what's inside."

Inside are the thirteen tiny pearls that the sisiutl gave me. I force myself to touch them.

"You're right to be scared," Madda says. "They're strong with spirit. They'll guard you. Next time you see that raven, you wave those pearls at him. He'll be leaving you alone. Raven and Sisiutl have never been friends. Put them in that pouch I gave you." She scratches her head. "Where is that pouch, anyway? I thought I told you to wear it."

"I did. I was," I say. My gaze flickers to the lake.

"Ah." Madda wrinkles her brow in thought, and I realize she thinks I lost the pouch the night of the sisiutl attack. "That's an even exchange, I guess. One thing for another. Well, you're good with your hands. Probably best you make yourself one anyhow." She reaches out and gives my hand a squeeze. "Tomorrow. After lunch. Don't forget."

I wrap my fingers around the pearls and clutch them tightly as Madda leaves the room. I have no pouch to put them in. That pouch, the one Madda gave me, is sitting at the bottom of the lake, where I should be right now.

I'm beginning to think the raven that's been dogging me is actually Paul. It's there, perched on the railing of the sundeck every time I wander into the sitting room. It follows me when I make my way down the hill to feed the chickens. I hear the whoosh of its wings outside my window every night. It haunts me, and makes me worry for my brother.

I've only seen him a couple times since the night of the attack. Last night, he crept into my room and sat on the floor while he thought I was sleeping, but I wasn't. Tension hangs between us. That's what woke me.

He's afraid of me.

And, if he really is that raven, I'm a little afraid of him, too.

• • •

My father rouses me early. "Get up," he says, grinning from ear to ear. "I've got something I want to show you."

There's magic in the air today. I can see it in the rosy glow of the early-morning sun and smell it drifting on the wind.

I dress quickly. The scabs on my stomach crack when I lift my arms, but it's a good feeling, a feeling that reminds me of nature's power to remedy wrongs. Breathing doesn't hurt, finally, and I feel so good I bet I'd be able to fly if I tried.

Paul and my father are outside, waiting for me. Paul drops his eyes to the ground as I wind my hair into a braid. I hate this distance between us, but how can I fix it when I don't know why it's there?

"Hey," I say, edging up to him and giving him a nudge. "Haven't seen you around much."

He shrugs and turns his dark eyes to my father, who gives each of us a forked willow branch. "Gonna teach you to witch," he says as he takes another branch from the back pocket of his jeans. "Figured we need a well. I'm tired of hauling water up the hill." He holds the tines of the branch in his hands. "Gently," he says as we copy him. "Let the willow talk to you."

I close my eyes and allow breath to slip in and out of

my lungs. The air around me hums. I feel open, a channel for the earth. The willow branch vibrates in my hands and when I open my eyes, I see the tip is bobbling up and down.

"That's good," my father says, nodding in encouragement. "Now, walk with it. When it points at the ground and doesn't move, you know you've found water."

I start off slowly at first, a step forward, a step to the side. The willow branch bounces and trembles, bending in impossible directions as it seeks out water far below the ground. Everything else fades away.

The branch continues to jerk back and forth as I make my way up the hill toward the back of the house, and then, all at once, it points straight down at the ground.

"Dad," I call. "I think I found something."

He comes racing up the hill. "Looks good," he says, holding out his own willow branch. It mirrors mine. My father pats my shoulder and drives his branch into the ground. "Good spot for the well—close to the house, but not too close. How far down do you think we'll have to dig?" he asks as he narrows his eyes.

I recognize that look—he already knows the answer, but wants to know if I'm a natural at this. It's the same look he gave me when he taught me to fire a rifle.

I close my eyes. "Not far down," I hear myself say. In

my mind, I see myself burrow into the earth like a root, a twisting, winding root searching for water among the rocks and the bones and the ghosts of dead things. And then I see the water—a deep, dark pool like the one in the spirit lands. It's fed by three streams. "About twenty feet down," I say. "There's a pool down there."

My father whistles under his breath. "Well, that's lucky. Sounds like an artesian spring. Huh. Surprising no one tapped it before." He smiles. "If there's enough pressure, we might even be able to pipe it into the house. Wouldn't that be something!" He takes the willow branch from my hand. "Good work. Let's go see how Paul is making out, huh?"

We go back down to the house, but Paul is gone. His willow branch lies on the ground, twisted in half. My father sighs as he bends to pick it up, and shakes his head.

I stare at the forest. I'm pretty sure that's where Paul's gone.

Why, for once, couldn't this gift have gone to Paul? He needs it more than I do, and if I could, I would give it to him. I would give him anything he asked for. But I can't, and no amount of wishing is ever going to change that.

CHAPTER TWENTY-TWO

I leave for Madda's after lunch. I'm worried about Paul. He didn't come back, and I can't help feeling that all the time he spends by himself isn't helping. Part of me hopes he's with Bran, and maybe he is. I like the idea of them working wood together. The thought erases some of the worry I feel for Paul, but not all.

The road is thick with shadows, and chickadees dart back and forth, chattering as they hunt for bugs. I pause to watch them. The basket on my arm suddenly feels very heavy, even though all it holds is Madda's herbal. But it's my gathering basket, and a good apprentice, says Madda, never goes anywhere without one. You never know when you might spot something valuable, she says.

I'm looking for something that I can use to hold the sisiutl's pearls when I spy a clump of wild ginger growing along the side of the road. Its ugly brown flowers poke out of the ground like alien creatures emerging from the primordial stew.

"Thank you," I whisper as I dig the plant with my hands, inhaling the strong, dank scent of earth mingling with the tang of ginger. The plant comes free of the soil with ease and as I tuck it into the basket, nestling it under a layer of fern blades to protect it from drying out, I hear the ratcheting of a bicycle coming up the road.

It's Cedar. He stops a few feet from me. "What're you doing?" he asks.

"Digging ginger."

He sniffs the air. "I can smell it." He smiles.

I notice he's missing one of his front teeth. I'm pretty sure he had it last time I saw him. "What happened to your tooth?"

"Oh, that." He rubs his jaw with an absentminded laziness. "Happened after the gathering. You know." He shrugs. "Where are you going?"

"Madda's." I walk past him, hoping he'll just leave me alone and continue on his way. He doesn't. Gravel crunches as he turns the bike around and then there he is, pedaling next to me.

"How did you like the gathering?" he asks.

I give him a sidelong glance. Does he know about the sisiutl? "Why?"

"Just making conversation."

"Why?"

"Are you always so bitchy? Shit, just trying to be friendly."

"Oh." I glance away. He's right. I am being bitchy and have no reason to be. "Sorry. I haven't been feeling well."

"I heard. You okay?" His eyes might be plain brown and a little too small, but they're squinting in what looks like genuine concern.

"Yeah." I shift the basket from one arm to the other. "Thanks."

He nods at it. "It's a long walk to Madda's. I could double you, if you want."

"No, thanks," I say as I pick up my pace. I don't know what it is—the look in his eyes, the strange smile pulling at his mouth, but the last thing I want is to go anywhere with him.

Cedar rides beside me. "Oh, come on. You can sit up here on the handlebars. I won't bite—promise."

"No, thanks. I'm still working on getting better. I don't want to risk falling off and getting hurt again." *Please, leave me alone*, I want to say, but the words won't leave my mouth.

"No; let me show you." He pedals hard, cutting me off with a skid of tire. "Here—sit here." He moves in to grab me, but I sidestep him.

"Cedar, I don't want to." I walk on, ignoring him as he curses and makes another grab for me.

"Come here," he says, this time without the pleasant air.

"No!" I glare at him, but something's wrong. I can feel it. No matter what I say, I don't think he'll take no for an answer. He catches my wrist and holds me fast, pulling me toward him, smiling, until I twist and wrench myself free.

Sparks flash around my eyes as I break into a run. I hear Cedar grunt as he pedals hard, but I'm off the road and into the woods. Brambles slash at my legs. Branches reach out to tear at my face, but I don't care. The sparks cluster around my head, blurring my vision as I fight to get away from him.

I can hear him crashing behind me. "Stop! Stop, damn it! Don't go in there! I'm not going to hurt you!"

I continue to run until he tackles me. We fall into a thicket of stinging nettle and I claw at his face.

"Jesus Christ, stop!" he says as he tries to pin my hands down.

"Don't touch me!" I strike at him.

"Stop it!" His hands are so big that he holds both of

my wrists at once. "You shouldn't be here. Ah, shit!" He stands up, pulling me with him, then lets go. Angry red welts run up his legs and more are sprouting up all over his face. He points at the spear-leafed plant crushed by our fall. "Stinging nettles? Why did you have to go through stinging nettles?"

"I didn't. If you hadn't chased me, we wouldn't be here." Welts are rising on my hands and arms.

"Come on. We need to get out of here. This is old burial ground—not a good place to be." He glances around and holds out a hand. When I don't take it, he rolls his eyes. "I'm not a monster, you know."

"Right," I mutter. "And all that stuff out there on the road? When I said no? Why wasn't that good enough for you?"

"Shh," he whispers. His eyes dart around, searching for something among the trees as I realize the birds have fallen silent. "We need to go—now."

I shiver and follow him back to the road.

"What on earth happened to you two?" Madda jumps off her ladder, newly severed blackberry cane still in hand, gaping at us as Cedar leans his bike against the gate. Our legs and arms are stained green from the dock I found along the roadside and used to take away the worst of the sting.

"Nettles," Cedar says. "On the old burial ground."

"What," Madda says, fixing Cedar with a piercing glare, "were you doing on the burial ground?"

I speak before Cedar has a chance to. "Cedar chased me into the forest."

"What?" Madda says.

"I thought he was going to hurt me."

Madda's face loses all its color. "Didn't you see the wardings, Cassandra?"

"What wardings?"

"Don't tell me you don't know what the wardings for a burial ground look like," she snaps.

I grind my teeth together. How am I supposed to know what wardings look like if no one has bothered to tell me? How am I supposed to know the rules and regulations of this place if they aren't spelled out anywhere? The words try to force their way out, even though I know I'll regret them later, but Cedar interjects first.

"The markers weren't there." His voice is hard. "I double-checked as we were leaving. They're gone."

"That can't be." Madda starts to pace back and forth, tugging at her chin. She stops and leans toward Cedar so suddenly that he sits back and hits his head against the wall. "You're positive?"

"Yes, Madda," he says firmly. "The markers are missing."

"Okay," Madda says. "Here's what we're going to do. Cedar, you're coming with me. We need to see the Elders. Cassandra, you're going to stay here." She fixes me with a stern look. "Go inside. There's a bottle of vinegar in the pantry. Use it to clean that green stuff off you. It'll kill the last of the nettle sting, too. Then go home and come back tomorrow. If anyone sees the two of you looking like this, well, talk'll spread all over town like wildfire, and not in a good way."

I notice that this doesn't seem to bother Cedar, but it sure bothers me. He got what he wanted, didn't he? I can't help feeling he's one of those people who taints everything he touches, and now I'm damned by association.

I've just finished washing my arms and my legs with vinegar when someone knocks on the door. Quickly I pull on my clothes and look up to find Avalon peering through the curtains. "I know you're in there," she calls. "Let me in!"

Her nose wrinkles when I open the door. "What's that smell?"

"Vinegar."

"Oh. Where's Madda?"

"Gone into town," I say, though I know perfectly well

that Avalon must have passed Madda on her way up here.

She motions to my green-stained and welted legs. "So, what happened?"

Like I'm about to tell her. "Long story," I say, waving her away.

"Huh. Looks painful." She trails her hand across the table, over the counter, touching the glass bottles of herbs lined up, waiting for Madda's return, as if she owns them all. "Do you like it? Being a witch's helper?"

"She isn't a witch." I cap the vinegar and set it back in the pantry. "She's a medicine woman. There's a difference."

"Whatever." She opens a cupboard and begins to paw through the contents.

"I don't think you should do that," I say.

She doesn't stop. "Why?"

"Because that's where Madda keeps her poisons. You should know that."

She cocks an eyebrow at me. "Really? Madda never taught me that sort of thing."

"Oh, well, that mushroom, the one in that container you're about to pick up? It's called fly agaric. It's so poisonous even the dew from it can kill you."

"Oh." Avalon closes the cupboard door and tries to pretend that she's not interested.

I can't help but smile as I turn away. For once I have

the upper hand. "Madda might be a while. Do you want to come back later?"

"No," she says. "I'll wait here."

"Fine. Just don't touch anything." Helen's left a half-finished basket sitting beside the fireplace, so I pick it up and start weaving where she left off. Madda did say I could go home, but that was before Avalon arrived, and I'm pretty sure leaving Avalon here by herself isn't a good idea.

"So," Avalon says, nodding at the basket, "where's Helen?"

"Don't know," I say as I join a new piece of cedar to the one Helen's already worked. "At the orchard, I guess."

"Really." Avalon snickers. "You know about her, right?"

My breath sticks in my throat. "Know what?" I say as I force myself to keep weaving, even though every muscle in my body has gone rigid.

"Let's just say"—Avalon gets up and peers out the window, smiling to herself—"that Helen isn't as innocent as you think she is. Ask Cedar about it sometime. I'm sure he'd love to tell you." She opens the door. "You know, we should hang out more. You, me, Bran, and Paul. Just the four of us."

I stop weaving and stare at her. Right. Just the four of us. "Maybe," I say. "I'll talk to Paul about it."

"Paul. He's a pretty sensitive guy, isn't he?"

"Yes," I say slowly. Just what is she getting at?

"I worry about him. He feels things too deeply. Takes things too personally. People like that, well, it's not hard to hurt them."

"Paul's stronger than you think," I say carefully. "You'd be surprised just how strong."

Avalon looks at me for a long moment. Neither of us has said what we mean, but I think we understand each other perfectly. "Well," she says with a lazy smile, "looks like Madda's going to be longer than I expected. I'm glad I got to spend a little time with you. It's hard to get you alone, you know." She hops off her perch and heads out, but not before stopping to pick a daisy. I watch her as she twirls it between her fingers, and then, pulls the petals from it, one by one, tossing them over her shoulder as she strolls down the path. *He loves me, he loves me not.* An innocent game, if played by anyone else, but Avalon is no innocent. If I didn't know that before, I certainly do now.

CHAPTER TWENTY-THREE

$\mathcal{M}$adda's attempt at discretion hasn't worked. Someone's been talking—two someones, with the names of Avalon and Cedar, no doubt—and the whole town's buzzing about the missing markers. Judging from the way people look at me as I walk down the street, I know there's been more talk than that.

"That damned Cedar," Madda mutters to herself. "Never could keep his mouth shut. Just hold your head high," Madda says, loudly enough for the people nearby to here. "Not your fault people are stupid enough not to know a lie when they hear one."

We've been summoned to a meeting with the Elders. Madda tried to get me out of it, but they insisted, and I can tell she's not happy about it.

I follow her past the watchmen totem poles and the forbidding stare of the thunderbird. My palms are sweating.

Madda stops and sets a hand on my shoulder. "Don't let them see your fear," she whispers. "Just be you. Tell the truth and everything will be fine."

I nod as we set off again. Dust motes catch in the light drifting through the smoke hole, casting the great room in a pleasantly hazy glow. Nothing remains of the gathering, none of the madness that gripped Madda, not even the ashes from the fire, but I can feel the songs in the air, the words that bring the old stories alive, turning myth into reality. The supernaturals press at me, wanting to take root in my body, wanting me to dance them back into this world, but I don't let them. This isn't the time or the place, and little by little, they back away, waiting their turn to be called forth.

Madda opens a door and we step into the meeting room, where the Elders wait for us. All men. That's the first thing I notice, and though Madda prepared me for this, seeing them here, staring me down, sets my heart fluttering. Henry Crawford sits at the end of a narrow table, leaning back in his chair. The others I don't know. Henry nods at me, and then looks down the line of men.

I glance around for a place to sit, but there is none.

Madda stands at my side, and I can tell she's uncomfortable too. This isn't a casual chat. It's the first time these men will test my resolve, and we all know this meeting will establish the dynamic between us from here on in. Right now, it's not so important. I'm an apprentice and will be for some time. But later, when Madda passes on? I pray that'll happen years from now. I can't imagine that I'll ever really be ready to face these men alone.

"So, you gonna stand there and stare, or are you gonna tell us what happened?" This comes from a man with fat jowls and gray hair. He leans forward and glowers like a great, fat toad.

Madda nudges me. I take a step forward and glance back at her. The truth is, I'm not entirely sure what I'm supposed to say because I'm not sure what they're asking about. Do they want to know about the sisiutl, or the incident at the burial ground?

"Something wrong with her, Madda?" another man says.

"Nope. You're just going to have to be a bit more specific. Speak plain, you old fools." She says this in an offhand, friendly manner, but there's a hint of warning about it, as if she's reminding them that we're here for their benefit, not the other way around.

Henry Crawford speaks up next. "So, do you wanna tell us what you were doing on the burial ground, then?"

My gaze flickers to Madda. They already know I was with Cedar and they already know his version of the story. So why do they want my take? What could I possibly tell them that they don't already think they know? The words I choose are important, that much I can tell. "I didn't know it was a burial ground," I decide to say. Keep it vague.

The men exchange looks. I can't tell if what I've said is the wrong thing or not, but I do sense that I'm on trial and they're my jury, and all the reasons I have for hating the Band come flooding back to me. What right do they have to judge me? Who says they're any wiser than I am? Who's elected them? Not me. I never asked for any of this.

Madda must sense I'm about to explode because she rests a hand on my shoulder again. "Tell them the rest, Cassandra."

I draw a deep breath. "I was on my way to see Madda. Cedar offered me a ride on his bike, and I said no—a couple of times—and I got scared because he wouldn't leave me alone. So I ran."

Henry Crawford nods, but he's the only one who seems to believe me. The rest have skeptical looks on their faces.

"You know what you're saying, don't you?" the jowled man says. "That's a pretty strong accusation."

"I'm not accusing anyone of anything," I say, drawing

myself up tall so I don't feel so scared. "I'm telling you what happened, just like you asked." I can hear my tone start to get lippy, and I know that's dangerous territory. These men have the power to make my life a living hell, and, by proxy, my family's, but when I see the corner of Madda's mouth quiver like she's resisting the temptation to smile, I know I'm doing okay.

"Teach her the wardings," Henry Crawford says to Madda.

And that's that. I'm not sure what's happened, for as Madda steers me from the room, I'm left bewildered. They brought me all the way down here just to tell Madda that?

Before we're out of earshot, the men start talking. "Stupid half-breed" is the first thing I hear. Followed by: "Idiot kid." "Pot-stirrer." "My son wouldn't lie." "Slut."

Madda walks faster, towing me along, but not fast enough. All I want to do is run back into that room to give them a piece of my mind, but Madda tightens her grip on my arm. "Let them think what they want," she mutters. "They're fools. The people who count will always know you for who you are. For the truth of you." She halts and turns me so we're looking each other right in the eye. "You know that, right? You know who you are? You know they're just a bunch of spineless, scared men?"

I nod. I do know, but that doesn't mean their words

don't pierce me like glass. I want to know what Cedar said. I want to know what his father believes, because I'll set him right. I'll show him who his son really is.

"Just don't forget who's on your side. They haven't done battle with a sisiutl, have they? Although it's just as well that they don't know about that, considering what just happened. No telling what they'd do if they knew your true power. Then they'd have real reason to be scared."

Maybe she's trying to make me feel better, but it doesn't help. Not one bit.

Bran is the last to know. It always works that way.

I'm sitting on the sundeck, staring out at the lake, watching for the sisiutl. I should be weeding, or mending my father's work shirt, or kneading bread, but I've found a length of rope. It's been some time since I've made something, and I can't stop myself. My hands are twisting and knotting, forming the rope and the stones I've gathered into a wind chime. That's when I hear Bran's footsteps rounding the corner of the house, and from the way they fall on the wood of the sundeck, I know, just from their rhythm, that he's upset.

"I should have been there." His voice is breathy, as if the words hurt his throat.

Should he have? I look up at him. For sixteen years

I've survived without Bran Eagleson. I stand, slowly, and lift my shirt to expose the scar on my belly before Bran can look away. "Look at this, Bran. Look. I don't need a protector. I am capable of taking care of myself, and if you can't handle that, then you should leave." I let my shirt fall back into place and sit back down. *Did I really just say that?*

"You want me to leave?" he asks. Surprise colors his voice.

"No." I sit back down and begin to work on the wind chime again, just so I won't have to look at him. If I did, I would want to fix his hurt, his confusion, but that's not for me. This, Bran needs to figure out on his own, though nothing says I can't help him along a bit. "I want you to stay, but only if we're equals. Not if you think I need your protection, that I'm your responsibility all the time."

He drops down beside me. Our shoulders touch. "That might be hard for me. I've spent most of my life taking care of my mother. I don't know how to do anything else."

"Yes, you do." I take his hand and trace the calluses on his palm. "You'll see."

"Okay," he says. And then, he leans in and kisses me. His lips are warm and taste like salt.

That's when Paul rounds the corner. "Oh hell," he says as Bran and I lean away from each other. "I'm sorry, I'm sorry," Paul mutters, backing away, pretending not to look at us.

"No, it's okay," I say. "Come back."

He looks at me from the corner of his eye, and then walks over to Bran and punches him hard in the shoulder. "That," he says, "is for kissing my sister. Just to keep things on the straight and narrow."

Bran laughs and gets up, then punches Paul back. "So, where've you been?"

"Nowhere." Paul eyes the welts on my legs. "I heard what happened. I'm going to remove more than Cedar's tooth the next time I see him. You with that fool? I laughed in his face." He smiles one of his brilliant smiles. "I think I'll kill him for you."

I don't know what to say. The words sound so light, so carefree, and yet I believe him.

"Well, it's hot." Paul rubs his hands together. "Swim, anyone?"

Bran nudges me.

I shake my head. "Not for me, but I'll come watch."

"Sounds like a good idea." Bran's voice is soft, as if he's suddenly a long ways away. He, too, is remembering.

Paul jumps up and is gone, racing down the slope, his raven shade chasing behind.

"He seems happy," Bran says. I nod. Happier than I've seen him in ages.

A kingfisher flutters at Bran's shoulder and for a moment, I don't know whether it's real or his shade. Its plumage is sleek, shining, glossy. Not a hint of disease, not a hint of anything other than health.

I close my eyes and smile into the sun.

"What are you grinning at?" Bran pokes me in the side.

"Nothing. Everything."

He kisses my nose, and then offers me a hand up. I take it, and together we walk down to the end of the dock. Paul is already in the water, swimming away from us.

It is a pleasant place, our little slice of Eden. We live beyond the world of noise and plastic, of searches and power cuts and microchips and disease. Here on the Island, we till our gardens, wander paths created by deer. We have forgotten what runs in our blood, have forgotten the Corridor altogether.

Forgetting is such an easy thing.

A week later, Madda finally gives me a day off. There are a million things I'd like to do with my free time, but the necessities of life need to be dealt with—the first being laundry. My father is already down the hill, heating water in our biggest pot, while I wander about the house, picking up dirty socks and underwear, pants stained red from the dirt, shirts stinking of sweat. My father makes a neat pile in the corner of his room. Paul? His clothes are strewn everywhere, forcing me to hunt for them. This makes me grin, because that's just the way Paul is. That's the way he's always been: messy, dirt on his knees, pants pockets full of rocks and sticks, and when I pick up his only pair of jeans, that's what I think I've found at first, a pocket full of rocks and sticks.

But it's not. Beneath the jeans are rocks and sticks and feathers joined together by lengths of twine. Seashells, too, and wood carved into images of thunderbird and raven. Symbols are painted on the rocks. I stretch the lengths of twine and stare at the objects fastened to them. I know what these are. These are the missing wardings.

Paul took down the wardings? Paul? But why? And why did he hide them where I'd find them? Because he wanted me to know. He must have. If he didn't, he would have hidden them better.

Paul, just what have you done?

It takes me a while to summon up the courage to talk to him. Things have been better between us lately, and

I hate the thought of ruining that. For days I put it off, finding one excuse or another, but today Madda forced my hand. We started to make new wardings this morning, binding stones and shells together with rope, while she chanted and anointed them with smoke. *The wardings*, she said, *are to keep bad spirits where they belong—in the burial ground.*

What bad spirits? I wanted to ask, but I was afraid. So was she, and I haven't seen Madda afraid of anything since the night of the gathering.

But Paul knows. He's always had a way with the dead.

I find him out back, digging the hole that will become our well. Twenty feet down might not be particularly deep, but when it's straight through time-packed clay, well, it's damn hard work. I bring him sun tea, hoping that an offering will start things off on the right track.

He smiles as he takes the glass and drains its contents in one long draft. I pour another. "I've been missing you," I say.

"I've been around."

"I know. Just, things seem a bit weird right now."

He wipes his brow and shrugs. "Lots happening."

"Uh-huh." I sit at the edge of the hole, letting my legs dangle. "So, I found something."

"Did you?" He starts digging again.

"Do you want to tell me about it?"

"No, not really." A clod of clay flies out of the hole, landing with a thud beside me. "You should probably move if you don't want to get hit."

"Paul," I say, not moving an inch, "what's going on? Why did you take the wardings?"

He stops and glares up at me. "Because they're not meant to be there." He slams his shovel into the ground. "You think just because you're Madda's apprentice that you know everything that's going on, that you're the only one who walks the spirit paths, but I do too, Cass, and they ask things of me as well."

"So they asked you to take down the wardings?" I don't understand. "Who's they?"

Paul bites his lip, as if deciding whether to tell me or not. I hold my breath, waiting. "The people in the woods. They're trapped there by the wardings. They wanted to be free, and for once I could do something about it. So I did." He starts digging again. "Why don't you go running to Madda and tell her what I've done. Isn't that what you want to do?"

"No, Paul," I say as I step away from him. "That's not what I want at all." *I just want you back*, I think.

I just want my brother back.

CHAPTER TWENTY-FOUR

Bran and I are pulling weeds from between bean plants in the garden. Bees buzz around us, flitting from flower to tiny purple flower while, above, the wind stirs the trees, sending a cascade of needles raining over the lake. Bran sits back on his haunches and swipes at the beads of sweat running down his forehead, leaving a smear of dirt in their place. He looks down at the water. "You can't avoid going in forever, you know."

I rip a thistle from the ground. "I know."

"Today would be a good day. I'm hot and dirty. I could use a swim."

"Tomorrow. Tomorrow sounds better."

"Cass." Bran turns toward me. "It's been almost a month."

He's right. It has. I can't avoid the lake forever. I pull my work gloves from my hands and throw them down. "Okay. Let's do it."

The wind dies as we make our way out along the dock. I stare down at the depths the entire time, looking for the shadow I know is there, but the only thing I see are dead fir needles, a sea of red giving way to silvered water farther out. Bran says nothing as I untie my shoes, sit down, and dip my legs in the icy cold.

I could stop there. Nothing says I need to conquer this today, but despite the glassy appearance of the lake, there's a sense of urgency in the air. If I don't do this now, I may never have another chance. I'm not sure why I feel so certain of this, but I do.

"Right," I say to myself. There's only one way to fix that. So with a deep breath, I tip myself off the dock and swim to the bottom. Darkness presses in on me as I remain there, treading water, waiting for the sisiutl. *Here I am*, I think. *What are you waiting for?*

The world above me is glass-bottle green. The dock sways to and fro and I can see Bran peering down, looking at me looking up at him.

Finally, when my lungs feel like they're about to burst, I push off toward the surface, breaking the glass bottle into pieces.

Bran's lying chest-down on the dock. "Wasn't sure you were going to come up."

I brush water from my eyes and swim toward him. "Me neither."

He tries to smile. "At least the monster didn't come back."

"That's what you think." I reach out and pull him in. I don't laugh. This is not a game. None of this is a game.

He surfaces and spits water at me. "I knew you'd do that."

"I knew you knew." I spit back and then, seized by impulse, I tug my shirt over my head. This is my lake. I claim it as my own, and nothing—not even the sisiutl—will harm me. My shorts come off next as Bran bobs and gapes.

"What are you doing?" he says.

"You wanted to prove the lake wouldn't hurt me? Well, I'm showing you it won't hurt me." I dive, pushing through the water, shattering it with my body.

When I surface, Bran is gathering up my floating clothes. He puts them on the dock, and then adds his own to the pile.

"Wait for me," he calls as I swim away, but I don't. If he wants me, he'll have to come get me. On land, Bran is master of his domain, like the stag who is king of the forest, but the lake is mine and I am its, and besides, I swim better than Bran. I toy with him, pausing just long enough to let him draw close. The moment his fingers graze my feet, I'm off, sliding through the water, melding with its currents. Slick like a seal. Flashing and fleeting, a salmon racing after prey.

Bran curses as he swims after me. I laugh and turn onto my back, floating naked under the sun, strangely unashamed.

We drift there a moment, golden and glorious, until his hand finds mine and he tows me toward a thicket of willow leaning into the water. His fingertips trace my body, marking the curve of my hips, the length of my arms, the rise of my breasts. I want to touch him, but I can't. Something that is fear, and yet, deeper, older, nameless, has stolen my body. All I can do is tip my face toward the sun, close my eyes, and breathe as his hands wander over my skin. *Don't think,* I say to myself. *Don't think. Just feel.*

I try, but I can't stop myself. *Do I put my hand here? Should I put it there? Is that too forward? Not forward enough?* I don't know this dance. I want to let go, to let myself feel him, to let his weight fall against me, to give myself over, but I can't. Every muscle in my body is tense as I fight—not against Bran, but against myself. What does this mean, giving myself over to him? What does this mean to him? Am I just another girl, or is it more than that?

"Cass," he whispers in my ear, "we don't have to do this." He lifts his hand from my body and pulls away. "If you're not ready, we can wait. There's no rush."

But there is. Just like the day of the earthquake when I kissed Bran on the lakeshore, I know that this is the moment. "I'm ready," I say. I know what I want.

"Then," he whispers between kisses, "do me a favor and stop thinking?"

And just like that, for the first time in my life, I do. I stop thinking, and just feel.

Sometime later, the siren starts.

Bran winces at the sound. "That's the emergency signal," he says, blinking. "Something's happened. I've got to go."

I reach for Bran's arm. "Wait. Not yet. Please."

But he's already swimming away, and all I can do is swim after him.

We dress in our soggy clothes and jog toward town. The sound of the siren is muffled by the trees, but it's still there, haunting our steps. We stop at the edge of town. Bran pulls me into his chest, kissing me hard. Neither of us want to stop, but Bran is the first to pull away. "If it's a search, go into the woods," he says. "Take Madda with you. I'll find you." He pushes me away and breaks into a flat-out sprint.

I wait until he rounds a corner, and then head toward Madda's, steadfastly refusing to look at the skies. A search? A search here, on the Island? It's not possible. How would they have gotten through the boundary?

Sparks begin to fly around my head. They're thick and bright, clouding my vision so it's harder and harder to see, but I must make it to Madda's before they take over. I can't risk losing myself here, in the middle of the road.

Madda is coming up her walk as I stumble through the gate. "Oh mercy," she says, "what is going on?"

"I don't know," I mumble as she pushes me into the cottage. "Sparks. The sparks have come. I don't know what they are."

Madda makes me sit down. I hear the strike of a match and the snap of something catching fire. "Here." She pushes a bundle of leaves into my hand. "Breathe. The smoke will ground you." She bustles around the cottage, bashing into things as I inhale the sharp, musty scent of burning sage. "We don't have time for this now," she mutters. "You breathe in that smoke until I tell you not to, and nothing else, got it? Open your eyes." She glares at me. "I don't know what's happening, and I can't find out until you're attached to this world properly. Here, put this on." She shoves a strand of purple beads into my hand. "And don't take them off until I say!"

I slip the beads over my head. Smoke wafts in my face, making my eyes water, but the sparks begin to float away.

Madda squints at me. "Better?"

"Just about," I say.

"'Just about' will have to be good enough." She pulls me to my feet, snatches the sage wand from my hand, and extinguishes it in a cup of water. "We've got to get to town. Who knows what ridiculous schemes they'll have cooked up by now." She throws the door open. "Honestly, there are times when I think I'm the only sane person left on this planet. At least you have a little sense about you." She sets off at a clip so fast that I'm forced to jog to keep up. "Men don't know what's coming and going half the time. When the Elders aren't jumping at their own shadows, they're creating half-baked excuses to go blow shit up." She stops, draws a deep breath, and then sets off again toward the longhouse.

For the first time, I catch sight of Madda's shade. It's not an animal. It's not anything I've ever seen before. It almost looks human, but it's not. I can make out swollen lips and bulging, bloodshot eyes. It's . . . grotesque.

"Got a bad feeling," she grumbles.

I've got to admit, I've got a bad feeling too.

CHAPTER TWENTY-FIVE

*W*e're at war. The siren wasn't signaling an emergency. It was a call to arms, a general muster. Word has reached the Band that the hospitals where they harvest Other blood were wiped out in the last earthquake, and now the Corridor is out of Other blood. That means they're coming for us.

Madda doesn't stay to learn the details. She pushes our way out of the crowd gathered around the longhouse and storms to the cottage without speaking a single word.

The cottage watches us with wary eyes. It knows we're leaving, and as if to reinforce that point three ravens fly overhead, a trio of black periods in the sky. Dot, dot, dot. What happens now . . .

Helen's inside, wide-eyed and pale.

"You're going to stay with Adelaide," Madda snaps at her. "Go pack."

Helen scurries off. "Why isn't she coming too?" I ask before I can stop myself.

Madda is half bent over, about to pull a basket full of bandages out from a shelf, when she pauses and turns back to me. "Because the first and last time Helen went on one of these things with me, I left her alone and she was raped. She was eleven. Does that answer your question?"

I don't know what to say. I just stand there gaping as Madda pulls stuff out of cupboards—bundles of cloth, packets of things that crunch, herbs, syringes, vials. She fires them all at me. "You wanted to know," she snaps. "Now you do. Let that be a lesson not to ask questions you're told not to ask."

"Who?" I whisper as I try to catch the jar Madda tosses to me, but it slips from my fingers and breaks, sending a rain of lavender rolling under our feet. I sweep it up as fast as I can. Madda doesn't even seem to notice.

"Don't know. She says she doesn't remember, but she's been afraid of men ever since. Can't say I blame her. Bran was the one who brought her back to me. . . ."

Madda stops speaking. Helen has appeared in the hallway. "I'm ready," she says.

Did she overhear us? I don't know. Maybe. Even if she didn't, it's all I can do not to rush over and hug her. But I don't. I also remember what Madda once told me, that Helen didn't want pity, so I say, "See you later?"

She nods and closes the door behind her.

Madda turns to me. "Thank you. That was kind." She points to her bedroom. "There are bags in there. Bring them both out, and start packing."

I find the bags stowed behind a set of drying racks, and set them on the table, stuffing bandages and clothes and whatever Madda tosses at me into their leather bottoms while she searches for something in the back of a cupboard. "There it is." She straightens up and hands me a cloth bundle. "You'll need this."

I hold the bundle in my hands. Whatever's under the cloth is hard and heavy. I peel back the layers to expose a silver barrel, and immediately thrust it back to her. "I can't have this."

She doesn't hear me. She's back in the cupboard. "I know I've got some bullets in here somewhere," she growls.

"Madda," I say. "Madda, I can't have this."

She's out of the cupboard and has a hold of my shoulders before I can blink. "Child, you have no choice. We're going into battle. If you want to come, you come armed."

"You don't understand," I whisper.

"Tell me what I don't understand." She peers into my eyes. "That your mother shot herself with one of these? I know that. She did it, not you."

And that's that.

What I remember is this:

A kitchen table.

One chair, knocked to the floor.

The door open.

A bottle of bleach, empty.

The apple tree outside.

Smoke from a smoldering fire.

Shadows behind it.

My mother's arm, blackened by Plague, piercing those shadows.

Her blood feeding the roots of the apple.

A letter on the refrigerator, tacked up with the letters *C* and *P*.

It reads: *I'm infected. I cleaned the house and burned my clothes. I'm sorry. I love you. I can't let it take you, too.*

A year later, just after I turn twelve, a scientist in Bangladesh discovers that those of aboriginal descent are immune to Plague. Our blood carries antibodies. Liquid gold.

I make my father promise he'll never have a gun in the house again.

And then the searches begin.

We gather outside the longhouse, a hundred head strong. My father stands beside me. We are grim-faced and silent. My father's not going. Someone has to stay behind, tend the crops, prepare for winter, and watch for our return. He's not the only one—a few of the Elders, most of the women, the children—they're also staying. The young, the infirmed. This is what the UA does to us: divides us into groups, makes us see who's expendable, who's not. Who's strong, who's weak. I've heard it said that conflict unites a nation, but I don't believe it, not for one second. All conflict does is break things apart and scatter the pieces so far that it's impossible to pick them all up again.

Paul hasn't been home in days, and when I spot him in the crowd, it's just as I suspected. He's walking hand-in-hand with Avalon.

"Did you know?" I ask my father.

"About the girl?" He shrugs. "Yeah, he told me. Not who I would have chosen for him, but that's love for you." My father nudges me. "Madda's over there. You should go to her."

I kiss my father's cheek and head off, not knowing what to think. The division has already begun. Does my brother deserve to be happy? Yes, of course he does. But with Avalon? Avalon, who will break his heart? Because she will—she's said as much herself. I wish I didn't know this, but I do, right deep in my bones. What will happen to Paul then? Who will tell him that his heartache will pass? Who will watch him slip into himself and disappear into the blackness that has haunted him since he was a little boy?

Please, let me be wrong. I have never wanted to be so wrong about anything in my life.

Madda is parked under a pine tree, ordering women around. "No, that doesn't go there," she says, scurrying over to snatch a bundle away from a flustered-looking woman. "What if someone takes a bullet? How would I get to it in time?" The woman mutters something and bends back to her work as Madda looks around and rubs her forehead with a grimy hand. She spots me and waves me over. "I need your help," she says. "Sort through the surgical gear and take out anything that's not essential. We'll be traveling light and fast." She nods at the pile of supplies behind her. "Anything that's too heavy, stick over there. The men will carry it." She marches off.

Avalon finds me wrapping bandages.

"You're going too?" she asks.

I force myself not to snap at her. What she said about Helen hasn't escaped my memory, and now, with what Madda has revealed, I'm not about to suffer Avalon's games. "Yes" is all I say, in hopes she'll just go away.

Avalon glances around. She sniffs and tries to pick up one of the backpacks, but it's clearly an effort for her and she sets it back down right away, even though I can lift it without any problem at all. "I could carry one of these." She sits down beside me, but makes no effort to help. "Healing isn't so hard. Maybe," she says as she gives me a sidelong glance, "you could ask Madda if I can come too."

"Maybe," I say, though I already know Madda's answer, and therefore won't bother. It's then I notice she's watching someone. Bran. He's walking across the park, a pack on his back, his eyes full of storm clouds. Avalon can't take her eyes from him.

Oh, Paul. If only you could see what I'm seeing now. I couldn't make him, even if he were here, but when Avalon breaks his heart, I will help him pick up the pieces and glue them back together again.

We spend the night outside the longhouse, sleeping wherever we can find a spot. Bran is beside me. The afternoon is still in my mind, and it's all I can do not to touch him. Instead I content myself with watching the rise and fall of his chest, the way his mouth relaxes, the thick lashes framing his eyes. I should sleep. But I can't. I pass the hours braiding a string of cedar bark on which I'll hang the little pouch with my sisiutl pearls and the feather Bran gave me. When it's finished, I drape it around my neck and smile. It feels good, though I can't help thinking that it should be the medicine bag Madda gave me.

My father is lying a little ways away. He isn't asleep either. I could ask him what will happen tomorrow, what being at war really means, but I don't. Tonight he has other things on his mind—one of which is Paul, who vanished earlier in the day and hasn't yet returned.

I turn over and find Bran awake, looking at me. "What's wrong?" he whispers.

"Nothing." I try to smile, but it doesn't work.

"Hmm." He scoots over and wraps his arms around me, pulling me close. The length of his body presses against mine. He's warm and smells of dirt and wood shavings. I yawn and close my eyes.

Madda wakes me just as an advance party sets out. The men are black shadows against the purple crush of dawn.

I see flashes of their shades, but they're too far away for me to make out what they are.

I'm tying a rope around my bedroll when Bran wakes. "Hi," I say.

"Hi." He sits up, rubs his eyes, and then fishes something out from under his shirt. "Hold out your hand," he says.

I do, and in it he places something cold and smooth. A stone. A green stone hanging on a leather thread. His green stone.

He smiles shyly. "It's a spirit stone. Will you wear it for me?"

I nod, and bend my head so he can bind it around my neck.

He touches it with one finger. "It looks like it belongs there." He's about to say something else when his attention catches on something in the distance. "Oh no."

I turn to see what he's looking at. His mother is standing on the other side of the park, wringing her hands. She spots Bran and comes streaking over, knocking aside anyone who gets in her way, tripping over sleeping men. "Too soon!" she cries when she reaches us. "It's too soon, and with so many things left undone!"

Bran grimaces as she throws herself into his chest and sobs. She stinks of whiskey. Bran mouths *Help* at me, but what am I supposed to do? I glance over at Madda, who just shrugs. The few eyes that look our way dart off just as quickly. They've seen this before, and there's nothing to be done. Grace Eagleson is a drunk. That's just the way it is.

"Come on, Mother," Bran says, brushing her tangled hair from her eyes. "Let me take you home."

"Oh, my love," she whispers as her gaze falls on the stone at my throat. Bran doesn't notice. He just takes her hand, slips it into the nook of his elbow, and leads her away.

I watch. That's all I can do: watch them leave.

And hope that Bran comes back.

CHAPTER TWENTY-SIX

*B*and business is slow business. Madda and I sit under a pine, listening to the men debate this, that, and the other, taking so much time that an onlooker might believe they were preparing for a horseshoe tournament, not a war. They're lucky that time doesn't spoil, because they're wasting it in huge quantities.

Something behind the longhouse catches Madda's attention. I look to see Paul standing there, a pack on his back, a rifle in his hands. He looks around as if the sunlight is blinding him.

Madda nudges me. "Go on," she says. "Might be a while before you get to see him again."

Paul is still standing in the same spot when I draw near. "Hi," I say, tipping my head to one side. "You okay?"

"I guess," he says, though he doesn't look it.

"Hmm." I turn and look back at the Elders. They're laughing about something. "I missed you," I say slowly, doing my best to sound casual. "Did you spend the night at Avalon's house?"

I don't have to look at Paul to know that was the wrong question. "What, exactly, is it that you want to know, Cass? If I was screwing her? What, should I have invited you along so you could tell me how to do it?"

"Paul!" I gasp.

"What?" He turns to me, and in his eyes I see something I haven't seen in a long time. Anger, and hatred, and something darker, something without a name. This isn't about me. I just happen to be the thing that's closest, the thing that's easiest to strike out at, but that doesn't lessen the sting of his words at all. "I don't need your help, Cass. Don't you get it? I don't need it, and I don't want it."

I don't know what to say, so I don't say anything as Paul storms off. Just as tears start to well in my eyes, Paul stops, turns around, and walks back to me. "Look," he says. "I shouldn't have said that. I'm sorry."

I'm sorry too, I want to say, but he's already stalking off to join the rest of the Band. Neither of us can undo what he's said. We both know it.

I stare at my hands, thinking of when we were little,

when we knew each other so well that we could finish each other's sentences. Now I don't know what Paul wants. I thought I did. I thought he wanted me to help him.

But I was wrong.

I was so, so wrong.

It's midmorning before we get under way.

Bran meets up with us as we head out, falling into place at the back of the group so I can't talk to him. He looks awful. His eyes are bloodshot and he walks bent, as if his pack is twice as heavy as it actually is. Paul falls into step beside him.

I focus on the road ahead of me. Paul and Bran are together. That will have to suffice for now.

Madda seems to know something's wrong and decides to quiz me while we walk, as if that will help take my mind off things—"How much borage do you need to lift a mood?" "Digitalis—what dosage is lethal?" "Primrose—how do you distill the oil?"—on and on until I have no idea where we are or what time it is.

The green spirit stone bumps against my chest, keeping time as I walk—*one, two, buckle my shoe; three, four, close the door.* My pack is unnaturally heavy, as if someone filled it with stones when I wasn't looking. The straps dig into my shoulders, worming their way down to bone, severing flesh from sinew, eating me alive. . . .

Madda snaps her fingers under my nose. "Don't you dare do that now," she says. "Not when there's people around." She leans in close. "When we get back, we're going to sort this out. Don't let me forget."

I nod as I blink myself back to the world of the living. Laughter echoes in my mind—not the laughter of a person, but of the raven. *I almost had you*, it says. *Never forget that you belong to me. . . .*

We reach the estuary around noon. The group divides into two. Half take to the enormous war canoes that were once ancient cedars. They'll go to the point on the water where the boundary is thinnest, the point where my family crossed. The rest of us, including Madda and me, will head south toward the land boundary, where waves ravaged the Island long ago and nothing now grows.

Bran and Paul are herded into a canoe before I have time to say good-bye. Bran stares at me and touches his hand to his heart. I draw the spirit stone out from under my shirt and press it to my lips. My brother rolls his eyes.

Then, with a shout, the men plunge their paddles into the water and the canoes shoot away, chased by a herd of shades, all vying to keep up.

"Come on," Madda says, taking my shoulder and

steering me away from the shore. "You'll see them again soon enough."

We find ourselves in the middle of the remaining men. Weapons can be fashioned, food can be caught, but healers are rare, and out here in the lands left behind, we are as precious to the Band as the blood in our veins is to the people of the Corridors.

Our path snakes through dark woods. Nature has reclaimed this place, burrowing her roots through the burned-out shells of houses, ripping through asphalt. No one speaks, but it's not from a need for stealth. Our silence is an offering to the spirits that live here, a sign of respect, a way to say that we will not stay.

We stop well after nightfall. Madda is summoned to a meeting with the Elders, leaving me to sit beside our packs and wait. For the first time, I notice Cedar. He's knee-deep in ferns, looking for a place on the forest floor to sleep. The other men do the same, but all of us keep an ear turned to what's going on with Madda and the Elders. They argue late into the night. I can't make out their words, but the tone of their voices makes it clear that Madda's not happy about something and the men don't want to listen to her.

I clutch my knees to my chest and think of Bran and

Paul. Where are they sleeping tonight? Are they together? Are they safe? For a moment I consider closing my eyes and reaching out to whatever seized me on the road. Perhaps the raven might tell me what I want to know. But I change my mind. It's been only half a day since I saw them leave in the canoes. What could have happened to them in that time? Not a whole lot.

Madda stomps back just as sleep is settling over me. I blink myself awake.

"Bloody pig-headed men," she fumes as she pulls her bedroll out from the top of her pack.

"What's wrong?" I ask.

"Nothing," she grumbles. "Just go to sleep. Tomorrow's going to be a long day."

But now that I'm awake, sleep is the furthest thing from my mind. I watch the midnight sky, where stars appear, one by one. The big bear, and the little one, chasing each other through time. The Milky Way, a wash of white. Serpens, his sinuous form bending through the darkness. Paul taught me the names of these constellations. I wonder, *Is he looking at them too?* Is he caught in their light, or in their shadows? Stars, he once told me, don't cast shadows, but how can that be? Everything has a dark side. Everywhere I look, I see outlines of trees, people, animals, and their shades, the hidden halves of their souls. All except me. I'm not vain enough to believe I'm so special that I don't need a shade, but . . . where is mine? Why can't I see that part of myself that connects me to the world of spirit? *Maybe I'm damaged,* I think, *just like Grace Eagleson said the first time I met her.*

"You're thinking too loud," Madda says as she rolls over. "Stop it. You're keeping me awake."

"Sorry." I force myself to close my eyes. "Where are we going, Madda?"

"The boundary." Her voice is raspy and sounds tired. "You know that."

"Yeah, but I feel like there's something else going on that no one's telling me."

"Honey, that's life." She draws her blanket up over her shoulders and closes her eyes. "Get used to it."

I dream.

I dream that the sky is alive, that the stars are anemones in the ocean and they're waving back and forth while waves wash over them. I try to touch one. Its sticky tentacles grip my fingers, and when I pull back, it doesn't release me. I'm trapped, halfway to heaven, halfway to earth.

It starts to rain sometime during the night. I wake shivering. It might be summer, but under the trees the world is cold.

We pack our sodden blankets and eat hard, dry strips of oolichan. The oily smell makes me gag, but I force the fish down my throat. Madda pushes a canteen of water at me and I take a long swallow. Water mixes with the fish oil until all I can taste is wet dog, and then I really do gag.

Someone pauses beside me. Cedar. "You're wet," he says.

"So?"

He hands me a blanket. "I'm used to this. You aren't. Put the blanket over your pack. It'll help."

"Thanks," I say. "But we did get rain in the Corridor, you know."

"Nothing like the rain here," he says with a shrug.

"That's true." This rain is thick and healthy, if cold. I drape the blanket around my shoulders. It feels like a peace offering, and maybe that's not such a bad thing.

Cedar takes a seat beside me—close enough to talk, but not so close that I'm uncomfortable.

"Did you like it there?" he asks.

"What? The Corridor?" I consider his question. Had he asked me this when I first arrived, my answer would have been very different, but now I can't believe I ever saw my future there. What was it I was going to be? What hope for my future have I forgotten? "Life was different there—easier, I guess. But not by much." I shrug.

"Hmm." He shifts his rifle from one shoulder to the other and looks like he's going to ask another question just as Henry Crawford shouts that it's time to move out. Cedar goes to take his place near the head of the line.

I'm struggling with my pack when he makes his way back toward me.

"You ever seen a searchcraft before?" he says.

"Once. Why?"

"If we see them, stay close to a man. They look for women first, but then, you're a half-breed. Your blood's diluted. Maybe that'll make a difference." He stalks off, his muskrat scampering at his shoulder, leaving me to wonder what that was all about.

Madda arrives back just as I'm hauling Cedar's blanket over the top of the pack. I'm not so sure I want it anymore. She eyes it. "Where did you get that?"

"Cedar," I say, nodding toward him. "Weird, huh?"

"Yeah," she says, narrowing her eyes as the first of the men head out. "I wouldn't trust him as far as I could throw him. Apple doesn't fall far from the tree." She twitches the edge of the blanket so it drapes over my shoulders to keep me dry. "Still, it was a nice thing for him to do." She pulls her knife from her belt, digging a fern from the moss on a maple before setting off. "Licorice root," she says. "Gather anything you think might be useful along the way." She cuts off the frond and starts to chew on the rhizome. "What's Cedar's shade?" she asks suddenly.

"A muskrat."

She nods. "And Henry Crawford's?"

I stare ahead at the man with the scarred face. "A weasel."

"And mine?"

"I still don't know." I feel my cheeks burn. "I'm sorry."

"Don't be sorry. That's what I hoped you'd say. So," she says with a deliberate pause, "have you seen yours yet?"

"No."

"Figured," she says. "We might have to address that while we're out here. There's not enough time to do everything in the proper way, you know." She stops to draw breath and then heaves herself over a fallen log. "Never enough time to do anything properly anymore."

Her voice disappears as a hemlock groans and topples to the forest floor before us, taking a man down with it. We both stand there, frozen in shock, until Madda comes to her senses and pushes me down into the ferns. Above us, wind parts the cedars and the sleek, bipod body of a searchcraft hovers over us like a great silver wasp, waiting to sting.

Madda drops down beside me. "Your gun," she says. "Get your gun!"

I fumble for it while the men start shooting at the searchcraft, though as soon as I've dug the pistol out of my pack, I drop it. My breath comes in short, rasping snatches as I fish for the gun, and when my hand finally falls on the grip, I shoot at the sky, hoping I don't hit anyone.

The sound of gunfire rips through the air, hissing and screaming as the searchcraft fires back, its energy weapons cutting across the forest, slicing trees in two. This isn't what I was told about searches. My father said they didn't want to hurt us, that they only wanted to stun us because a dead Other is no good to them, but now I see that's not true. I watch a man fall to the ground a short ways away, one leg severed from his body, his precious blood spilling on moss.

Madda scrambles past me, rushing over to the man, dropping down beside him, the blanket Cedar gave me pressed to the man's wound. She thinks she can save him, but she can't. Even through the smoke and the gunfire, I can see he is fading. "Madda!" I scream as sparks begin to block my vision. Still, I grope for her, to draw her down to hide in the ferns. She's going to get killed. The only way to survive is to get down low, hide, become a stone, a worm, a root . . .

And then the searchcraft's engine starts to whine, and

thick black smoke billows into the air. A cry goes up from the men as the searchcraft banks and vanishes from sight. A few moments later, the sound of its impact reaches our ears, and then, the forest goes still. Rain drops onto tree, onto leaf, onto fallen body. No one moves.

Henry Crawford stands, slowly, and speaks. "Tom, Ron, Cedar—go chase it down. It won't be far."

Cedar catches my eye as he jumps up. His face is flushed with excitement as he follows the older men off into the underbrush.

Madda touches my arm. "You okay?"

I nod and brush the last of the sparks away from my eyes.

"Good," she says. "We've got work to do."

I start to take a step after her, but my feet won't move. Sparks return to float around my face while beneath my feet, the earth shudders. *Breathe*, I tell myself. *Just breathe.* The sparks recede. The shuddering stops.

Madda frowns at me but doesn't say anything. What is there to say?

We step out of our hiding place to find an arm waving at us, except it's dangling from a cedar branch. The owner of the arm is nowhere to be seen.

Madda kneels. A man lies in the rich humus, his head cradled by bracken. He has two arms, so the one in the cedar isn't his, though a livid burn crisscrosses his chest.

Madda touches my hand. "I need my medicine bag. It's in the top of my pack."

I bound away. *Medicine bag, medicine bag, I must find her medicine bag.* I repeat the words to stave off the sparks that chase after me. Their drone fills my ears, making it hard for me to think.

The pack sits in the mud, half open. I root through the top for the bundle that contains Madda's most potent medicines. *Why doesn't she have it with her? She always carries it with her.* And then I see it poking out from under the pack. I seize it and I'm back at her side within a few quick strides.

The rain has stopped. Mist descends, wrapping the forest in a shroud. Men walk back and forth, half-ghosted, carrying the wounded closer to Madda. She still sits beside the man with the burn, stroking his brow, and she doesn't look up when I approach. I open the medicine kit. She waves her hand at me, as if I should know what she needs, but I don't. This man is dying. Nothing will stop that now.

She reaches across, retrieving a bottle herself. WATER HEMLOCK, the label reads. And then I know. Madda doesn't mean to heal this man. She means to ease his passing.

"Hold on, Ben. Open your mouth," she says. "This might be a little bitter, but it will kill the pain."

I turn away, but Madda yanks me back. "Get over here," she hisses. "You're a healer. Act like one."

So I kneel next to Madda, remembering the day she told me I'd face difficult decisions, that there'd be times when I'd have to do things I'd rather not.

Yes, she told me, but maybe deep down I didn't believe her.

But I'm here now, with a dying man beside me and none of that—what I believed, what I wanted, what choice I made—matters. If it were me lying there, what would I want? I'd want someone to stay with me, to talk to me, to take my hand and wait until I left this world. So I do that. I pick up the man's dirty hand and cradle it in my own. Madda nods and walks off to find her next patient.

The man stares at me with vacant brown eyes. He's about my father's age. His hand is ice-cold. I have to force myself not to shiver. He has no shade. "Cassandra," he says. "That's your name, isn't it?"

"Yes, it is. And yours is Ben?"

"Yep. Never got a chance to know you. I'm sorry about that." His eyes flutter closed as his breath rattles in his chest. "So much I never got to do."

I don't know what to say, so I sing "Alouette," like my father used to sing to Paul and me when we were little, and smooth Ben's hair away from his eyes. Death is coming. I can feel its arrival, this raven that walks the spirit world with a black mask and a cape of rattles. I can hear him dancing, shaking his cape.

Ben clenches my hand. "I'm not long for this world. I hear the Great Spirit calling my name."

I squeeze my eyes shut and nod. I hear it too. *Don't go,* I want to say, but the decision isn't mine. Ben wheezes, "It's time." A smile pulls at his lips and then, he's gone.

I don't know how long I sit there, singing, holding his hand. Long enough for his skin to take on a tinge of yellow. Long enough for his mouth to fall slack. There is no beauty in death. Ben is no longer Ben, but a husk sloughed off by his soul.

All around us people rush back and forth, setting guards, slashing bush, tending fires, bearing hastily made stretchers. I know they're busy. I know there is much to do, but the fact that no one stops by, no one marks Ben's passing, leaves me feeling so sad. These men knew him better than I did. They would know if he has children, a wife, someone who might be waiting for him to come home.

I pull a strip of bark from a nearby cedar, and then

pick ferns. I will weave Ben a garland to wear. My hands make the knots as part of me starts to withdraw. I see the mist hanging in the air, but I don't truly feel it. I know rain falls on my head and drips down my neck, but I am not cold. I see the men moving through the undergrowth, their faces grim and serious, but I don't hear them. The rain. The mud. The forest. The broken tree, stabbing up from the earth.

Ben, lying on the ground, except he isn't. Only his body is. The rest of him is gone, off on the long journey to the land of our ancestors.

And then, blood rushes in my ears. Something snaps, and the cocoon protecting me from the noise and the cold and the truth breaks.

It's Madda, calling me.

Reluctantly, I let Ben go.

CHAPTER TWENTY-SEVEN

Three dead. Six seriously injured. Two of those will likely pass into the spirit world before dawn. Many with minor cuts, contusions, scrapes, burns. By all accounts, we've been lucky. *It could have been worse*, the men whisper. *Much, much worse.*

If we lived in the Corridor, if we weren't Others, the injured men would be treated in a hospital with the best drugs the UA government could muster up. In the Corridor, a broken bone is a painful nuisance. A little plaster, a few pins, maybe surgery, some rest, and you're all better, sonny. Right as rain.

Out here, we have splints. Honey. Garlic. Boneset. That's it. The two men who may still pass over? They've been burned by the searchers' weapons. They might still have died if we were in the Corridor. But then again, maybe not. Maybe if we were somewhere else, they'd wake up tomorrow in a hospital room, smile at their family, comment on how lovely the lilies are, *May I have a sip of water? Could you bring the bedpan, please?*

Darkness descends around us. It's not true night yet, but the shadows of the rain forest don't know that, nor do they care. I'm sewing up a bone-baring gash in a man's arm—I asked him his name but I don't remember what he said—as I wonder why we're still here. If the searchers found us once, what's stopping them from finding us again? Maybe I should wish for that. If they came, we could send these men back with them. The searchers have reason to get them back to the Corridor quickly, to fix what we can't. But then what would keep them from taking all of us? I don't know. I still don't understand why that searchcraft attacked or how it found us to begin with.

I think these things over and over and over because I don't want to think about what's happening beyond the canopy of the trees. I don't want to think about how the searchers penetrated the boundary. I know Madda said there are gaps now, but still—gaps big enough to allow a searchcraft through? That means the boundary is failing. How long until it's gone completely? And what will stop the UA from coming and rounding us up then?

Madda brings me a steaming cup of tea. "Drink it," she says when I wave it away. "Healing is hard work. If you don't, you'll regret it later, and you're dangerous to everyone, including yourself, if you're exhausted." She glances at the row of stitches that run up the man's arm. "Nice work."

I sip the tea. It's bitter, but warm. "She'll bring some to you later," I say to the man when he glances at my cup.

"I hope not," he says as he closes his eyes. "That smells awful. Hurry up. I want this over with."

When I'm finished with his arm, I start mixing a poultice for a man who's lost most of his right ear. While I pound and grind, Cedar returns with the two older men. They go to join Henry Crawford.

"Well?" I hear him say.

"Found it. Killed the two still alive," says one of the older men.

"And the searchcraft?" Crawford says.

"Salvageable."

"Did you mark its position?"

"Cedar did the triangulation. We'll be able to get to it again. Disabled the tracker and covered it well, so the UA won't find it unless they stub their toe on it." He grins.

Cedar glances my way and I drop my gaze back to my

work. The last thing I want right now is his attention.

Later, as the men are settling down to sleep, Madda comes and sits beside me. "So," she says. "It wasn't what you thought it would be."

"No." It wasn't. It was harder, and scarier, and yet . . . good, too, in a way that tastes both bitter and sweet.

"I remember the first time I watched someone die. I want to tell you it gets easier, but I'm not sure it does." She gives me a kind smile. "But it's necessary, you know. Death—it's not the end. Something happens afterward." She points up at the single star that has poked its way through the clouds. "Some say that's what we become. Others, they say we become part of the wind until the day we're born again." She shrugs. "We all get to find out sooner or later."

"Madda," I say as I tug my blanket closer. I'm suddenly very cold. "The boundary. You said that there are gaps now. Do you know why?"

She scratches her cheek. "Not exactly. I've sensed it for a while, that the boundary isn't what it used to be, though as far as I know, this is the first time a whole searchcraft has come through. Before, they only managed to drop their soldiers through the gaps. Maybe . . . maybe it's just that nothing lasts, you know?"

"But if that's the case, Madda, shouldn't we be ready to leave? If it's not safe here?"

She looks at me from the corner of her eye. "Remember when I told you there were things you'd have to say that no one would want to hear? Well, that would be one of them. I've said it. No one wants to listen." She sighs. "They'll come around, though—soon, I hope. Before it's too late. But don't you worry about that now, Cass. You've had a long, hard day. Get some sleep."

I shuffle around, and when I'm mostly comfortable I close my eyes, but it's some time before Madda's words leave me. *Before it's too late. Before it's too late.*

What if it's already too late?

I dream.

I dream of Paul sitting by a fire, staring at the embers. Bran sits across from him, a rifle resting across his knees. I float between them, a wraith called up by the depth of Paul's vision, or maybe the dream's merely a manifestation of my mind, a hopeful projection of what I wish was happening.

I touch Bran's cheek and he shivers. It's then I know that this is real, that Paul's called me into his world for some reason. I sit by Bran's side, rest my head on his shoulder, and watch my brother, wondering why he wants me here. What does he need me to see?

Something shifts in the shadows behind Paul. I'm not

the only one he's summoned. Faces peer out of the darkness, contorted in suffering. They moan and reach for Paul with crippled, wasted hands.

I scream at them to leave him alone, though my voice carries no weight in this place, and neither does my body, for when I try to push the faces away, my hands pass right through them and I stumble into darkness.

It's all right, Cass, I hear Paul say. I had to try. He shakes his head and I spiral through the darkness until I feel my body jerk awake.

We set out for the boundary around midmorning. I'm not sure why we're still going. Surely we should take the injured men back to town and see if the searchers attacked there too. But the order is given to move out and that's what Madda's doing, so that's what I do too.

Three men, not two, passed during the night and Henry Crawford decided not to leave until beds had been made for the deceased high in the tops of the cedars where they can see the sky. I feel the dead men now, looking down over our shoulders as we leave them behind.

The men around me sing as we walk. I don't know what they're saying, though I can understand the gist of it—a song of mourning. A song that will accompany the deceased on their journey to what comes after. The men sing in their soft, rustling language, a language that I don't know, though the sound of it makes my head swim. Madda places a hand on my arm and squeezes it from time to time, probably to make sure I'm staying with her.

We walk well into the night, and rise early the next morning to walk again. The day passes without incident, and by late afternoon, we arrive.

The forest just stops. One minute, we're in the trees, and the next, we're not. Legend says that a long time ago, the earth just slipped away into the ocean. My father said it was too full of sorrow over the land lost to the earthquakes, so it wanted to die too. Now it sits at the bottom of the ocean, looking up at the stars.

My gut aches at the sight of the ground stripped bare of every living thing. No birds. No trees. No water. Just the red stone running like an artery, bleeding all over the place, red stone as far as I can see.

I press my hand to my mouth, biting down on my knuckle hard to stave off the panic surging inside of me. Cedar pulls my hand away. "Don't," he murmurs. "They're watching you. Want to know what you're made of, whether they can control you better than Madda. Don't let them do it." He lets go of my elbow and walks away without another word.

Men approach from the east. They talk with Henry Crawford, who shouts at us to move out. A path traces the edge of the forest and leads to a makeshift camp, where mildew-stained tents huddle close to a cabin tucked into the tree line.

Madda drops her pack on the ground. "Leave yours too. They won't need us for a while. We've got other business."

I set my pack down and follow her into the woods. I'm so relieved to be away from the red stone that I'd happily follow her anywhere.

We walk north for a good long while, long enough for the shadows to drape themselves across the trees. Madda doesn't speak. I don't speak. Whatever we're doing needs to be done in silence.

Our path runs uphill to where the forest thins. Madda pauses, scans the mountains, and then turns west. We scramble down an incline of pebbles, and then I see it: a tall, black stone, so polished our reflection ripples across its surface. It stands in a crater where nothing grows.

"What is it?" I whisper. Sparks buzz around my head, drawing closer and closer until I'm afraid to breathe, for fear of inhaling them.

"The source of the boundary," Madda says. She takes a deep breath. "Gather some firewood, but don't wander too far. I don't want to have to go searching for you."

Windfall litters the edge of the crater and it isn't long until I've collected a fair pile of kindling. Madda's built a fire next to the monolith. She digs several strips of oolichan out of the pouch at her hip and offers them to me. I shake my head. Hunger has left me. Madda nods and starts taking other things out of the pouch: eagle feathers, twine, a moonstone with a drop of red right in its center, a rattle, a needle, a jar of ink. She sets them in a row, and then crumbles sage onto the fire. "Drink up the smoke," she says.

I inhale deeply. The smoke winds its way into my lungs.

"Now, take off your shirt."

I do as she asks, shivering as wind touches my sweaty skin.

"Hold still." The pungent fumes of whiskey fill my nose as she touches a cloth to a flask and then rubs it on my shoulder. Then she dips the needle into the ink, but pauses. "This isn't right," she murmurs to herself, shaking her head for a moment before raising her gaze to meet mine. "I need to ask you a question. Do you want to become my daughter?"

"Your daughter?" I echo.

"Yes. I want to adopt you. The Elders aren't sure about

you, and if you're my daughter, well, that gives you some protection. You're without clan, you see. Clan structure is a lot more lax now, not like the old days, but it'll help if they see I've claimed you as my own."

"But my father . . ."

"That doesn't change. We've actually had this in the works ever since you got hurt. Had to wait for the full moon, though." She points to the haze of white that's beginning to rise over the eastern horizon. "So?"

After a deep swallow, I nod. Madda and my father decided. Without even asking me. It's all predestined, out of my hands, decreed. I want to be angry, I really do, but I'm not. I just don't have the energy.

It's then that I notice the monolith is humming. "Couldn't we have done this back at the camp?" I ask. I have the weirdest feeling that the monolith is looking at me.

"We need its power. We've got more to do tonight than your adoption." She frowns. "Time to figure out your shade, I think. I'm pretty sure you'll find a sisiutl. It's rare to have a supernatural as a totem, but not unheard of. Besides, everyone's special in their own way, you know? But let's not get ahead of ourselves here. First things first." She nods toward the monolith. "Time you know the story of this land. Comfy?"

"Comfy enough."

"Good." She dips the needle again, holds it close to my shoulder, and then stabs. At first I feel each pinprick deep in my flesh, as if Madda is burrowing the needle to the bone, but slowly, as it bites into me again and again, the pain fades until it's little more than a dull ache, like an ember trapped under my skin. Madda sings under her breath as she works, sweat beading on her brow, and all the while, the monolith watches, humming in counterpoint to Madda's tune.

"There," she says at last, sitting back to admire her work.

"What is it?" I strain to see, but my skin is angry and swollen, marring the image. All I can make out are grotesque, protruding lips, a squat torso, and huge, swollen breasts.

"Some call her an earth mother, and some the wild woman of the woods. She has other names too," Madda says as she rubs more alcohol over my skin. "I got her from the medicine woman before me, and she got it from the medicine woman before her. Sort of like our own clan, you know, a clan of women. Lots of power in her, the woman of the woods. Strong medicine. She'll protect you, watch over you. She looks ugly, but that's the way she likes it. Ugly demands respect." She takes a swig from her flask and then hands it to me. "Just a mouthful," she says when I shake my head. "We have more work to do, and pretty soon that shoulder of yours is going to be hurting bad. Don't be a martyr. Have a little. Go on. It won't kill you."

I pull my shirt over my head and take a swallow. The whiskey burns its way to my gut.

"So." She puts away her supplies and then shifts around until she's comfortable. "Part of what comes with being my daughter is learning the stories that were passed on to me by my teacher, so pay attention. You're going to have to pass this stuff on one day too, because without it, we lose sight of where we came from, and if we've lost that, we aren't anything. These stories are living things, as alive as you and me. Just in a different way, that's all." She picks up a pebble and inspects it. "Like this stone. It's got a soul, and I've got a soul, so in that, we're the same, but what houses the soul, that's completely different. The stories are like that—alive, just housed in a different body, a body our words give them. And our voices are their food. They need us to keep them alive."

I nestle myself into the gravel, pull a branch out from under my rump, and nod that I understand, though I don't, not really.

"Let me explain. In the days before the treaties that

formed the territories, people knew what was coming," Madda says. "They knew there would be a time when the world would be hurt bad, so bad it would actually cry. But knowing isn't enough. It has to be more.

"So, some of the medicine women back then, they knew that the earth was tired and unhappy, and pretty soon, things would happen that would scare them right down to their bones. They knew that the old creatures, the supernaturals, were fed up with humans. They had taught us everything we knew, and we forgot to be grateful for their gifts. The few of us who remember, who honor their teachings by living the Old Way, well, there's still hope, right?"

I nod. Yes, there's always hope.

"Anyhow, those women, they got together and made a big magic. Back then, there were still lots of spirit stones, you know, like the one I wear inside this amulet, like the one Bran's given you. They had a different name back then, but that's the thing about time—it transforms everything. Names change, but the essence of something doesn't. So, the women gathered up the stones, as many as they could find, and brought them here, and when they had finished, they had a pretty big pile. 'Course, all the men were upset that the women took the spirit stones, but the women did it anyhow because it needed to be done.

"They met here and once they placed all the stones on the land, they started to dance and after a while, Raven came to see what was happening. Well, he took one look at all those spirit stones and decided he wanted a few for himself, because everyone knows Raven loves shiny things."

She pauses to make sure I'm listening, and I am, though my hand has found its way to a stick. My fingers curl around it and I scratch in the dirt. It's not the same as knotting or weaving, but I need something to hold me here.

Madda clears her throat, and continues.

"Raven, he landed on the pile and watched the women dance for a bit, because he liked their dancing too, the way women sway and all, but he was so interested in the dancing that he didn't really notice when they started to sing. He just got a big, happy smile on his face and stood on the pile of rocks, watching the pretty women, and then got to thinking about which one might make him a good wife, because it had been a long time since Raven had taken a wife. One of those pretty stones might make a good wedding gift, too. Some of the other supernaturals joined him—Sisiutl and Dzoonokwa, for example. Not Thunderbird. He just watched from high in the sky. Smart, that Thunderbird. The others, what they didn't

notice was that as the women were dancing and singing, they were weaving a web of spirit right over top of
those spirit stones, binding them all together, and when
Raven picked up a stone and tried to fly off, he couldn't.
He was stuck, bound here on the Island, along with the
other supernaturals. Raven started to struggle, and as he
struggled, two of the stones fell out of the web and rolled
toward the dancing women. One of them is the spirit
stone you wear around your neck. I have the other one
here in this amulet I wear. The woman who picked them
up was the first medicine woman here on the Island,
after all the tribes came together and formed the Band
and the treaty lands were made.

"Anyhow, the women saw that Raven was trying to
steal the stones, so they danced faster and faster until
the spirit stones were coated in sticky spirit threads and
Raven and his friends were trapped inside. And so Raven
swallowed the stones, thinking the spirit threads would
dissolve in his gut, but when he swallowed the first stone,
his left foot turned to obsidian, and with the second
stone, the right. He tried to stop, but a powerful hunger
came upon him and he gulped and swallowed and gulped
and swallowed until he had eaten all the spirit stones.
And here he stands, after all this time, and I imagine he's
pretty mad that he's still stuck here, but that's what you

get when you go taking things that don't really belong to you."

My skin rises into goose flesh. The raven is trapped here. Is that what he's been after, all this time? He wants me to free him?

Madda rubs her temples. "So now you know, and you'd better not forget. It's time to get some work done. Close your eyes. I'll guide you through the rest."

I do as she asks, though the image of the monolith doesn't leave my mind. It pulses behind my eyelids, sings to me: *My sweet doe, my gentle dove,* and when I realize it's my mother's voice, I let go. I slip into the monolith and let it consume me.

I float between the stars, carried by the currents of the night. The stars smile down at me. Each has a face; each has wings. Behind them I can see a double-headed serpent swimming among them. I only know it's there because stars disappear when it draws near. It swallows them whole.

"What are you?" I say.

You, it replies as it stretches forth and swallows me too.

I spiral in the icy cold of nothingness, down and down and down, slipping through the great serpent's bowels, screaming as it pushes me through its body. I rake it with my fingers; I bite, I claw, I try to grab hold of anything, and then it expels me and I'm falling, falling, falling . . .

Back into myself.

Above me, the serpent slithers down from the stars to wrap itself around the moon. It tastes the night with its tongue.

I reach for it. My fingers touch its scales as it winds itself around my wrist, twisting my arm. It rears back, and before I can stop it, sinks its fangs into my neck. *Be careful what you look for*, it whispers just before dropping away into the night.

I hear the hum of the monolith and from far away, a woman's scream. Me? Madda? I don't know. I can't tell. I begin to cry. I've learned nothing. I've failed.

No, a voice says. *You are the serpent that flies by night.*

And then the real world falls away once again and I'm stretched across the sky until I am the sky, I am the air, I am the fire of stars and the water of rain. A kingfisher flies with me and catches me in its bill and I know Bran still lives, but behind us, racing through the dark, is something else. I can't see it, but I can smell it, a foul stink, like rotting flesh. *Faster*, I say to Bran. *We must go faster!*

The kingfisher releases me and vanishes in a burr of song.

I fall, but I don't hit the earth. Instead I open my eyes.

The horrible smell is still in my nose, my mouth. I grab the bottle of whiskey and drink, hoping it will burn the smell away, but I swallow wrong and cough it back up instead.

Madda doesn't help. She just sits across from me, waiting. "Well?"

I struggle to find my voice. "I saw Sisiutl," I say, though my throat is hoarse and my neck burns where it bit me.

"I suspected as much. He wears many skins, that sisiutl, and has many names. Dragon, Wyrm, Wyvern, those are some of them. Doesn't really matter what you call him. He is what he is," Madda says as she presses a cup of water to my lips. "Drink. Come on, open up and drink."

I push it away. "I'll be sick."

"No, you won't. Spirit is trying to pull you back under. Drink."

The water sends my stomach into spasms and the pain on my neck gets worse. I touch it and discover blood on my fingers. "I'm bleeding."

"Let me see." Madda moves in close to inspect it, so close I can smell the stink of her perspiration. "How did that happen?"

"Sisiutl bit me."

"Hold still. Don't move a muscle." She thrusts a knife

into the fire and then pulls it out, pressing it against my neck without warning.

And all goes black.

I dream.

I dream that I'm surrounded by people I can't see because it's so dark, though I can feel them. They're pushing me, shoving me, kicking me. All of us are fighting for room, for we're contained within something that's small, far too small for all of us. And then the tapping begins. Someone is drumming outside the dark space, drumming so loud my ears ache and we begin to moan.

A beam of light breaks the darkness. An eye is peering at us—a black eye, so highly polished it reflects my face. The eye blinks, and then a beak reaches in. The others around me scream and try to hide, but they needn't worry. It only wants me.

I see you, *the raven says as it tries to pull me out.* I've got you now.

I wake. The fire is dead. The moon hangs above my head like a great pearl in the sky. The monolith is silent.

And Madda?

She's gone.

CHAPTER TWENTY-EIGHT

This has been the longest day of my life. The monolith started humming again hours ago, keeping me company as I wait for Madda to return.

Am I to stay here? Is this some kind of test where I'm supposed to try to find her? I don't know and can't find any trace of where she went, or even how to get back to the boundary, so I bide my time walking around the crater, searching the woods surrounding the clearing while the monolith watches.

The wound from the sisiutl throbs. I clean it with the water left in Madda's canteen, and then clean it again—anything to stop myself from dwelling on the fact that Madda is missing. *What if she's hurt?* The thought makes my throat grow thick. I call her name over and over until

I'm hoarse. No reply. No sound at all, save for the hum of the monolith. No bees. No birds. No frogs. Nothing but the monolith's incessant hum.

I dream.

I dream of Paul, floating in the ocean. His hair fans out around his shoulders and moonlight catches in his eyes. He spreads his arms and legs until he is a star, a spinning star in the sea, a starfish, a sea star. He looks at me and says something, but I can't make out his words. I lean close, and realize I'm in the water too, swimming toward him, when a great fin pierces the water and a creature swallows Paul whole.

And then I scream until water fills my lungs and I wake, drenched in sweat.

Night comes and goes, and still no Madda. I stuff moss in my ears, but it doesn't stop the hum.

Could I find my way back? Maybe, if I had paid closer attention, but the woods all look the same to me and I'm just as likely to end up back here at the clearing as at the camp. But the humming is getting louder and I can't shake the feeling I'm being watched.

I pass the time first by drawing concentric rings around the monolith, as if that will stop the hum, and when I grow tired of that, I use stone to make a great wheel, radiating out and away from the slab of obsidian. The stones are heavy, and before long, my hands are blistered and sore, but I don't stop. I just keep on working, doggedly, as if that will bring Madda back.

And then, something changes. A sound breaks through the monolith's hum. The snapping of twigs. I freeze. I can't make out where the sound's coming from, and all at once the entire world seems to spring to life with noise. Twigs snap, birds call, and my head reels. The humming ceases—a blessing!—but my nerves are shot and I whirl around, trying to find the source of the snapping. Something's coming.

I squeeze my eyes shut and when I open them, I see Cedar, Henry Crawford, and another man—I don't know him—standing at the edge of the clearing, staring at me. They hold rifles in their hands.

Cedar takes a step forward. "Are you okay?" he calls.

I realize they don't want to come close to the monolith. They're afraid of it. Their fear rolls off them, down into the crater. The monolith drinks it up.

I run toward them. "Madda's missing!"

"We know," Henry Crawford says. He slings his rifle over his shoulder. "We've come to take you back."

"But Madda . . . ," I say as the men exchange looks. "What? What's happened?"

Henry Crawford shakes his head.

"What does that mean?" My voice is flat with anger. "What's going on?"

Cedar reaches out and takes my arm. "Come on, Cass. Let's get back to the boundary and talk about it there."

"No," I snarl, pulling my arm back. "You tell me what's happened."

The men won't look at me.

"I have a right to know," I say. "I'm her daughter."

This startles them. Henry Crawford scratches his head. "She adopted you?"

I pull up my sleeve, exposing my shoulder to show him the tattoo as proof.

Cedar shakes his head. "Cass, no. Just come back, okay?"

I glare at him. "Don't you treat me like a child. You don't know me." I lean toward him. "But I see what sits on your shoulder."

Cedar's muskrat peeks out at me.

"I see all of your totems," I say, nodding at the other men—Henry's weasel, the other man's frog. "I see more than you can imagine."

Henry Crawford sighs. "Well, okay then. Showing you is probably the best way."

Cedar looks like he's about to disagree, but a warning glance from Henry seems to change his mind.

They give me a second to gather up Madda's belongings down at the monolith, and then we set off. I can't tell if I've won a battle or suffered a terrible defeat.

Madda is at the bottom of a cliff. I want to go to her, but I can't seem to make my legs work.

Madda, wake up. Wake up and ask me how to make a poultice for croup, or how much willow is needed to stop a headache, or what's the best way to fight a cold—anything. Just wake up. Please, wake up!

She doesn't move. She just lies there, her leg twisted at an unnatural angle, her head turned away from me. *Go help her!* my mind screams. *Get down there and make her better!*

But I know there is no helping Madda now. Deep down inside of me, I feel something break. I don't know what, but as it does, tears begin to sting my eyes. I squeeze them shut. I won't cry. Madda would want me to be strong.

One step. Just take one step. That's all you need to do, I tell myself, *one step to get started.*

So I do. Scree gives way beneath my feet, sending a cascade of stone and dust toward Madda as I scramble down the cliff. *Stop thinking*, I tell myself. *Stop thinking, don't think, don't think, you cannot think!* But my mind already is—*How long has she been here? How long has she been alone? How long did she suffer? Please, please say she didn't suffer. Please say that whatever did this to her did it after she was already dead. Please.*

I carefully turn her toward me. She stares up at the sky with eyeless sockets. One of her arms lies a man's length from her body. I collect it and set it where it belongs, and then begin to search for her eyes, scouring the ground, pushing stones out of the way, heaving them across the clearing, kicking at the dust, grappling at the broom leaning out from the cliff face. Where are they?

"Help me!" I scream at the men who are still standing at the top of the cliff, looking down at me. "Come down here and help me!"

I can't find them. I can't find Madda's eyes. I fall to my knees beside her and close her eyelids. She will never see the sky again.

This isn't Madda, I tell myself. *Madda is strong. Her tongue is sharp. She doesn't suffer fools kindly. This, this doll, broken and cast aside, isn't her.*

But that's only partly true. This was that person, once. Once was. Won't be again.

I rest my cheek on hers and cry.

After a time, someone makes their way down the cliff and sets his hand on my shoulder. "Come on, Cass." It's Cedar. "We need to go."

I wrench myself away from him. "No, we don't!" He tries to take my shoulder again, but I shake him off. "Don't you touch me! Don't any of you touch me!" I take Madda in my arms and hold her close. "I'm staying here with her!"

Cedar kneels before me. "Madda's gone. She's gone, Cass." He looks over his shoulder, and then off at the forest beyond the clearing. "We have to go. Madda would want you to leave."

"You don't know a thing about what she wants!" I hiss.

"Cedar," Henry Crawford calls from the top of the cliff. "Bring her up."

"Not until I know who did this!" I shriek at him. When I find the one responsible, I will grind him to dust. "You know. You know who it was. Tell me!"

Cedar takes a few steps back. "Not here," he whispers.

"Now you've seen," Henry Crawford says. "Time to go."

"We can't leave her here like this! We have to do something for her—build her a nest in the trees. Something!"

"No," Henry Crawford says. "She stays where she is."

I stand up and set my hands on my hips, like Madda would've done. "She deserves a proper place to rest, just like what we did for those men she tended back in the forest. Have you forgotten that already?" How dare he! How dare he suggest we leave Madda's body here, exposed, for carrion-eaters to pick at! How dare he look sad! She will be alone, so alone here. In the trees she'd have the wind and the rain and the sun. Her bones would bleach. Her skin would dry. She'd be with the stars, the moon. What better place to rest than under the heavens? How can they think of leaving her here? After all she's done for them?

Henry Crawford draws a deep breath and crosses to me until we stand nose to nose. "We are being watched," he says. "I'm sorry, but they want her to stay here." He casts his gaze to the trees. "They've claimed her."

"Who is they?" I say.

"You're the medicine woman, aren't you?" He narrows his eyes at me. "Shouldn't you know?"

The hair on the back of my neck lifts as I scan the tree line. I have no idea what, or who, is watching us, but I realize he's right. I can feel the eyes again, boring into my soul.

"You tell me," I demand. "You tell me right now who did this."

Cedar exchanges worried glances with the other men. They know, and they don't want to say.

We climb the cliff, and when we reach the top, just as I'm about to demand answers, something behind us screams. I've never heard such an unearthly sound. I jump and try to bolt forward, but Henry holds me back.

"Walk slowly," he says. "If they wanted you, they would have taken you already. They won't hurt you now." But his hand trembles.

"What . . . what is that?" I whisper.

"Dzoonokwa," Henry says. "A supernatural, from the old stories. The wild woman of the woods."

"Women," the other man says. "There's more than one."

"What are they?" I ask.

"Later." Henry Crawford nods at Cedar, who sets off again. "We need to get back before dark. But now you have your answer."

The screams follow us into the woods, though they grow fainter with time. Only then, when I can't hear them anymore, do I realize tears are streaming down my face again.

We arrive back at the camp at nightfall. I find the place where Madda and I abandoned our packs, and it hits me that the packs and all they hold are now mine. I sink down beside them, rest my forehead on the stiff, rough canvas. I don't cry. I feel like I should, like I need to, but I have no more tears. My eyes feel dry and raw and cracked. So, too, does my heart.

No one approaches me, though I feel many gazes resting on my back. What the men think, I don't know. I don't care. Staying away from me is the best thing they can do. I want blood.

Cedar dares to approach a short while later. He holds a bowl of stew out to me. "You should eat," he says.

"I'm not hungry."

"Suit yourself." He sets the bowl beside the packs and turns to leave, when I stop him.

"Tell me about the dzoonokwa."

He pauses midstep. "They're the wild women of the woods."

I groan. "Henry already told me that. I'm not in the mood to play games."

Cedar whirls around and glares at me. "I'm not playing a game," he snarls. "Dzoonokwa claimed Madda's soul, and now we're stuck with some stupid, half-trained half-breed who doesn't know a damn thing about the spirit world or the creatures of the forest." He storms off.

I throw the bowl of stew at his back, but I miss and the bowl bounces off into the bracken. I can smell the stew, and only then do I realize how hungry I actually am.

CHAPTER TWENTY-NINE

I can't see the stars. A fog has swept in, smelling of salt and kelp, and I'm so soul-sick, my chest aches. The sparks ebb and flow in swarms, washing in and out of my vision on a strange tide.

The men go about their business. A few of them sit around a fire. Someone plays a drum. Faint laughter echoes through the fog. All of it reminds me that I'm alone. I close my eyes and search my mind for Bran, for Paul, even for those damn ravens that never leave me alone—until now.

I've never minded being alone, but now I realize there's a huge difference between being alone and being lonely. No Paul, no Bran, no father, no mother. And now, no Madda. Who will I look to for help? Who will teach me what I need to know?

"Madda," I whisper to the stars, but I can't say anything more. How do I say that a piece of my heart broke when I saw her body? How can I walk this path knowing that creatures of the spirit world took her life? Madda, who is so strong. Was so strong. Tears push at my eyelids as, in my mind, Madda's face turns into my mother's, and then I'm no longer able to hold them back.

Later, Henry Crawford comes to crouch beside me. "I have work for you," he says.

My body is so heavy it takes all my strength to stand, but I make myself do it, and then follow Henry to the cabin. I won't let him see how much I'm hurting, though maybe, he knows.

The cabin is filled with a light so bright that my eyes burn when I step inside. Four men sit on hunks of wood, watching me. None of them speak.

Henry Crawford steps in and stands beside me. "Well?" he says. "You don't expect her to know what's going on just by staring at her, do you? Fill her in." He pulls up a rickety chair and nods at it. "Sit."

I drop into the chair and lean back, letting it support my spine. I'm so tired.

A rat-faced man frowns at me. "We have a problem, girl."

I force my eyes open. "My name is Cassandra, not Girl."

He blinks at me. "I'm Chris. Chris Johnson."

I nod. "So? What's the problem?"

"Plague. At least, we think it's Plague." His gaze shifts to the other men. "Got two men quarantined outside in the lean-to. Sick as dogs. Pocks on their face."

My heart stops beating. Plague among the Others? "Do they have chips?" I ask.

He nods.

"But you're sure they're Others?"

Henry Crawford nods once, slowly.

"How can that be?" I ask.

Chris Johnson shrugs. "We don't know—a new strain, maybe? We found them wandering around outside the boundary this morning. They've been in and out of consciousness since we brought them back."

"Oh god," I murmur. "So you've all been in contact with them?" They nod again. I shake my head. "We all have to be quarantined, then. Why didn't you stay away?"

Chris shrugs. "We thought they must be from the Corridor at first. Never seen Plague in one of us. We didn't know . . ." His voice drifts off as he glances down at his skin. I do too, before I can stop myself. My mouth fills with a sour taste, like I'm about to be sick. How long? How long until we start to show the signs?

"Anyone else been in contact with them?" I say.

"Just us."

"And now me, too, because I've been in contact with you."

"You're the healer. If you aren't protected, none of us are."

I lean toward him. "What's that supposed to mean?"

He sits back. "Nothing. Nothing at all."

A small, balding man who sits in the corner speaks next. "You look tired. You want something to eat?"

Yes, but I shake my head. "Later. Do any of you have symptoms?"

Chris shakes his head. "Not yet."

Maybe they're not really sick. Maybe everyone's made a huge mistake. My skin crawls and I look at my arm again, half expecting the black marks of Plague to be worming their way across my skin, but nothing's there. "I guess you'd better take me to them."

Chris steps outside, blows a single blast from the signal horn to let everyone know to stay away, and then leads us out. I notice Henry Crawford's brought his rifle with him.

The lean-to is directly behind the cabin. Chris enters it first, holding a lantern before him as he beckons me inside. I pause, draw a deep breath, and step across the threshold. Henry Crawford leans against the doorjamb and peers at the men on the floor. Even in the flickering light, I can see they're in bad shape. Only one of them is conscious.

Everyone's watching, waiting for me to perform some sort of miracle. *Think*, I tell myself. *Pretend you're Madda. What would she do?*

"Cassandra?" Henry says. "Need something?"

"Give me just a second." I draw a couple of deep breaths, trying to steady the pounding of my heart. "Okay. I need Madda's medicine kit. It's with the packs. Ask someone to leave it outside. We don't want to contaminate anyone else." Henry nods and disappears, closing the door behind him, sealing us away from the night.

I kneel beside the man who's still conscious.

"Am I dying?" he says. His voice squeaks like a rusty hinge.

"I don't know yet."

"You look awfully young to be a healer."

"I agree, but you don't have much of a choice, do you?"

He manages a rattling laugh. "I'll take what I can get."

I draw a deep breath and start examining him. Maybe, just maybe, I might be able to heal him. I unbutton his shirt. Pockmarks stud his chest. I touch one. Liquid ripples underneath. His forehead burns with fever. I move to the other man. The black spots have burst all over his body. They're seeping through his clothes, into the earth that he lies on. It's all I can do not to gag. I know that stink. I smelled it back at the monolith, when Madda sent me on the journey to find the sisiutl.

Just a coincidence, I tell myself. *Doesn't mean a thing.* Or does it?

The door opens and Henry steps in, interrupting my thoughts. "Well?" he says.

I shake my head. I don't know. "I'll have a better idea once I try a few things," I say, but it's more for the benefit of the conscious man than anything else. Hope works wonders, and when there's none to be had, sometimes we have to make our own. "You can go back to the cabin if you want."

"I'll stay," Chris says. "You might need someone to get stuff for you."

"Thanks." I smile. His thoughtfulness is a welcome surprise. "We'll need water. Leave a bucket outside and have someone pour water into it. Make sure they don't touch the bucket."

Chris and Henry head out. I'm left with the two sick men and a medicine kit full of plants. What am I supposed to do now?

I lift the lid and scan the contents. Devil's club. St. John's

wort. Mint. Lavender. No silver bullet. No secret anti-
dote. No magic potion. Nothing that will eradicate
Plague. Others just haven't had to worry about it, and
now, because of that, we're all contaminated. We may
all die a slow, painful death, just like these men. Or we
could do what my mother did, and end it right now.

That's just grief talking, I say to myself as I take a pinch
of each herb and begin to mash them together in a bowl,
working them with the knob of antler Madda once used.
St. John's wort for the pocks, lavender and mint to calm
and soothe the mind. *Don't get ahead of yourself. First
things first. See to the men. Do what you can. Worry about
what comes after later.*

Chris returns with the water and I add a little, mash-
ing the herbs into a fragrant paste.

"That smells good," he says. "Reminds me of what my
grandmother used to rub on my chest whenever I got a
cold as a kid."

The unconscious man starts coughing and the sweet
tang of St. John's wort is replaced by the stench of excre-
ment. Chris gags as I draw my shirt up over my mouth.
"Here," I say, offering him the mortar. "Breathe this in."

He does and hands it back to me. "Thanks."

I spread the paste over the conscious man's sores and
spoon a little water mixed with willow powder into his

mouth, but his gaze is already glassing over. Soon, he won't see anything anymore.

That leaves me only one option—to cross and see if I can find answers in the spirit world. The medicine kit contains sticks of sweet grass and sage, so I light them. Smoke drifts through the cabin as I close my eyes. Sparks pulse at the edge of my mind. I let them come.

I see a raven. He cocks his head, glancing at me, and hops away. *Come along,* he croaks. *Follow me. I can show you what you want to see.*

I take a step forward and realize my feet are not feet, but talons. Wings beat at my back and my tongue is that of a serpent. I stare at it, cross-eyed, in wonder.

Now that you know, you can shift, the raven says, dancing his jig across the path. *That's sisiutl's gift. Come. You must come now.*

He leads me into a thick forest, where I see a shadowy figure of a man on a path. *So,* the raven says as he lands on my shoulder to whisper in my ear, *you thought I was a trickster.*

"What do you mean?"

He shrugs as only a raven can.

The figure starts down the path, moving away from me.

"Do I follow?" I ask the raven.

Do what you feel is right.

The man begins to run as I draw near, forcing me into a run too. Thorns reach toward me, tearing at my skin, tangling in my hair. Thunder stirs the air and the sky breaks with lightning. The forest gives way to the twilight-lit lake. Gray fingers of rock reach out into it and on the end of one finger is the man. He's waiting for me.

I know who you are, he says.

Lightning flashes, exposing skin that is seeping and raw. Is this one of the infected men?

Why don't you come closer and find out? The man takes a step toward me.

"Get back," I growl.

The raven flutters down beside me. *You think he'll listen to you?* he cackles.

What have I forgotten? Something is clawing at my mind, trying to remind me that there's something I need to know, something I can do to save myself, but I can't think of what it is.

I'll offer you a deal, the man says. Lightning flashes again, this time exposing a man's face laced with scars. He smiles, baring a mouth full of fangs, and then blows a mouthful of breath at me.

It's such a strange thing to do that I don't react at first, not until the smell hits me—that terrible, rotten stench, sweet and sickly and noxious. My stomach flips as I pinch my nose shut, but the smell is in my mouth, in my throat, in my lungs. This was a bad idea—a terrible, terrible idea. I want back into my body, into the hut with the diseased men. I want away from this being who would devour my soul.

You're right to fear me, he says. *You don't know the paths of the spirit world. I do. I've walked here for ages, waiting for you.* He smiles. *I have your brother.*

"You lie," I say.

The raven hops up and down. *Oh-ho, I didn't expect that!*

Do I have your attention now? the man says.

"You do."

Good. I want you in exchange for your brother.

"Who are you, exactly?" I narrow my eyes. This exchange is not in good faith. I can feel it.

Does it matter? I have him. You don't. Simple as that.

Something in the water catches my eye. There, in the center of the lake, the sisiutl rises from the depths. Is it coming for me or the man? The raven cackles and lifts into the air. *Use your power,* he says. *Make the earth dance to your drum.*

What the hell is that supposed to mean? I wonder as the man crouches low to the ground, exposing a great dorsal fin rising from his back. He's primed to strike. And yet, something is making him wait. Why hasn't he attacked me already? He's said I'm weak, that I don't know the ways of the spirit world, so why is he stalling?

The sisiutl stares at me with its obsidian eyes. *Dance*, it says. Then, with a smack of its great head-tail, ripples race across the lake, right to where I stand.

I lift one foot and set it down, and then the other, more firmly. The earth shudders. I do it again, with greater certainty, and the shudder becomes a tremor. The tremors radiate out from me, running through the earth, sending rock and plant and tree rippling as if they are borne upon waves. Again and again, I dance and jig, lifting my feet higher and higher, crowing as I jump at the sky and drop back down, the earth trembling and quaking beneath me. This is my answer. *This man has my brother, and I will come for him. Oh, I will come for him and his captor will pay!*

And then sparks fly at my eyes and I'm back in my body. The hut is alive with fire. Screams fill my ears. Mine? I don't know. Someone drags me out and a blanket is thrown over top of me. The earth shakes. Trees shudder and groan as they topple. Men run across the red earth, trying to escape.

The hut and lean-to collapse in a burst of flames,

like bones of a long-dead animal trampled underfoot.

That's enough, I think, and the shaking stops.

I can smell the horrible scent of singed hair and I hope it's not my own. I touch my face. It's been spared, but a fierce claw of pain is coming from my right shoulder. I don't touch it. I don't want to know what's there.

Someone picks me up. Pain rips through my body, burning down veins and arteries, turning nerves to ash. I hear someone scream. Me. It's me. I scream and scream as I am burned to dust.

"Hold on," a voice commands. "Hold on to me, and don't you let go."

CHAPTER THIRTY

Sleep, Cassandra. Go back to sleep. You aren't ready to wake yet.

Madda?

Yeah, it's me. Don't worry about that right now. You need to rest.

Madda, it's all gone wrong.

Things are changing, that's all. Everything changes.

Am I burned?

Yes. The spirit world needs sacrifice. They need to see what we're willing to give up in exchange for their help. Nothing comes of nothing, you know. There's always a price to pay. Listen to me for a second. I never told you about my last apprentice. I'm with her now. She was taken by the dzoonokwa first, and she wanted me with her. I didn't protect her as I should have. The dzoonokwa know what it means to be mad, and they seek that insanity, flock to it like the way you and me are drawn to spirit.

So that's why you died?

I'm not dead, Cassandra. I'm still alive, in a manner of speaking. Just different now. You ever see my totem?

Only a bit.

Well, it's a dzoonokwa. Always knew I'd be with the wild women eventually—I suspect all of us end up with our totems sooner or later. Didn't expect it to be quite like this, though. Now I'll walk Dzoonokwa's paths, work her medicine. She doesn't have good eyesight, and she wants my eyes to see better in the world of the living.

Madda, did I cause that earthquake?

Yes. You did. Earth's lent you some of her power, because she needs your help. Just like the dzoonokwa taking me. They need my help, and I'm not sure they're done with you, yet, either. That's why I haven't crossed over to the land of the dead yet. But that can wait. Right now, you need to heal. So sleep. Don't dream. Do you think you can do that for me?

Yes.

Good girl. You got to stay grounded, stay sane; and rest, real rest, will do that for you.

• • •

When I wake, the first thing I see is the monolith. Its gaze is an accusation: *You should not have lived.*

And then I blink. The monolith is in my mind. Only my mind. Somehow that doesn't make me feel any better. My chest aches. I try to move, but I can't.

Someone dabs my forehead with a damp cloth. Cedar. "Shh," he murmurs. "You're going to be okay."

I try to nod, but my lungs are full of smoke and sweat and fear, so full there's no room for air. I take another breath, and another, until I'm gasping and my sides hurt.

"Slow down," Cedar says. "You'll hyperventilate."

Another face peers down at me. Henry Crawford. He doesn't speak. He just looks at me, his face creased into its angry river, and then walks away.

"You're on a stretcher," Cedar explains as he gently runs the cloth over my forehead again. "Your right shoulder—it's burned. You kept on having bad dreams where you were lashing out at something. We thought you'd hurt yourself, so we bound your arms. You're safer this way."

I don't believe him. There is something wrong in his voice, something he isn't telling me. "I want up," I say, struggling against my bindings even though it hurts so badly. "Let me up. Let me up right now!"

"Okay, okay. Just hold still," he says, but his voice

trembles. He unbinds the straps that hold my arms and helps me sit up.

My head spins. Cedar steadies me until the spinning stops, but the pain inside of me, the invisible pain of losing Madda—will that be with me forever?

And then I remember: Plague. I pull up the sleeves of the old work shirt someone has dressed me in so I can inspect my skin for the telltale black pockmarks. Nothing. Through the pain and the dizziness, I try to remember how long it takes for the first symptoms of Plague to appear, but my mind is fuzzy, unfocused. I can't seem to find the right piece of information. "The other men?" I force myself to say, because they're the only things I can see clearly, lying there on the floor of the hut, the Plague marks marring their skin. "The men in the hut . . ."

"What about them?" Cedar's voice is harsh, as if he's fighting to control it.

"They had Plague."

"Did they?" He squints at me. "That's not what Henry Crawford says. He says they were sick with starvation."

"But . . ."

Cedar leans in. "Starvation. That's what Henry Crawford says. That's what I say too."

I close my eyes. How long? How long now, until the men begin to get sick?

If they get sick.

Maybe I was wrong, just like Cedar says. Maybe those men didn't have Plague after all. Maybe they had something else, something I didn't recognize, because I'm hardly a doctor. I don't know everything. Starvation would be so simple, so easy to pin blame on. After all, we're supposed to be immune to Plague. No wonder everyone believes Henry. I want to believe him too.

And yet, when we return to town, we carry the infection to everyone there. Hasn't Henry thought of this? Hasn't anyone?

"Cass." Cedar brushes my hair back from my face. "It's done. What's done is done."

He's right. If we're to die from Plague, we will. I can't do anything about that, medicine woman or not, even if I wasn't in this condition.

But infect everyone else? I can try to stop that.

I must stop that.

I dream.

I dream I follow Bran and Paul through an ancient forest. Tendrils of silver Old-Man's Beard reach down to brush their heads. Their hands are bound. Their backs bear the stripes of a whip's bite. Paul is hurt; he limps. Bran holds his head high, forced back stiffly in an effort to appear unafraid, but I can smell the truth.

Who leads them? I peer into the shadows of the forest to see men without souls, without totems. Shadowmen with teeth that gleam in the moonlight.

And then the ravens come, swooping through the cedars in droves, beating me with their coal-black wings, driving me back.

Away, away, they shriek. Away!

I smell the fire before I see it. Smoke licks at my skin like a snake tasting the air. I should run. But I can't. The ravens fly around my head, shrieking, but I am rooted to the spot like an ancient tree. I will die here.

But the flame doesn't come. A shadowman comes instead, with his ragged dorsal fin, his face that is part man, part orca.

Sea wolf, sea wolf, the ravens shriek.

"I'm not afraid of you," I growl.

Oh no? the man says as he crouches down, primed to strike.

But before he does, I wake, drenched in sweat, panting, and with a mouth full of smoke.

The trip back is terrible. They feed me alcohol laced with willow bark so that when we stop at night, stars whirl above my head while my stomach heaves back and forth.

Three days ago I regained consciousness. How many days since we left the boundary? I don't know. All I know is that I won't take the whiskey anymore. Cedar pours it into a cup. He's decided he's my nurse.

"No," I say when he eases me up and puts the cup to my lips. "It's making me sick."

"It's making you better," he says. He doesn't take the cup away.

"I said, enough." This time I use my good arm to push the cup away.

He sits back on his heels. "You'll regret it later."

"Maybe, but I don't want any more. It's poison."

"Suit yourself," he says, setting the cup on a stump. "I'm going to go hunt." He grabs his rifle and stalks off.

Men mill about. An air of brooding hangs over them as they get ready for the night. Few look my way, but I hear them. Oh, I hear them as they whisper that the earthquake was my fault. It's almost laughable. How could a girl cause an earthquake?

Until I hear one of them whisper, *I saw her dancing. It was the dancing that did it.*

Was it?

I don't know. I remember becoming the sisiutl, and seeing the shadowman and the stench that accompanied him. I remember feeling sick, and then, yes, dancing—why dancing? It seems a strange thing to have done, though that's what I did—but I was in the spirit world. How would dancing in the spirit world equate an earthquake in this one? I know that what happens in the spirit world has repercussions in ours, but an earthquake? It just doesn't seem possible. Or plausible.

And yet, it happened.

What does that mean? What am I supposed to do with a power like that? Healing is one thing, but this? The ability to set the earth shaking?

They're wrong. They're crazy. It wasn't me. And just to prove it, I lift my foot and gently set it down. Nothing—no shudders, or tremors, or swaying trees. Nothing at all. I try it again, fearing what might happen, but I need to know. I need to know if it was me, if I'm capable of such destruction.

I wish Madda were here right now. I don't understand this. I don't understand how I could have done such a thing. I didn't know! If I had, I would have stopped dancing. . . .

And then what? The sisiutl told me to dance. It wanted me to do it, and it had to have known what would happen, even if I didn't.

Why would it want me to cause an earthquake?

But it's not just the earthquake, if "just" is even the right word at a time like this. It's what happened after. I haven't seen Chris Johnson. My heart hopes he's off hunting too, but something tells me he's not, that he's back there at the boundary, left behind. Was it the fire or the earthquake that took him? Doesn't matter, I guess. Both, I think, were my fault.

The men watch me. They've seen what I can do, and any lingering doubts why Madda chose me as her apprentice have been erased. I walk with greater care. I'm afraid of my own feet, and I almost laugh. How ridiculous is that? And yet . . . what if it was me? Why would I be given the power to cause earthquakes? What's the trigger? Anger? I remember being angry, but if it is anger, what if I can't control my temper? What if this power uses me, rather than me using it? What if I start something and can't make it stop?

One by one, I look at the men, making note of the faces. Who is missing? Who was lost in the fire?

The two men in the lean-to. The two men with Plague. Is that why the sisiutl had me dance? To destroy them before they . . . what? Before they destroyed me? No. Why would a supernatural need me, if that's all it was? They were dying anyway.

But the smell . . . the smell that made me gag when I

entered the lean-to. I encountered it again in the spirit world, a stench so intense that it almost had form. It followed the shadowman like his very own shade. Is that it?

I'm not sure, but I'd like it to be. Then all of this would be his fault, because if I caused that earthquake, if I caused that fire, if I set the world shaking by just danc- ing, what does that make me . . .

I remember Madda saying I was special, but *special* isn't the right word. *Freak* might be closer to the truth. And a danger—to everyone—if I don't figure out what this all means.

I squeeze my eyes shut. Madda once said that there is a duality in everything. We need water, but too much will kill us. Fire warms our bodies, but too much? My aching shoulder is proof of that. Too much food can be just as bad as too little. Too much sun? Too much wind? Too much rain? Life is about balance, she said, about walking that thin line between what is right and what is wrong. How will I know which is which? How will I know if this next footstep is the one that will set off another earthquake? If my next breath will cause a hurricane and destroy us all?

I don't. So for now, I keep on walking. Carefully.

The men have set their packs at the roots of a great maple. I spot Madda's among them and ease myself down beside it, carefully unwrapping the bandage wound around my right shoulder. I go slowly, the bandage crackling as dried blood breaks apart. It doesn't hurt, more or less, until I get to the final layer. What was once skin has adhered to the linen of the bandage. I stare at my shoulder, wishing I didn't have to do what I'm about to do. I can already tell that Madda's tattoo is gone. The skin has been burned clean away. My hand creeps up my neck, slowly, testing the remaining skin. The wound from the sisiutl is gone now too, but not because of the fire—because it's simply not there. I squeeze my eyes shut. First the earthquake and now disappearing wounds?

Henry Crawford walks by and sees me trying to pull the bandage from my shoulder. "That's gonna hurt." He crouches beside me. "Do you want me to do it?"

I nod. My voice has disappeared.

"All right. It's gonna bleed. You got something to stanch it with?"

I show him the handful of sphagnum clenched in my fist.

"Good enough. Take a deep breath. On the count of three, let it out and I'll pull. Ready?"

My forehead is damp with the cold sweat of fear, but I do as he asks. "Ready."

"One, two . . . three."

I scream as pain seers my body. Fire, fire, it's eating me alive, my body, my eyes, my brain . . .

Henry takes my hand and presses it to my shoulder, sending a shower of sparks through my mind, like cinders lifting on an updraft. The spirit world wants me. It wants me to cross over, and this pain is paving the path. Henry Crawford leaves, unnerved, as I try to blink the sparks away.

Slowly the pain subsides, leaving me with a thirst in my throat, a thirst that probably would have been quenched by Cedar's whiskey. But instead of going to get it, I remember something else. My hands find my throat. Bran's stone, and the pouch holding the sisiutl pearls. They're both gone.

"Please," I say to the next man passing by. "Who pulled me out of the fire?"

The man tilts his head toward Henry Crawford.

I make my way across the clearing, ignoring roots, the sparks, the humming in my ears, the insistent burning of my shoulder. "Please," I say to Henry Crawford. "Please, in the fire . . . when you found me . . ." I can't catch my breath. "Please," I try to say again, but it's nothing but air. Henry Crawford's face puckers into a puzzled frown. I tap my throat, my chest, pull my collar back to expose the notch of my neck. *Bran's spirit stone. Please, tell me you have it. Tell me it's safe.*

Henry retrieves something from his pocket and presses it into my hand—the cloth pouch, stained with soot. I roll it between my fingers, feeling the sisiutl's pearls inside, and then look at Henry. "My necklace? The one with the green stone?"

"You were holding that in your hand," he says. "That's the only reason it survived. Everything else was destroyed when the cabin collapsed."

"Oh." I run a finger over the hollow of my throat. My gut aches as my pulse collides with my finger. The spirit stone is gone.

CHAPTER THIRTY-ONE

I dream.

I dream I am sitting on the edge of the ocean, staring out at open water, looking for my brother, for Bran, but all I see is the sisiutl. Its head rises above the seafoam as it swims toward the shore. All at once, the ocean draws back, rushing away as if repulsed by the sisiutl, and I draw back too, for I've never seen it without water surrounding its body. Folded close to its back are a set of wings, glistening like mica, and as the sun beams down on it, I am forced to shade my eyes. This is no eel, no sea serpent. This is a creature of ages.

Drop your hands, *the sisiutl says in a voice that's as deep as the ocean, as thin as air.* Drop your hands and look at yourself.

My arms fall to my sides as I force my eyes open and stare at nothing.

We set out at daybreak. Cedar carries one end of my stretcher, a man named Joe Potter the other. I am permitted to walk for short intervals until my breath comes in shallow gasps and then they force me back onto the stretcher.

Ravens wheel above us, but they don't follow. They're content to watch from a distance.

A whistle breaks the silence and we draw to a halt. Six men, armed to the teeth, emerge from the ferns.

Stop! I try to yell to the men, but my words don't carry. Henry gives Cedar a quick glance. He nods, and my stretcher is picked up and moved out of earshot so I can't do any damage. I want to laugh, but I only choke. Damage. What damage can I do, compared to what Henry is doing at this very moment? He's shaking hands with one of the men, spreading contagion as if it's nothing to him, as if he's forgotten our history. Smallpox. Tuberculosis. Addiction. All brought into our communities by outsiders. I clench my hands. I will not allow this.

"Settle down," Cedar says, putting a hand on my shoulder to steady me. I'm so angry I'm trembling. "Cass," he says again, more deliberately this time, "get a handle on yourself."

"No," I say as I struggle against him. Doesn't he understand? Doesn't he get what Henry's doing?

But then . . .

I realize. The earthquake. The last time I was this angry, I caused an earthquake. All of a sudden I can't make myself calm enough. I hold my breath, bite my tongue, grab on to the sides of the stretcher so tightly that my fingers go numb. Despite what Henry could do, despite what he *is* doing, I am capable of far, far worse.

Henry steps back from the men and storms over to us. He points at me. "You," he snarls, "are to keep your mouth shut."

"We need to be quarantined," I say, every word as pointed as his.

"Do we? I say we don't. None of us shows signs and the incubation period is just about over. You've been so out of it that you've got no idea how much time has passed."

Is that true? Maybe. Possibly, but still . . . "But we've never seen this before, Plague in Others. What if this is a new strain? What if it behaves differently?"

He doesn't allow me to continue. "There's been no new cases since the earthquake. No new cases. We're safe. Got it?" He leans in close, so close I can smell his stinking breath. "And, in case you need reminding, don't forget who allowed your family to come here and gave you that nice house of yours. I can change my mind about that, you know."

"Go ahead," I say, though fear is thick in my throat and it's hard to force words past it. "See how well you do without a healer."

"Oh, I won't send you away." His smile deepens. "I need you. I've seen what you can do. But your father? Your brother? They're *expendable*." He leans on the last word, and I draw back. "I think you know what I mean." He waves a couple of the newcomers over. "Relieve Cedar and Joe. They've been carrying this stretcher all morning."

The stretcher swings as the men lift it up. I know what Henry is doing. He's keeping me from those who might listen. These new men, they don't care about me one bit. But why? Why is he doing this? Yes, it's true that the incubation period could be over, but why put the entire community at risk? How can he not understand this?

But, as we enter town, it's clear that it no longer matters. It's too late. People are waiting for us, and the moment we're sighted they come running over, hugging their husbands and sons, kissing their cheeks, welcoming them home. I turn my head and refuse to watch. What did this trip accomplish? Nothing. No refugees arrived at the outpost. The searchcraft? As far as I know, it's still in the woods. Maybe it's salvageable, but probably not. Madda? Dead, along with how many others? I still don't know. So what was it that we were supposed to have done? It doesn't make sense. None of this—my burns, the earthquake in my feet, the sisiutl in my mind—none of it makes any sense at all, especially when I open my eyes to see Henry Crawford throw his arms around a woman and a little girl.

I look away, sickened.

"Where are we taking you?" one of my stretcher-bearers says.

"Home." I want to go home. My father isn't here. I want to see him before I quarantine myself.

They lift the stretcher up and set out. The man at the foot of my stretcher keeps sneaking glances at me, until finally he says, "Pretty sorry to hear about your brother. I was out on the water with him. Nice guy."

"My brother?"

His gaze drops to his feet. "Oh. Um . . . well . . . he was in the canoe that didn't come back."

My heart stops. "What?" I whisper. Paul's canoe? It didn't come back? *Are you sure?* I try to ask, but when I open my mouth, nothing comes out. This man is wrong. He must be wrong. Paul? Missing? Does that mean Bran's missing too? I try to get up so I can run back to town, but my arm gives out and I almost fall off the stretcher.

"Whoa," the man says. "Take it easy. You'll hurt yourself."

I'm already hurt. I can't tell you how hurt. "Tell me what you know," I finally manage to say. My shoulder is aching so badly that my vision's gone spotty and my ears are ringing, but I force myself past it. I must listen. I need to know.

"Well . . . we're not sure what happened," the man says. "The canoe went out on patrol and didn't report back when it was supposed to. No one thought anything of it at first, because sometimes currents can mess things up." He won't look at me. "By the time we figured out that something was wrong, too much time had passed. There was nothing to find."

"So what's been done?" I blink, hard, trying to clear the spots from my eyes. "Who's trying to find them?"

I wait. And wait. And when no answer comes, I tip myself off the stretcher and fall in the dirt, but I don't care. I have to go back to town. Paul and Bran are missing. We need to go find them. We need to get them back.

All I manage is two steps before the blackness overtakes me.

• • •

Sometime later, I wake. They've bound me to the stretcher, so I'm forced to stare at the sky as they carry me toward our house. A few puffs of clouds cling to the blue. I want to touch them. I want to touch what's untouchable.

"No," I say when they start down the driveway. "No, leave me here."

The men exchange puzzled looks. "Here?" one of them says. "You sure?"

I nod. "Just go down and tell my father I'm up here, okay?"

He looks at me like I've lost my mind. Maybe I have. "All right," he says. "Will do."

A few minutes later, my father jogs up the hill toward me. My stretcher-bearers head off without a word, leaving my father and I to stare at each other. He's trying not to cry. So am I.

"Don't come closer," I manage to say. "I've been exposed to Plague."

"But you can't catch Plague." He's clearly puzzled. "None of us can."

"We can now." Something inside of me cracks. I think I'm going to cry, but instead, it's laughter that spills from my mouth. My ribs hurt and my stomach is clenched in knots and all I want is to stop, but I can't. No matter what I do, I can't stop—until I do. Just like that. But the tears streaming down my cheeks? They don't. They keep on coming.

My father kneels at my side and unbinds my hands. "Oh, Cass." He's about to say something else but can't, so instead, before I can stop him, he leans in and kisses both of my cheeks.

And that's that. Whatever happens next, we'll face it together.

CHAPTER THIRTY-TWO

We sit in the living room. A pool of sunlight surrounds us. I wear one of my father's old flannel shirts and a pair of his woolen socks, for despite the summer heat, I just can't get warm. My bones are so cold.

No pocks yet. No fever. No Plague. We both pretend we aren't waiting for its arrival, but I catch my father searching his arms whenever he thinks I'm not looking. I do the same. *How long, how long?*

My father tries to smile. "So far, so good," he says. "I went into town this morning, and before you ask, I was careful. I didn't go near anyone. As far as I can tell, no one there has come down with Plague yet either." He shrugs. "Maybe it was nothing."

What he means is maybe I was wrong. Maybe. That

certainly would be the easy answer. But I'm not ready to dwell on that longer than necessary. I have other things I need to know about first. "What did they say about Paul?" I ask.

He gazes out at the lake. "Not much. They don't seem too worried, or maybe they just don't care." His voice is bitter. "Grace has been hassling them too. I don't like that woman, but I have to admit, she's a force to be reckoned with. But the Elders, they're not budging. Not one bit. I get that it takes time to mount a rescue and that they don't know where to look and all that . . ." He takes a sip of his tea, but chokes on it. When he stops coughing, his words are raspy. "If it was their kid out there, I wonder if they'd be doing what they're doing right now."

"Dad," I say carefully, "did they tell you about Madda?"

"Yeah."

The lake is watching us, gauging our responses, mocking us with its serenity.

"She had a feeling, you know." One corner of his mouth curls up in a half-hearted attempt at a smile, but it fails and drops. "All that stuff about adopting you . . ."

"She said you agreed."

He shrugs. "I did, but I didn't really believe her about what was coming. I mean, she never spelled it out, either, but now that I think about it, she knew. There's a big difference between knowing and believing, though." This time, his smile is more successful. "Guess that makes you medicine woman now, huh?" His voice breaks and he gulps down another mouthful of tea to hide it.

"Yeah." My shoulder aches. "Dad, what are we going to do? How are we going to find Paul?"

He doesn't say anything at first. Instead he gets up and retrieves a blanket from his room, and drapes it around my shoulders before taking a seat beside me. "I don't know, Cass. That's a huge place, the ocean. I want to believe they're still alive, but I've spent too much time on the sea to think differently. And yet . . ." He takes a deep breath. "I think I'd know, wouldn't I? Wouldn't we?"

Yes, we would. Paul is not dead. Neither is Bran. For the first time, I think I can understand how Bran's mother must feel, holding on to hope when everyone else has long since bid it farewell. "We'd know, Dad," I say. "We'd know."

He nods. "I know you're right. Just . . . I've asked the Elders, before Henry came back, and they said they had to wait for him. And now that he's here? I've got to pray that he'll let me take a boat out, and then I'll have to pray for a miracle, because that's what it would take to find a canoe out there."

I close my eyes and try to see them, but all I can see

in my mind is the great gray expanse of the ocean. "We'll find them, Dad. We'll find them."

We sit that like for a while, my father trying to convince himself of something he doesn't believe, and me trying to figure out how to make it happen. We would need a boat, which we don't have, and we would need fuel, which we also don't have. But supposing we did, what then? The strait between the Island and the Corridor is more than thirty miles wide, and if they got caught in a current and were taken south? They could be anywhere by now.

No. I won't think that.

I will find them. I will.

Except . . . I am medicine woman now. *Sometimes you'll have to make hard decisions.* Madda's words come crashing down around me. I can't just go off in a boat. I have a responsibility to this community now.

Does that outweigh my responsibility to Paul and Bran?

I don't know. I'm not even sure I can *be* medicine woman. My training's hardly complete, for one thing, and for another, just because I was Madda's apprentice doesn't mean I'm medicine woman—or does it? Henry said I was, and he's an Elder, so maybe I am, and yet . . . "Dad," I say. "Do you think I can do this? Be medicine woman, I mean?"

"Yes, yes, I do." He nods to punctuate his words. "Madda wouldn't have taken you on if she didn't think you could do it. Me, I'm glad it's you and not that Avalon girl. At least Paul's away from her," he mutters into his cup.

That's a small mercy. A very, very small mercy.

I want to stay here forever, in this house perched above the lake. I want to wake to my father singing in the kitchen. I want to spend my days washing windows and picking rocks and listening to the blackbirds warble. I want to twist my hair into a thousand braids and whirl in circles, dancing like I did when I was small.

I want my brother to come home.

But my father is standing in the doorway, speaking words that I don't want to hear.

"You're needed in town," he says. "A boy's been hurt."

I'm not ready. Madda said not to heal when I wasn't well myself.

And yet, a boy is hurt.

"They're waiting for you down at the dock. I've got Madda's medicine kit ready for you," my father says.

This was my choice. I chose this path. So why can't I move?

My father takes my hand in his. "You can do this. I know you can. Put on a brave face and tend that boy like you've done your brother all his life." He touches my hair. "Don't let them see you like this, Cass. You aren't weak. Don't give them reason to think you are."

I want to tell my father he's wrong, that I *am* weak, but the look on his face—the one that says he believes in me—convinces me otherwise. "Okay," I say. "Okay."

My father smiles. "That's my girl."

He walks me down the hill to where two men bob in a big rowboat. Neither says a word in greeting. My father helps me in, hands me Madda's medicine kit—my medicine kit—and the men begin to row. I clutch the kit to my stomach and try to ignore the pain in my shoulder, the lump of stone in the pit of my stomach. How can I do this? I don't even know what's inside the medicine kit at this point. How much of the St. John's wort did I use back at the boundary? How much willow bark remains? What if I need to suture a wound and there's no gut? What if the kit's completely empty, so that when I arrive at this boy's side, I'll find I can't do a single damned thing? I should look, but I can't. I can't move at all. What kind of medicine woman will they think I am, wandering around with an empty medicine kit? What then? Will they laugh at me? Kick me out? Stone me?

The men dip their oars into the dark water and pull, dip and pull, and there, beyond the wake, is the sisiutl, watching me with its glassy black eyes. He's coming along to see what unfolds, and when I fail, he'll swallow me whole.

But the sisiutl stops swimming and floats there in the water, just under the surface, as the boat draws toward the opposite shore. If anyone looked at it, they'd probably think it was a dead-head. Maybe it is. Maybe none of this is really happening. Maybe the shades aren't really shades. Maybe the sisiutl isn't really a sisiutl at all, but a trick of light that my brain has interpreted as something supernatural because that's the only way I can make sense of this twisted reality I live in.

I turn my gaze to the sky. I don't want to look at the lake anymore. If this world is a figment of my imagination, shouldn't I be able to look at these two men in this rowboat and see Paul and Bran at the oars instead? Shouldn't I look back at the dock and see my father standing there with Madda?

The man across from me frowns. "You okay?" he says.

"Yeah," I say. "Just fine."

And I will be, I tell myself. *Just wait and see.*

They beach the rowboat on the southern end of the lake, not far from Bran's house.

"That way," one of the men says, pointing toward the

neat rows of an orchard. He helps me out of the boat. My feet sink into the sand as I watch them paddle away.

I turn my back on the lake and head to the orchard.

Women cluster around my patient. They part as I approach. I recognize some of them from that day in the park, when Helen invited me to make baskets with them. They watch me with blank expressions, as if they don't know me. And they don't. They don't want to, either. I'm here to heal, and then leave. I'm an outsider. I know it. They know it. And that's just the way it is.

Helen is kneeling beside the boy who's lying on his back unconscious. I almost drop the medicine kit. Helen. Who has lost Madda too. I draw a deep breath and walk toward her, hoping she'll look at me. How could I have forgotten Helen? Who told her?

Doesn't matter who told her, my mind whispers. *It should have been you.*

It should have. Yes, it should have, but I was too lost in my own grief, my own pain, to think of anyone else but myself. The need to apologize, to make amends, to make everything better is so strong that I have to bite back the words, because now isn't the time. Right now, that boy on the ground needs my help. Fix him first. Fix the rest after.

A dark-haired woman sits beside Helen, cradling the

boy's head, weeping. She looks up at me. The woman from the park. The one who shunned me.

Doesn't matter, I repeat to myself. *Fix the boy. Fix him. Concentrate on that. Put the rest away.*

I crouch beside Helen. "What happened?"

"He fell," the mother says.

"From how high?" I glance up at the tree above us.

"I wouldn't know, would I? I wasn't here when it happened." Her eyes are angry and red. "You're the healer. Heal him."

Someone behind me snickers. Suddenly I can tell that this is a test. Heal the boy, and I pass. If I don't, I'm nothing more than a half-breed outsider. My shoulder is throbbing. I pry the boy's eyes open and find the whites staring back at me. His pulse is light and fluttery; his forehead cold. I gently check for broken bones but find none. No contusions, no scrapes, either. If I didn't know better, I'd say he was sleeping, but he isn't. I can feel it. "Someone must be able to tell me what happened. You don't expect me to work magic, do you?" I say.

Helen gives me a worried look. "We aren't sure what happened, actually. He was climbing trees, but no one saw him fall."

"Okay," I say. "How long has he been lying here?"

"About an hour."

An hour. I sit on my heels and bite back a groan. An hour. An hour! And I haven't the faintest idea what's wrong with him. Did he have a seizure? Is he in a coma? And if he is, what can I do about it? I open my medicine kit and stare at the bundles of herbs. What powers do they have? What latent magic do they hold within their petals, their fragile leaves, macerated and broken into pieces as if that might give them sway over life and death?

Helen touches my arm. "What do you need?"

I try to convey my gratitude in my smile, hoping she'll understand, and maybe, forgive. "Water. A fire."

She nods and goes to talk to the other women, leaving me alone with the boy and his mother.

Madda said that if all else fails, look for the source of physical ailment in spirit, and right now, that's all I think I can do. Madda also said I shouldn't go into spirit when I'm not well, and goodness knows I don't want to, but I have no other choice. Maybe there I might be able to see what's wrong. I hang my head. This is a bad idea, but what am I supposed to do with nettles and mint?

All I know is that I have no choice. I must heal this boy.

Helen brings me a bucket of water as the smoke blows past me. "I'm so sorry," I whisper to her as the other women mingle around, looking worried and frightened.

"Not now." Helen holds her breath. "I can't. Not now. You can't either." She tips her head in the direction the other women. "We've all heard about what happened at the boundary. You're going to do spirit medicine?"

"Yeah." I scatter a handful of sweet grass over the fire. It bursts into flames and the air fills with its perfume. "I can't tell what's wrong with him physically. I figure a look into spirit might be of some help."

She squeezes my hand, taking me by surprise. "Good luck."

"Thanks." I hope my hair hides the blush burning on my cheeks. "The boy—what's his name?" I ask.

"Saul," his mother mutters. "You going into spirit?"

"Yep," I say as I draw a big breath. "I don't know why he's unconscious. I might be able to find out in the spirit world."

"Look for an elk." She nods at me. "That's his totem. Bring my boy back."

"I'll do my best." Smoke swirls around my head. I waft it over my face, over my body, down toward my feet, and around my womb. Silence—the strange, otherworldly silence that accompanies a shift from the here-and-now into spirit, the silence of a passing season, the silence of death dancing, drops around me like a cage. I close my eyes as the sparks approach, and cross . . .

. . . and open my eyes to find myself sitting beside the fire, right beside the boy, still surrounded by Helen and the other women. I'm not in spirit. I close my eyes and try again, and again.

I fight back tears of frustration. I can't let him die. I can't. *Madda, help me. Help me help him!* I close my eyes, and try again.

This time when I open my eyes, I'm in spirit, but floating far above the lake. I stretch out, trying to drop from the sky, but I'm suspended there. I can't move a muscle. Below, I can just make out something crawling along the lakeshore, something that feels . . . wrong. A fog has risen, a black, poisonous, stinking fog. It slinks along the ground, past the lake, winding its way past willows and stumps.

A stench rises up to where I hover, that foul, putrid stench I've smelled before, but this is the first time I've seen it take form. I stretch my wings wide, ready to plummet back to the earth and do battle with it, but before I can, a star drops toward me. A second follows. I hover, transfixed, as stars continue to fall, showering me, scorching my skin. Starlight sears my wings, cuts through my flesh, drives into my soul, and then the heavens shake and all the stars come loose, diamonds slipping through the hands of time, and me slipping with them.

No! I scream, though all that comes from my mouth is a hiss. *No, don't send me back yet! I need to stay. I need to find Saul!*

But something in this spirit world has made the decision that Saul is not coming back, that I must return without him, and if I don't do so willingly, it will send me back against my will—the hard way.

The smell of woodsmoke comes first, followed by onions. They linger on the breath of the person standing over me, shaking me.

"Cassandra, wake up. Open your eyes."

I try, but sunlight burns them and they shut on their own.

"I mean it. Open your eyes and keep them open."

I try again, and this time, have a little better luck. Helen's face swims before me.

And then the wailing begins.

Time slows as I turn my head in infinitesimal degrees toward the boy. I did not find him. He has died while I was gone. He has died.

The women rush past me to his side as I watch, dumbstruck.

His mother raises her head and howls, and when she brings her gaze back down, her eyes fix on me. "You! You did this!" She claws her way through the other women, struggling to reach me.

Helen steps between us and I almost push her aside. I want to feel this woman's pain. I want her to beat me, to hurt me. I failed, but Helen takes the woman's flailing hands and holds them. "She tried," I hear her say. "She tried."

The woman snarls and pushes Helen away. She seizes my arm and twists it, trying to wrench it from its socket. I feel a searing pain as the newly healed skin on my shoulder rips. She shoves me to the ground and leaps on me. I don't struggle. I let her push my face into the dirt and hold it there.

"You die too!" she screams, slamming a knee into my kidney. "You go with him!"

All right. I will. There's nothing left for me here. I am the reaper of lives, not a healer. They're better off without me.

I want her to do it.

The woman laughs. The sound is high, distraught with lunacy, and then, someone pulls her off me.

"What the hell do you think you're doing?" a man says.

I know this voice of salvation. Cedar.

I lie in the dirt while the woman stares at me, blinking. Tears slip down her cheeks. "You're just a girl," she says, as if she's seen me for the first time. "Just a girl." Her head bows as she walks back to her son, drops down, and gathers his limp body in her arms.

Cedar helps me up. Blood has stained my shirt, but I no longer feel the pain in my shoulder. I don't feel anything at all.

"Are you okay?" he asks as he glowers at the other women. "Jealous cows. Didn't lift a finger to help her, did you? Just let her get beat down, and whose responsibility was Saul? Not hers. She crossed into spirit even though she almost died a week ago, and you blame her? Who was supposed to be looking after Saul? Why aren't you beating that person?" He brushes dirt from my face.

"It's okay," I mumble. "It's just a bad situation."

Helen hands me my medicine kit. "I think you better go," she says as the mother begins to howl again. "She'll be all right, but still, I think you'd better go. But I know, Cass. I know you tried. I saw."

CHAPTER THIRTY-THREE

I sit in the prow of Cedar's rowboat, staring at my palm. A burn the shape of a star is there. What does that mean? It's like the lines are blurred between the spirit world and this one, but why? And that fog—what was that? How could I have any hope of succeeding when faced with something like that?

Maybe I wasn't meant to succeed. Maybe this was something beyond me. My job is to heal. If something— something more than me—decided Saul wasn't to be healed, then maybe I couldn't have done anything anyhow.

But that doesn't feel right either. That fog—it's wrong. It's . . . polluted. Evil.

The sun warms the air around me, but I don't feel it. A chill has seeped into my soul and it's from more than the lingering effects of spirit. Helen. Who told Helen about Madda? It should have been me, and it wasn't, and the fact that I completely forgot all about her is eating at me as much as losing the boy and the fog and the fact that I wasn't any help at all.

Cedar doesn't say a word during the crossing, and when I get out of his boat and stand on the dock, he just rows away. It's just as well. There are no words for what happened this afternoon.

I climb the hill to the house, dragging a bucket of water along with me, and when I'm sure I'm alone—really alone—I strip down and wash my skin carefully, as if I was preparing a body for burial. Ashes to ashes, dust from my skin. I dab water onto my poor shoulder, ripped and bleeding. It stings like fury, but I'm glad. Maybe some pain will drive sensation back into my heart.

I dress in a plain white nightgown, climb the stairs to my room, slip into bed, and wish for sleep.

But it doesn't come. The memory of Saul, as pale as wax, lying under that tree, washes through my mind. His mother follows, angry and red-faced, staring at me with her accusing eyes. I try to call to mind those I love to replace her. Madda, so I can ask her why she left me before I was prepared to take her place. Bran. Paul. The point to my star.

But only tears come, so I cry myself to sleep.

• • •

I dream.

I dream I am walking in another time, another place. Bran and Paul are here. I can feel their presence, but I can't see them. I search and I search, and nothing. Paul has shut me out. He doesn't want me to follow, and I can only imagine what terrors he and Bran face.

I shut my eyes and try again.

The house is dark. I rise and tiptoe downstairs. My father stands outside on the balcony, staring at the stars.

The wood is warm under my bare feet, and I hardly make a sound as I steal outside and rest my head on his shoulder.

He gently tugs my hair. "Difficult times are ahead for you, Cass."

"I know, Dad."

He wraps an arm around me, taking care not to touch my shoulder. "This isn't what I had hoped for you or Paul."

"I know, Dad. It isn't your fault. No one could have known any of this would happen."

He draws a deep breath. "I know. But still . . ."

"Don't worry, Dad." My hand finds his. "We'll find Paul. Don't know how, but we'll find him."

He kisses my forehead. "We will. But we won't do much finding if you're falling down exhausted. Go to bed, starshine, and get some rest. You're going to need it, because tomorrow, I'm taking you to Madda's . . ." He pauses, dropping his chin to his chest. "Your place. It's your place now."

My place. The words ring hollow. My place. *I have no place*, I want to say, but I don't. I just turn to go back to bed, but then change my mind. "Dad," I say slowly, "do you know who told Helen? About Madda?"

He scrubs his chin. "I did. She's still staying with Ms. Adelaide. Figured you weren't in any shape to, and I didn't want it coming from the Band men."

"Oh, Dad. Thank you."

He ruffles my hair. "She'll still want to talk to you about it, you know."

I do. And I will.

But right now, all I wish for are words strong enough, words deep enough, to tell my father how thankful I am, how lucky I am that he's my dad.

We leave for Madda's at noon. I carry a basket of clothing, nothing else. Everything I need is already there waiting for me.

My father doesn't speak. Neither do I.

When we finally arrive at the cottage's gate, I half expect Madda to poke her head out from the blackberries, shears in hand, to wave us in. I know she's dead. I know this in my heart and I know it in my bones, but I still can't quite believe it. My brain has stubbornly decided that it will rule me, and what it says goes. Madda is not dead. She's just off in the forest, or working on the blackberries, or puttering around the cottage, and any minute now, she'll stroll over to the truck and ask why I look like I've seen a ghost.

"Best get it over with and go in, don't you think?" my father says, though he's not anxious to get out of the truck either.

Still, one of us has to make the first move, and since I'm the one who will be living here, I guess the task falls to me. I slide out and push the gate open. Blackberry canes have come loose from the arbor and have twisted over the walk to the cottage.

"Good thing Madda has a machete. I'll go get it," my father says with a quick smile—too quick—before he rushes off to collect it from the woodpile.

When he returns, I pace while he hacks the canes back. Each stroke is a reminder that I don't belong here. This is not my place, and each step down the path reinforces that Madda is not coming back. Ever.

The air is soon sweet with the scent of the ripening blackberries. *How long until autumn?* I wonder as I look at the canes my father has hacked down. I can't afford to be this wasteful. I should have found a better way— tied them back, maybe, or picked the berries first, even though most of them are still hard and red. Will they still ripen? They must be good for something, mustn't they?

My father sees the panic that's spreading through my body. He stops and wipes the sweat from his brow. "You don't need to live here, you know. Madda would understand. She'd be disappointed, but she would understand."

I want to ask him why. Why me? She could have chosen anyone, so why me? If I left now, would I be free of all of this? No one would miss me here. Hell, they don't even want me here. Someone else could do this. Someone else could take my place.

But that's not true. Madda *did* choose me. That meant she had faith in me. Leaving, even if I had somewhere to go, would be dishonoring that faith. I'll find a way.

A raven lands on the apex of the roof and glares down at me. I glare back and inch toward the door.

"Almost there," my father says. "Just one more step."

My hand falls on the handle and with a held breath, I turn it. The door swings open. "Okay," I say.

"Good girl." My father pauses to wipe his brow again. "Do you want me to come in with you?"

I stare into the darkness. Time to face the ghosts that lurk within. "No," I say. "But maybe come for dinner tonight?"

"Sure," he says. "That sounds good."

I turn then and notice he's on the verge of tears, but he ducks his head, sets the machete on the doorstep, and trots down the path before they can slip from his eyes.

I don't know how long I stand there in the doorway. Long enough for my shadow to stretch out across the floor. Long enough for my legs to begin aching.

Finally I force myself to step inside and set my basket down on the table. Everything is just as Madda left it. Herbs are strewn on the workbench. Bundles of bandages spill out of a box. A sweater is draped across a stool. Two pairs of old shoes sit by the hearth. A walking stick. An empty glass, complete with fingerprints. A half-eaten biscuit. A hairbrush. This is what remains of Madda.

"Stop thinking," I mutter as I roll up my sleeves and pick up the bucket by the door. If I work, I won't think.

The rest of the day is devoted to cleaning. Tomorrow, I'll go to Ms. Adelaide's and talk to Helen. I'll understand if she doesn't want to live here anymore, but I'll ask her just the same. And then, once I've done that, I'll figure out how to persuade the Band to send out a search for my brother and Bran. I'll lead it, if I have to.

I scrub the little kitchen with its polished enamel sink and tiled floor. Dust motes float in the air as I sweep the floors. Night approaches, so I build a small fire in the cookstove. Madda's garden is full of squash and corn, and I'll feed my father some of both.

My arms ache, but it's a good ache, the ache of hard work. My face is smudged with dirt and so are my hands, but oddly enough, I'm also happy—so happy that when my father arrives, he looks shocked for a moment, as if he doesn't recognize me. We eat in silence, each of us offering careful smiles, because I think we're both afraid to break the mood.

Later, after my father has left, I open every door and window in the house to invite the night inside. Evening air permeates the cottage. I pull a chair close to the fire, pretending that I'm not tired yet, but I am. I just can't bring myself to go into Madda's bedroom. It's too soon. I'm not ready.

But the chair by the fire is comfy and warm. Good enough for now.

More than good enough for now.

• • •

I startle awake. Moonlight paves the floor and the fire has died.

Something isn't right.

I scramble to a window and peer out at the forest.

I can't make out a thing, but I am certain, beyond doubt, that someone, something, is watching me. Every hair on my body stands at attention.

Nothing moves. There is no sound. Even the crickets have ceased their singing.

I steal through the house as quietly as I can, shutting the windows, barring them in place, locking the doors. Tomorrow, I will dig through Madda's notes and set up every warding I can find.

CHAPTER THIRTY-FOUR

*F*irst thing in the morning, I start making plans: Get the Elders together. Talk to them. Figure out how to find Bran and Paul. And make them take me along. It all seems manageable. I'm medicine woman here now—I must have some say!—until I think of Saul. My first duty as medicine woman ended in tragedy, and the Elders will have heard of that by now.

Doesn't matter, I tell myself, but suddenly I'm overwhelmed with a desire to do anything but walk into town and face the Elders. It feels like Madda's here, working in the garden or grinding herbs at the table. I can't see her, but when I close my eyes, I can sense her. *Help me, Madda. Give me the strength to face those men. Help me convince them that we need to do something, that Paul and Bran are still alive, and they need our help.*

But that's not what she wants.

What she wants is for me to go into her room.

I fight it, but no matter what I do, I keep finding myself standing at her bedroom door, hand on the doorknob. Three times I turn away, but on the fourth, I grit my teeth and make myself open the door.

Time has stopped in here. The bedcovers are rumpled. A robe lies on the floor. Underwear dangles from the arm of a wicker-backed chair. The wardrobe stands open, its arms wide, ready to receive me. The windowsill is jammed with books. I run my hand over the spines, leaving tracks in the dust as time begins to beat again. A cardigan has fallen behind them and I pick it up. It smells of earth and roses—just like Madda. This is how I will remember her.

I shake the cardigan, loosing a layer of dust, and a letter flies from one of the pockets, skittering across the floor. The envelope is made of thick, homemade paper, speckled with rose petals and lavender. My name is scratched across it in Madda's spidery hand.

I pick it up and crack the beeswax seal.

Cassandra,

If you're reading this, then I haven't had a chance to burn it, which means I'm not around. I'm really sorry that I've left you with such a burden, but even if you don't believe it, you're ready. Now you just have to trust that, which is the real test.

There's a loose board in the floor of the pantry. My herbal is in there, along with a couple of bottles of opium and some whiskey. Don't leave the herbal out in the open. There's a lot of stuff in it that's not for ordinary eyes— stuff that's a bit dangerous, especially if used by someone with less than honorable intentions. The knowledge in there is generations old and once it's lost, that's it.

And, for god's sake, if you decide to go rambling around in the spirit world, protect yourself. There's a whole section in the herbal on wardings and bindings— learn them, memorize them, LIVE them. You're strong, but you're still pretty green, and it wouldn't take much for a creature of spirit to use you as it wants.

This is going to be a trying time for you. Everyone's going to test you, especially the Elders. Speak your mind. Trust that you know right from wrong and don't let anyone ever tell you otherwise.

I know I don't need to warn you about Grace, but I'm going to anyhow. She's going to be hell-bent on

separating you from Bran. Keep him close. Marry him
if you have to, though that's not any guarantee, but ties
that bind are useful, you know?

And be wary of Avalon. Darkness always resents
the light. Besides, you know what they say about
keeping your enemies close. That's what I would do,
if I were you. I thought she would be my apprentice
once, after my failings with the last one, before you
came. But you know, as she never could, that all this
stuff—healing, the spirit world, these paths we walk—
it's not about us. See past yourself to the things that
need doing, and do them when no one else will. Don't
choose the easy route. Choose the one that's true.
You'll know which that is, because when you close
your eyes and feel your choices, the right one always
feels open, even though you know it's going to be hard.
And don't forget—you're a survivor, Cassandra. Look
at what you've been through. You keep on going, keep
on fighting, even after your mother and your home
and your teacher were ripped away from you. And I
have a feeling there's more to come. That's what sisiutl
can give you—the power to endure when you think
you can't. But you can. I know you can. That's why
Dzoonokwa was keeping her eyes on you too. Everyone
wants you on their side.

If I had time, I could fill a book with all the things you need to know, but I guess some of them you'll just have to figure out for yourself. The last thing, and maybe the most important: If you think you're being watched from the woods, you are; and if you're reading this, you probably know what, or who, those eyes belong to. Talk to Adelaide. She can tell you about them. She's the only woman I know of who has faced the dzoonokwa and survived. Go and check the wardings on the burial ground—if they're still missing, get them back up as soon as you can. I should have done that myself, but there just wasn't time. It's probably not a bad idea to set up a few on the forest side of the cottage either. Whatever you do, show them you're strong. They'll probably respect that. After all, you've got the sisiutl on your side. Not everyone can make that claim.

I wish I could have been a better teacher to you. There just hasn't been enough time. There's never enough time for anything.

Madda

The letter is dated the morning after the gathering. So this is what she saw when the madness took her—that she had no time left. Madda knew. She knew. I read the letter again, and again, and then, when the words are etched in my mind, I feed it to the fire. An immolation seems the proper way to send Madda off.

When all that's left is ash, I wrap Madda's sweater around me and head out.

Time to pay Ms. Adelaide a visit.

Ms. Adelaide peers at me from over the top of her cracked cup. "Madda said what?"

I hold an equally cracked cup between my palms, inhaling the smoky greenness of real tea. How long has it been since I've had a real cup of tea? I don't remember. The scent almost makes me forget what I'm here for, so when Ms. Adelaide clears her throat, I have to force myself to look at her. "Oh. She said to ask you about the dzoonokwa."

She frowns. "Why would she say that?" Her voice has lost its customary friendliness.

"Because they're watching me."

"How do you know?" She narrows her eyes. "You seen them in spirit?"

"No. I think they're in the forest, just behind the cottage. Madda said to talk to you about them."

Her teacup rattles on its saucer as she sets it down and looks out the window. "Good thing Helen's off at the orchards this morning. . . ." Her voice trails off. "Well, this changes plans."

"Plans?"

"Yep. If the eyes are on you, sleeping alone isn't such a good idea. I'll stay with you tonight, to see what's what. I'm no Madda, but I'll do my best. Besides . . ." She smiles at me. "I killed a chicken and I baked a blackberry tart this morning. Chase them down with a glass of my parsnip wine and you'll forget all about the eyes. I've got a few things to do here, and then I'll bring them along this evening."

"And Helen?"

Ms. Adelaide frowns at her teacup. "I'm not sure. She might need some time, see? Madda took her in after her stepdad kicked her out, and Helen—well, Helen needs a mother. Her own didn't do a very good job." Ms. Adelaide picks at a loose thread on the tablecloth. "I never had children—never wanted them at first, and by the time I did, it was too late. I guess if that's what Helen needs me to be, I'll be that, because you aren't ready yet, Cass. Not for this. You got enough on your plate, don't you think? Oh, and by the way, the Elders are meeting at the longhouse right now. Figured you'd want to know."

"Thanks," I say. I'm about to head out, but I stop and turn back. "Ms. Adelaide? Would you tell Helen . . ." I pause and draw a deep breath. "Would you tell her that she's always welcome at the cottage?"

Ms. Adelaide smiles. "Sure, Cassandra. I sure will."

The first time I entered the longhouse, I was summoned. This time, the watchmen salute me as if we have been friends for a very long time. They're on my side, and they'll back me if anything goes wrong.

The men are sitting on the benches in the great room, clustered around the fire. They don't notice me at first. They're bent over a map, pointing at this and at that, talking about rebuilding the outpost at the edge of the lost lands. It's the stupidest idea I've ever heard. The land has made it clear that it doesn't want us there.

Henry Crawford is the first to notice me standing in the doorway. He sits up and nods. "What can we do for you?"

I take a step forward. "The lost canoe—I want to know what's being done about it."

The rest of the men look at me as if they're seeing a ghost. Good. They should fear me. Cross me, and I'll dance those stories right out of the longhouse walls, line up the supernaturals and get them to dance too, right over these men who think they know what they're about.

"We're not doing anything," the heavy-jowled man that

I now recognize as Cedar's father says. "Not the first time a canoe's gone missing."

"And if it had been Cedar in that canoe?" I say. "Would you be saying the same thing?"

"Look here," Henry Crawford says, rising and coming to stand by my side, blocking the other men from my view. "I know you've had a hard time. You've gone through a lot. We haven't forgotten—it's just that other things have got to happen first."

I look at him and the angry river on his face. Rage wells in my gut, and I only have one response for him. "No."

He drops his voice. "You aren't making this easy for yourself."

I whisper back. "You aren't either. You've forgotten I know those men had Plague. Have you told the other Elders that? That you've risked everyone's life? And for what?"

He rocks back on his heels. "You were sick. Delusional."

"Don't you dare try that with me," I spit. "I know. I stayed away. I waited until I was sure I wasn't sick. But what about you? Did you tell the others from the boundary to quarantine themselves? To not go near anyone until you were sure? Did you hug your wife? Kiss your children?" I lean toward him. "What kind of man would do that? What kind of chief does that?" He takes a step back. "Help me bring Paul and Bran and those other men home, because they're still alive. I've seen them. Please, help me."

Henry Crawford doesn't say another word. He just stares at me for a good long minute, turns, and goes back to the other men. They return to what they were doing, pointedly ignoring me as if to say, *See, girl? This is what power looks like. We hold your fate in our hands. We'll do with it just what we like, and don't you dare think otherwise.*

A line has been drawn in the sand. A line that I have no fear of crossing.

As soon as I get back, I start making plans, beginning with laying out all the contents of Madda's medicine kit on the table, making careful note of what's missing, what's depleted, what's stale. Once that's done, I head outside to the garden to replenish my stock. Bran and Paul might be hurt, or sick, or both. This time, I will be prepared. This time, I won't fail.

I'm in the middle of picking lemon balm when someone says, "I heard you were back."

I sit up so suddenly that my head spins. Avalon stands on the other side of a trellis, laughing at my reaction. "So, this place is yours, huh?" she says, rounding the end of the trellis to give me a curious smile. "Pretty lucky."

"I'd hardly call it that." Lucky that Madda's dead? I wonder if Avalon is aware of what she's saying.

She isn't. She picks a daisy, tucks it behind her ear, and turns to regard the cottage. "Well, this should be fun."

"Fun?" I peel off my work gloves and suck out a thorn that's found its way through the stiff leather. "Not really. Just a lot of hard work."

"Depends on how you look at it." She whirls around, her skirt fanning out around her. "Are you hurt?"

I almost laugh, but catch myself. She means my hand, not the burns, or Paul, or Madda. What must it be like, I wonder, to only see the surface of things? "Just a scratch," I say.

"Let me see." She takes my hand into her own and examines the drop of blood, and then presses the flesh around it.

"Hey," I say. "That hurts."

She shrugs. "My father says that's the only way to get the germs out. You're not the only one who knows about healing, you know."

"Right." I pull my hand away. She's up to something. "Come inside. I want to put some salve on this," I say.

Avalon smiles, and I'm pretty sure those words are exactly what she wanted to hear.

She pokes around while I dig out a jar of salve, and as I dab some on my finger, she sidles up to the door to Madda's bedroom and sets her hand on the knob.

"Don't go in there," I say.

"Why not?" Her smile is innocent and beguiling, but I can hear the challenge in her voice.

"Because."

She shrugs as if she doesn't care and turns to pick at a bundle of sage that sits on the hearth. "So, how is Cedar?"

"Cedar? I don't know. Why?"

"No reason." She puts the sage back and moves to inspect a basket of speedwell. "Grace was glad to hear you're back."

"I'm sure."

"She's been making me read to her, but I'm not a very good student." Avalon flops down into the battered arm-chair in the corner. A cloud of dust frames her like a halo. "I mean, I like to read well enough but not those stories. And not to her. She has some strange ideas. She's decided I'm her student."

I arch an eyebrow. "Student? Of what?"

"Oh, this and that." She yawns and stretches out. "I like it here. Maybe I should study with you instead. Madda was teaching me before you came." She picks up a bundle of pennyroyal. "She said a tincture of this stuff can get rid of a baby. And other stuff can help you get one."

"You shouldn't mess with that sort of thing. If you don't know what you're doing, you could end up bleeding to death. Something you want to tell me?"

"Nope," she says, crushing a leaf between her fingers before setting the bundle down. "I'm just making conversation."

Right. Now I'm seriously annoyed. "Avalon," I say, "what do you want?"

She turns toward me slowly. For a moment her eyes are clouded by mist and for the first time, I catch sight of her shade—a fox. A cunning vixen. It's never occurred to me that she might have a shade, but there it is. She must have been hiding it all this time, a skill I would never have imagined Avalon to possess. Just what did Madda teach her?

"I want," she says, "what everyone wants. I want a place to be. I want something to belong to. I want my life to be normal." Tears well at her eyes and she brushes them away quickly. "Do you realize how incredibly selfish you are? Do you think you're the only one who's lost something? Lost someone?" Her words fly from her mouth, darts laced with venom, and each strikes me squarely in the heart. "You think you're so special, but I'm sorry, you're not."

She storms out, slamming the door behind her.

I watch her run down the lane, dumbstruck. She's right. I'm not the only one who has lost someone. Avalon has known loss too, and that's shaped her into the person she is now. Does she have a mother? What does her father do? I don't know. I've never thought about it. I've never thought about Avalon in any way except how she might harm Paul, or what threat she is to me.

Does that erase what I know of Avalon? No. I can't forget the night when I saw her push that bottle into Bran's hand. What kind of person would do that? Nor can I forget the way she treated Helen the day we arrived here on the Island. Or what she said to me about Paul.

But there's a reason Avalon acts like that. Maybe, once, she was just a girl. Maybe, once, she was like me.

As Avalon vanishes from sight and I turn away from the window, I find that maybe I don't dislike her as much as I did. Maybe I even feel a little sorry for her.

Thunder rumbles in the distance. It's going to rain.

CHAPTER THIRTY-FIVE

*M*s. Adelaide arrives at the cottage just as the sky is turning a dusky purple. Helen's not with her. My heart sinks as I rush to the gate and try to pull it open, but Ms. Adelaide just shimmies her way through. "Well," she says, looking at the garden as we make our way back to the cottage, "you've got lots of work to do, huh? Gonna need some help."

"I can do it."

She raises an eyebrow at me. "Honey, those are foolish words. No one gets through the cold months on their own around here—not even Madda. You'll need a winter's worth of food, because when the snows hit, no one goes anywhere. If you don't have a healthy cache stashed away by the end of summer, you'll starve before the thaw comes. Make sure you trade healing for a portion of the salmon run. I'll teach you to smoke it. And get that Cedar to hunt you some venison."

I startle at the mention of Cedar's name. Why am I the only one who's certain that my brother and Bran are still alive?

Ms. Adelaide stops by the door, waiting for me. I jog the last few steps. "Sorry," I mutter.

"No apologies," she says. "You got a lot on your mind."

She lights the fire while I gather onions in the garden. When I return, she's boning out the chicken, tossing skin into a bowl, humming to herself. I stand by the door, feeling like a trespasser. She's the one who seems at home here.

She looks up at me. "You okay? You look like you've seen a ghost."

I smile. "Not today."

She takes the onions from me. "See them often?"

"What? Ghosts?" I shake my head. "No. Just people's shades. Ghosts are Paul's thing."

"Hrumph," she grunts as she halves an onion and drops it into a pot. "Now, let's see." She glances at the mess on the counter. "I need some garlic. Got any out there?"

"I think so. I'll go check."

A driftwood fence is the only thing that separates the back garden from the salmonberries creeping in from the forest, and they've decided a little driftwood isn't going to stop them. I make a mental note to tackle them tomorrow before they run riot.

Garlic flowers twist like tormented swans at the far end of the fence. I rip one from the ground and the air blooms with sharpness. The bulb's still a little small so I pull a second, straightening up just as a bat darts close to my head. A bat. *I haven't seen one of those in ages*, I think, as it dips and weaves its way toward the forest, veering off just before it hits . . . a dzoonokwa. I rub my eyes, and blink. Yes, she's there, almost hidden in the twilight shadows. I can just make out her bloodshot eyes and the flecks of spittle at the corners of her enormous lips. Gnarled knots of hair fall over her shoulders. A bark skirt hangs at her hips. She takes a step forward and in a rasping voice calls, *Hoo, hoo.*

I cannot move. My legs are clay; my tongue, gone. My hand pulls the pouch that holds the sisiutl's pearls out from under my shirt and some small part of my brain has the wherewithal to hold it up so the dzoonokwa can see it.

She cocks her head, considering the pouch, and then takes another step forward. Another dzoonokwa joins her, and then, another.

"What do you want?" I whisper. "What do you want from me?"

"Cassandra?" Ms. Adelaide's voice floats out of an open window. "You okay out there?"

"No," I say. "Close the window and bar the door."

"What?"

"Just do it." My voice trembles. "There are three dzoo-nokwa standing at the edge of the forest, watching me."

"Cassandra, come inside," she says. "Just walk away like you never saw them."

"No." My voice stops trembling. My hands stop shaking. I hop the driftwood fence, garlic bulbs in hand, and walk toward the dzoonokwa. They murmur and mumble as I approach. My heart flutters in my chest. Which heartbeat will be its last?

The first dzoonokwa snarls as she fishes something out of a basket on her back.

How will they kill me? With their hands, like they did Madda? With a club hidden in that basket? Will they wait for me to stop breathing before they begin to gnaw on my bones? The dzoonokwa straightens up and howls. The others join in. Then they fall silent as the first one lobs something into the air. When it falls at my feet, they turn and run into the forest, the darkness swallowing them whole.

My heart thuds against my breastbone as I scan the trees and wait for them to return, but they don't. My teeth have started to chatter, and only then do I realize just how scared I actually am.

Grass rustles behind me and then a hand falls on my shoulder. "Girl, whatever possessed you to do that?" Ms. Adelaide says.

I can't answer.

"Damn stupid girl," she mutters, shaking her head. "The stupidest and bravest thing I ever saw. Take that damn bundle they left you and let's get inside."

"The garlic," I say, holding up the tiny bulbs.

She laughs. "The garlic? You come face-to-face with three dzoonokwa and all you can think about is garlic? Clearly we need to get some food inside you, because you've gone crazy." With that, she steers me back into the safety of the cottage.

Once we're inside, with the door locked and the windows shuttered, Ms. Adelaide sits me down and goes back to what she was doing as if nothing happened. The bundle rests on the table before me. Cedar bark, bound by rotting string, covers it. I close my eyes so I don't have to look at it, and listen to the clank of Ms. Adelaide setting the stew pot on the cookstove, the pop of a cork being pulled from a bottle, glasses clinking together, and the rush of something being poured.

"Here," she says, slipping a glass of parsnip wine beneath my nose. "Drink it."

The wine is sweet and musty, a strange taste in my

mouth after the sourness of fear. I'm aware of Ms. Adelaide waiting for me to swallow, but I can't. I just swirl the wine around and around my mouth, because I'm not sure that I'll be able to keep it down.

When I finally swallow, the wine drops into my stomach, and a burst of warmth rises up. I sigh, a deep, releasing sigh that makes my bones go slack.

Ms. Adelaide smiles. "There," she says, settling back. "My parsnip wine will fix just about anything." The words are light, but I see the cloud of worry in her gaze. "Good thing no one else was here to see that. Best not speak of it. You've got a mighty strong way with the supernatural world, that's for certain, but this . . ." She gestures at the bundle on the table. "I've never heard of anything like it."

"Should I open it?"

"Suppose so."

A shiver runs down my spine. The last thing I want is to touch the bundle. Grease on the bark glistens in the candlelight. Where did that grease come from? Some poor animal? An unsuspecting child? Madda?

Ms. Adelaide cuts the string with a paring knife. "The rest," she says, "is up to you." With a faint smile, she picks a tangled skein of wool, sits down across from me, and begins to unravel the knots. "Staring at it won't make it go away."

"I guess not," I say, but that doesn't mean I'll touch it. A pair of tongs rests by the hearth. I grab them and fish the bark away. The pieces come off, one by one, to reveal a smooth, translucent moonstone hidden beneath the layers.

My breath catches in my throat.

The chair creaks as Ms. Adelaide reaches out to me. "What's wrong?"

It takes several minutes before I can tell her. "That's Madda's," I whisper. With a single finger, I reach out and touch it. It's icy cold. "What am I supposed to do with it?"

"Now, don't panic. Just sit for a bit. But first, burn that bark. The dzoonokwa touched it."

I fling the bark into the fire where it bursts into blue flame. "That's not normal."

Ms. Adelaide snorts. "Honey, when you're dealing with supernaturals, nothing is normal, and it's unreasonable for you to expect it to be. You probably want to know why it's you they've chosen. I wondered the same thing once, back when Dzoonokwa came to see me. You're young, you're strong, you're as smart as a whip. And you're pretty—the gods like the pretty ones."

"Gods?"

She shrugs as she rummages around in the pantry. "Gods, spirits, Elders, whatever you want to call them.

Shining Ones—that's my own favorite." She emerges triumphant, a kettle in one hand and a canister in the other. "Aha! I knew Madda had a stash in here!" She sets the kettle on the stove. "Whatever you call them, they're the same thing, and they're all part of this land. They're waking up and they're not happy. If I was a bettin' woman, I'd bet you're their voice."

I let my head fall to the table with a dramatic *thunk*. "They? Who's they?"

"The spirit people, the ones from the old stories, Cassandra." Ms. Adelaide looks at her hands, turning them over to expose her palms. "These hands are supposed to tend the land, care for it, nurture it. This voice? For telling the old stories, for keeping our way alive, and it's not just our way—it's *the* way. Look at the Corridor. Do you think what's happening there is a coincidence?"

"It's a big leap from Plague to gods and myths, Ms. Adelaide," I say.

"So it is, but how does it feel to you?" She cocks an eyebrow at me as she sets the kettle over the fire. "Take a second. Feel it out."

I close my eyes and think about all that's happened, about the shades I see, about walking the paths of spirit. I think about the sisiutl and the earthquakes and how ravens haunt my every step. I think about Bran with his shifting shade and my brother's relationship with lost souls, and how we came to the Island. I think about Plague, and the sea wolf, and the poisonous cloud that works with him. Everything happens for a reason, and nothing—absolutely nothing—is without meaning. I stretch my hand out toward the moonstone, hesitating for one moment, and then wrap my fingers around it, claiming it. This has been given to me. I don't know why, but there's a reason. There's a reason for everything.

Ms. Adelaide nods as if she knows my answer.

"So," I say, "what do I do now?" My fingers wrap around the moonstone, tracing its smooth, cold planes, over and over. *What do I do, what do I do, what do I do?*

Ms. Adelaide sinks into the armchair, shuffling back and forth until she's comfortable. "I'm not sure, but what I do know is that the creatures of the old stories are seeking you out." She points at the moonstone. "Madda told you about the making of the boundary?" I nod. "Well, here's a bit more of the story for you. Back when that happened, the women who made the boundary asked the supernaturals for help, you know, all the old ones. Raven, Thunderbird, Sisiutl, Wolf, the ones from the old stories, except, that's the thing. They aren't stories. They're living myths, and those creatures, they're as alive as you and me. You know that now. Anyhow, some of them agreed to help, those that still had hope for humans. Some just wanted to cause trouble, like Raven, and look what happened to him. And the dzoonokwa, well, my guess is they just don't care anymore. People have been hunting them for ages, trying to take their picture, making up all sorts of lies about them, so I don't blame them for ignoring us. But when the boundary went up, they got stuck in it."

"In? Like, they *are* the boundary?"

Ms. Adelaide nods. "And now the boundary's failing, which tells me that the supernaturals aren't going to last much longer, either. They don't belong to us, Cass. They aren't ours. This place, this haven we've created?" She casts her arm around me. "It isn't for free. Everything costs something. I know we think we're safe here, but are we?" She peers at me. "Are we really? Or do we just think we are, because that's what we want to believe?"

I'm not sure she's really talking to me anymore, but her words hit me in the face just the same. "So what exactly am I supposed to do?" I ask. All the hair has risen on my arm. "Free the dzoonokwa? Just how do I do that?"

"I don't know, but then, it's not for me to know. It's your task." She reaches out and squeezes my hand. "But I think you'll be okay. One dzoonokwa could have killed you in the blink of an eye. Three? They could have torn you limb from limb, but they didn't. They need you for something. Just remember that Dzoonokwa's not bad. She just is what she is. She takes the life of some people; she gives others beautiful things. Special things. You know what that spirit stone is, don't you?"

"Sort of. Madda told me the story, but I'm not sure I understood it entirely."

"Well, I imagine you know that there are only two left—that we know of, at least. That one was Madda's. Now it's yours. A little bit of the wearer stays with the stone forever and ever, so your ancestors are always with you. You just have to listen, and they'll help you along, but you have to know how to listen first, and that's the hard part. The monolith was a gift from the supernaturals, and so is that stone. You have a piece of spirit, and now, by wearing that stone, it has a piece of you."

"So Bran's . . ."

"Is similar, though his stone is bound more to the land." Ms. Adelaide yawns. "Now, stir that stew, would you? Don't want it to burn." She goes back to her wool while my mind spins. Spirit stones. Supernaturals. Old stories. The land. And the task Dzoonokwa has set before me.

Then it dawns on me—Bran's spirit stone. If I've lost it, the thing that binds Bran to this land, where, exactly, does that leave him?

CHAPTER THIRTY-SIX

I dream.

I dream I stand in a circle of light. Across from me is Paul, standing in his own circle, and when he turns around, I see he's changed. One half of his body is covered in black feathers. They're dull and ragged. Some have fallen out and lie at his feet, leaving white, pebbled bird flesh exposed at his shoulder, his flank. His right arm is a wing. He stands with his shoulders slumped, his back curved, as if at any moment he'll curl into the fetal position.

I reach out to him, stretching my hand across the circles of light.

Paul raises his head slowly. When he sees me, his lips form the word no, *and when I don't stop trying to reach him, he brings his winged arm across his face and pushes me back. Again. And again. And again. And again.*

Leave me alone, *he says.* Leave me alone. Why won't you ever leave me alone? Leave me, leave me . . .

I can't, Paul, *I say.* I can't.

Then I leave you.

And just like that, he's gone.

I wake to the sound of a flight of geese making their way south. The seasons are beginning to shift.

My back aches from a night curled up in the chair and my head is still fuzzy with sleep, but something has changed. If Paul doesn't want me in his dreams, that's one thing, but if he thinks he's turned me away, he's mistaken.

I've just finished dressing when my father's truck pulls up outside, laden with firewood. He gets out and starts unloading.

I dash outside to help.

"About time you got out of bed," he says, laughing at first, until he sees the look on my face. "Everything okay?"

"No." I feel like I want to hit something. "I met with the Elders yesterday."

"Oh." My father scowls. "Why don't you go put the

kettle on? I've brought wood for you—figured I wouldn't use it all myself. Let me get it stacked, and then we'll talk, okay?"

But putting the kettle on doesn't do anything to assuage my anger, so a few minutes later I'm outside, helping my father pack alder and fir to the far side of the house. We don't talk. Not yet. I'm still too angry, and my father? I don't know. Sad, maybe. There's something about the way he moves, the way he balances each piece of firewood so carefully on the one below—too carefully, maybe—that tells me something's not right.

The shriek of the kettle's whistle calls me inside to make tea. There's still some blueberry pie left, so I put it on plates and take it out to my father. He rolls up his sleeves and washes his hands under the spigot of the rain barrel, thoroughly, thoughtfully, like he used to back in the Corridor, and then sits down on the chopping block. I hand him a cup of tea.

"It's real," I say when his eyebrows shoot up in wonder.

He takes a sip and sighs in appreciation. "Real tea. And blueberry pie. Did you make that, too?"

"No. Ms. Adelaide did. She came by yesterday."

"Did she?"

We continue making small talk, because we're not ready to change the mood just yet. But we must.

CATHERINE KNUTSSON

"So," my father says. He sets his teacup down on the woodpile and spreads his fingers wide over his knees. "What did the Elders say?"

"What do you think? They gave me some excuses about needing time, that this isn't the first canoe to go missing, that I need to be patient."

My father draws a deep breath. "Cass, we have to be careful with this. Really careful. It isn't that they're doing nothing—they're doing something. Just not what we want them to do. I want Paul back as much as you do, I promise you that, but . . ."

"But what, Dad?" My father's shade, his robin, has appeared at his shoulder, dragging its wing. Wounded, or just pretending to lure a predator away from its young? Which is it? I can't tell. "What is it that you're not telling me?"

"Cass," he says, "they don't want to find that canoe. I get the feeling they may know where it is, or, at least, where it was, but . . . it's not Paul. They don't care about him. It's Bran." He sits back. "Grace Eagleson has been hounding me every day, begging me to make the Elders listen, because they won't to her, but I've gone to see them twice now. Paul and the other men in the canoe are insignificant—innocent bystanders, if you will. They haven't come right out and said that, but . . . think about

382

it, Cass. With Bran gone, where does that leave them?" He balls his hand into a fist. "Without anyone who has a claim to be chief." He sighs. "There wasn't much hope in finding them anyhow, Cass. Even if the Elders knew where they went, a single canoe out on that sea? They could be halfway across the ocean by now, if they got caught in the wrong current. I fished out there when I was young. That ocean? She's unforgiving."

"So," I whisper, because I can scarcely believe what I'm hearing, "are you telling me that I shouldn't try? That I should give up? That you've given up?"

"No." My father fixes me with a steely look. "But we've got to be smart about this. You just can't go running off on a fool's chase. I'll help you if I can, but it has to be you, Cass. If I do it, well—let's just say the Elders aren't afraid of hurting you. I think Henry knows you've got some power, but the rest? They think you're just some girl. Who knows what they'd try to do to you if I weren't here. I can't take that risk." The steely look begins to fade. He's fighting tears too. "I'm sorry, Cass. I'm sorry this is the way it is."

"You could come with me," I say.

He shakes his head. "I could, but then, once we found them, what would we do then? What would we have to come back to? Besides, there's always a chance Paul will find his way home. Someone needs to be here for him."

There's more to it than that. I don't know what, but if my father says I have to do this alone, I will. I trust him.

I hug him. He smells like sawdust and tea. "I'm going to go tomorrow, Dad."

He kisses my cheek. "Then I'll see you soon."

The remainder of the day is devoted to preparations. Spirit's my destination. The journey begins when I pick up Madda's stone, douse it in salty water, string it on a leather strand, and fasten it around my neck. It feels different than Bran's spirit stone, cool and soft, nothing like Bran. Nothing like Madda. Maybe that's because this stone's mine now, and Bran's never was.

My next stop is the forest, Madda's herbal in hand. As I give thanks and sever a bough from the nearest cedar, I remember Madda's advice about putting wardings at the burial ground. Helen will know where the boundaries are, but on the other hand, maybe I'll just take my sweet time and see how the Elders feel about that. Then we'll see who holds the real power.

Two ravens fly overhead. They circle round and land on the limb of an alder.

If I can face the dzoonokwa, I can face anything, I decide. "Shoo!" I yell, and they burst into flight, voicing their raucous opinions as they wheel away.

I dig for wild ginger and scrape moss from a maple tree, thanking each plant for its gifts. Before long, my gathering basket holds rocks and branches, roots and mushrooms. And then, I gather stones. They'll be for more than marking the boundary of the fire ring. The herbal says to mark the boundaries of now and not-now, of here and spirit, so that when I want to return, they'll guide me home, just like the breadcrumbs left by Hansel and Gretel, except this trail won't be gobbled up by ravens. Granite is for the quarters, marking out the directions of the wind. Quartz is for the cross-quarters to provide protection against anything or anyone who would seek to harm me. This time, I will do everything exactly right because I must, I *must* find what I'm looking for. There is no other option.

As I strike flint against steel, I think of the lost ones, the souls who speak to my brother and drift between worlds. What of them? Maybe there's a way of helping them after all—if I could only find a way into their twilight. Smoke puffs from the handful of moss in the center of the fire ring as I wonder if Paul's already found a way there. Maybe that's why he was so strange before he left. Maybe that's why he doesn't want me in his dreams anymore.

Smoke circles around me as I finger Madda's spirit

stone, and that's when I realize I've got the means to find Bran and Paul right in my hand. All I need to do is ask the spirit stone the right question, and it'll give me the answer.

Dusk tiptoes off, making way for the heavens. It's a perfect night, this night without a moon. I close my eyes, inhale the smoke, and feel the shift. I'm no longer where I was a moment ago. When I open my eyes, I am in the strange twilight world of spirit.

A raven cackles and hops down from a tree. *I know what you're looking for. I can lead you to what you seek.*

"For what price?" I ask. I know this raven—it's not just a raven, but *the* raven, the one who found man, the one who is the monolith. He does nothing for free.

He cocks his head this way and that, considering me. *I wouldn't mind that stone at your throat*, he says, bobbing his head.

I touch the spirit stone. "No."

Croak, he says as he hops toward me. *I thought as much. Perhaps a favor—not now, but when I need it most. A favor. That's my price.*

"And how do I know you won't ask for my left eyeball, or my firstborn, or some other awful thing?" There's no way I'm making an open-ended deal with this trickster.

You don't, he says, flapping his wings as he begins to

hop from foot to foot. *But you and I have been friends for a long time, Cassandra. There was a time when no one would listen to you except for me. Have you forgotten that time? Should I help you remember?*

I'm about to tell him that I don't understand when he flies at me. Before I can cover my eyes, his wings strike my face and a flood of memory washes over me. I see a world torn to pieces by fire and war. I stand apart, watching as the gates to a mighty city open, admitting a wooden horse taller than the firs of the forest. I scream and scream to stop, to burn the horse where it stands, but no one listens to me, for I have no tongue.

The vision shifts and I see a man on a barge. I can't tell if he's alive or dead. I slip into the water, shape-shifting to the sisiutl, and follow the barge. I know this man. Silver stains his auburn hair. It is Bran, an older Bran, worn thin and haggard by time. He is guarded by four women in black robes, and I know they are taking him to his resting place. He reaches out to me, but before I can touch him, someone strikes me with a sword and I sink back into the water, the sword embedded in my side.

The scene shifts again and again. I am a maiden standing in a field, calling the name of god. I am Sybil, Brigid, Skadi, a thousand names in a thousand tongues, proclaiming the truth of a thousand mysteries, and no one will listen to me.

The vision passes and I fall to my knees on the gravel shore beside the twilight lake.

The raven hops to my side. *Did you find what you were looking for?*

"I'm not sure. Do you know what I saw?"

Oh yes. He hops closer and pecks at my hand. *You have much work to do. This time, we all have too much to lose.*

"What does that mean?"

He cackles. *You'll see.* The raven opens his mouth wide. It stretches into a gaping maw and when I look inside, I see he has no tongue. He snaps his bill shut. *Even I am bound by laws, Cassandra. They bind you, too. But there's a way around them, if you have the courage to break what cannot be broken.*

"Stop speaking in riddles," I say.

The raven croaks again and bobs his head, then takes to wing. *I've spoken as plain as I'm permitted,* he says, now circling around my head. *Shall I show you what you're looking for?*

I don't want to trust him. I know I shouldn't, but in this world, I have just as much power as the raven, and if he tries to trick me, I'll find a way to trick him right back. "Yes," I say as I feel my body begin to change again. "Show me where my brother and Bran are."

The raven waits as I lift from the ground and fly after

him. We cross immense forests of thick fir, rising on warm currents, skimming the peaks of a mountain range. Beyond is the ocean and behind us, the mainland, with the yellow haze from the Corridor clinging to its coast like the slow creep of fungus.

There, the raven says, *where the sea wolves swim. Find the sea wolves and you'll find what you seek.*

I turn to thank him but he's gone, and I find the trees rushing up to impale me as I plummet back to earth.

When I wake, the fire is dead and my clothes are damp with dew. My head aches. My throat is raw and sore. I find my way to my feet, stumble toward the rain barrel, take a drink, and then go inside and fall into Madda's bed.

My bed.

It's my bed now, and I plan to stay here until I have slept away every last bit of fatigue and sorrow in my bones, because tomorrow, I will leave to find Bran and my brother—no matter what.

CHAPTER THIRTY-SEVEN

$\mathcal{I}$'m awake well before dawn. The cottage is quiet. Outside, the sky is pink and gold. A good day for a journey.

I've just put away the breakfast dishes when someone knocks at the door. When I open it, Helen is standing there, a pack on her back.

"Helen," I say, "you don't need to knock. This is your house." I move out of the way so she can step inside, aware that she knows the cottage better than I do. She's the one who belongs here.

She sets the pack down on the table and turns to face me. "No, it isn't. It's your house, Cass. I have something I need to tell you."

I open my mouth so I can apologize properly, so I can

tell her all the things I've wanted to say since I got back, but she shakes her head. "No. Sit. Listen."

So I do.

Helen takes a seat across from me and folds her hands on the table. "Cass, I knew. I said my good-bye to Madda before she left."

"You knew?" I can scarcely believe what I'm hearing. She nods.

"Madda told you?"

Helen shakes her head. "No. Do you remember that day at the store, the day you came to the Island? When I told you I knew you were coming?"

It's my turn to nod. I had just assumed that Madda had told her.

"Sometimes I just know things. I can't say how, exactly. Just . . . they pop into my head, and I know that they'll happen. Not all the time, and not as often as when I was younger, before . . . well, before. But I knew about Madda. She told me not to tell you. She told me you'd try to find a way to stop it, or give yourself up in her place, or something like that."

For several moments I can't do anything but blink at Helen. I can't believe what I'm hearing. "You knew," I say again, because it's all I can say. She knew.

Somehow that doesn't help, and I find myself looking at a knot in the wooden tabletop so she doesn't see my tears.

That's when I remember the pack.

"What's that for?" I say as I touch the stiff leather.

"You're going on a trip. I'm coming too."

I brush my tears away and look up at her. Her jaw is set, and even if I said no, I'm pretty sure she'd still follow. "Okay," I say. "I'll be glad to have you." Though *glad* doesn't even touch on the relief that I won't be alone.

"You'll need a boat," she says.

I can't help chuckling. "You've got this all planned out, don't you?"

She shrugs. "I've had some time to think things through. Madda's skiff is in the estuary. Henry's claimed it but, well, I have the key." She digs it from her pocket and dangles it in front of me. "Not much good to him if he can't start it, is it?"

"You know how to pilot a skiff?" I ask.

"I helped Madda run hers during herring season," she says. "I think I can make do."

"We might have to go out into the strait."

"As long as we've got the fuel . . ."

"Oh." I hadn't considered that. It's one thing to steal a skiff that's rightly ours, but fuel's something else. "Any way around that?"

"We could siphon some from the other boats," she suggests.

"No way. We'll have to figure something else out."

We pack quickly. I have no idea how long we'll be gone. All I know is that we're going. The rest will fall into place. I stuff the pack with sweaters, blankets, jackets, Madda's medicine kit (I'm sure I'll need that), and whatever food we can find in the kitchen—mostly the dreaded smoked oolichan, but it'll have to do.

"Does Ms. Adelaide know?" I ask Helen as I lock the door.

She's about to answer when something out in the lane catches her attention. I swing around. Cedar. He's standing at the gate, giving us a quizzical look. "Going somewhere?"

"We're headed to the estuary." Which is the truth. I don't have to tell him what comes after that.

"Hmm," he says. "That's a pretty long way. I could take you down there in my boat."

I cock an eyebrow at Helen, as if to say that would save a lot of time, but I'll leave the decision up to her.

She bites her lip and considers. I do too. Is this a good idea? Cedar has never been a friend to either my brother or Bran. What if he wants to come along? How do I explain that away? Still, a whole day of travel shaved off . . .

Helen takes a deep breath and nods.

"You don't have anything else to do?" I ask Cedar.

"Nope." He nudges a stone with his foot. "Was just coming by to see how you were feeling, that's all. So?"

"Sure," I say as guilt gnaws at my gut. "That'll be great."

He takes the pack from me. "I meant your shoulder," he says. "It's better?"

"Getting there."

An awkward silence settles over us as we set off. Helen glances at me from time to time, as if trying to gauge my feelings about Cedar. Hell, half the time I don't know how I feel about him, and that makes me wonder if I'm using him right now. Still, he offered. He wouldn't have offered if he didn't want to help, though it occurs to me that he never asked what we're up to. Maybe, if he knew, he'd change his mind.

Cedar's house is not far from town. It's a neat blue salt-box with daisies growing up against it—definitely not what I'd imagined for him. A woman peers out the window at us, but Cedar doesn't stop. He just picks up the pace and leads us down to the water's edge, where his rowboat lies upside down on the shore. He flips it over, tosses the packs in, and pushes the boat out knee-deep. "Get in," he says.

Helen takes the bow, leaving me to sit in the middle, closest to Cedar. He plunges the oars into the water and we're away, shooting across the lake. "It'll be a bit tricky once we get to the dam," he says. "We'll have to pull the boat out and portage to the river, but it'll still save us some time."

"What are you going to do once we get to the estuary?" I ask.

"Depends," he says with a shrug. "You'll have to get home somehow."

"We might be gone for a couple of days," Helen says.

Cedar nods, but, curiously, doesn't ask where or why. He just keeps on rowing.

Once we're across the lake and on shore, Cedar flips the rowboat over and heaves it onto his shoulders in one swift move. His head disappears into the ribs and when he talks, his voice sounds like it's echoing through a tunnel. "To the west," he says, picking his way up the beach. "There's not much of a trail, so you'd better let me lead."

Helen and I fall in behind the rowboat with legs. No-see-ums buzz around our heads as we hike through the dark, swampy forest. Corpse plants spring out of the loamy ground, their ghostly flowers a warning that we're in strange territory now, and wandering too far from the path might lead us into a sinkhole full of mud.

After an hour of pushing through marsh, I hear the rush of the river. We're soon back in the rowboat, speeding downstream. The boat glides past ancient granite outcrops that watch us pass until we reach a fork in the river. Cedar rows us up the smaller branch that leads to the wharf. Skiffs and war canoes bob on the ebbing tide. No one's around. We paddle up to a dock and get out.

"Well," Cedar says as he lifts his boat out of the water, "we're here. Now what?"

"Now," I say, "we steal a boat."

Cedar laughs as Helen walks down the wharf and hops onto one of the skiffs. "This one's Madda's," she says, grinning. "The tanks are full!"

"You're serious," Cedar says.

"Dead serious." I meet his gaze. "But it's not really stealing. Madda left the boat to us. Henry Crawford appropriated it, so really, he's the thief."

Cedar runs a hand through his hair, shaking his head. "Do you have any idea what you're doing? Helen, are you actually going along with this?"

Helen shrugs.

"Look," I say. "You've got a couple of choices here. You can hightail it back and tell Henry, and by the time everyone gets here, we'll be long gone. Or you can keep it to yourself and when we get back, well, we'll do the explaining."

"Or I could come with you." He scratches his ear. "My mom saw us, remember? My dad's in Henry's pocket, and if he finds out that I was part of this . . . well, I'll get a beating either way." He smirks. "Might as well do something to deserve it."

I find it incredible that anyone would beat Cedar—he's the stockiest boy in the town—but I don't say so. After all, Paul knocked out his tooth. He's not invincible. "Don't you want to know what it is we're doing before you sign on?"

"I guess."

Helen, standing where Cedar can't see her, pretends to swoon. "We're going to find Bran and Paul," I say in my most matter-of-fact tone, even though I feel awful. Cedar would probably do anything I asked, beating or not.

Cedar's gaze falls to his shoes. "I see."

"We'd better get going," Helen says. "We need to be out of the estuary before the tide changes."

"Okay." I step around Cedar, who's still staring at his feet. "Coming?"

"Hell," he mutters. "Why not? I've got nothing else to do." He sighs. "Get onboard, Cass. I'll cast off."

CHAPTER THIRTY-EIGHT

*H*elen steers the skiff from behind its dodger. I stand next to her, watching the gray expanse of the ocean. Cedar sits at the stern. Neither of them have asked what we're looking for, and I'm not entirely sure myself. It's one thing to have a raven in the spirit world show me sea wolves, but another thing entirely to head out onto the open ocean to find them, but at least I know where to start. Madda's spirit stone is pushing into my hand like a needle on a compass. "North," I say to Helen. "We need to head north."

She gives me a sidelong look. "Okay. We'll have to go east a little ways first, because of the currents. Got to conserve fuel if we want to make it back. I don't know what Henry will be more mad about—the boat or the gas." She gives me a wicked smile. "Do you know how much the gas in this boat is worth?"

"Not more than Paul and Bran," I tell her.

Her smile fades.

Gulls swoop down to keep pace with us as Helen turns the wheel. With the Island a shadow of blue far to our left, I begin to wonder if this is the stupidest idea I've ever come up with. I have no clue how many miles will we have to cover. How will we find them in this huge expanse of gray? Luck, fate, and mercy will all have to be on my side if we're to spot Bran, Paul, or the sea wolves that are supposed to guide us to them. "Sea wolf" is the old name for a killer whale—orca. How, exactly, are they supposed to help, and why didn't I think about any of this before I sent us off on this crazed mission?

The gulls mew as they wheel away and I wonder why they've chosen now to abandon us. What do they know that we don't? The sight of them disappearing into the distance leaves me ill at ease.

The hours drift away. Dusk falls as we continue north. Helen rubs her eyes. "We need to find a place to camp," she says. "It's not safe out here after dark, not without proper night gear."

Cedar leans into the dodger. "Over there looks pretty good," he says, pointing toward a cove.

Helen nods and shifts gears, the whine of the engine dropping to a low thrum.

We are far from people now. If something happens to us, there's no one to know. I should have been better prepared for this.

Helen shuts off the engine as she points the skiff toward the shore and lets it coast through the shallows, as close to the shore as the hull will allow. "Tide's on its way out," she says. "We'll have to wait for it to come back in before we can leave."

Cedar digs a fishing rod out from under a seat while I jump down into the water and wait for Helen to throw me the mooring line. "I'll see if the salmon are biting," he says as he straddles the rear gunwale. "You probably didn't bring food for me."

I hardly brought food for Helen and me, but I don't say so. I just nod and wonder how much fresh water we've got as I make my way up to the shore and tie the line around a solid old stump. Helen seems to read my thoughts, and brings two empty water jugs with her. "There'll be water here somewhere with all these maples," she says as she points above us.

She heads off into the woods while I gather wood for the fire. Cedar has a little luck on the boat. He bludgeons something and then starts casting out again.

By the time Helen returns, the fire is going. Cedar joins us, bringing two small salmon with him. "I should have fished while we were out in open water," he says with an apologetic shrug. "These guys are pretty small. Feel kind of bad taking them."

"They're great," Helen says shyly. "Thanks." She splits them and sets them to roast on cedar boughs, and soon we're picking pieces off and sucking the juice from our fingers.

"How do you think you'll find them?" Cedar asks after he sets the fish bones back to the ocean and we all give thanks.

I stare out to where the water is turning purple. "I don't know. All I know is that we're looking for killer whales. Where we find orcas, we find Paul and Bran." I pull Madda's spirit stone out from beneath my shirt. "But this seems to help too."

Cedar whistles. "Where did you get that?"

"Long story."

Helen's staring at it with widened eyes, and I tuck the stone back under my shirt. She and Cedar exchange enigmatic looks. "The Elders won't like that you've got it," Helen murmurs.

"They don't have much choice." The spirit stone warms my skin. "And when we find what we're looking for, I doubt they'll object. Besides, let them try to take it from me. We'll see what happens then."

The tide goes out, leaving the sea bottom exposed, a graveyard of rocks and barnacles. We light firebrands and go exploring, looking for crab hidden under the kelp. Salt and seaweed scent the air, an intoxicating perfume. Soon we're punch-drunk on it, stumbling into tidal pools, falling into one another, giggling. Cedar stubs his toe on a barnacle and swears as Helen and I wade in the shallows. Luminescence clusters around our ankles and we take to kicking water high in the air, creating our own falling stars.

"We should go skinny-dipping," Cedar says.

We both stop and look at him. The moon casts his face in shadows, highlighting his eye-sockets so I can see what he'll look like when, one day, his body is lifted into the canopy of the forest to be scourged by the wind.

"No," Helen says as she starts kicking the water again. A heron fishing nearby grows tired of our antics and flies away, squawking at us.

"So? Cass? What do you think?" Cedar says.

"It's pretty cold," I say, though even if it weren't, there's no way I'd skinny-dip with Cedar.

He shrugs and peels off his shirt, but when he unbuttons his shorts, Helen and I run off, making our way back to the fire. Cedar is no more than a black shadow from there.

Helen holds her hands out to warm them. "He isn't all bad," she says. "He's just . . . not good, either. I don't know what he'll do when he realizes he isn't going to have you, Cass."

I stare out into the night, listening to the waves. They're a long way off. "I know."

"I've known Cedar all my life. He's my cousin, did you know that? We grew up together. He's always been a bully, but he's . . . different . . . when he's around you. It's almost like he wants to try." She shrugs. "Like he's hoping he could change. If you wanted him to."

Like he could change. The words leave me feeling incredibly sad, as if Cedar's fate rests in my hands. "I do want him to change," I say. "But if he did—for me—I mean, that wouldn't be right. It wouldn't be true. If he wants to change, he has to do it for himself."

Helen nods. "I know. I think he does too, but it doesn't mean he's stopped hoping." She stirs the fire. "Hope's a pretty powerful thing."

"Yeah," I murmur. "I know."

We sit in silence for several minutes, me thinking about what to do about Cedar, and Helen—who knows what she's thinking about. Every time I've seen her near Cedar, she's looked as terrified as a mouse before a cat, but which Cedar? Cedar now, or Cedar past, or some Cedar yet to come? Is it just him, or all men? I wish I knew.

Above us are the three stars of Orion's Belt—Mintaka, Alnilam, Alnitak. The last time I saw them was the night Paul and I sat on the windowsill at our house, before we left for the Island. The stars look different now, bright and shiny, like someone spit-polished them, and I realize Helen's right. Hope's a pretty powerful thing, and taking hope away from a person is the surest way to destroy him.

We decide to sleep by the fire, but Helen gives up, abandoning the warmth of the flames for the silence of the skiff because of Cedar's snoring. I consider the same thing, but I'm caught in an awkward place. If I leave, Cedar might think I'm snubbing him, but if I stay, I'm never going to fall asleep and right now, sleep is the thing I need most.

I sit up and add a little wood to the fire, but when I lie back down, I find Cedar watching me. "What's up?" I say, unnerved by the intensity of his gaze.

He doesn't reply, so I turn my back on him, gazing out to the ocean as he shuffles under his blanket. Somewhere out there is Bran. I can feel it. The spirit stone can feel it. Maybe tomorrow will be the day. Maybe tomorrow, I'll find Paul. Maybe tomorrow, we'll be together again. Maybe tomorrow, they'll be safe.

The moon casts a spotlight on the ocean, a straight, brilliant beacon that leads right to me. How could they miss it? The heavens are conspiring with me for a change, and if they're on my side, how can I fail?

I draw in a deep breath and realize that Cedar's snoring hasn't returned. The hair on the back of my neck lifts as I roll over and find him crouching right beside me.

"You okay?" he whispers.

"Oh. Yep. I'm fine." I give him a quick smile. "Just watching the moon." A cold sweat breaks on my brow. Something bad is about to happen.

He sits down so close to me that we're almost touching, and then reaches under my blanket, putting his hand on my thigh. I reach down, pick up his hand, and put it on his own leg. He returns it to mine, and I return it to his. "I think it should stay there," I say, giving his hand a light pat.

"Give me a break," he murmurs. "We're finally alone."

I sit up and move away, trying to keep things light, friendly. "Not really—Helen's just over there."

"That's not what I mean, Cassandra." The way he says my name, my full name, makes me realize this is really serious. He's not just making a pass at me. He's got something in mind.

I'm suddenly aware of his physical presence. There's a musky scent about him that I've never noticed before, and his bulk looms next to me. I stand.

"Where are you going?" he says. His voice is deep and throaty.

I pick up my blanket and give it a shake. "The sand fleas are getting to me. I think I'll go sleep on the boat too."

"Cassandra," he says. A hand extends toward me, but I step back.

"Cedar, you know it's not like that."

"He'll hurt you." His words are hard and tight and all the throatiness is gone. "He'll hurt you and ruin you. One day, you'll come back to me and say, 'You told me, and I didn't listen.'"

"Maybe," I say as a knot forms in my stomach. *Is he right?* "But right now, I can't be anything more than your friend. I'm sorry. I'm so sorry. . . ."

He throws a log on the fire and suddenly his face is illuminated with orange light. He doesn't look like the muscle-bound goon I once met. He's a boy—just a boy. A boy who's heartbroken, and as I edge away toward the skiff, I wish I could take that hurt away.

CHAPTER THIRTY-NINE

I wake to a raven's rasp. It perches on the dodger, bobbing up and down at me.

"Shoo," I whisper at it. Helen doesn't stir, so I say, "Shoo," a little louder.

The raven still doesn't budge. It just continues to caw and bob at me, until I caw back. Then it flies away, sailing straight down the beach to the edge of the water, almost running right into Cedar, who's standing in the shallows, watching something.

I stand, stretch, and decide to let Helen sleep a little longer. The tide is licking the bottom of the skiff, so we could leave now if we wanted, but it's a shame to wake the one person still asleep when there's no immediate rush. I settle on the prow and watch Cedar. In another place, in another time, maybe things might have been different. Maybe. But maybes aren't very useful because they're not real, and all that wondering about what could have been, if only . . . it never leads anywhere.

The sun turns the sky a red so violent that I can tell the weather's going to change. That's going to make our search difficult, and my heart sinks a little—until I notice the black shapes in the open water just beyond the mouth of the cove. That's what Cedar's watching. Orcas. Sea wolves. Our sign.

And he was going to let them pass without telling me!

Anger rages through my veins as I shake Helen awake more roughly than I should. "I'm sorry, I'm sorry," I say as she blinks at me. "They're out there—we have to go."

"Okay," she says, pushing her hair away from her face. "Okay. Give me a second—do I have a second?"

"One," I say.

"Where's Cedar?"

I freeze. I'm so angry I could kill him. I'm tempted to leave him here, but I call him anyway. "We're going!" is all I say. He'll have to figure out the rest.

Fortunately for him, it takes Helen several minutes to wake up fully, and a few more before the skiff is truly floating—enough time for Cedar to hop onboard. He doesn't look at me. I don't look at him, either. We both know that something has changed between us and that the friendship we once had—if it could be called that—is irretrievably lost.

But I have no time for that now—only the black dorsal fins of the orcas as I pray that they don't disappear, that they're not just some strange optical illusion—that they're real.

Helen revs the motor and the skiff plows the water. I grip the gunwales, boring my gaze into the ocean, willing the orcas to surface. And then, just off our port side, one breaches, sending a flume of water high into the air. Others join it, and then they continue their migration south, dipping and diving through the waves as I thank them silently.

The wind whips up a stiff chop as we round the point, and dark clouds are billowing in the southeast. "Where to now?" Helen yells.

I don't know. I somehow thought that when we found the sea wolves, we'd find Bran and Paul with them, but I scan the ocean and can't make out anything. My hand finds Madda's spirit stone. It's silent too. "Still north, I guess," I say.

Helen gives me a grim look. "We can't go far. We need to save enough fuel to get back."

"Do your best" is all I say.

The shoreline has been painted red by rising sun, so

the whole world seems coated in blood. I shudder and push the thought away. There will be no blood spilled this morning. And then, from the corner of my eye, I spot a blur of blue—a kingfisher. It ducks into the shadows and there, where a creek runs out to the ocean, I spy a war canoe.

We've found them.

In my mind, this is what I envisioned: Bran would run to me and spin me in his arms. Paul would greet Helen, and love her as much as I do. Maybe as a sister. Maybe as something more. We'd return home, triumphant. Our family would be whole again.

None of this happens.

The canoe is empty and badly damaged. Bullet holes riddle one side. Rusty bloodstains coat the ribs, as if the canoe was a living creature stripped of its flesh. My heart thuds against my breastbone. One of them—maybe both—is hurt.

"It had to get here somehow," I hear Helen say as I run to get the medicine kit.

"Currents, probably," Cedar says.

"Currents, my ass." With the kit slung across my back, I duck into the forest. Standing on the beach staring at the canoe isn't going to find them.

Helen chases after me. Great firs tower above us, watching as we wade through the sea of ferns on the forest floor. I look for signs that they passed this way—broken branches, crushed fronds, something, but there isn't anything to find. When we reach a creek, the only sign of life is a doe and her fawn drinking.

"Good water source," Helen says. "Maybe they came up this way."

We wait until the deer leave, then scour the banks, looking for tracks. Nothing.

"Looks like tidal flats on the other side," I say, nodding at the bright light behind a screen of willows. "Maybe they're out there?"

"Maybe," Helen says.

We search the flats, calling for Bran, for Paul as we go, but no one answers. My throat has gone dry. *Where could they be? Did the raven lie to me?* I pick up my pace, jogging down a stretch of beach, hoping each time I round a stand of sea grass, I'll find them stretched out in the sun, but there's nothing but stone and sand and forest.

"What do you want to do?" Helen asks when I draw up, panting. She glances up at the sky, now thick with clouds, with a worried look.

"Just a little longer," I say.

"Okay," she says. "But not too much longer. I don't like the look of that storm."

We head back toward the skiff, searching every log, every rock, every outcropping of beach oats. My brother is here. Bran is here. I know it. I can feel it.

The skiff comes into sight. I can just make out Cedar kneeling next to it, and then a shock of auburn hair appears next to him. "Over here!" he yells when he spots us. "I found them. Over here!"

I break into a run, scrambling over the seaweed, slipping, falling, and taking all the skin off my knees, but I don't care. I cannot be fast enough.

And then, I round the prow of the skiff. Bran and Cedar are standing over a man lying flat on the ground. *Where is Paul?* I look on the other side of the canoe, and then at Cedar, who just shakes his head.

The man on the ground groans in pain, and I push the questions about my brother away. The man's hurt. So is Bran, judging from the way his eyes are tinged with yellow. *See to them first. Then they'll tell me where Paul is. Maybe he's off hunting. Yes, that must be it. Hunting.* My heart settles into an even rhythm as I reach out to touch Bran's cheek. It's filthy. "You're back."

He trembles at my touch. "Hi."

"Hi, yourself." I wait for him to draw me into his arms,

and when he doesn't, I take him in mine. He smells terrible, but I don't care. He's alive.

"Okay." I turn my attention to the man on the ground. "Who is this?"

"This," Cedar says, "is Arthur Eagleson."

"Your father?" I whisper.

Bran nods. "He's hurt bad."

I unsling the medicine kit from my back and drop to my knees beside the man. "What happened?" I ask as I check his father's pulse. Fluttery. Weak. Not good.

Bran just shakes his head. He's on the verge of tears.

"Bran," I say as I touch his hand, "if you want me to help him, you'll have to tell me what happened. And where's Paul?"

Bran furiously rubs his eyes as if that'll make the tears go away. "He's not here."

My heart stops. "Bran, where is he? Where's my brother?"

"Cass," he whispers, "they came and took us. Took us all. They took us north. They had my father . . ." His voice breaks and he turns away so we can't see him cry. "Paul offered himself for us," Bran finally says. "So my father and I could come home."

"Who took you, Bran? Who?"

A sound comes from Bran's throat, a growl, primal and

bizarre. "They call themselves the sea wolves," he says through bared teeth. "And they're hunting you, too."

I treat the cuts and abrasions as best I can, and then we get everyone on the boat and out to sea before the tide's completely gone. It's a long way back to the estuary, and the sea isn't happy to see us go. The ocean is whitewashed with waves. The skiff lurches over them, slamming into each trough so the whole boat shudders. I know I should feel this, but I don't. My entire body has gone numb. All I can think of is that my brother is gone.

My brother is gone.

My brother is gone.

Cedar struggles into the dodger and tries to help Helen keep the skiff on course. Bran huddles beside me and stares at his father with vacant eyes. His shade fades in and out, guttering like damp tinder. He needs spirit healing as much as his father, but I can't help either of them until we're back on land.

The skiff hits another swell. The engine shrieks as we hover in midair before crashing down, throwing everyone off balance again.

"Put into shore," Cedar finally yells over the wind. "Over there!" He points to a sandy spit. "There's a burial ground there, and an old longhouse. We can get out of the wind, at least."

Helen turns the wheel and the skiff banks, cutting through the water, drenching us with spray. My stomach can't stand it any longer, and I vomit over the side. Cedar grabs hold of the waistband of my pants so I don't fall overboard.

Helen runs the skiff up onto a beach. The waves lick at our heels. The ocean's hungry today, and not happy that we've managed to elude her.

Cedar and Bran lift Bran's father from the skiff as Helen and I frantically try to figure out a way to moor it. I have no idea how far we are from home, but if we get stuck here, that's that. We finally decide to wrap the mooring line around the biggest log we can find and hope the storm's not bad enough to take the log out to sea. It's the best we can do.

The longhouse is a little way off, set into scrub pines just beyond the beach. It's in a bad state. Most of the roof has fallen away, but enough remains to keep us out of the worst of the weather. Cedar's already left to search for wood, taking Helen with him, leaving me alone with Bran and his unconscious father.

We sit on the ground, staring at our feet. I want to ask Bran a thousand questions, but I fight to keep quiet. He's not ready to talk yet. I'll have to be patient. I know how to do that. I've done it a hundred times with my brother.

Who is gone.

A sob lodges in my throat, but I swallow it away. *Not now. Later.* Paul will have to wait for later, even though all I want to do is scream at the skies that my brother is gone.

I glance up to find Bran watching me. For a moment he looks like he's going to take me in his arms, but then Cedar and Helen arrive with driftwood and the moment passes. Bran returns to looking at his feet. I rise to help Helen and Cedar with the fire.

We are strangers once again.

CHAPTER FORTY

Rain slashes sideways through the gaps in the roof. We huddle in the only dry space as the fire hisses and pops in the strange, shifting wind. Bran's father lies on the ground, bookended by Bran and me. His breathing is slow and shallow. His heartbeat? Jumpy and faint. It could be his heart that's the problem, but there's no way for me to tell for certain. He's not running a fever, nor does he bear any major physical injury that I can find. That means one thing: If I'm to help him, I'll have to cross into the spirit world to do it, and the last time I had an audience? It didn't go so well.

I sit back on my heels and rub my eyes. I can feel Bran watching me. Hope radiates from him. But what if I can't fix his father? I couldn't help Saul.

"Cass?" Helen says. "What do you need?"

"Nothing," I say. "I'm going to have to cross over."

Helen bites her lip. Bran clenches his jaw and drops his gaze. Cedar sits back in the shadows so I can't see him at all.

I try not to think about any of them. There's a man beside me who's really hurt, so hurt that I can't let myself think of last time. My gaze drifts out of focus as I look for where his totem should be, but it's gone. He had one once, though. I know because I can feel it, and I can also feel the wound left behind, a raw, gaping hole in his being, a wound that must be stanched before it bleeds him dry.

I draw a deep breath and force my gaze back into focus. Delaying isn't going to make this any easier. "Bran," I say. "What happened to your father? Do you know?"

He won't look at me.

"Bran, please," I say. I want to touch him so badly, but he draws away from me. "I need to know what I'm dealing with."

Bran drops his head. He's on the verge of tears again.

In the shadows, Cedar groans.

"Shut up," I snap at him. "Just shut up." I slide closer to Bran. "I need to know what I'm looking for when I cross."

He raises his gaze to mine. His expression is blank, but

in his eyes, I see the shadow of fear. "There's a man. The leader of the sea wolves." His voice is weak and hoarse. He's fighting for every word.

"Go on," I say, giving him a smile.

He clears his throat, making way for his voice. "They've broken away from the Bix'iula. They live on their own, somewhere up north, along the coast."

"Okay," I say, trying to be patient. I'm not sure what this has to do with his father. "Just take your time."

He coughs again, and I start to worry. The cough is heavy and thick. I want to check him out, but I force myself to sit there like a rock and wait for him to speak.

"They came for us when we were patrolling the boundary," Bran finally says. "Put us in the hold of a ship. Beat us, but the beating wasn't as bad as what came later. That's when the man came." He draws his knees into his chest. "We stopped somewhere, I don't know where. There weren't any windows in the hold. That's when he took our men out one by one, and when he brought them back . . . they didn't talk anymore. They didn't even look like men—more like . . . shells. Like their life was burned out of them." His gaze shifts to his father. "Paul said the man was taking their souls. Paul . . . he spoke with . . . ghosts, and that's what they told him. That's what they had done to my father. That's what they were going to do to us. I don't know what they do with the souls, Cass, but our men . . . we should have killed them. I should have. Put them out of their misery." He finally looks at me, eyes so full of agony that I have to force myself not to look away. "Except I didn't have the courage."

"Oh." The urge to curl into myself is overwhelming. I know the depth of failure he feels, the knowledge that life will never be the same again because every time you close your eyes, the people you failed are there, staring straight at you—not with accusation, but with sadness, with regret that they chose the wrong one. But I won't give in—not without a fight. I sit up straight, put on a mask that says *I'm fine, I can handle this*, that I'm not scared to the pit of my stomach. That I'm not terrified for my brother. That I'm not torn between raging at Bran for leaving Paul behind and wrapping him in my arms and rocking him until his tears fade away and never come back.

Bran grimaces and looks up to the sky. He can't stop crying, no matter how hard he tries.

"What a pussy," Cedar mutters.

And then, just like that, Bran launches himself at Cedar. Helen screams as they roll toward her, kicking and biting and fighting like bears. I yell at them to stop, but they don't hear me. Battle-frenzy has taken them. Cedar lands a good, hard punch to Bran's kidneys, but

Bran doesn't even seem to feel it. A growl rises from his throat. He twists, pinning Cedar in the dirt, and then his hands are around Cedar's throat, choking the life right out of him.

I grab Bran's shoulders and try to pull him away, but he shakes me off. Cedar is gagging and wheezing as he claws at Bran's hands.

"Stop it!" I scream. "You're going to kill him! Stop it!"

Bran ignores me. Cedar's face turns purple as he tries to punch Bran, but each punch is weaker than the last. His eyes bulge in his head. He opens his mouth, gasping for air.

"Bran," I say, crouching beside him. "You've got to stop. That's Cedar you're killing. Listen to me. Come back. Bran, please come back." I set my forehead against his shoulder and whisper to him. "Please. Come back. You have to come back."

I feel him shudder, and when I look up, he's watching me as if seeing me for the first time. Slowly he releases his grasp on Cedar's neck, leaving brilliant red welts that mark the outline of his fingers. Cedar wheezes and spits as he tries to breathe.

"He deserves to die," Bran says. "I saw what he did to my father. I know what he'll do to Paul." His voice sounds like the wind.

"But it's just Cedar, Bran. Not the man who hurt you." I take one of his hands and hold it in mine. "It's just Cedar."

Cedar lies there on the ground, staring at us. He doesn't move. "Yeah, it's just me, man," he croaks. "I'm sorry. I shouldn't have said that."

Bran drops his chin to his chest, panting. I close my eyes and see things swirling around him, things I've never seen before. His kingfisher is barely attached to him and there are other things now—sea wolves, for one, but not the healthy black-and-white orcas we saw in the ocean. These are depraved creatures, bloody and mutilated— monsters. And I must get them away from Bran before they take him, too.

My hand finds one of the strings at my neck and I pull my pouch, the one holding the sisiutl's pearls, over my head. "Wear this," I say, closing his fingers around it. "I want to give you a little sisiutl medicine, just for a while, just until you've found yours again."

Bran just stares at the pouch, so I take it and string it around his neck. "There," I say, patting it against his chest. "They can't come for you, and if they do, sisiutl will eat them." I smile, hoping he will too, and I'm rewarded with a quiet chuckle.

"Thanks," Bran says as he gets to his feet. I'm not sure he believes me.

Cedar pushes himself away and creeps back to his seat in the shadows.

"I'm so sorry, Cass," Bran says. I've never seen him look so lost, so uncertain.

"Apologize to Cedar," I say. "He's the one you attacked."

Bran shakes his head, as if what I've said isn't true, but he goes to where Cedar sits, crouches, and offers him his hand. "I'm sorry, man. So sorry."

Cedar grunts something I can't hear and after a tense moment, I see a hand extend from the shadows to take Bran's. They sit there, hand in hand, until Bran nods and releases Cedar's grasp. "Thanks, man," he says.

He waits a second, takes a deep breath, and then moves back to sit beside his father. "They took my father's totem," he says. "He was a bear. Now he's not. That's what they did with all the men, except Paul and me. They were saving us for the man who fragments souls—that's what they called it—and when Paul came back, he told me about the exchange. He gave up his totem, Cass— gave it to my father so he could come back to this world. The others? They're all lost. That's what Paul said. Lost."

"They took Paul's shade?" I whisper.

"No," Bran says as his eyes change to storm clouds. "I don't know what that man said to him, but Paul gave his totem up. Willingly. He came back afterward to tell me to tell you. He said he didn't need it anymore, so he was giving his to my father to replace the one he lost. He said to tell you not to look for him. Not to try. He said he's beyond help now. Beyond hope."

I edge closer to the fire, hoping its warmth will ease the chill that's seeping into my heart. Paul chose to stay. What could this man have said to make him want to stay?

Solace, I think. That's the one thing Paul's never had. Solace. Peace.

But I can't think about that now. Something's changed with Bran's father. His breath is coming in short, shallow gasps, as if our words have unleashed something from the spirit world and it's begun to steal him away.

I take sage from my medicine kit, but before I set it on the fire, I look at Helen, and then Bran. "This isn't going to be easy," I say. "I'll need you guys to watch over me while I'm gone."

Helen creeps closer and sets a hand on my back. "We can do that, Cass. Don't you worry." She smiles. "We'll be your anchors."

Bran nods. "I know you can do it."

I try to smile, but my lips quiver and all I can manage is to clench my teeth together. I hope they're right, because if I can't find Bran's father, I might not come back either.

CHAPTER FORTY-ONE

The wind throws itself against the longhouse. Rain drives down from the sky. We sit in our corner, staring at the clouds, as our fire fights for life.

Every bit of me has been scraped thin. I can't cross into spirit like this. I'll be fodder for whatever's hunting me, for now I realize that's what's going on—the wolves I've seen in the spirit world are tied to the man who has taken Paul. I'm going to face him down, that man—there's no doubt about that, but I'll do it on my terms, not his.

Helen looks up as I stand and dust my hands on my filthy pants. "Where are you going?" she asks, wide-eyed with fear.

"Out." I duck out into the slanting downpour before she can stop me. Rain soaks me to the skin in an instant, but I don't care. I open my arms wide and run, run as fast as I can down toward the crabbed pine forest where the burial ground sleeps, where platforms with old bones watch the sky. I have no idea where I'm going. All I know is that I must run, and the faster I run, the faster I will find myself because that's what I've been looking for all along. That's the one thing I need before I cross into spirit to find Bran's father.

I run until my pulse screams in my ears and my lungs cry out for breath. I run until my legs ache and sand blisters my soles. I run until sky and earth become one and until the storm blows through me and past me and over me. And then I drop to my knees, turn my face to the sky, and let the rain wash me clean.

Above me, the clouds shift back and forth, rubbing together, and a low rumble comes from the east. A flash of light, and an answering rumble, and another flash. The skies are alive. When I was very little, my father would say the gods were bowling whenever I was frightened by a thunderstorm, but now, what I know is this: The gods don't bowl. They dance. They writhe and twist and meld together until positive and negative become something more, something without a name, something that gives birth to lightning and her sister, thunder, and that's when I know what I have to do.

I rise and run back to the longhouse. This time, I won't fail.

• • •

Helen dashes to my side the moment I step into the long-house, draping a blanket around my shoulders, leading me to the fire. "You need to get warm," she says.

"No," I say, though I draw the blanket close with a shiver. "What I need is to get started."

Bran's face is pale with worry, but whether it's for me or his father, I don't know. It probably doesn't matter. I'm no longer the Cassandra he once knew. I don't know who I am, but I know what I need to accomplish and that's all that's important right now.

I drop more sage into the fire, sit down, and as soon as I close my eyes, I'm gone. When I open them again, the twilight lake is before me, and in its center is the sisiutl. It nods. I nod in return. We are two halves of a whole, two sides of a coin, and it will help me do what I need to do.

I scan the sky for the raven, but it's not there, nor did I really expect it to be. The raven I'm looking for is injured, and injured animals hide. The place that's darkest in this world and therefore the best for hiding? The lake.

I step into the water, wading deeper and deeper until the lake fills my mouth, my nose, my ears, enveloping me. I am the sisiutl. I can fly through the sky and swim through water, and nothing will harm me, save my second head at the end of my tail.

I walk to the center of the lake and look up to the sky.

Stars wink at me, so I reach up and pluck one, cupping it in my palm. It shall be my beacon in this underwater world, for the brightest stars cast the deepest shadows, and the deepest shadow is exactly what I'm looking for.

The bottom of the lake is littered with bones. Some I recognize: skulls, knuckles, rib cages, but some have come from creatures I've never seen, for they've never existed except in this place where all things are possible. I walk through the boneyard, looking for a raven, star glowing in my hand, until the star's light catches on something cowering behind a pile of pelvises. I creep forward, and there it is: a raven, plucked bare, its wing broken. It looks up at me and tries to hop away, but it's too sick and all it can manage is a feeble croak.

"Don't fight," I say as I pick it up. "I'll help you."

It fights anyhow, pecking at me as I tuck it under my arm and retrace my steps. I set the star back in the sky and walk ashore, carrying the raven that bleats like a lamb. It struggles against me with each step I take, but no matter how hard it tries, I won't let it go.

Another raven is waiting for us on the beach, this one the large raven I've spoken with before.

He cocks his head. *I see you've caught my little brother. What are you going to do with him? Cook him up? Make a little raven soup?* His caws sound like laughter.

"Nope," I say as I raise the little raven above my head and close my eyes. "Watch and see."

Oh-ho, the raven says. *A show!*

I smile, but in my mind, I call wind and rain and clouds and all the power the sky can muster. Thunder rumbles across the twilight lake and I know it's working—I'm going to make a storm. The rain hits me next, blowing in on a wind so strong I can feel its fury pierce my skin, letting blood, and why not? This requires a sacrifice, and what better one can I give than the most valuable thing I possess—my blood.

I take the plucked raven in my arms. "Hold on, little one," I whisper to it. "This is going to hurt." And with that, I scream to the skies and call the heavens down on me. They answer with sheets of light that strike me asunder.

I am lying in the sand. My head hurts. I reach up to touch my hair, but there is none. All I feel is skin.

A face swims before me and when my vision steadies, I can just make out Bran's worried gray eyes.

"Did I do it?" I ask.

Bran helps me sit up. His father is beside me, asleep. At his shoulder, cast in the strange light of spirit, is the raven, battered and mewling, but there. I did it. I brought his totem back.

Bran eases me back down. "Now you," he says, "are going to sleep."

I try to answer, but I can't. I'm already gone.

They let me sleep for two days before we set off toward home. They feed me clams and seaweed, the ocean's bounty, when I wake, as if this is its way of making amends. The lightning singed most of my hair off. A small part of me hates to think what I look like, but when I run my hand over my head, I can feel fine stubble there already. Bran says he thinks I look beautiful like this, like an Egyptian goddess. I want to ask him how he knows what an Egyptian goddess looks like, but I don't. For now, a goddess is what I choose to be, and I don't really feel like breaking that spell.

Bran's father sits next to Cedar, watching me. He's stopped saying thank you now, but his eyes speak for him. After all, he was marked by the lightning too. His hair was once dark brown. Now it's white.

We're both lucky to be alive.

No one else has spoken of what happened. There will be another time for that. Right now, we're just glad to be going home.

Before we dock in the estuary, we can tell there's going to be trouble. Two armed men patrol the wharf, and as we approach, they load their weapons.

"Put them down," Art, as he's asked us to call him, says.

They gape at him until Bran stands beside his father. "Yeah," he says. "He's back."

"I found them," Cedar quickly adds.

None of us contradict him. If Cedar wants to lay claim to finding Arthur Eagleson's body, that's fine. We all know we did this together—all of us.

We're driven into town and soon, word spreads. Someone thinks to fetch Grace, and I fade into the background as she throws herself into the arms of her husband and her son. I have my own family to see to.

The walk home feels longer than before. My legs are heavy. I can barely lift them. Long ago, the day we left the Corridor, I remember thinking that my father looked as if he carried the weight of the world on his shoulders. I now understand what that must have felt like, because the news I carry now? It has left me feeling the same way.

My father finds me halfway back and when I tell him what's happened, his knees buckle. We sit there in the dust as the shadows stretch across the road. We can't cry. We can't move. There is no measure of our grief. My brother, our Paul, is lost to us, and I have no idea how to get him back.

CHAPTER FORTY-TWO

*W*e keep close to our house at the lake and spend days sitting on the sundeck, thinking of Paul. There are so many things we should be doing—the list is endless—but neither of us can figure out how to start without Paul. The ship Bran was on was a large ocean-going vessel. There's no way we could follow a ship like that, a ship that can cross waters our little skiffs aren't built to weather.

My father thinks they must have a base—even a ship like that needs to put in to shore for supplies from time to time, but where? The coastline north of here is two thousand miles of inlets and fjords and islands, crisscrossed with treacherous currents and riptides that terrify even the most seasoned mariners. We will find him, my father says, but not just yet. With autumn approaching, with the storm season on the horizon, now it just isn't the right time. We must turn our attention to surviving the winter so there will be someone to mount a rescue in the spring.

While we talk about this, we listen to the dancing and singing celebrating the return of Bran's father on the other side of the lake. It goes on for four days. A celebration like that is an event that will be talked about for years, but how can my father and I celebrate?

Every day, a man arrives, asking us to attend the night's fire. On day five, he says that my attendance is required. I am medicine woman now. I have responsibilities. And, he adds just before he leaves, the Elders will not take no for an answer.

So we go. The fire roars. The drums throb. The celebration continues.

My father and I sit at the edge of the circle, watching, outsiders for a whole new reason: We're the only ones whose cup does not floweth over, though we're doing our best. Helen sits beside me. I'm glad she's there.

The men start to dance, slowly at first, weaving and hopping around the fire. Tongues of flame flicker over them. I blink, and when I open my eyes again, I don't see men. I see ravens streaked with blood, and it's then I know that spirit isn't done with us yet.

Bran dances beside his father. He alone is not a raven. I can see his kingfisher and something else just behind it, but I can't say what. I could close my eyes and pass into spirit to find out, but for tonight, I'm staying grounded on earth. I'm done with the spirit world for now. I've got nothing left to sacrifice.

Bran turns and smiles at me. He steps from the dance and holds out a hand. "Come," he says. "Come dance with me."

I shake my head. Once, a long time ago, he told me he wouldn't dance until his father returned. Now I will not dance until my brother is at my side again. Bran looks hurt, but I think he understands. He goes back to dancing, at least. My grief is not his. I will not share.

The dancers spin through the firelight, hopping and jumping so fast that when the first rock flies, no one notices. But then, a man close to me is struck. He stops, glances around, and goes back to dancing, but then another, and another, until rocks are raining down all around us. The drums fall silent. People scream and run for cover. Bran crouches beside me, protecting me from the worst, but not one stone touches us, and when I peer through the rain of stone, I know why.

The dzoonokwa have gathered.

They have come for me.

The dzoonokwa shriek and drive anyone who tries to flee back to the fire. When a man approaches them with a gun, the nearest dzoonokwa snatches him up and tosses him into the darkness as if he weighs no more than the rocks they've been throwing.

A little girl presses herself behind me. I let her, though there's no point hiding now.

"What do they want?" a woman screams. "What do they want?"

"The wardings!" someone else says. "Why have they come through the wardings?"

Henry Crawford's gaze finds mine. His face is almost expressionless—almost. His scar twitches. He's got no one to blame but himself for what's happened. Maybe now he'll recognize that I'm not just a girl. No one is just anything.

Bran squeezes my hand. "Don't move," he whispers. "Dzoonokwa's got bad eyesight. If we don't move, they might not notice us."

But I do move. I take a step toward them. Bran grabs at me, but I will not be stopped. "I know you," I say. The people around me murmur as I walk right up to the nearest dzoonokwa. "What do you want from me?"

The dzoonokwa points at me, and then Bran. She closes the gap between us, and reaches out. I don't move a hair. I don't even breathe as she pulls Madda's moonstone out from underneath my shirt, gently pressing it into my chest before gesturing at Bran again.

"What does she want?" Bran whispers.

"Your spirit stone, I think." My heart sinks.

"But I gave it to you," Bran says. "You have it, don't you?"

"I lost it." I can't look at him. "I didn't want to tell you."

"No," Bran says. "No, it's here. I can feel it." He whirls around. "Who's got it? I know someone here has it. You'd better cough it up right now before I let the dzoonokwa search for it."

The dzoonokwa mutter among themselves as Bran walks from person to person, staring at each one before moving on to the next. He finally stops in front of his mother. "Mother? You've got it, don't you?"

Now she's the one who won't look at him.

"Give it to me."

The dzoonokwa go wild, screaming at the sky as Grace clutches her chest. "No!" she says. "You'll just give it back to her! She doesn't deserve it. I need it for the one who will wake your past. . . ."

"Mother," he says, "give it to me, or I'll let them take it from you." As I hold my breath, Bran takes his mother's hand and forces it into her pocket. When he pulls her hand out, it holds his spirit stone. "You had no right," Bran growls.

"They gave it to me," Grace says, her eyes wildly turning to Henry Crawford. "It binds you to the land, Bran. You shouldn't have given it away."

"I didn't." He curls his fingers around the stone. "I was sharing it." He turns on his heel and pushes his way back to me. "Now what?" He leans closer to the dzoonokwa. "Don't you think we've been through enough?"

The closest dzoonokwa steps toward us and ushers us forward. I take Bran's hand. "Don't let go. It'll be all right," I say.

But when we follow the dzoonokwa into the darkness, I hear someone laugh. Not a man, or a woman, but a raven, laughing at me.

We walk all night. All but one of the dzoonokwa fade away into the forest, but I know they haven't left us. I catch glimpses of them from time to time. They watch us with their bloodshot eyes, and their voices accompany our footsteps. *Hoo, hoo.* That's what they say. I wish I knew what it meant.

Bran and I stumble along, tripping over roots as fatigue presses down on us. We are permitted to stop at intervals to catch our breath or take a sip of water when we encounter a stream, but never long enough to rest. Our stomachs grumble, for we've had nothing to eat. At morning's first light, one of the dzoonokwa offers us a freshly caught rabbit, its body still warm. I push it back. The sharing of food is a sacred act, and I know I may have offended these creatures, but what would be worse? Biting into fresh, bloody meat that drew breath only a few seconds ago and vomiting, or just pretending I'm not hungry?

The dzoonokwa doesn't seem to care either way. She tears the rabbit in two and chews it up, bones and all. *Fee-fi-fo-fum.* Will these creatures crush our bones to make their bread? I doubt it. They've kept us alive so far. They need us for something. That much I've figured out, but for what? And what happens when we've performed whatever task they need—what then?

"Don't think," Bran says, touching my arm. "Just keep going."

And so we walk. I catch sight of the sun late in the afternoon, streaming down through the needles of a hemlock, and I can tell from its position we're heading south. South, and east. My skin prickles. Unless I'm very much mistaken, we're heading toward the monolith. The place where they took Madda and tore her limb from limb.

Bran, walking with his hand on my shoulder, gives me a questioning look.

"Just tired," I whisper as a dzoonokwa's gaze falls on me.

Bran cocks one eyebrow. He knows I'm not telling the whole truth, but there are some things that should not be said aloud. That we're heading toward the monolith, the site of Madda's murder, a place that reeks of a power that almost overwhelmed me? Those are things I'll keep to myself.

The second night, we're permitted to sleep. They keep watch over us, tall sentinels in the dark, and when I close my eyes, I can hear them slowly whispering to one another, the soft, lowing *Hoo hoo*, that, strangely, is as beguiling as a lullaby. Bran sleeps with his arms wrapped around me. I feel the slow rise and fall of his chest against my back, and though I fight sleep, it draws me down anyhow.

Dawn still clings to the cedars as the dzoonokwa force us to wake, rise, and push on. My gut aches from hunger, and my head is fuzzy with fatigue. The dzoonokwa set a grueling pace, leaving Bran and me struggling to keep up. We don't want to find out what will happen if we fall behind.

I sense the monolith long before we reach its clearing. The spirit stone at my throat begins to vibrate and I hear the monolith's hum in my mind. It knows we're coming.

Bran walks as close to me as he can. "I feel strange," he whispers.

"I know," I say. "The veil between the worlds is thin here. Hold on to me. I'll keep you from passing over." I'm not sure when I became so certain of myself, but Bran nods and slips his hand into mine. If he believes in me, then I'll have to find a way to believe in myself.

We step from the forest into the clearing, where two dzoonokwa block our path, motioning for us to stop. Bran glances at me and chews on his lip as we wait.

I've forgotten how still the land is here. The humming from the monolith is one thing—I'm not even sure it's really sound. I think I hear it only in my mind. Everything else is silent, as if the land has ceased to live. There is no birdsong. Wind doesn't touch the trees. Even the subtle, near-silent pulse of the earth is absent. Bran senses it too. His shoulders are set and full of tension.

A howl breaks the silence in two. It's answered by the dzoonokwa guarding us, and then they gather, emerging from the forest, circling the clearing as Bran and I clasp hands and stare. I lose count at thirty. Thirty? How can it be that so many of these creatures exist here, unseen by the rest of the world?

"You see them too, right?" I whisper to Bran, just to be sure.

"Yeah, I see them," he whispers back.

Okay, then. I'm not losing my mind. That's something, at least.

The last dzoonokwa to step from the forest is taller than the rest, and holds Madda's partially decayed face in her hands. She turns the skull this way and that, as if using it to see. My gut churns, but I will not let myself be sick. I don't know what these creatures intend, but I have power in my own right, and I will not give it away by being weak.

Madda's eyeless skull stares at me, for I know that eyes are not all we use to see.

Our guards push us forward. We stumble down the scree before finding our feet, and turn back to face their circle. The dzoonokwa don't follow. They stand in their ring, edging the clearing. The tallest points at the monolith, so we make our way to it, the black center in the middle of their shadow ring.

"Now what do we do?" Bran asks. He peers into the monolith. His face stares back.

"I'm not sure," I say as I touch Madda's spirit stone. "I think this must have something to do with it. Hold yours up."

He pulls his spirit stone from his pocket and thrusts it out toward the monolith. The dzoonokwa begin to shriek. Bran flinches and presses his hands to his ears, almost dropping the spirit stone in the process. "Why are they doing that?" he yells.

"I don't know," I scream over the din, "but I think you were doing the right thing!" I lift my spirit stone closer to the monolith. Bran copies me, and then all at once, light shatters my vision and all goes dark.

CHAPTER FORTY-THREE

When I open my eyes, I'm no longer standing in the clearing. I'm in the spirit world, and Bran is standing next to me. The bright red spikes of a kingfisher run down the crest of his head, and his arms have turned into slate blue wings.

He flaps them and gives me a worried look. "What's happened to me?" he asks. "What's happened to you?"

I beat the mica-scaled wings of a sisiutl. "We're in spirit," I say, pitching my voice to sound matter-of-fact and in control, even though this is a place in the spirit would I've never visited before. There's nothing under my feet. There's nothing above my head. All there is is darkness, though I can see Bran well enough. "You're just manifesting your shade."

"I am?" He flaps his wings again, this time with a bit more strength so he lifts into the blackness. "But my totem is a bear."

"Not that I've ever seen," I say. "Who told you that?"

"Madda," he says.

I don't know what to say. Bran's followed around by a bunch of stuff, but I've never seen a bear in his entourage. So, who is wrong? Me, or Madda? Doubt raises its ugly head. Maybe my abilities aren't as strong as I think they are after all. I sense this is somehow important, but right now, we've got other things to tend to. The darkness at the edge of my vision shimmers, and when I turn, the monolith emerges from a bloodred mist. It's not alone. Behind it, in the shadows that aren't shadows, is a creature that's part wolf, part whale, and something else that has no name. It blinks in and out, disappearing only to reappear with some new physical configuration. Depraved eyes, decaying flesh, and a stink of such foulness that I choke when I breathe. I know this creature. I know that stink. It doesn't come from the sea wolf—it comes with it.

"Now what?" Bran says, edging close to me. I can feel his fear, and so can the monster behind the monolith.

"I don't know," I say, though as the words leave my mouth, I start to boil with rage—not my own rage, but the rage of the sisiutl and of the raven and the dzoonokwa and all the creatures of the spirit world, and that rage is directed squarely at the sea wolf, who is also the man who has my brother. *Hunt him, hunt him,* they whisper in my mind. *You must destroy him before he destroys you; before he destroys us.*

I reach inside myself and search for a storm, but there's nothing in this place to draw on. This is not the world by the twilight lake, where nature still has a role, where I've figured out how to wield what power I have. This is another place, a place of darkness and shadow, with little substance and no rules. "Have you still got your spirit stone?" I ask Bran. If the dzoonokwa sent us here with the stones, we must be meant to do something with them.

He dips his head to his chest so the spikes of red feathers on his skull shoot straight up in the air while he picks his spirit stone up with his mouth. "I have no hands," he says with a frustrated grimace.

The sea wolf laughs as Bran fumbles with his stone. *Is that what you mean to defend yourselves with?* he growls.

"Not exactly," I say as I move closer to the monolith.

Yes, yes, the creatures of spirit whisper in my ear. *The monolith, the monolith!*

But the monolith senses our approach. Its hum crescendoes, filling my ears with such a sound that I'm sure my mind will explode as the monolith begins to recede into the void.

"Quickly!" I shout at Bran. "It wants to get away!"

The sea wolf snarls and wraps his tail around the monolith. *Come and get it*, he says.

Bran mutters that rocks can't move, but that's exactly what the monolith is doing. It's a living, breathing entity, and it's trying to run from us.

"Faster," I say to Bran. "Faster!"

He rises into the air. I follow, speeding after the monolith, which is fading, fading . . .

And then we slam into it, headlong. Bran crumples to the earth, unconscious. I hover in midair, screaming in pain. One of my wings is badly torn, but somehow I manage to land safely, only to find myself face-to-face with the sea wolf.

I've been waiting for you, he says. *And now it looks like I've got you and your boyfriend after all. Time for you to give your totem up to your brother.* Grotesque, mutilated fin-hands reach toward me, but he pauses, reconsiders, and turns toward Bran. *I think I'll take him first. Easy pickings, you know . . .*

"Leave him alone!" I lash out with my battered wings but hit nothing. The man has disappeared.

Is that the best you can do? he cackles when he reappears on the other side of Bran. *Why don't you give up now, before you really cause problems? I'll let the boy go if you do.*

"No," I say, because there's a reason this creature suddenly wants to strike a deal. He has Paul. I think fast—what do I have that *he* wants? I stare at the moonstone hanging at my throat, and suddenly I know. It wants the monolith to remain intact. That's why the dzoonokwa brought us here, why the raven has helped me along. They're trapped by the monolith, trapped in the boundary that protects the entire Island, just like Ms. Adelaide said. And the sea wolf wants to keep it that way.

But why is it that he can come in, and yet the creatures of spirit can't leave?

Because of whatever that stink is that follows him. I see it now, curling there, looming in the darkness, taking form. It rises up, a great maw and nothing else. This is what the creatures of the spirit world fear. I can sense it, rippling out toward the dzoonokwa, coursing through the nothingness around us. They are trapped, and while they are, the sea wolf and his denizen can hunt them as they desire—and us, too. I've already seen the poison gas take one person already. Saul. I thought it was my fault. But perhaps it wasn't after all.

And now, I am here—because I share the power of

sisiutl, the strongest of the spirit creatures, and if I want to break the monolith, there is nothing the sea wolf can do to stop me.

I rest against the monolith, pressing my head to its cold, shining surface and listen, turning so I can see my eyes reflect back at me. *Do it*, my mind whispers. The searchers have already found their way through. The monolith is failing. If the creatures of spirit die altogether, what then? And what if this creature gains their power first?

Your brother, the sea wolf says.

Yes, my brother. Me, for Paul. If I do this, if I take Paul's place, I will save him.

But I can't. Even as a great sob rips through my throat, I know I can't. I must stop the sea wolf and whatever it is that follows him, no matter what the cost.

And that cost, for me, is my brother.

So before I change my mind, I seize the moonstone with my mouth and press it to the monolith. At first, nothing happens, but then from far off comes a faint noise, like the sound of ice cracking under the warmth of a spring sun. It has begun.

"Bran," I say, turning just in time to see him begin to shift back into his human form and vanish. "No!" I scream, grabbing at him. "You have to stay here!"

He slowly opens his eyes and the plumes of red reappear on his head. "I hurt," he moans.

"I know, I know," I say, helping him up. "We're almost done. Just one thing left to do."

Pain rockets through my bad shoulder as I fold my wings and help Bran stand, ignoring the sea wolf, who is poised to strike. Bran leans into me, and with the last of his strength, he presses his stone into the monolith just as the sea wolf leaps toward us.

The world shudders. The monolith screams, a sound that defies description. My ears feel like they've been shot with glass and I'm forced to drop the spirit stone so I can press my hands to my head. My ears—I've never felt such pain! Bran falls to the ground and vanishes. It doesn't matter. We've done what we needed to do. Cracks appear, turning the surface of the monolith into a spiderweb. I see my face fragment into a mosaic of selves, each one skewed, each one me.

No! the sea wolf howls. *Do you know what you've done?*

I ignore him. Smoke seeps out of the cracks on the monolith and I drink it in, greedily consuming its power. Its power is now mine, and I will devour it whole and turn it on this creature of nightmares beside me.

The sea wolf rushes to the other side of the monolith, lapping at the smoke, trying to claim what he can for itself, but it's too late. With each breath I take, the cracks widen, until chips slough off. The creatures of the spirit world rush forward, catching them in their maws and swallowing them before disappearing from sight. The dust left behind I swallow myself. I don't know what this will do to me, but I do it anyhow as my sisiutl self takes over and drives me on.

When the chips stop falling, all that's left is a single obsidian shard. It slices my palms as I seize it and turn it over and over, watching as my eyes stare back at me.

I don't see the sea wolf lunge at me, but I feel him. Before he can tear flesh from my body, I lift the obsidian shard high in the air, and with all the strength I have left, I rip the veil between the worlds apart.

CHAPTER FORTY-FOUR

Bran and I lie on the ground, head to head. I can't tell if he's alive or not, and I'm not ready to find out. I close my eyes, and in my mind, I see that it's raining, but it's not water that falls from the sky. I see the boundary falling in jet-black rain drops, and with it fall the creatures of the supernatural world. Eagle. Thunderbird. Wolf. Sisiutl, on wings that glitter in the sunlight. Raven.

The last drops down beside me and hops onto my chest. He cocks his head from side to side, and then pokes his beak right in my face. *Bet you didn't expect you could do that, did you?*

I don't answer.

He chuckles. *This won't be the last we see of each other.*

He hops off my chest and takes to wing, flying after the horde of supernatural creatures that have now descended into our world.

I reach out with my senses, testing to see if the spirit world still exists, and it does, just beyond the mist, just beyond reason, but that mist is thinner now, and maybe one day it'll evaporate so that the spirit world and the physical world will be one again, just like they were a long, long time ago, in the time of the old stories.

After a while, I sit up. The obsidian shard is still in my hands, bound to me by a crust of my own blood. Bran wakes shortly after, and we realize, after speaking words that we can only see, that our hearing is gone. There's always a price to pay in the world of spirit, and a sacrifice to be made. I should have known that right from the start.

The dzoonokwa have left, except for one. She stands just beyond the tree line, watching us, hidden by the shadows so she's hard to make out. She's shorter than the rest, closer to my height, and thinner. Her hair finer. Her hips not as wide. She raises a hand for one fleeting second, and then vanishes into the forest.

Bran and I rise from the ground, and leave too.

EPILOGUE

$\mathcal{I}$t takes several days to get back. When we arrive, we skirt around the village, stopping at Ms. Adelaide's so she can send word to my father before heading to Madda's the long way so no one else will know we've returned. Before we left the clearing where the monolith no longer stands, we decided that after all we've been through, we deserve a little time to ourselves. Time to heal the wounds we both bear.

Healing is more than medicine. Madda always said that healing starts with the heart, and though we aren't healed yet, we're on our way. Some of our hearing has returned, but not all, and I don't think it ever will. A small sacrifice, I suppose, for freeing the creatures of the spirit world. Maybe one day they'll return to give thanks, and I'll be able to ask for my hearing back. But maybe not. We talk about these things, Bran and I, between the moments when we stare at the fire, sleep, look at the stars when the sky is clear. We talk about what it means that the boundary is no longer there. We talk about the guilt we feel, and what will happen when we tell the Elders what we've done. We talk about if there had been another way, if we could have tried something else, if we were somehow mistaken about what the dzoonokwa wanted us to do. We talk about Plague, and the men it infected, and wonder, *Have we just been lucky, or is there more yet to come?*

We talk and we talk, but in the end, talk doesn't matter. What's done is done. We can't change that. No one can.

The only thing we manage to decide in all our talking is that we must find Paul. How, we don't know, but we will. Together, we will.

But for now, we exist in our little spell, for soon it will end.

And, as fate would have it, it is Avalon who ends it for us.

We are in bed, beginning the slow process of finding each other. We touch each other's scars, the half-healed wounds, the bruises that mark our histories. Bran kisses the sisiutl's bite, slowly, one dot at a time, as if his mouth can take away the pain that still lingers there. He's about to slide lower when someone opens the cottage door, and before either of us has time to react, Avalon wanders into the bedroom as if she owns the place. We look at her; she looks at us. If she's surprised to see us, she doesn't show it.

"Get out" is all I say.

Bran laughs as she slams the door shut. It's the first time he's laughed since I found him, and if it weren't Avalon he was laughing at, I might laugh too. But I don't. I reach out and pull him toward me, and then we pick up where we left off.

Word spreads from there, and it isn't long before we have to explain ourselves and what happened.

The Elders are arguing over the Band's next step at this very moment. They can argue all they like, but there are two things I know. The first? We can't stay here anymore. The boundary has fallen, and this place is no longer safe. The sea wolf knows where we are, and the creature that follows him does too.

The second? I'm going north, and Bran's coming with me.

There's a story among people—not my people, for I am, and will always be, one apart. But there's a story of how people came to be, how Raven dropped from the sky to pry open a clam shell, and found humankind inside. They say that this story took place a long, long time ago when the earth was still young, when Raven still spoke words that were lies and truth at the same time.

So I say: This is the story of the way things once were, and now are, and how they will be, for if there is one thing I've learned, it's that we are not bound by the myths created for us. It's time for my own myths, and those myths will take place in the land of ravens, the land left behind by time—the land of the Bix'iula.

These are my truths, my myths, my lies. This is my story.